I0817769

Once…,
The Once Trilogy, Vol. 1

Once...,

Bryan Ó Muimhneacháin

Paladin Books
2019

Once... is a work of fiction. Names, places, and incidents are products of the authors imagination or are used fictitiously.

First Printing: 2019

ISBN: 978-1-7334083-0-1

Paladin Books, LLC
PO BOX 574
St. Clair Shores, Michigan, 48080

www.oncestories.com

v1

Dedication

For my wife, who told me to try it,

For my friends who told me to keep at it,

For everyone who chimed in to support it,

And to everyone else that put up with it,

This book is dedicated.

Contents

Foreword

To the best of my knowledge...

... King Ronald does not exist. Comes to it, the Kingdom of Lochhaven is a fantasy, too.

... The Talte Bruite, or Crushed Lands, are a myth. If there are existing forbidden places where monsters dwell and all that is sacred is ignored; where ancient hubris has brought disaster and carnage to the world; where all is nightmare and horror — I didn't write about it here.

... The Empire of Yorch; a land of wonders and pinnacle of civilization; exists only in my head.

In other words, all of the above is imaginary, just as the story to follow is. A fantasy world that helped a young boy fall asleep at night when the real world conspired to prevent that very thing. It's nothing more, and nothing less.

Unless.

Unless, on some level, we tell ourselves stories to remind ourselves who we could be. To let the secret person that lives in us out into the light. For good or ill. It could be that this tale is a glimpse into the author's private world, where good and evil easy to identify, a hero can be a hero, friends are true, and the future is up to each of us.

Or maybe not. You, dear reader, may decide that for yourself. Or you may choose to read the story and laugh at the jokes and forget the whole idea of 'meaning'.

Whatever you decide, I hope you enjoy this story that may – or may not – have happened...

Once...,

CHAPTER ONE

– AERYK –

Were you to ask me, I would not be able to relate to you a more pleasant ride than the one the morning it all began. The sun had risen in a cloudless sky, and hours later, it remained the only feature in the azure expanse. Shafts of piercing light played through the canopy of leaves above my head, shifting and twinkling in the crisp autumn breezes. Cool, but not cold. Winter was still some way off. All was quiet and beautiful. In fact, the only thing disturbing the natural beauty of the day was me.

From a distance, I intended to look like any of a dozen merchants and tinkers from the area, on my way to buy or sell or repair or whatever it was that they did. As I would shortly find out, the effect didn't hold up very well up close, but then, the intent wasn't to be looked at too closely. The road from Castle Claire, which was now several miles behind me, to my destination was not without its dangers, and I was trying not to draw attention to myself.

My 'disguise' was actually my father's idea. Since I was to go alone, being invisible was my best defense, he believed.

“There are too many random bandit clans these days. You should have a guard, though I know you won’t,” he counseled, “This journey is too important to have you run afoul of some low-birth looking for coin.”

Far too cavalierly, I had said, “Let them come.” I would regret that, as it came to pass.

But on that road, in the beauty of that late morning sun, with the steady ‘clop’ of my horse’s footsteps lulling me into a reverie, I had no idea I was about to receive a lesson on overconfidence — the first of many in this story.

Something moved in the roadway ahead of me. Tugging on the reins, I brought my horse to a stop several feet from a man that had seemingly appeared out of nowhere, brandishing a worn long-sword at guard. *Precisely how lost in thought have I been*, I wondered. I felt the first pricking of anxiety and scanned around. To either side of the path – which I now realized had narrowed to little more than a cart’s width –, there was a rustling as from each direction a man with a loaded bow rose from the brush. To the rear, a fourth man now stood brandishing a dagger. I rested my right hand on my staff, which was lying at an angle across my lap.

“Hold!” called the man in the front, which was a ridiculous thing to say, as I had obviously already stopped. It occurred to me that I could spur the horse on and try to rush past, but the bowmen gave me pause. My back would be a tempting and easy target if either of them knew even which end of the arrow went against the string. I decided to try the other way out.

"'Ello," I called, passably affecting the accent of the commoners, "what's y'r happin'?"

The de facto leader was short, but almost as broad at the shoulder as he was tall. He wore a dark green shirt and pants with a rough-hewn leather vest over it. His face, like his clothes and close-cropped blonde hair, was dirty and twisted into a smirk.

"C' mon," he said disdainfully, "let's not play. Just hop offa yer horse and gimme that purse there and we c'n all move on." As he spoke, he gestured with the tip of his sword. I noticed he had a casual, practiced manner with the weapon that bespoke his comfort with it.

"C' mon," I said back, still trying to play my role, "Lemme on. I jes' got this one ol' horse 'ere, an' me purse is paltry. Lemme on, eh?"

There were sudden barks of laughter that took me off guard coming from all four men. When the leader spoke again, his accent had receded to the point that he almost sounded like my father's steward back at home. "'Let you on'? Listen, fancy boy, no one with a 'paltry' purse has such a finely bred horse as their 'one ol' horse 'ere.' And your clothes are far too clean and well-fit. Now either you're a thief yourself, in which event you just got four partners to share with, or you're some fancy-pants noble boy and a wicked liar. Either way, you give me the purse. Or...,"

It's odd to say it now, but at that moment, I found myself noticing that he didn't mention me getting off the horse again. As the strangeness of that tiny detail rang in my head, I saw his eyes dart over to the bowman to my left. There was a soft 'twang' sound, and I felt my seat drop almost instantly. On instinct, I pulled my legs up and rolled with the motion as a thousand pounds of now dying horse collapsed beneath me. I hit hard on my shoulder and tumbled forward, stopping on my knees slightly ahead and to the left of where the horse collapsed and now comfortably in the range of the leader's blade.

"... you'll be next!" he finished.

I got one of my feet under me and brought my staff – miraculously still in my hand – to guard position between us. I surveyed the situation. The bandit leader had softened his stance and was bringing his blade up to attack. Behind me, there were two more with arrows no doubt trained on me. Oh yes, and a fourth bringing up the rear with a dagger in his hand. I thought of my father's warnings again. *I hate this,* I thought, *I am going to die, and he is going to be right.*

Just then, I heard a new sound. It was similar to the bowstring from seconds before, but higher pitched and came from entirely the wrong direction. I flinched anyway, sure that I was about to feel an arrow tearing through me, but it didn't happen. Instead, a groan erupted from the bowman that hadn't yet fired. With a glance over my right shoulder, I saw him turn away from me and topple over, his bow now beside him on the ground. I turned back to the leader in time to see a fog of confusion on his face. Behind him, from a low branch off to the side of the path, a figure dropped to the ground with the crunching sound of gravel and twigs. The bandit leader spun at the noise, only to find himself unexpectedly and somewhat desperately parrying the thrusts of the newcomer's black-bladed sword.

There was no time for thinking, and I began to move on training and instinct. I dropped to the ground and rolled sideways toward the body of my horse. Where I had been, I heard an arrow skip across the road. Shifting my staff to a javelin grip, I launched it at the remaining bowman, where it smashed satisfyingly into his face with a sound like wet wood snapping. *That's for my horse, back-birth,* I thought. Still crouched, I turned back to the bandit leader and his mysterious attacker. The new figure was clad entirely in black, the most noteworthy aspect of his garb being a thick, military-grade leather breastplate bearing no standard. He was, oddly, looking over towards me rather than at the bandit, as if checking to see if I were in any peril.

At that, I spun to find the fourth man advancing toward me and having produced a second dagger to match his first. From my crouch, I sprung up, retrieved my staff from where it landed and whirled it into a defensive position. He stopped, bringing his blades forward toward me. I spun my staff expertly before me in a wide figure-eight pattern before bringing it back to guard position. It was a flourish, and wholly unnecessary, but it had the effect I wanted. He looked at the barely stirring form of the bowman I had felled, gave a second glance toward the other who was now crumpled on the ground holding his wounded shoulder and finally one up to the sword fight behind me. He made a nervous shuffling of his fingers on the hilts of his daggers. We eyed one another over the dozen or so feet between us. And abruptly, he turned and bolted back into the woods. I grinned to myself before turning back to the bandit leader and his opponent.

I was in time to see that the stranger in black had also noticed the retreat of the fourth man. Seemingly satisfied, he turned his full attention to his fight. With three quick slashes, he moved inside the bandit's defenses and with one last strike with the flat of his blade, he slapped away the other man's sword, sending it spinning away. He followed with a high snap-kick centered on the bandit's chest that sent him sprawling into the middle of the road. The stranger moved in and held his blade to the bandit's throat.

"Do what you must, pilgrim," growled the fallen bandit leader, though the fact that he was struggling to get air back into his lungs after the kick had driven it out hampered his intended ferocity.

"I'm not going to kill you," the stranger in black said with a hint of exasperation in his voice. The man on the ground, his breath now returning to him, looked confused. "I mean," the stranger continued, "I will if I have to, but I'm not planning on it."

The bandit eyed the black blade still resting at his throat and looked back up to the stranger. "We'd have killed you," he said, almost as if to give permission.

The stranger shrugged slightly, though his blade never moved. "I imagine that's important to have clear," he said, "Must be tough to be a thief if you don't establish some kind of reputation. You're a touch unconvincing, though." The man on the ground shifted, his eyes never leaving the stranger, but a renewed look of confusion alighting on his face. "Let's be honest," he continued, somewhat nonchalantly, "if you were the killing sort, you wouldn't have shot the horse, you'd have shot the man. Fact is, shooting the man's horse instead of the man is exactly the kind of thing you'd do if you want a reputation. Vicious enough, but still doesn't make you a murderer. So let's cut right to it, eh? No one here is killing anyone today." With that, he let the sword point drop away and extended his hand.

The bandit's eyes went wide as he stared at the outstretched hand. He shot a look over at me, where I'm sure he found my expression was as baffled as his own. He looked back at the offered hand and tentatively took it and stood up.

"Now," the man in black said, "get your stuff, get your boys, and go home."

"You shot my brother," mumbled the bandit leader with some of the growl back in his voice.

"Yeah," said the stranger, nodding, "I did. He won't die. Might do well to get him some doctoring, though. Here, let's go have a look."

I can't accurately tell you how confused I suddenly felt; the only way I can only describe the situation was surreal. I stood stock still and watched as the stranger and the bandit walked together over to the archer that had been the first to fall. The stranger reached down and took hold of the crossbow bolt. After a moment where he appeared to be twisting it gently, he pulled it out of the wounded man's shoulder with one quick motion. Again he offered his hand, and the injured man took it and got to his feet. The stranger produced a cloth, pressed it into the open wound, then stepped aside and away from the two men.

"On your way, then," he said, waving his hand in a dismissive gesture.

Without another word, the two failed bandits walked over to the unconscious form of the one I had felled with my staff and together they grabbed him by his arms and dragged him off into the brush, heading in much the same direction as had been taken by their fourth member; the one who had fled moments before.

I looked at the stranger who was himself watching them go. He stood there without moving for several moments – well after they were no longer visible. Then as if noticing me for the first time, he turned and looked at me. He held up the crossbow bolt he had retrieved from the bandit's shoulder.

"Waste not, you know?"

And those were the first words Kelly ever spoke to me. I had no idea at the time what things our future together would hold, but looking back I think it's significant that the very first words my friend ever said to me were something that ordinary. I looked more closely at him as if somehow his talking about the value of a crossbow bolt made it okay for me to do so. His clothes, as mentioned, were black. So black was it that the cloth seemed to swallow even the rays of sunlight that reached him. I was close enough now that I could see that they were expertly made and of the highest quality. The leather armor appeared as finely crafted as the clothes; articulated in such a way that he moved smoothly in it. He went back toward the tree from which he had initially dropped and retrieved several items – a small quiver of bolts, a baldric and scabbard, a black cloak, and from a couple of feet away, a black crossbow. He returned all of these to his person as he walked casually back over to me. I became acutely aware that I was staring and suddenly felt awkward, so I turned to the body of my horse and retrieved my supply pack.

"Nice throw," he said, close enough now for quiet conversation. "Do you do that sort of thing a lot, or did we just get lucky?" he asked, nodding at my staff.

"I've had some training," I said, "Thanks."

He shrugged his shoulders a couple of times to settle his equipment into position as he spoke. "So tell me, mi'lord, what brings you out on a wild road alone?"

"'My lord?'" I challenged. *I'm a tradesman,* I thought forcefully, *there's nothing to see here.* I gave him a feigned look of confusion.

He looked at me for a long moment, and then he decided to let it pass. "Either way," he said.

I wasn't sure what that meant, but his apparent awareness that there was more here than met the eye unsettled me. I decided that keeping as close to the truth as possible would give me a better chance of staying discrete, and too much pretending had nearly gotten me killed moments before.

"I'm on the road to Clemons for business. It's a very personal matter, and I'm trying to be inconspicuous."

"Inconspicuous is one thing," he said, "and you appear to be wicked dangerous with that staff, but if I could give you a little advice? I might suggest that you keep a little more company about you in the future. This lot were amateurs, but against a few more determined or seasoned robbers...," he shook his head a little.

"You make a decent point," I said. *Shut up, father,* I thought at the voice in my head. I looked down at my horse's body. Somewhere under the massive pile of horseflesh, I now realized, was my purse and the only money I had been carrying. He will never let me live this down. After a moment, I looked back up at the stranger. "What about you? Aren't you alone in the woods too?"

"Fair observation," he said. "What do you say we travel together to this city of yours? Could be a touch safer."

I thought about it. The Duke – my father – had all but demanded I have the militia along with me, but that would include too many people; be too public; for a clandestine task. This man, though, wasn't a local. His accent, while slight, placed him as an easterner, and not from any of the provinces of Lochhaven or even its environs. Perhaps the road, where I would be for at least another day and a half, would be safer with two of us.

"Where were you headed?" I asked.

"Just passing through," he said, "Eventually I was thinking of heading further west, but I was hoping to see some of this land before I went."

"Clemons is a seaport," I said, "you might find a ship for passage west, or wherever you'd like."

He stood for a moment and looked up at the leaf-shrouded sky. To this day, he has never told me what was going through his mind at that moment. What finally made him decide to double back from his journey to go to Clemons. What motivated him to attach himself to me. Were I asked about it now, I'd say that he's never told me because he doesn't himself know. Whatever his reasoning, he finally turned away from the sky and looked over at me.

"You've got a deal, sir. Actually...," he said as he turned to the forest and whistled four notes. Before I could even ask why he did so, a magnificent stallion emerged from the forest brush. It was dark brown with a blonde mane and tail. Packs of equipment hung evenly across its back. The animal approached and stopped right next to him as he patted it on the flank. "... I think you're going to need me if for nothing more than a ride." Casually, he climbed up onto the horse's back. "This is Locksley. For the rest of this trip, he is our transportation."

"Excellent," I said. Kelly shifted his bedroll forward from where it rested on the horse's back, and I was able to mount up and take position between it and the other bundles.

"It's rude not to introduce yourself," he said, tipping his head to the horse.

"Oh. Right," I said. I was caught between the odd feeling of talking to the horse and an unforeseen sense of rudeness if I didn't. I chose the former. "I'm Aeryk Escrios, son of Rojer of Castle Claire," I said, leaning aside to look at the animal.

My host chuckled. "I knew it. Nice to meet you, Lord Aeryk."

I felt my face flush. *You used your real name,* I thought suddenly. *Very clever, Lord Idiot.*

I did not want to be outdone, of course, so I said, "Fine, well, 'It's rude not to introduce yourself.' So, who are you, mi'lord?"

He chuckled again in a way that I would come to identify as indicating that he knew more than he was letting on. "No title, sire. I'm just a seeker, looking to see what's around the corner. But," he paused, then said, "you can call me Kelly." He smiled as if at a private joke. "Yeah, that will do nicely."

Whatever was that about? I thought. I decided to accept it at face value and the name as well. "Well then, Kelly," I said, "just call me Aeryk. It's good to know you."

He nodded and nudged Locksley forward before he finally said, "You know? I think it really will be."

We rode on through the afternoon without ever seeing another soul. We rode quietly for a while; a boon, as I still felt myself calming down from the bandit attack. In the course of the next few hours though, we found ourselves in the rhythm of discussing the sorts of things that strangers do when they're thrown together by circumstances – the weather, the condition of the road, the desire for a hot meal, and so forth. Long stretches of silence then punctuated these discussions of such profound and personal subjects.

"Y'know…," Kelly said, his voice ringing out after one particularly long period of quiet, "I think I understand what you were trying to do with that outfit, but you look like a real mark."

I looked down at myself involuntarily. I had explicitly gotten the rough-spun tan pants and broadcloth shirt so that they would be unremarkable, and my leather vest, while not light, wasn't in any way something that observers would mistake as armor. The dark green cloak I wore was untrimmed, and my boots – duplicates of the ones worn by the men in Castle Claire's stables – were extremely uncomfortable, which I had concluded did explain the bad moods the horsemen typically had. I looked back up. "What do you mean by that? I meant to pass as a tradesman of some kind. I think I'm pretty close."

Kelly snorted, then said, "Mi'lord, typical tradesmen do not have freshly laundered and unsoiled clothes when they travel. And most particularly," he jutted his thumb toward my staff, "they very much don't ride alone on groomed horses through bandit-infested woods carrying gold-inlaid quarterstaves."

I felt a little heat in my cheeks. I don't like dirty clothes; that was non-negotiable. I supposed that I really should have covered the staff, though. "But maybe one could be. There are a lot of tradesmen among the common people," I protested weakly, defensive of my careful planning, regardless of its ineffectiveness.

"True," he said with a slight smirk, "but they would have been robbed too."

Despite myself, I started to laugh. The day had not gone as I had expected, for sure. And now here a random pilgrim was poking holes in my carefully crafted – if not entirely father-approved – disguise. It was an irony that doesn't come along often.

"So tell me a little about this kingdom of yours," Kelly said. "I've only ever passed through the Western Kingdom; never spent any real time here. What's the story?"

'The Western Kingdom.' He was from the east, I thought. "First thing," I said, "is that you are currently in the kingdom of Lochhaven, under the authority of King Ronald Kastellian."

Kelly glanced back over his shoulder at me and shrugged a little. "Important tip. See, I'm learning already."

"As you surmised," I continued, "I am Aeryk, Marquess of Claire and the son of Duke Rojer Escrios. My father's province is one of twelve that make up the whole of the Lochhaven. Each province has a local ruler like my father, for a total of eleven. Over them is the King, Ronald, who directly rules his own province as well as being our monarch. The provinces stretch from the Esterwynn River in the west to the Teardrop Sea on the east, and from the Talte Bruite on the south to the northern mountains, which are known as the Superiors. The port we're going to is on the southwest coast of the Teardrop Sea."

"I see," Kelly said nodding. "and the kingdom – Lochhaven – ends at the coast?"

"Right," I said. "The other side of the sea is wild land from the far coast to the mountains. From the sea, you can head north; eventually, you would reach the channel; and take that further north and east until it exits onto the Great Eastern Ocean."

"So you're bounded by two mountain ranges, north and south, the Esterwynn, and the sea? That sounds like a recipe for a fairly secure land."

I shuddered a little without meaning to. "It is," I said. I decided to change the subject; we were veering too close to things I thought it best to avoid discussing.

"Ah ha," I said, looking up just then. I pointed to where, ahead and just off the road, a large inn stood.

"Why is there an inn in the middle of the forest?" Kelly said.

Finally, it was my turn to chuckle. I explained, "Not exactly 'in the middle.' I think if we look at the sign over there, we'll find that we're probably a short ride from some small village or another. Often the locals come out of the town proper to build these inns for travelers. It's lucrative for —," I stopped as Kelly got off the horse.

I was puzzled, but I followed suit. Kelly gathered the packs from off the animal's back, handing me mine. Then he removed the bridle and lightly smacked the horse's hind end. With a sudden lurch, the great brown stallion leapt forward and disappeared into the forest. I felt my stomach drop, and my eyes go wide. As he collected the gear and slung it over his shoulder, he noticed my expression.

"He doesn't much care for stables," was all he said before turning and walking toward the inn.

"But—" It was the only word I was able to get out before I realized the futility of the effort. "Oh," I finished to nobody in particular.

The inn was a typical if spartan affair, with a large main room, two stories high, built of stone around a central rectangular fire pit that stretched nearly the full length of it. Over the pit hung various pots and kettles that could be retrieved with metal hooks and in which a variety of soups, stews, and water for tea were being kept warm. Along the sides were the small rooms that the inn offered for rent. Up an open stairwell near the door was a walkway around the second-floor balcony that lead to more of the rentals. There were probably a total of nine or ten rooms total, though it wasn't likely all of them were for rent. Along the sides of both floors were small tables and stools, and at the far end of the ground floor, opposite the entrance, was a worn wooden bar. The fire illuminated the entire room and was kept burning by the ministrations of a young boy who was apparently in charge of stoking and feeding it. The entire place smelled like smoke and beef and damp wood.

We walked the length of the room, and Kelly dropped his packs on the floor beside an empty table. I sat down while he went to the bar. An old common woman appeared as if from nowhere, and they talked for a few moments. He handed her some coin and returned to the table with two large metal mugs, one of which he put in front of me while he settled down on a stool and faced the fire, leaning back on the table.

"So what's the rush?" he said after a few minutes and a couple swallows of his drink. "There some fancy lady waiting for you in Clemons, or what?"

"I wish," I said, swallowing a mouthful of my beer. The best I can say about it was that it did not make me cringe excessively. It tasted like wet wheat and alcohol, but it was better than nothing. "No, it's more business than pleasure."

Kelly nodded. I thought he might push, and I prepared myself to dance around the truth, but he just leaned back and looked at the fire. "So," he said, "you were telling me about your homeland here. With eleven vassals, is there a lot of infighting? That's usually the way of such things."

There was a weariness to his tone that made me think that he didn't have much patience for politicking. I couldn't help but notice too that he had a very high-born way of speaking, even beyond his accent. He may protest, but he wasn't a simple commoner.

"Not in my lifetime," I said. "King Ronald is a remarkable man and a very diplomatic one. He keeps all eleven of the other royal families directly involved in the running of the kingdom. Since everyone has a seat at the table, and everyone seems to be prospering, no one feels like they have reason to challenge things." I drank a little. I wanted to change the subject again, so I asked. "You don't seem to be a stranger to the halls of rulership. How is that?"

Kelly sipped for a moment, then said, "I've had my share of dealings with the ruling classes. You pick it up pretty quick." I watched him for a moment as he seemed to get lost in a memory, then blinked himself back to the present. "There is a dance that you people all do that would frankly exhaust me," he said with a smirk.

"Indeed," I said, thinking on my own business for a bit.

An older man had seated himself at a table near the bar and was strumming on some sort of stringed instrument that looked like it either once been or wanted to be a mandolin. We talked a bit more about lighter things and listened to the musician play while we nursed our drinks.

“All right, then,” Kelly eventually said as he stood, “we should get a little sleep and get ourselves off to an early start.” He finished the last of his beer in one swallow. Grabbing his things, Kelly went back to the stairs and up onto the second level while I followed. We passed several rooms until he stopped, looked at the door we were standing in front of and, satisfied, handed me a key. Bidding me good sleep, he went to the next room and disappeared inside. I went into my room and locked the door behind me. The conversation had been nicely vague, but it still stirred up all of the uncertainty I had about my mission and the many circumstances that led to it. Many little doubts sang in a chorus in my mind about my assignment as well as my place in it. And then, of course, there was the new uncertainty; the mysterious stranger that had inserted himself into the situation. Trusting him too far didn’t seem wise, but there was little doubt it was better to have him along on the road than it was to go alone. He had helped me get away from the bandits, but I was fairly sure that he hadn’t told me his real name. That was a lot of unknowns, and it made sleeping that night a challenging thing to accomplish.

We left at dawn the next day, with only the fire boy to see us go, and he did so only because I accidentally kicked him where he lay at the near end of the fire pit.

"Whhuu—?" he said, stirring himself from the pile of skins and blankets that apparently served as his bed.

"Go back to sleep," I said my voice low so as not to rouse anyone else, "We are leaving. Take these." I held out our room keys to him.

Groggily, he held up a soot-stained hand and accepted the two keys. He stared hard at them. Slowly, the fog of sleep began to clear from him, and understanding began to infiltrate. He looked up at me, and his eyes seemed to focus somewhat. I heard the door open as Kelly went outside, leaving me with the boy.

"You're leavin'," he said. It came out as if he had just solved a very complicated puzzle.

"Yes," I said, "and I gave you–"

"Keys!" he said with tremendous excitement. "I've to get yer keys!"

I pointed to his hand. He looked down at the two keys, then slowly back up at me with a smile. Suddenly he jumped up. "Och! I've to get yer horses outta th' stables!" He looked back and forth as if he suddenly noticed that snakes were surrounding him. "M'boots...," he mumbled, "got to get m'boots..."

I reached out and touched his shoulder, causing him to freeze in place. He looked up at me with wide eyes. "Don't worry," I said, "Just relax. You don't need to get our horses.

We—"

"Oh, ya I do, sire," he said, "It's me job. I'm to make yer stay a fine one. I jes' need m'boots..." He started looking around again, and my mind filled with the image of a chicken pecking for seeds.

"No, no," I said, grabbing both of his shoulders more firmly, "You don't. We don't have any horses in the stable."

He looked up at me. "No horses?" he said, deeply confused.

"No horses," I said, reassuring him. The confusion seemed to drain all of the manic energy out of him, and he stood staring at me.

"But," he said, his brow furrowed in deep concentration, "how did y' get here?"

I knew what I was about to say wasn't going to help, but if I had to deal with the ridiculous nature of my travel plans, it seemed just that someone else should too.

"Oh, we had a horse," I said, "We just let it go free into the forest last night after we arrived."

He stared at me, and I began to be concerned that the furrows in his brow might be permanent. I patted him on the head.

"So go back to sleep," I said, "and take comfort that at least your life makes sense." I turned toward the door just as Kelly reopened it and gave me an impatient look. Flashing my new young friend one last wave, I walked to the door and out into the morning.

We had gone a hundred yards or so from the inn, with Kelly all the while humming quietly to himself and admiring the dawn light in the sky when he gradually slowed down and became very interested in the ground along the roadside.

“Problem?” I asked.

He held one hand up as if to shush me and peered very carefully at the edge of the brush. A long moment passed, then he whistled four notes which I recognized as the same four notes from the day before. Almost immediately this time, the brown and blond stallion emerged from the shadowy brush. Kelly began slinging his supplies back into position on the horse and putting the bridle on him.

“That is an honestly impressive trick,” I said, choosing to ignore the part where he ‘shushed’ me. “How long have you owned it?”

“Oh, we’ve been together for a long while. It’s not really ‘ownership’, either. More like ‘companionship.’”

I mumbled something in the affirmative that I thought was polite, but asked, “Where was it trained?”

Kelly shot me a sidelong glance, veiled annoyance in his eyes. He said, “Not sure what you mean. He does what he wants; it just happens that it’s what we both want most of the time.”

“Yeah, but,” I protested, “how does it–?”

“Look,” Kelly said, hopping into place on the horse’s

back, “He is my friend and a magnificent one at that. You’ve now heard all there is to say about him.” He emphasized his use of each pronoun to clarify the point. He spent a few moments readjusting the supply packs again and waited for me to climb up.

I was silent as I mounted and we began to ride, realizing that my experience with animals was nothing like the bond of – well, friendship – that my new companion had with his steed. I had been rude without meaning to, and felt, not for the last time, that I was privy to something to which I could not yet relate.

In point of fact, as I have learned more about Locksley, it is a wonder he didn’t throw me off his back right then. Truthfully, he would not have been wrong to do so.

Kelly chose to follow the main road that morning with some confidence. He explained that we would likely be safe for some time because, as he put it, “Bandits hate early.” As a result, we made excellent time. This part of the road veered away from the dense forest and went off through low, grass-covered hills overlooking a view of the Teardrop Sea. The afternoon sun bounced gently off distant waves as we rounded one last bend, and the city of Clemons came into view. The sea breeze, no longer deflected by the final hill, hit us full on with the briny smell of the water. It was warmer than the day before, a day my father would call ‘false summer’, and after a long day on horseback, I was grateful for the coolness of the shore wind as we rode.

The town of Clemons is built low, with few buildings over two stories, and is surrounded by a modest stone wall, perhaps no more than ten to fifteen feet high on average. From the road on which we were approaching, the two features that drew attention most were the waterfront and the Lord's Tower. The wharf was relatively small, but even from a distance, we could see it was bustling with fishermen and traders. The reason the lords had chosen Clemons for my clandestine business was precisely that; it was large enough for a foreign ship to be unnoticed, but small enough not to be noticed itself. North of the city and the docks where a small outcropping of rock formed the highest point in the city was the other principal feature – the Lord's Tower, the home of the Lord of Clemons and his family.

I pointed to the tower, "That's where we're headed. Baron Myk Peralta, the lord of the city, will be waiting for me. He'll be able to provide you with lodging as long as you like." I looked at him directly. "He'll be able to pay you back for the lodging at the inn, too."

"I didn't think you noticed," Kelly said slyly.

"I probably owe you more, considering the ride and all," I admitted.

"Ah, don't give it another thought," he said. We rode for a couple more minutes, then he said, "So we're going to the big tower there."

"Yes."

"I'm taking a Marquess of these lands to the big tower in a port city."

"Yes."

"I'm taking a Marquess of these lands to the big tower in a port city to meet its Baron."

"Uh-huh," I said.

"For personal business."

"Yeah."

He shook his head. "God's teeth. This has got to be about a woman."

I chuckled as we made our way over the last stretch of road.

There was no fanfare when we entered Clemons proper. Kelly had dismounted and released Locksley again beyond the city wall, and we walked in on our own two feet. I was acutely aware that I was still wearing the wretched uncomfortable and unconvincing 'tradesman' boots, and I was looking forward to getting back into a proper pair. We made our way through the center of the town and up through their market district. The sounds of animals and carts, of people selling and negotiating, of crunching foot on stone, and of criers shouting their news mixed together into a senseless background cacophony. I wondered then and still do, how do people live in such a manner?

By and by we reached the grounds around the Tower and were met by two smallish guardsmen dressed as members of Clemons' militia. Their livery was the dark navy blue that was standard for the guardsmen in King Ronald's lands, with black leather breastplates and boots. They held long spears in their right hands that they extended across the door to the Tower itself at our approach.

"G' day, mi'lords," said the one nearer to me on my left, "What's your business in the tower?" He had longish red curls that peeked out from beneath his conical metal guard's helmet onto his face that struck me as very distracting.

"Er," I said, recalling myself, "I'm Lord Aeryk Escrios, Marquess of Castle Claire. I request an audience with Baron Myk Peralta."

"Ah," the guard replied, seemingly confused by something I said, or maybe that I had an answer at all. "I'll have to check. Wait, um, wait here while...," he looked at his companion who seemed no less confounded.

"It's all right," came a loud but casual voice from within the doorway, "let them in."

We walked into the gray stone entry chamber that I recalled from my last visit to the Tower years before. Five equidistantly spaced torches mounted on the walls provided light, but otherwise it was completely unadorned. Two other doors led out of the room, forming a triangle with the entry. Each had a guard stationed beside it wearing the same blue and black combination of the two outside. The voice had come from the man in the center of the room.

Lord Myk was a short, stocky man with kindly eyes and an easy smile. His hair, which I remembered as midnight black, was shot through now with wisps of gray. He was dressed similarly to the guards, but in more ornate if still practical fashion, and with a silver vest of chainmail replacing their leather. His warhammer hung from a baldric that was little more than a tied off rope. On seeing me, he bowed stiffly and then approached.

"Hi Aeryk," he said, clapping me on the shoulder, "I'm glad you made it."

"Me too," I said with a smile, "but I might not have if it weren't for my friend here." I pointed over to Kelly. "He helped me out with some brigands on the road. We made the remainder of the journey together."

Myk, ignoring or not comprehending that I had involved a stranger in my clandestine mission, turned and extended his hand. "Hi. I'm Baron Myk Peralta. Welcome to Clemons."

Nodding at first, then taking the proffered hand, Kelly replied, "My pleasure. I'm Kelly."

"Kelly...?" Myk said, expecting more.

"Just Kelly."

"Hunh," Myk said, then turned, dismissing whatever Kelly's lack of pedigree had brought to his mind. "Hey, come on in and have something to eat." He walked toward the right most of the two doors opposite the entrance. I felt Kelly looking at me and turned to him with a shrug. Together, we followed the Lord of Clemons.

Beyond the door was a small stone passage that curved around to the left and opened through a door at the end of a large banquet room which seemed to follow the outer wall of the tower. The outside wall, which was opposite the entrance, held large glass windows overlooking a balcony over the inner side of the bay. On the other walls were decorative tapestries and paintings depicting scenes of sailing vessels and the sea. Arranged in the middle of the room were semi-circular tables positioned opposite one another with an offset, effectively forming a single, winding table the length of the room. It gave me the impression of a large chain that bent back and forth through the area. Chairs were placed around the outside of the curve of the individual tables, thus providing seating for a large number of people should there be the need. Around the rest of the room were sideboards with various stacks of dinnerware, candle holders, and other miscellanies for hosting feasts. Myk told us to have a seat and pointed to the near end of the closest of the tables as he went to the nearest sideboard and rang a small bell. Before he even had time to return the few steps to us, a serving girl appeared from some hidden entrance at the opposite end of the room. Myk requested that she bring some food and wine, and then he sat down with us.

"Lord Myk," I began.

"Aeryk, it's fine. Just Myk. It's fine," said the Lord of Clemons, "I've known your family forever, and you nearly so. Let's not be all fancy, okay?"

I smiled at him. He was right, my father and the baron were of similar age, and had been allies – and friends actually – longer than I had been alive. It was strange, I thought, how rarely I had been there over the last few years. Clemons had been the site of many boyhood vacations, and almost a second home. There had been some falling out between them, I knew, but that wouldn't have affected my own ability to come. The truth I didn't see then was that I had become far too high-minded to go off and associate with my father's friends. Of course, as will become apparent, I know that very well now.

"Myk," I said, correcting myself, "I do owe Kelly here for paying for an inn along the way. Unfortunately, my purse was...," I glanced at Kelly, "... lost during the business with the bandits."

"That's no problem," Myk said with a grin. He looked at Kelly. "I'll make sure to have some coin brought up to you."

"And," I continued, "I also offered him lodging here until he is ready to be on his way. He wasn't coming to the city, and only agreed to join me for mutual safety."

"Of course," Myk said again with his easy smile, "we have plenty of room. We already have one visitor from Traverse Bay. The more, the merrier."

"Thank you for both," Kelly said, "I should be heading on shortly, so I won't overstay my welcome."

The kitchen staff brought in a couple of platters of cold meats, cheeses, and loaves of bread, as well as wine. We sat and talked until the sun's reflected light was long gone. The tower's staff had just lit the candles when Kelly stood.

"Lord Myk, I want to thank you for your kindness," he said with a curt bow, "but I should leave you two to your...," he shot me a glance, "... business. I am leaving as early in the morning as I can manage, so I should bid you good night. If someone is available to show me where I will be staying?"

Myk called one of the stewards over and instructed him to lead Kelly to an open chamber on the second floor. Kelly thanked him again and turned to me.

"It's been a pleasure, your lordship," he said with a bow. "If I don't see you before one or the other of us leave, I bid you safe travels." The formality of the good-bye seemed strange from Kelly after our two days traveling together, but his invoking of such proper manners seemed to be a natural reflex for him. I stood and clasped his hand.

"My pleasure as well," I said, "and I wish you the same. Thank you again." I paused, then said, "And thank Locksley too."

He laughed and shook my hand once more. "I will. And if we cross paths again and you have a need, I would consider it a privilege." With that, he turned and followed the steward out of the room.

And just to underscore how clueless I was back then, I honestly thought that would be the last I saw of him. But, as was made clear to me just a short moment later, that was not to be the case.

"Aeryk," Myk quietly said after Kelly left, "I have an idea."

The next morning at dawn, I dressed quickly and went downstairs from my chamber to the entry hall. There I found Kelly with all of his equipment bundled, preparing to leave. He looked up as I entered the room held up a hand.

"Well, that was a lot briefer farewell than I expected," he said.

I nodded a response, then said, "Could you come with me for a minute? Lord Myk and I would like to talk to you."

Kelly pointed to a small pouch. "It's fine. I was brought the coin last night. The stewards took care of it."

I shook my head, "No. It's something else. Can you join us?" Just then, Myk came out of the stairwell behind me. He had hurried, obviously having rushed to be down before Kelly left just as I had.

Kelly looked from one to the other of us thoughtfully

for a long moment before he sat down his pack. “Very mysterious,” he said to neither of us, “Okay, so now I’m curious.” He followed us as we led him back through the door and upstairs.

The stairwell was a polished, well-lit affair that took us up around the circumference of the tower floor by floor. The walls were painted in a sky-blue color that, coupled with multiple narrow windows, gave the stairs an unexpected feeling of openness. We continued up the stairs for two flights, passing the floor where we had lodged the night before, and exited into a large furnished room dominated by two ample windows framed by golden velvet curtains overlooking the whole bay. The morning sun streamed in from over the sea, illuminating the entire room in a golden glow. The floor was overlaid with dark polished wood and covered with a large woven rug. An immense black tapestry with a rearing white warhorse emblazoned on it hung on the wall to the left. In front of it stood a large round table and several chairs. On the opposite side of the room was a bookcase, a hearth, and several pieces of padded furniture.

Also near the hearth was a woman. Her back was to us as we walked in, so all we saw was the bright pink of her dress and the immaculate weaving of her braided dark blonde hair. She spun around as Kelly and I entered.

“Oh,” she said, putting her hand on her chest, “My lord Baron, I didn’t know we had visitors. I only came up to watch the sunrise." She looked us over with large blue-green eyes and an impish smile. She was a small woman, but definitely a woman and quite stunning in the pink dress.

"Aeryk?" she said suddenly and with unveiled excitement. She moved over to me in a swirl of pink and grabbed me in a tight – if brief – embrace. She stepped back to a more 'proper' distance and looked down with perhaps a hint of color in her cheeks.

I felt Kelly move close behind me. "You sure that she wasn't the reason we had to hurry?" he whispered in my ear. I shoved my elbow back into his chest, glancing back to him with a frown.

"Lady Sherilyn," I said with complete formality and propriety, "How have you been?"

"Oh," she said, still recovering from the hug, "okay. I really want to go home, though." She brightened abruptly and asked, "Is that why you're here? Can I go home now?"

"I'm sorry, no, not yet. The consensus is that it is still not safe for you in the north. As I understand it, your mother is still very concerned. Hopefully, though, it shouldn't be much longer. Anyway, I'm here to meet with someone that may be able to help."

She dropped her eyes to the floor but a moment later looked back up, this time at Kelly.

"Hi," he said, smiling slightly.

"Hello," she replied with a graceful curtsy. "I am Lady

Sherilyn Voelkel of Traverse Bay."

Kelly stepped forward and took her hand. As he bowed, he kissed it before he said, "I'm Kelly. It's a pleasure to meet you, my lady."

I stepped forward, suddenly feeling very intent on getting on to business. "We have important matters to get to, Sherilyn. Kelly," I said, giving him the slightest glare, "is here to help with them."

"Am I?" Kelly said, very quietly.

She turned back to me slowly and said, "In that case, my lord, I will leave you to it. But will the two of you be here long?"

"I actually don't know," I said, "I expect to be here at least overnight."

She seemed to brighten up again. "Okay!" she said, elongating the 'O' sound, "I will look forward to seeing you later today then." She paused a moment to smile first at Kelly, then at me before she walked out the door behind us.

Kelly watched her leave then turned to look at me. There was a smirk across his face.

"Really, just don't," I said with all the gravitas I could muster. It wasn't much.

Lord Myk, who had been standing to the side and watching this exchange with a smirk of his own, walked over to the large table. He sat down in one of the chairs and indicated the other two for us to sit. As we did, Kelly spoke first.

"So tell me," he said, "why am I here?"

Myk looked at me. Throughout our conversation the night before, he was cautious to point out that the decision we reached and how best to enact it would be mine; that he was just a counselor.

"Do you remember why I said I was coming here?" I started.

"Sure. 'Personal business'," Kelly said, glancing over to where we had talked to Sherilyn.

I gave my voice a low, conspiratorial tone, "Actually, I'm to meet up with an ambassador."

"Ooo. Very serious," he said, mimicking – if not mocking – my hushed tone. "Where from?"

I narrowed my eyes to underscore the seriousness. "The Empire of Yorch."

A long moment passed as he stared hard at me. I felt like he was trying to burn a hole through me with his eyes. Just as it was becoming too uncomfortable for me not to say something, he looked over to Myk.

"Long way," he said, turning back to me, his voice very flat. "That would make me think that there's something big going on in your quiet little kingdom."

"There is," I said, "You remember how I described Lochhaven as peaceful. That's primarily because of King Ronald. He's a good man and a noble king, and the other lords know it. In that strength, he's kept the peace here for his entire reign – all of my life and more. All of the local rulers, like my father, have sworn a pact of peace, so none of them has a standing army."

Kelly cocked his head to the side, his brow furrowing. "No standing armies? What about defenses? Peacekeeping?"

"Each hold, like my home in Claire, has a small local militia that is strictly for policing the land. It's...," I took a breath to punctuate the seriousness, "... it's not much."

Kelly shrugged and sat back, "Actually it sounds great, though. If it's worked for so long, what's the problem?"

"The problem's name is Mathu. Or I guess more accurately now it's 'King Mathu.' To the north beyond the Superior Mountains has been wilderness for generations. At least, we thought so. Apparently, that wilderness has been tamed now by a young general named Mathu who's effectively united all the people up there under his thumb. He's young and hungry, and we don't believe he's done." I looked down. "He's established his throne in Chateau Flint. It was an old ruin that he's rebuilt. It is very close to the mountains and therefore, very close to us. It's just a matter of time before he realizes we are just a fat, lazy cow. A cow ready to be slaughtered." I looked at Myk, and if he had any objections to my characterization, it did not show on his face.

Kelly was quiet for several moments. Looking back, I see now that it was because I had unwittingly become very intense and grim. He was letting the cloud pass. Eventually, he spoke.

"So how does Yorch fit in?"

"King Ronald believes that we can negotiate a treaty with the Empress. Yorch's armies will secure our borders in return for trade and token."

"So he wants Imperial troops to secure the border, and for that, the Empire gets goods and coin, which it's always looking for," Kelly said with more certainty than I expected.

"That's the plan we are pursuing," I said, "With Imperial forces behind us, Mathu would be a fool to come here. He hasn't yet built his army to the point to invade us alone, never mind if we have Imperial backing. But he's certainly building to that point, and he won't want us to get the support that would make his efforts worthless. The king and his counselors, including my father, believe that he will try to stop or delay the treaty by intercepting the ambassador before they can meet. I was sent to greet him and discreetly get him to the king without incident."

"So that was the hurry," he said with a nod, "you needed to get here to Clemons so you could meet up with the ambassador before Mathu's people can find him and stop him."

I nodded. Kelly looked back and forth from Myk to me again.

"You're looking for help," he said as he realized our purpose.

"Myk and I talked last night," I said, "and the experience with the brigands was a good reminder. In seeking to be discreet, I might have opened the door to dangers other than just being discovered. It's clear that this is a job for two."

"Or more," Myk interjected with a mumble. I looked at him, and he quieted. He had suggested the night before to use a whole unit of his men. In truth, he had argued quite strongly for it. I told him, though, that unless he knew of a way for me to take his city guard and not leave his city without law and order, that suggestion was off the table. He had relented, but not happily.

"But you're here, and you're already on the fringe of the whole plan," I continued. I didn't say what had ultimately convinced me the night before; that there was something about Kelly that I naturally felt could be trusted. It was a gut instinct, and as I spoke with Myk that night, it was more and more apparent that it was one in which I held faith.

It marks, as will again become evident, one of my few good 'gut' decisions.

"Okay, I'm in," Kelly said after a moment's pause, "if for no other reason than because I saved your life, and now I feel responsible." He smiled broadly.

"I had it under control," I shot back.

"Sure," he said, "where is your purse again?"

Myk laughed and reached over to retrieve a small bundle of papers from the far side of the table. Just then, the red-headed guard we had met at the Tower door came rushing in.

"My lord!" He said too loudly. He was out of breath from the stairs and took two rasping gasps, during which he realized he had barged into a private meeting. "Oh! Sorry!"

Myk, who was never much of one to stand on ceremony, said, "No, no problem, Phranc. What's wrong?"

"A message, sir. A messenger from the lookouts says he saw an Imperial ship passing near Auron – the lands of Duke Duglas. There were three ships following it!"

I looked at Myk while the implications settled on us both.

"Look!" Kelly said, suddenly. He had gone to the window and had been scanning the horizon while the guard was talking. He was now pointing at four small dots off to the northwest, barely visible in the dawn light.

"Mathu's ships," I said, my teeth gritted, "They have to be. They're trying to stop the ambassador before he even gets to the harbor."

CHAPTER TWO

— DANA —

By far, the majority of the voyage had been uneventful, even if we take into account my more personal discomfort. Travel by sea was never something I particularly enjoyed in the best of circumstances, there were a few instances – more than enough, actually – where our voyage had been particularly unkind to me. Our transition from the openness of the Great Eastern Ocean to the narrows of the channel that led west had been tempestuous, and the ship was rocked severely for much of it. The turbulence that we endured had, quite characteristically, lead to my feeling an equivalent restlessness in my stomach that I did not enjoy at all. Of our vessel, however, I can say that it was pleasantly appointed, and my lady and I were well looked after by the Imperial captain and his crew. Though our quarters were small, for what they were, they befit our station. Even had my stomach's discomfort been the worst we faced on the entire journey, I would already have categorized the trip as a qualified success. Before we reached our destination, though, I would find that queasiness was far from the worst thing, and that 'qualified' is a very appropriate word.

We had been several days at sail when we finally reached the famed Teardrop Sea; an immense freshwater lake far to the west of the Empire and beyond our western mountains. From there, we continued south and west for another day before we began to close in on our destination. It was then, however, that the captain came down and gave us the disturbing news. Three ships were approaching from the northwest, he said, which were rapidly approaching as if to intercept us. The crew had made several attempts at signaling them, but no reply had come, and it was now his belief that they were hostile. It was impossible to say precisely when they would intercept, but he believed that we would not make our destination port – a small harbor known as Clemons – before it happened. Presuming they meant us harm, and we agreed with his conclusion on this immediately, there would likely be conflict. He directed that it would be best for us to remain below decks while he and his crew would do their best to evade them or defend against them by whatever means they could. My companion protested, insisting she and I should be helping in some way above decks. For Princess Julea Niconnal bar Ardallah, daughter of the Empress herself and royal ambassador, the protest was as typical of her personality as it was inappropriate.

"Surely, captain," she said, acting as if he had already

agreed with her, “another pair of hands would be helpful. We are no strangers to hard work. Granted, we’ve not the experience of the crew, but we can help, certainly.” She stood and squared off against the captain, bringing the full pressure of her presence to bore.

The captain was a seasoned sailor. Over several of our dinners with him, he had entertained us with tales of the years he had spent at sea in the service of the Empire, facing pirates, the mysteries of the Great Ocean, stormy seas, and rebellious crews. Now though, the grizzled veteran stood in place with a look of near panic on his face as he tried desperately to tell the Imperial heir why she should not go on deck and work with the crew.

I moved up behind her and touched her arm. “I’m sorry, Imperial Highness, but I have to agree with the captain,” I said, well knowing how little she liked it when I used formal titles with her in any circumstance. “Your safety and, therefore, your ability to potentially escape this threat is my main responsibility. Working on the deck in these circumstances is not tactically wise.”

Julea eyed me gravely, flashed a glance to the captain, then relented. “Very well,” she said with a resignation that it was apparent she didn’t feel, “Captain, do what you must.” He bowed low to her, nodded a quick nod to me that I interpreted as a heartfelt thank you, and left the room.

“Dana–,” she said, wheeling on me the moment the

door closed. I raised a finger and cut her off.

"Jules, you can chastise me all you wish," I said gravely, "but your mother would have me drawn, quartered, burned at the stake, and buried in a manure pile if I let you go work a ship in a crisis like this. And not necessarily in that order."

It was evident that she was still flexed to pounce, but as my words sunk home, I could already see her settling back. I had known her for most of my life, as she had me, and I well knew that being kept out of the action was maddening to her. It was for me as well, for reasons that were not dissimilar. And yet, while my heart might be up there, my duty was down here. I was not born to the silver spoon; my parents having been free landowners and wealthy, but not of the royal class, and so duty had become the cornerstone of my life. Combat and peril I had been eminently trained for, and it gave me a better perspective in such times. But then, I knew her to be so much more capable than me in so many other ways, consistently poised, intelligent, and beautiful. And I'd seen her on those mornings after when the nights before had included far too much wine.

"Fine," she said, with actual resignation this time. She looked at me hard for a moment, then said, "but 'Imperial Highness?' Ugh."

"I do what needs to be done to arrest your attention, Imperial Highness," I said, this time with a small, mischievous grin on my face. She punched my arm in a very un-regal way. It was not the first time.

"Seriously though Jules," I said, "the Imperial Navy trains the best seamen in the world. We only need to wait patiently for—," I stopped; she was glaring at me, a twinkle in her eye.

It took me a moment to realize what caused the glare. I rolled my eyes, "Oh good grief, Jules. We're adults." She was snickering now. "Fine," I said, flushing a little, "The best sailors in the world." I sighed in a way that was meant to be disapproving but didn't hide a slight snicker of my own.

"I know," she said, her annoyance now replaced with resignation. "And of course you're right. The best thing is to stay here. If the ship is taken, we might yet sneak away in the confusion that ensues, and if not, no harm was done. It's the wisest action. But that doesn't mean I like it." She sat down and looked out the large rectangular windows at the sea rolling behind us. It was obvious that she didn't like it; that she'd rather be doing anything else. The imperial heir or not, she tended always to be the first to get her hands dirty if she could. And yet, I also knew that my friend had made a life of doing what needed to be done and not what she wished to do. I stepped over and put my hand on her shoulder.

"Thanks, Dana," she said quietly. We watched out the glass at the three small dots that were growing in the distance.

It was hard to tell how much later it was when the uproar began. The ship had been tacking into the wind which seemed to have developed the will to drive us into the laps of our pursuers. Only the aforementioned skill of the crew kept them at bay. The princess and I passed our time going over the treaty protocols that the Empress had sent with us and skimming the books we had taken from the Imperial library that described the Western Kingdom – apparently referred to locally as "Lochhaven" – which was our destination. Our Imperial instructors, both Julea's and my own, had only briefly mentioned the place and its king, Ronald. Never once had this idea that they maintained no standing army been discussed. Perhaps, Julea mused, to the great minds of the Empire's tactical schools such a thing sounded like a fantasy. I simply commented that it would seem that their request for this treaty was substantial evidence that it was a fantasy.

During this time, the dots on the horizon gradually resolved themselves into three large ships as they got closer moment by moment. Julea and I began gathering our most needed possessions and otherwise making whatever preparation we could in the face of what now seemed to be inevitable conflict. We had occasional glimpses of the shore as our vessel tacked its way in, but such only afforded us vague estimates of when we would arrive, and the pursuers were very close indeed.

Our pursuers – three tall warships at full sail – had

gotten very close, with the lead ship only a handful of yards to our aft. Suddenly, our vessel rolled hard over, tilting the floor of our cabin to a high angle and causing us both to stumble. We steadied ourselves by holding on to the side tables in the room, fastened as they were to both the floor and the walls. Most of the fixtures in the little cabin were affixed in this fashion, an obvious precaution on a ship, so only our personal items – ones that we had carelessly left unattended – were tossed about. If either of us had thought to see to them, we had no time to do so, as the ship rolled again just as suddenly, but to the opposite side. Going from so far one direction to the other exaggerated the motion, making it feel as if the ship was rolling over. My stomach, ever eager to remind me that it disliked sea travel, did an exaggerated roll of its own. The discomfort must have shown on my face.

"Easy…," I heard Julea say to me in a gentle, almost motherly tone, "Keep looking out the windows. It will help." She had already seen me return one previously eaten meal on this ship when we entered the western sea passage mentioned earlier, and so was well aware of how low my tolerance was for shipboard acrobatics.

Obediently, I looked out the window, just in time to watch a fantastic sequence of events. To the right of us, what appeared to be a derelict ship slowly drifted into view. It looked to be barely afloat, abandoned in the harbor with gaping holes visible in its hull just above the waterline and tattered sails hanging dubiously from its masts. The lead ship of our pursuers, by now directly behind us and uncomfortably close, began to pass it and was just a few yards away when the derelict erupted into flames. The shock of the blast of fire was still in effect when a dozen spears flew through the flames from the vessel, embedding themselves in various places in the side of the pursuing ship. The spears trailed lines which were aglow with fire and that went almost immediately taut. The pursuit ship, now effectively bound to the derelict, was pulled off course by the weight and into the other vessel.

"Jules!" I said, but she was already looking, both of us now edging closer to the windows as we watched. The two ships bumped gently together and began to spin in a tug of war between the waves and the wind. The flames, at first concentrated on the derelict craft, spread like unnatural wildfire up the side of the pursuit ship and crawled onto and across its deck. Unable to look away, we saw figures climb from the midst of the flames up onto the ship that had so recently been a threat to us with fire trailing behind them as they went. Within moments, the two vessels had merged into a single mass of flaming timber as men, indistinguishable now as to which ship they had been on, leapt into the water and swam desperately away from the inferno.

I looked over at Julea to see that she was white as a

sheet. “No. That would be impossible...,” she muttered under her breath.

I waited as long as I felt was acceptable, then said, “Jules? Princess? You look like you’ve seen a ghost. Are you all right?”

She turned toward me slowly, returning from wherever her mind had gone as she did so. “Maybe,” she muttered. There was more, but we were both compelled to turn back to the scene outside. The strange hungry fire had by now nearly consumed both ships, and they formed one giant pile of charcoal and ash feeding the flames that coughed clouds of gray smoke into the air. The mass floated on what was left of the ships, the small amount of their timber hulls that remained below the surface. In the water, in every direction we could see, figures swam hard and fast away from the carnage; the majority of them swimming out and toward the other two pursuit ships which had now turned away from the chase to focus instead on rescuing those in the water. There were, though, some number of the men who swam the opposite direction, disappearing from our view as they passed too far to the side of the windows to see. The distance between us and the remaining two ships was growing now, and I surmised that we would soon make the shore without difficulty, even if they attempted to resume their pursuit, which they seemed unlikely to do. I still couldn’t see what happened to the men in the water that had so deftly rescued us, and I hoped that their plan had included their escape.

Julea backed away from the windows, and the vacant look returned to her face. She had been staring at the flaming wreckage on the water, and only now turned away. I looked at her closely, deciding that this time, I would wait out her meditation. Her green eyes were unfocused as they darted back and forth, watching something only visible in her memory. After what felt like a very long time she looked up at me, though she still had that a faraway look. "Did you see that?" she said, a little breathlessly.

I nodded effusively. "I did. That was amazing. I can't imagine how that happened; what causes a fire to light and spread like that?" I shrugged, "It was incredible."

Julea narrowed her eyes at me as if I was missing something. "It was. A miracle, in fact. It's almost like there was something in that fire that made it behave like something else. Like it wasn't just fire." She stared at me.

I looked at her askance. "Are you talking about the legends," I said, "or those weird stories we all heard a few years ago? Come now; those were just stories. That's not what you think this was, is it?"

She looked at me; her attention again turned inward. I thought back. It had been some six years ago when for a brief time the people of the city had begun whispering of miracles. The rumors had reached the court; stories of magic and impossible feats from the very edges of the Empire. Some of the nobles had even asked the Empress herself, though she had dismissed the subject entirely. Then, just as abruptly, the stories stopped, as stories often do.

Of course, that was also during a time when my friend had been very distracted by something much more personal.

"There's no way," I said confidently. There was more to it, though. Something that had embedded itself in the princess's mind deeply enough that I wasn't going to be able to remove it.

"There's more to this than we're seeing," Julea said, looking back to the windows, "I know it."

We dropped the subject then and turned back to our preparations. Answers, the princess agreed, would have to wait. There were proprieties to be observed when we made it to the docks, and we had roles to play. No longer needing to prepare for some rushed escape, we set about putting ourselves together properly for the meeting with the representatives of the king of Lochhaven. I had brought a couple of worthy dresses among my travel clothing and armaments, and now faced the task of choosing between them. As bodyguard to the princess, I had a broader wardrobe than many, even most, royal women. A fair amount of it was what I think of as 'working clothes' – britches and tunics, armor, pauldrons and vambraces, and the personal weaponry that accompanied it – that was unique to my role. These supplemented the many dresses and fineries that being often stationed in the Imperial court demanded of me. I selected a deep burgundy dress which went nicely with the black bodice that doubled as my 'dress armor.' The dress was made of a crushed velvety material, which gave it an illusion of depth and warmth. The sleeves were tailored at the shoulder, but expanded out from there in a narrow bell shape, and would have been quite full by the wrist save that they were cut at an angle from the elbow down. This design suited me perfectly, as they camouflaged my bracers without hampering my freedom of movement. The neckline was high by my request, as my armor came up high on my torso and I found that a lower neckline chafed. The dress itself was relatively simple, hanging straight to brush the top of my boots, and the whole affair – sleeves, hemline, and neckline, were trimmed with gold over-stitching. Over this, I draped my gray velvet cloak which hung, expertly tailored, to precisely the top of my booted feet as well. I drew it around me and test fitted the hood. It did as intended and hid all detail of my clothing beneath, as well as covering my rapier – my preference over the typical Imperial long-sword – which hung at my left hip.

Julea too draped her gray velvet cloak over her shoulders, but not before I saw the deep emerald green dress she had selected. It was cut similarly to mine, angled bell-like sleeves and gold over-stitching, but as her duties didn't require the same kind of equipment, it made no concessions to armor or exertion as mine did. As such, the neckline came down generously and tastefully; the front was laced together with a golden cord. The shoulders were open from her neckline to the midpoint of her upper arm, and the sleeves were fuller. The color was a perfect compliment for her honey-blonde hair and picked up the green in her eyes. It was an unusual choice for her, far more likely to be worn to an affair of state than a formal meeting. I considered it.

"Do you think," I said cautiously, for the first time in a while unsure of my freedom of speech with my friend, "that a different dress might be more suited to the occasion? Something more suited to the business at hand?"

She shot me a look which inspired in me a genuine concern for my future. "Or, not," I said quickly. "Your choice, certainly."

Princess Julea Niconnal bar Ardallah of Yorch looked at me for a heartbeat, then said, "You look lovely, Lady Dana. I think that red compliments your dark hair nicely." It was an honest compliment, delivered in a stilted tone that was meant to remind me that some things weren't open for input. I bowed my head.

"Thank you. And the green is an exquisite choice." I smiled gently.

"Thank you," she said and paused for a long moment. She looked at herself in the mirror and fussed with her hair one last time. She wore it down, with two small sections near her temples swept back and braided together behind her head and hanging down her back. A small golden chain stretched across her forehead to complete the look. She turned back to me, the odd irritation having dissipated. "I know," she said. "It's just...," she looked down, then back up, "I have the strangest feeling. Do you know how people say when something feels off that it's like someone stepped on their grave? I feel that. Something is," she paused, "off. I just need you with me, okay?" She was almost rambling as she spoke, something I had never seen her do. There was, I realized, something that she wasn't telling me; something that was troubling her. I put my hand on her shoulder and smiled.

"I am always with you, Jules," I said, and I meant it. I can still hear my voice giving that promise before I knew anything of what was to come.

A knock came at the door, and with our permission, it opened a moment later to two of the crewmen. They were wearing their full Imperial Honor Guard uniforms in preparation for our disembarking. They greeted Julea with a bow, snapped a practiced salute to me, then turned without a word to escort us out. We put up our hoods, wrapped our cloaks around us, and followed them through the ship. We negotiated the narrow halls and steeply angled stairs to finally emerge onto the deck of our transport ship and into the late afternoon sun. Stationed at various assigned positions across the vessel were the crew, each fully festooned in their dress uniforms of gold trimmed maroon, topped with white waistcoats prominently bearing the stylized wolf's head that was the standard of the Empire. Their golden helmets glinted in the sun as they stood at attention with their hands resting on the hilts of their sheathed long-swords. At our appearance, they drew the blades and held them aloft at a high angle in salute. I thought for a moment how few of them there were. The Empress had instructed that the crew be small and the ship we traveled on be unassuming for purposes of remaining unnoticed in our passage, but after being pursued as we had been, it gave me pause. If they had overtaken us, there would have been very little hope of fending them off. But it didn't happen, I reminded myself, and thinking like that is unproductive.

We walked down the gangplank and up the dock. At the end stood a group of about twenty men clad in navy blue and black. Ten or so on a side, they formed an aisle which ended before a small, stocky man with graying hair. He was dressed as they were, but instead of leather, he wore a silver chain mail vest that glinted in the afternoon sun, and a blue dress-cloak over his one shoulder. At his side hung a medium-sized warhammer with silver inlays. I considered him for a moment, then the hammer, and decided that it had likely never seen use.

The men we passed seemed very nervous, even tense. At first, it put me on edge, but I quickly realized that these were men for whom official visitors from the Empire was the highlight of, potentially, their lives. I straightened my back more. If this was a thrill for them, then it was my responsibility to play my role well. I flashed on the idea for just a moment that this feeling, new to me, was how the princess felt all the time.

We stopped before the short man, Julea a pace in front of me. He bowed awkwardly, looking down at his feet, then back up. We returned the gesture, then removed our hoods.

A look that I can only describe as one of unveiled confusion replaced the friendly open expression on his face. He stood frozen for just long enough to be awkward, then extended his hand as if nothing had happened. I smirked slightly with the realization that he hadn't been expecting women.

"Uh," he said, admirably continuing while still recovering, "I'm Baron Myk Peralta, Lord of Clemons. I'm representing King Ronald Kastellian of Lochhaven."

"I am Lady Julea Niconnal, ambassador of Yorch, and this is my companion Lady Dana Lunavale," Julea said, smiling politely and taking his hand. I noticed what she specifically didn't include about herself by not using her full title or the Imperial form of her name. She was careful, even with – at this point still potential – allies.

Lord Myk, shaking her hand and then releasing it quickly, said, "It's great that you could make it. How was the trip?"

"Just fine until the last stretch. The pursuit was concerning. From what my captain tells me and from what I saw from my quarters, we wouldn't have made it without the assistance of your men. I offer my gratitude."

Lord Myk nodded.

"How long before we are to meet with your king?" she asked, lowering her voice so that only the closest to us could hear her.

"You can't leave until the morning," he replied, "You wouldn't get very far with the light that's left today. Besides, it wouldn't hurt for you to rest a little from your journey and all of the excitement," he said, nodding a little toward the bay. "We've got a room in the Tower for you all prepared." He swept his hand toward the large stone tower overlooking the bay.

"Again, my thanks," Julea said with a nod, every inch the professional noblewoman.

The Lord of Clemons turned and gestured two men forward. He turned back to Julea and said, "These two men led the group that rescued your ship. They are also assigned the privilege of guiding you to our king. Let me introduce you."

Julea nodded again as the two figures came forward. The first was a tall man with dark brown hair, not dissimilar from my own, and narrow features. He was not quite fully dry from his adventures in the water and looked bedraggled as a result. In spite of that, he carried himself with a quiet sort of seriousness.

"Lady Julea, Lady Dana," Lord Myk said, indicating each of us in turn, "this is Lord Aeryk Escrios, Marquess of Claire."

Lord Aeryk bowed deeply and deftly, then stood and offered his hand to Julea and me, giving each a gentle squeeze and bow as he took them in turn. He was high born, that much was evident, and his manners seemed impeccable, which was a surprise to me. I had not seen nor expected that in a rural kingdom like this one. "My pleasure," he said to each of us.

"Mine as well," we both said in reply.

"And this is Kelly," Lord Myk continued then, turning to the other man.

Kelly stepped forward. He too was still wet; his black clothing damply clinging to him as he stood came forward. His dark brown hair appeared to have been combed back with nothing more sophisticated than his fingers and flopped on his forehead in an unruly tangle. Recognition swept through me, and I barely restrained a shocked intake of breath. He and Julea looked at and through each other for just a moment longer than seemed comfortable, and I realized that some private, wordless communication was taking place. It was over in the flash of a second, though, and she extended her hand. He reached out, took it carefully, and gave it the gentle squeeze of custom as he bowed.

"I'm honored, my lady," he said, never taking his eyes off her. "And may I say, that is a lovely green you're wearing." I felt a wave of tension wash off my friend.

Releasing her hand, he turned to me and took mine as well. I nodded to him as he did so, and caught the faintest grin as he looked at me. Then he stepped back to his position behind the marquess. Julea – the consummate professional – turned back to the Lord of Clemons.

"Shall we go?" Julea said to Lord Myk, her voice formal and – if only to me – several degrees colder than before. The baron nodded to her, obviously unaware that something unrelated to the official meeting was happening. He clapped his hands twice, and the columns of guards formed up and walked us up the pathway toward the Tower.

I looked back over my shoulder once to see Kelly and Lord Aeryk standing on the end of the dock. Kelly was half sitting on a post and saying something while the marquess looked confused. He glanced up, saw me looking, and shrugged. I turned away and followed my princess.

There was a dinner not long after, and while the food may not have been what I was accustomed to in the Imperial

Palace, I can honestly say that after days at sea and fighting waves of nausea, it was delicious. Julea and I decided to wear our less formal apparel for fear of seeming like we intended to lord over our hosts. As such, we dined in our traveling clothes – dark brown britches and tunics. Now, of course, even they were very finely crafted and easily the equal of the best of the clothing we saw on display that night in the Tower. Little did we realize that our fashion choices, such as they were, would affect the style of the women of Clemons for long after we had left.

I have ever been a quiet person, content to listen and watch others. My friend is much more gregarious, as befits her station and its requirements. She held conversations with all those at the meal, even speaking for a while with one of the serving boys. Still, through it all, she kept her formal facade firmly in place, and I followed suit as I was called on to do. We were in a foreign land, she had said while we were still on the ship, and we will not quickly know who our real friends are. Therefore we will be cautious and reticent, but polite and cordial. It was a knife's edge that she balanced on with apparent ease, while I found it much simpler to remain observant and laconic. In due course, the meal came to an end, and we retired to the room set aside for us.

It was noteworthy to me that Kelly had declined the party; instead, he took his meal in his room. I did not comment on this to Jules. Somehow the subject did not seem a safe one to broach.

Much later that night, I heard the soft creak of the bed frame from across the room and opened one eye. In the dying light of the fire, I could make out the shadow of Julea slipping on her shoes and slowly creeping to the door while throwing her woolen day cloak about her shoulders. I waited for what I believed was a fair amount of time before I got up, slipped into my boots and cloak, and followed. The light scuff of distant footsteps above me told me that she was going up, and so I followed. I had a moment's pause. Should I be doing this? I dismissed the thought and continued, chastising myself. Her safety is my responsibility. Physical or emotional.

I followed the sound of her footsteps as they led to the top floor of the Tower. The hatch that led to the roof was open, and I came out both carefully and noiselessly. Outside in the cold night air, the world was silent except for the distant lapping of the waves below. The waxing half-moon was high in a cloudless sky, and everything was bathed in soft bluish light. Across from me, I could see Julea standing by the castellated parapet and watching the water. I started toward her when I heard a footfall from down the stairs behind me. Moving as quickly and silently as I could, I slipped into the shadow of a small supply shed off to the right of the tower roof; it was likely used for siege storage, though I doubted it had ever seen use. A black-cloaked man came out of the hatch and stood almost exactly where I had been a moment before. After a short pause, the figure began to move toward Julea. I tensed, quietly sneaking around the shed so that I could see and hear; and intervene, if it was needed.

"Good evening, Princess," came Kelly's voice. "Pretty view isn't it?"

"It is," she said, too quickly but quietly. She didn't turn and remained silent. He walked up even with her at the parapet, but a few feet to one side to keep a polite distance.

"I meant what I said earlier," he said, watching the sea, "that green dress really did look good on you, Jul—"

"Why are you here?" she said suddenly, cutting off his last syllable, "I mean, what are you up to?"

Her voice was flat and cold as the wind. I swear I saw Kelly shiver at the tone even from my spot several feet away. Her question hung for a long moment. Finally, he sighed and looked up toward the moon.

"Coincidence," Kelly said finally, in a monotone that matched hers. "I met Aeryk by accident on the road as he probably told you by now. We traveled together for a bit and became friends. He said that he had business with the Empire," he paused, thoughtfully, "I guess my curiosity got the better of me. Old habits, you know."

"Coincidence," she muttered, almost as an accusation.

There was another pause. He continued, "There was no way I could have known that the ambassador he was meeting would be you. It isn't like your mother to send you out on something like this."

"Keep your estimations or imagined insights into my mother's decisions to yourself," she snapped. I felt my own eyes go wide. After years of practice and conditioning, Julea had a nearly superhuman control over her reactions, so seeing her on edge was unsettling.

Another moment passed and then, realizing she had reacted a little more harshly than intended, she said with a small chuckle, "Though that's not entirely unfair."

"So. I suppose we'll just have to make the best of it?" he said, more warmly this time, as if her choice to back away from the burst of anger had broken through some barrier. He had phrased it as a question, but it was not a request; it was more of a statement of intent, but still, one seeking a confirmation.

More silence followed. There was an unspoken negotiation going on, I could see. Not the one on the surface between them in the present, but rather one that lived in the past. A tug of war between need, responsibility, desire, and pain. Finally, Julea spoke.

"You're planning to stay then," she said. It was a statement, not a question.

"I said I would. That's what I do," he said.

She spun and looked directly at him, a breath drawn in to respond. The look that passed between them carried meaning, and history, and even a challenge. It was again apparent that there were volumes of things that weren't being said. Finally, and a bit slowly, she turned back to the water, and let the breath go.

"I don't trust you," she said.

A beat. "No, princess," he said, "you probably don't at that. But," and here he took one small step toward her, "maybe you'll learn to again. I mean, you did know to meet me up here. We still have a history that wasn't all bad."

She turned back to him, and again they locked gazes.

"They call you 'Kelly,'" she said after another silence, an eyebrow arched.

"People have for a while now; I needed something," he said, flashing a quick grin.

Julea nodded; an explicit acceptance of the arrangement now in her expression. She returned to the controlled and practiced role she played. "Okay," she said, "but here, especially in this situation, I'm not the 'princess.' Stop calling me that."

"Whatever you say," Kelly said. He turned at that and walked back toward the trapdoor. "'Til morning," he called back, "good night, my lady." He opened the door and began to walk down the stairs, but just before he disappeared into the Tower, he looked directly at where I was hiding in the shadows. And smiled.

I froze there for a long time. Julea went back into the Tower a few minutes later. Still, I waited. I thought about the memories I had myself of the man now called Kelly and the princess.

The past ever seeds the present, and in the now we have the fruit of the past with which to deal. The master of my tactics courses said that long ago. He said that when facing an unknown – enemy or friend – the best thing to do was always to try best to understand what brought all parties to the present moment. I didn't know many of the details of the time when they had known one another; as close as the princess and I had always been, that was an aspect of her life that she had chosen to keep her own counsel about, even on those nights of wine and revelation. I drew conclusions, of course; I'm not a fool; but I didn't know what the full story was. I worried for my friend, but I knew that she, perhaps more than anyone, would do the right thing. My responsibility hadn't changed. I would continue to protect her, whatever that may mean. Eventually, I returned to our room. The princess was fast asleep, making my entrance easier. I wondered if I would have to explain my absence in the morning. Did she even notice that I was gone when she returned? But that was a question for then, I decided. Rolling over and settling again into the first bed I'd been in on dry land in far too long; I let sleep take me.

CHAPTER THREE
– AERYK –

I rose at dawn on the day following the ambassador's arrival. I intended to oversee the packing of our supplies for our coming journey. The capital of Lochhaven and home of the high court was Castle Sterling, the ancestral home of the Kastellian family. The ancient palace in the middle of that sprawling city was, in particular, our destination. While the distance between the two holds was not so far as the crow flew, such a direct route was impossible. Even were we to manage the less than friendly terrain, there was still the Aosta Forest, a wild and untamed tangle of confounding plant and hungry predator. It stretched over much of the northeastern part of Lochhaven – covering much of the province of Sterling in particular – but it qualified as our lands in name only; it was untamed wilderness. The local militias patrolled its borders; the denizens inside thwarted all efforts to go deeper. The king believed, with the approval of the court, that the cost to create and maintain any reliably safe passages through would far outweigh the effort required simply to go around. As a result, our company could expect at least three days on a gradually ascending road with a few sparse settlements on the way. Thus, I went to the stables with the intent to be sure that Myk's horsemen had made sufficient provision for the expected length of the trip. The more profound truth was that I was motivated by a lack of confidence in Myk's men, and even more by a need to make myself useful as more than a glorified bodyguard to the ambassador. Yet, I entered the main door of the stable only to find Kelly, standing with Locksley in the middle of the open area between the stalls. He was tightening the straps that held a new leather saddle on the stallion's back.

He didn't look up as I came near, but said, "I got the idea that we would want to leave as soon as we were able. So, I went out of the city early this morning and caught up with him," he tilted his head toward Locksley, "We came back here, and I've been giving him some attention before we get underway." He patted the horse's flank. I saw a brush nearby and noticed that Locksley had been brushed down; his mane and tail combed out. If the stallion had been impressive before, the grooming only served to highlight that the horse was a stunning creature.

"I, ah, thought along the same lines," I said, slightly off balance but not wanting to seem so. "I also thought it might be good to oversee the loading of supplies."

Kelly nodded and turned his attention back to his ministrations. He remained quiet as he loaded up his personal belongings – his bed-roll and packs – and then added a couple of the supply bundles that Myk's servants had provided, draping them evenly over the horse's hind end. Once finished to his satisfaction, he went around to the horse's head and spoke quietly for a few moments directly into Locksley's ear before giving him a gentle pat.

"I also had a thought," he said, stepping away from his steed toward me.

"Oh? What's that?" I said, half listening. I had begun busying myself with counting the remaining supply bundles even as the stable hands were loading them onto the horses Clemons was providing for the journey. After a moment, I noticed by his silence that he was waiting for more of my attention. I turned to him, inwardly annoyed that I was now losing count.

He looked out the stable doors through which the light of the dawn gently glowed he spoke. "I've been thinking about our route. After what happened yesterday, it's a sure thing that the road is going to be watched; and without a doubt, by those it would be best for us to avoid."

I bounced my shoulders in a feeble shrug. The thought, correct yet useless at the same time, had already occurred to me. "Sure, but we don't have many choices, do we? It's the only way to the king."

He looked at me and cocked his head. There was a kind of mischief playing in his eyes. "Is it?" A moment passed before I took the meaning of his words and all but laughed.

"That's madness," I said with a shake of my head. "Trying to take a path through the Aosta is suicide. Even with everything considered, we'll have a better chance on the road."

"See, that's the problem," he said. He ran his fingers through his hair as he spoke. "I'm not convinced that's true. Not after yesterday. This King Mathu is sparing no expense to stop your meeting."

"Three ships is a commitment, I agree," I said. He had my interest now, as the undisguised attack on the sea the day before was still very much on my mind for several reasons. He was already shaking his head.

"That is part of it, sure," he said, "but not just that. When we were on board that ship, I ran into the captain."

I blinked, "You did? How do you know it was the captain?"

Kelly said, "You don't see Edword Ribald on a ship where he isn't the captain."

I felt my eyes go wide. "Ribald? The pirate? Are you sure?"

"No question," he said, "Let's just say that we've crossed paths before."

My mind reeled. Edword Ribald was the bogeyman; the scary story sailors told to keep the night watchmen awake. He had slipped in and out of the shipping lanes for years, a shadow over the seas that was always there. Over the last year, he had drifted further into legend by having seemed to disappear. Some said he retired, and some said he died, but the one thing that no one believed was that he had been overcome. A cold fear ran through me so sharp that it seemed to be trying to make up for being a day late.

"He's a mercenary," Kelly continued after a beat, his tone almost consoling. He had seen my thoughts play across my face and waited until I was able to focus again. "An elusive one, but a mercenary nonetheless. More importantly, he works for others rarely and only for the highest price. If he was commanding the ships that pursued your new Imperial friends, that means there is many a ducat to be had."

In short order, I found myself at the same conclusion that he must have reached. "So you're thinking that if Mathu is spending enough to attract Edword, he'll be spending enough to have the road from here to Castle Sterling watched by the very best sell-swords in the business," I said.

He nodded. "Mercenaries come a dime a dozen, but the good ones come a dozen dimes each, so to speak. I'm guessing we should expect the best of the worst on that road. So I say, let's not give go on the road. We don't have the manpower or the time to secure it, so we don't use it."

I shook my head, but without much enthusiasm. I knew what he was suggesting, but my heart was clawing at me to find any other solution. “You are underestimating the dangers of the forest,” I said.

“That could be,” he said, “but what I’m not underestimating is what’s likely on that road.” He looked at me, waiting. “It is your call, your lordship. I’m just advising. Should we talk it over with Lord Myk?”

I thought for a long moment while he waited. There were so many more dynamics than he knew. Talking it over with the Lord of Clemons was not something I could allow. Would I prefer to be shot or hanged? I thought. More like shot or mauled. “I did hire you for your help, and you’ve been worth it so far,” I said to him, “Are you sure about this?”

“I’m never sure,” Kelly said, more honestly than I would have preferred. “This could all bottom out at any minute. But it seems like our best option, and we may yet have some surprises up our sleeves.”

“Perhaps you could lie to me now? Just a little?” I said. I looked back and forth, but nowhere I looked provided a quick answer. I blew out a breath, then said, “Fine, we’ll do it your way. But if this goes wrong—”

“One bit of good news is that if this goes wrong, there will probably be very little either of us will get to say about it,” he said, cutting me off and grinning at me. I shook my head, knowing full well he was right. Then I had a thought. A question.

"What surprises did we have up our sleeves yesterday, by the way?" I asked, "I still don't know how all that worked."

Kelly turned toward the packs of supplies and grabbed one. "It worked really, really well, in my opinion," he said.

"No, no," I shook my head, "I mean, how did it work? You can't just set a ship on fire like that; warships have a treatment that slows the spread of fire. Otherwise, every battle at sea would only be a matter of getting off the first volley of flaming arrows. That fire acted as if it had, I don't know; intent."

He handed the pack to one of the stable boys nearby. "Intent, eh? That would be bizarre," he said. I waited. He kept moving the packs.

"You're really not going to tell me, are you?" I said.

"I can't think of what I would tell you," Kelly replied. "You were right there. What did you see happen?"

With that, I thought back to the afternoon before. After spotting the ships from Clemons's tower, I immediately sprinted for the docks though Kelly hung back, keeping pace instead with Myk. I heard Kelly asking him for a few men, any small ship that could be sacrificed, though most of the rest was lost to me as I rounded the flight of stairs. I did hear Myk's voice bellow out some orders from behind me, though the specifics were also lost to the jumble of echoing sounds in the tower. I reached the ground floor and headed out across the courtyard and down the hill, cursing the wretched boots with every step.

By the time I got to the docks, a dozen of the city's militia were already gathered there, having been summoned by the horn I now realized had been blowing from the tower. Kelly came up from behind me, and together we waited until one of the tower steward's came up and pointed us to an old barge lashed to one of the moors. Kelly started barking out instructions – calling for a barrel of lantern oil and ropes – while I made directly for the barge. It was a dilapidated thing, with gaping holes above the waterline that had been patched with misfit boards and mold encrusting the corners of the deck, but it was still afloat, and that was what we most needed. As soon as the men bearing the supplies Kelly called for were aboard, we shoved off. He selected six of the men and had them rushing about various tasks – kicking out the patchwork of planks, cutting down the threadbare sails, and pouring out some of the lantern oil along the side of the deck. He took the ropes they had brought and tossed them in the barrels with the remaining oil in them.

Meanwhile, I had the other six men take up the oars and steer us toward the oncoming ships. As the first men wearied, the other six traded in, and thus we closed the distance rapidly as the tide and wind – even without functional sails – was in our favor. Kelly took the spears that each of the men carried and tied the now oil-soaked ropes to them and to whatever fixtures there were left on the wreck that seemed secure. I was fixated on our approach to the enemy, but could not fathom what he was intending.

Shortly, we judged we were close enough that we might be seen from the enemy craft, and Kelly called for the oars to be pulled in and for all of the men to duck down and hide. Trusting in the barge to drift the right way on its own – and on the Imperial helmsman's intuition – we waited to draw close to one of the pursuing ships. It was a successful gamble, for the helmsman did the best possible thing, rolling their transport in as sharp an arc as the ship could manage. It passed very near us and left us scant yards from its pursuer's path.

Up until then, everything seemed – if not absolutely insane – at least mostly understandable to me. I was terrified, make no mistake, but at least I was terrified of things that I understood. In the ensuing moments, that was no longer the case. Kelly had been prowling up and down the deck on his knees, and as he went, he quietly nudged the crouching men to back away from where they had spread the lantern oil shortly before. At last, he stopped, pulled two small stones from a black bag, and struck them together. A single little spark hit the oil, but instead of the gentle spread of a new fire, a great gout of blue-green flame erupted and spread in seconds down the side of the barge. The men jumped back, but already Kelly was shouting for them to throw the spears. Their throws had less expertise than I would have hoped, but there had just been a terrifying burst of flames less than half a dozen feet in front of them, so guess I can forgive their loss of focus. The spears though, trailing the ropes, wedged themselves into the side of the other ship stoutly; much more so than I anticipated. I felt our barge suddenly jerk hard from the momentum of the other ship as the ropes now connecting us to her went taut, pulling against the tie-points violently. The force threw me hard against the railing and sent us into a tight spin that brought the two vessels crashing together.

Of course, the ropes also carried the unnatural fire, soaked as they had been in oil, and where they touched the sides of the other vessel, it began to burn as well. Kelly told the men to charge, and we ran forward, catching hold of the flank of the pursuit ship and climbing up. I credited it to my imagination, but I swore I saw twinkles of fire, like falling fireflies, falling off of the men as they climbed, and where the little sparks landed on the deck more flames came into being. By now, the fire had changed to the considerably more normal orange and yellow color of a nice, sensible inferno, and clouds of smoke billowed all around. From the choking smoke came the call from somewhere to abandon ship. It sounded like a very rational voice, I decided, and I moved to follow its direction. I found my way to the opposite side of the deck from where I had boarded, and as I prepared to jump into the water, I turned to see that the path I had taken was also ablaze, as if the fire was coming off of me as well. I had no time to think what that might mean, though, as the blaze was growing at an unearthly speed. I jumped into the water. Together with the other men from Clemons, we swam as best we could from the conflagration until a small rowboat; somehow having followed us from the dock; picked us up.

"I saw two ships go up in flames that were not possible," I said, coming back to the present and looking at Kelly.

"Well that can't be what happened," he said with a casualness that was quite infuriating, "The flames had to be possible. Seriously." He looked around at the horses now gathered for us. "Ready to go?"

"Impossible flames, impossible man," I muttered though he was already walking Locksley and another horse away. I took two of them by the reins and followed him out into the new day.

Kelly then led the way around the side of the Lord's Tower from the stables to the front courtyard where we had first arrived. We had a total of six horses, including Locksley, between the stable hand, Kelly, and me. That would be sufficient for us, the two Imperial women, and two of the Lord's Tower guards that had been assigned to accompany us despite my protests.

"I can't spare any more men," Myk had said at dinner the night before, "but I won't feel right without offering some help." I thanked him, though based on what little I had seen of his men and their training, I wondered exactly how much help this was indeed going to be.

The courtyard had a full complement of the city's militia in place, and we waited in the center for our eastern guests. Myk's servants had already brought down their personal belongings and sundries, and these were added to the packs on the horses. There was a heaviness to the air, and the thick clouds in the sky seemed so low that I felt like I needed to duck my head or be swallowed by them. I stole a look toward the sea, and it too seemed to feel the heaviness of the day; only the slightest ripple marred it, and it mirrored the gray sky so perfectly that it was hard to see where one ended, and the other began. I turned back toward the Tower and saw Lady Sherilyn was standing nearby to see us off. I smiled at her, and she favored me with a return smile and a brief wave. I took a step toward her when I heard Kelly mumble. I glanced at him, then saw that he was watching Lady Dana and Lady Julea come out of the Tower.

"What was that you said?" I asked him quietly.

"I said, 'Oh good, we can get moving,'" he said without inflection.

"Funny," I said, "it sounded like it was, 'Oh god, can we get moving?'" I raised my eyebrow at him.

He looked at me and maintained his deadpan expression. “Of course not,” he said. “That would be disrespectful.” To his credit, he never cracked a smile. I did, but just a small one.

The Imperial ambassador and her bodyguard were garbed now in tunics and britches – dark green for the former and burgundy for the latter – covered with black scale armor and boots. At the princess’s side hung a standard Imperial long-sword, while Lady Dana bore a silver-handled rapier. Rather than the fashionable gray cloaks from their arrival, they wore heavier ones, woolen and meant for travel. Draping these over an arm, they mounted their horses with quick, fluid motions and in perfect unison. Out of the corner of my eye, I saw a smile pass over Kelly’s face.

“Is there –” I started, but second guessed myself. Too late, though; Kelly had turned.

“Is there what?” he said.

I looked over to the Imperials and back to him, making a show of it. “Is there something I should know?”

“Hunh?”

The discomfort in my mind took center stage. I had to address at least some of the mysteries surrounding me. “Look,” I said, “I decided to trust you when I hired you. You haven’t given me a reason to doubt that choice yet, but I feel like something is –,” I let the sentence hang as a question.

He put his hand on my arm. “Aeryk, it’s fine. Like I

told you yesterday, I am a little uncomfortable around people from Yorch. I have some..., history there. But there's nothing to worry about. My blade is at your side."

I thought for a long moment, then mirrored his hand on my arm with mine on his. "Okay," I said, "That's good enough for me. Let's get on our way."

Once we were all mounted, we let the two militiamen lead the way out of the city through a smaller north-western gate. The two young men, brothers by the name of Rindros, were eager, and given the opportunity spoke far too much and too freely for guardsmen. The older of the two, Markh, had been the red-haired guard that had greeted Kelly and me when we arrived and was under the impression, it seemed, that it made us friends. I suspected that it was because of a general lack of discipline in Clemons; Myk's casualness as to protocol seemed to be evidence of that. But they were pleasant, and seemed somewhat awestruck to be leaving the city on an 'important mission.' We followed the road due west for some time. I didn't know precisely what Kelly planned as far as turning off into the Aosta Forest, but I knew we would be safe within sight of the city and while still in Myk's lands, so we were able to settle into the ride for a bit. The two brothers split up, one taking a position in front of us and the other at the rear, allowing the four of us to ride together for a bit and talk.

Well, we could have talked. Despite their mannerly

and gracious behavior at the dinner the night before, neither of the women seemed at all interested in talking to either Kelly or me. While I could occasionally get some small response to a direct question, there was no conversation forthcoming. Eventually, I found myself trotting along with Markh at the rear and discussing autumn birds for some reason. Just ahead of me, Kelly rode alongside Dana, and I noticed her stealing glances in his direction, though quick to look away if he happened to turn. I realized that she was surreptitiously admiring Locksley.

"He's a *rugah capall*," Kelly said suddenly, giving away that he was aware of her stolen glances, "Wild born. I came upon him when he was in the middle of teaching a wolf pack not to think too much of themselves."

She stiffened, and I thought maybe the fact that she had been noticed would make her trot away. I was starting to think of our two eastern visitors as I think of cats; barely tolerant of others, and inwardly confident in their superiority. Lady Dana, particularly so. At dinner the night before, Lady Julea displayed a very polished, if formal, cordiality to all, but her companion had said very little for herself. There on the road, though it took a moment, she relaxed and looked at Kelly.

"A wolf pack?" she asked, honestly curious.

"Yeah, four or five, by the time I got there," Kelly said, "Blood wolves. They'll kill and eat anything, and they don't fear anything either. There was an older mare dead on the ground, and a couple of the wolves were dead too. I assumed the mare was his mother. I – well, we – chased the rest of the wolves off and I took care of his injuries."

"Did you take him to a horse-master?"

"No. Well, not officially. I meant to leave him free, but he followed me. After a while, I sort of took him in and trained him myself."

"You?" Her eyes grew, then something like understanding flashed over her face. "Oh, sure. That makes sense."

Kelly didn't reply to that. He just rode in silence until we heard Julea call for Dana. Kelly nodded to her, and she hastened up next to the ambassador. I guided my horse up into the slot left open next to him.

"Nice chat?" I said, not at all snidely.

"Lovely," Kelly said, pretending not to notice my tone. "She's actually very nice. Little quiet."

I snorted, then after a moment, said, "Is that really how you found him?"

Kelly nodded.

"That's incredible," I said. "You could have told me."

"True," he said, "but she is much prettier than you."

Shortly afterward, Kelly moved up to the front of our little group and called us to a halt. After carefully surveying the area around us, he explained to the rest of our party the plan that he and I had discussed that morning. I watched our visitors closely; sure there would be a protest over what seemed – even to me if I'm honest – a foolhardy plan. But neither the ambassador nor her bodyguard seemed at all reluctant. The Rindros brothers, though, looked to one another with expressions ranging from confusion to outright fear, and ultimately turned to me as if hoping that I would stop the madman and his ridiculous plan. I painted a look of calm confidence on my face and nodded to them reassuringly. It may not have made them happier, but it seemed to be enough to calm them. Kelly gave some further instructions.

"I'll be in the lead," he continued, "Lord Aeryk and Lady Dana will rotate flanking Lady Julea, and you two," he pointed to the guardsmen, "will have the rear guard. When I stop and raise my hand, we'll sort to a single file march, and you will need to follow exactly where Locksley and I go, step by step. Lord Aeryk will step ahead of Lady Julea and Lady Dana behind. I'll lower my hand when the path is wider, and we can revert to normal order." He looked up, gauging the sun behind the cloud-shrouded sky. "I would say we have a good couple of hours before we will need to spell the horses and take a short rest. While we ride, we will need to stay as silent as possible; no more chatter until we break. Everyone understand?" He paused, but no one spoke. "If you see anything moving in the trees and you think I need to see it, snap your fingers once."

Kelly looked from face to face to verify the instructions had been heard, then turned around on Locksley and the two stepped off the road and through the brush. We all sorted ourselves as directed – Dana alongside Julea to begin – and followed.

The first hour or so was very like the ride Kelly and I had taken through the underbrush on the way to Clemons. From the road, and even from horseback, there seemed to be no trail or path ahead. But each time it seemed we had lost the trail, Locksley would turn into some branches, parting them as he walked through to reveal an unseen path. I realized that these hidden routes were just the sort of things that woodland outlaws used to ply their trade, and I wondered again how Kelly seemed to be so familiar with them. Then, as we passed into the second hour, the texture of the forest changed. I can't explain it adequately, but it was as if the woods themselves became darker and more..., unfriendly. I knew what it meant; we were in the Aosta Forest itself now. It was here that Kelly first raised his hand into the signal for us to change our march, and we moved into a single line behind him, each horse nearly touching the one in front. I could see Kelly focused on the ground in front of Locksley's footfalls, gently nudging the stallion's steps as if on a tightrope. After a few tense moments of this, he again signaled, and we moved back into our usual positions. This went on as we passed, incredibly slowly it seemed, through the dark and evil-feeling woods. After what felt like an eternity, we came through a tangle of vines and branches to a clearing at the end of a long, narrow lake.

"Time for a break," Kelly said, his voice jarring after such a long time in silence. The group dismounted, opened some of our supplies, and had a small lunch. The lake water was cold and suitable for drinking, and it felt good on my dry throat. The ride had been so tense that I had forgotten to even drink from the skin I had brought. My legs and back screamed their appreciation to be off the horse. After stretching for a few minutes, I walked over and sat on the ground near where Kelly had settled, scanning the edge of the forest.

"That armor is very loud," he said with a smirk.

I glanced down. I had taken one of the silver scale mail vests from Clemons to wear with the dark blue livery Myk had provided, and when I moved, the individual plates made a tiny clinking noise. I looked back at him, "Really? That's a problem?"

He looked at me; the smirk solidly on his face. I rolled my eyes. "Anyway, I've been thinking," I said.

He went back to scanning the forest edge and said, "I feel like I should be concerned."

I pressed on, "This lake is a good place to stop for a

break, but we obviously can't stay here long."

"Agreed."

"Sure. But then I have to ask; where are we going to stay for long? I mean to say, we're going to have to camp somewhere; this is untamed wilderness. There are no inns or lodging anywhere in the Aosta Forest. And if there were, I can't imagine what they would be like."

"I have a plan," Kelly said. It wasn't a revelation; he said it as if he was simply stating a fact.

"Oh?" I said, trying to be as annoying nonchalant as he was being.

"Yep," he said, and started to stand, "but for it to work, we've got to get going. Long ways to go yet." He brushed his hand off on his pants and headed for Locksley.

"Oh, we're done talking. I see," I said to myself since no one else was listening.

The afternoon went much as the latter half of the morning had – dark, tangled forest branches brushed and clawed; mysterious dangers on the forest floor caused Kelly to warn us to change our marching order, then just as mysteriously change it back again; and always the heavy silence that seemed over time to have physical weight. Which is why, when shortly before sunset Kelly began to whistle loudly and happily, the remaining five of us were gobsmacked.

"What the hell are you doing?" Julea hissed at him.

He paused and looked at her. "Whistling," he said, and then continued right on where he left off.

Before anyone could react in any way beyond that, the forest around us came alive with movement. And by that I mean to say that it seemed like the literal forest came alive; bushes and trees that had moments before been part of the background suddenly began moving around us, surrounding us in an unbroken ring and revealing themselves to be a crowd of camouflaged forest people. To Kelly's left, a tall, dark-skinned figure appeared as if from nowhere.

"Nice of you to drop by," said the figure in a perfect high-born baritone.

With a sudden leap and a barbaric yell, Kelly leaped off of Locksley's back at the figure, who instantly crouched into a ready stance as the full weight of Kelly's leap fell on him. The collision knocked both men to the ground and into a pile of leaves. I was reaching back for my staff when I realized there was a sound coming from the mound of leaves — the strangest possible sound. The sound of laughter. After a moment, Kelly and the other man stood up and gave one another an embrace. After which, each began brushing errant leaves and other detritus from themselves and one another while their laughter continued.

I couldn't take another second of that. Was this some manner of ploy? Had I entrusted myself and all of our plans into the hands of someone that had now betrayed us into the hands of bandits? For the briefest of moments, I felt the sting of being played for a fool, and it fueled my anger. Staff in hand, I swept off my horse in a single motion and marched over to them, forest people be damned.

"What in the name of the nine hells is going on?" I said.

Kelly held up his hands in a calming motion, but the stupid laugh was still coming out of his mouth. Through the foolish laughter, he said, "Whoa there, your lordship. Let me —"

"Let you what?" I said, not even remotely calmed. "Who's this? What is going on here? What's this about?" I was building up momentum, a thing that only rarely happens to me and, once it does, I have found that I usually can't stop.

"Hey!" barked the dark-skinned man. "Shut up!"

Whether it was the incongruity of the apparent high-born accent coming from such a rough and tumble looking forest dweller or whether it was just that he actually yelled at me and I'm not used to it, I don't know, but I immediately stopped talking.

"Is he always like this?" the man said to Kelly.

"No, this is new as of just now," Kelly said as if I wasn't even present. I could feel my anger building the momentum again, but before I could speak, Kelly continued, "Lord Aeryk, Lady Julea, Lady Dana; I'd like to introduce you to Gadai Marran, best man of the woods."

"He's a thief," I heard Dana mutter quietly. Julea shot a look at her, then at Kelly, who looked at Gadai.

"My pleasure, lords and ladies," he said with a slight bow, "though I prefer to think of myself as more of a highwayman."

"That means thief," Dana said.

Gadai smiled widely, amused. He turned to Kelly. "What in all the realms brings you my way in this gods-forsaken place?" he asked.

"I am on an important mission," Julea piped up suddenly. "My companion and I are expected at Castle Sterling, and there will be dire consequences should we not arrive."

An interesting card to play, I thought. It was a tacit threat; nothing overt, just an implication that could be easily passed off if she chose. I turned back to Gadai and Kelly.

"It's important," Kelly said, "Imperial business." Gadai gave Kelly a curious look, but when no more was forthcoming, he nodded. The tall bandit looked back at the rest of us.

"Well, if it's important, you'll need a place to stay for the evening. The Aosta Forest isn't known for its kindnesses to guests. It is your choice, of course, but it'd be my privilege if you'd lodge with us tonight," he said, making a sweeping gesture that encompassed all of the men around us. A low cheer of agreement went up from them.

"We're in a hurry–," Julea said with evident exasperation.

"But we have to stop somewhere," Kelly said, finishing her sentence. He looked at Gadai, "You've got a deal."

Gadai's face split into a wide grin. "Excellent! Let's make an evening of it. You two," he pointed at two of the men near where he was standing, "hurry back home and make the arrangements. We're playing host tonight." The two nodded and disappeared back into the forest, which had grown even darker with the slow setting of the sun. Gadai said a couple more things to Kelly that I couldn't hear and then turned to his men while Kelly returned to Locksley. I followed him, still seething with a combination of residual anger and confusion. Kelly remounted Locksley, and I did likewise with my horse. The crowd of forest bandits around us began to move, guiding us through the forest while giving us a wide enough berth to ride up to three abreast.

"You want to explain this?" I said after a moment. It came out heated, but I didn't care; I was heated.

Kelly sighed, then spoke loud enough for everyone in the party to hear. "Gadai is an old friend. We've known one another for a long time." Kelly paused wistfully, "A very long time, come to think of it. He and his people have used the northern forest of Lochhaven – Aosta – as a summer base for many years. They have learned to manage the inhospitable nature of the forest, and its reputation is a boon. No one comes here; that allows them a relatively secure home. Of course, we're rapidly losing what's left of summer, so it was a gamble to try to find him. It's the safest option for us while we're in the forest. While we could have taken our chances; and would have if this didn't work out; the dangers of this forest are not unearned. Building a campsite of our own would have been dangerous at best. This," he shrugged a little, "well, this is the best case."

"From a certain viewpoint," Julea said suddenly, "you just got us captured by bandits."

A look of steel passed over Kelly's face. "You don't know him, your ladyship. Gadai is one of the most responsible and loyal men I've ever met. Trusting him with my life – and yours – is not a question at all."

A new kind of tension passed between them. "Fine," Julea said, "but spare me your dissertations on 'responsibility' and 'loyalty'. Between you and your bandit friend there, I cannot imagine anything you can contribute to the matter."

A lot was going on in that exchange that, at the time, I didn't understand. I only knew then that Kelly fell utterly silent; his face stony.

There is very little I can write that could truly express the surreal nature of the evening that followed. After the initial meeting, we were guided along paths even more obscure and hidden than the ones we had been on all day. Our guides led us with complete confidence, though I couldn't see how. I also can't say how long or far we marched; the encroaching darkness and the strange state of anticipation I felt conspired to disabuse me of my ability to tell time or distance. At ends, we came through a particularly dense wall of brush and found ourselves in a large clearing under a high canopy of trees, greeted by one of the most amazing sights I've ever seen.

The clearing was illuminated, it seemed at first, exclusively by torches affixed to the base of the numerous large trees that dotted the area and a large fire-pit in the center. Suspended over the fire were slabs of meat – venison, had I to guess – and many pots and cauldrons. More, the entire area had numerous mats and makeshift tables scattered throughout. Dozens of people – men, women, and even quite a few children – were hustling about, checking on the food at the fire, adjusting the tables and mats, and ducking in and out of a sizeable hut-like shelter at the far end of the clearing. We were bid to dismount, and the forest dwellers led our horses away, including Locksley. I thought for a brief moment of challenging Kelly on that, but that's when the music started.

Across the clearing, from the other side of the fire pit, the sounds of a pipe, a drum, and strings drifted to us. I looked at my companions, all of whom seemed as bewildered as I felt, except for Kelly. He seemed oblivious to the music and was instead staring upwards. I turned to see what he was looking at and let my mouth drop open in awe. The tree canopy above us was honeycombed with wooden walkways suspended between the trees, each of which seemed to have one or more sophisticated tree-houses suspended in it. At various points, lanterns were hanging that gave light to the suspended platforms and, I now could see, added to the torchlight below.

At our arrival, many of those that had guided us had dispersed into the larger group, but some few remained near our little party and, after having given us some time to take in the vista, led us to one of the small tables nearer the fire where we settled on the benches provided. The location was also very close to the musicians, and while they were not dramatically loud – I have been near deafened by the minstrels that have come to the halls of Castle Claire – it was just enough to discourage quiet conversation. That was fine, as at least from my point of view the surreality of having what was apparently going to become a full banquet in the middle of the Aosta Forest was just about all I could cope with at that moment. The music went on for a while until as if responding to a cue, the musicians stopped and the attendees began a rhythmic clapping. The other tables and mats around us in the area were now occupied by people as well; easily two hundred souls were now around us of every description, and all of them were clapping in rhythm. It was thunderous. I resisted at first the strange compulsion to join in until I saw that Kelly, the men from Clemons, and even Julea and Dana were all already clapping along.

The clapping went on for several moments, until suddenly a stream of people burst forth from the large hut, carrying huge trays of food. At their appearance, the rhythmic clapping changed to straightforward applause, during which the platters were brought to each mat and table. Apparently, as we were guests, we were cared for first; trays of meat and bowls of soup and stew were put down on the table before us. I watched, waiting for the remainder to be served before I partook. To do otherwise would have been rude, at least according to the manners of the halls of Castle Claire. I noticed, though, that all of our hosts – every single table, in fact – was waiting as well. It was not a long wait, however, considering the size of the crowd, before even the servers had settled down to tables will a full spread of food on them.

Gadai then stood up from his seat on the opposite side of the clearing from us and walked out to where he was visible to everyone. The gathering fell utterly silent. At this, he raised a mug, and all of the forest dwellers did as well. It looked like it was going to be a toast, so I reached for my own cup when Kelly's hand fell on my arm. I looked, and he quickly and subtly shook his head, then nodded as if to indicate Gadai. The bandit leader looked around at the raised mugs, and still in silence, poured the cup out on the ground in front of himself. He bowed his head. No one moved. I felt strangely like I was intruding on something sacred, even though he was the one that brought us there. I didn't want to look around, but I couldn't help it. Every person was stock still with their mug raised and watching Gadai. A breath. Two. Three.

Gadai lifted his head, and the entire gathering let out a deafening cheer. The mugs came down, returned to their places. Gadai nodded once more and then went back to his table.

And at that, the meal commenced. Sounds of conversation, laughter, and all of the expected sounds of a banquet filled the air quite abruptly after the silence of a moment before. I turned toward the table and along with the rest of my companions, filled a plate. The food was spectacular, and all the more so it seemed for the environment from which it came.

I would describe the feast leisurely, I suppose, as there was no rush and plenty of food. When, though, it was evident that the majority were finished, a different group of Gadai's people – since that's how I now thought of them – rose and took all of the various dishes and leftovers away. Others of the forest dwellers began rolling up the mats, and it was only then that I noted that they had been concentrated in an area near the fire-pit, and therefore near the musicians. Once the mats were gone, they began to play again, and a crowd started to form in the open area and dance.

If anyone had attempted to tell me before that day that while I was protecting the ambassador from Yorch from assassins, I would find myself at a dance party with outlaws in the Aosta Forest, I would have immediately had them taken to the madhouse. But it was when I joined in with the dancers myself that I realized that perhaps I probably also belonged there. Yet, whatever madness I had, it was not so pervasive that I didn't notice, from the corner of my eye during a dance with one of the women that had served us, that Kelly was dancing with Lady Julea. Without question there was more there than either one was saying, I knew. But what that might be I couldn't guess.

Despite the revelry, the fact was that we were all exhausted from the long and tension-filled ride of the day, and before long I was sitting back by the fire and feeling that weariness from head to toe. Kelly walked over, having left a discussion he was having with Gadai, and slumped down on the bench by me. He stretched his legs out and leaned back against the table.

"He says they've got one of the larger chambers prepared for us," he said, pointing up, "Up there."

I nodded. "All of us?" I asked.

"Yeah, though the Rindros brothers are already sleeping in the food cabin, I think," he said with a grin. "Gadai is showing Dana and Julea up now, and he'll be back for us shortly."

I nodded again. I was tired, but I felt like playing a little with my new friend. "You danced with her."

He shrugged. "I did. She didn't seem to like it."

"But she still danced," I said. I was probably pushing my luck, but I kept going. "I have to ask again, is there anything you want to tell me?"

"Not a thing," Kelly said flatly, "it was just a dance. She's just too well-bred to say no."

"It seems like there is something about you specifically that bothers her," I said.

He looked alternately at me and past me before finally answering. "That seems fair. You know what, you should ask her," he said with a sigh, "It's not my story to tell either way."

I considered that for a moment, then relented. "Fair enough. As long as it isn't a problem?"

He shook his head, "Absolutely not. I already told you. Keeping you all safe is the job, and that's what I'm going to do."

Standing, I turned and gave him a sober look before I clapped him on the shoulder. "Then your business is yours, my friend."

Shortly thereafter, Gadai came over and directed us to

a rope ladder that led to the suspended hut where we would sleep. Kelly went up first, and reaching the underside of the shelter itself, he pushed open a small trap door and climbed inside. I followed, closed the trap door behind me, and looked around.

We were in a large wooden chamber that encircled the massive trunk of an old oak tree which came through the floor in the center of the room and continued out through the roof. The outside walls were about four feet high. The top foot of each wall panel was an opening that served as a window; all of which were currently shuttered and latched against the colder night air. The roof ascended at an upward angle from the walls to the tree trunk, giving plenty of headroom near the center. There were, though, layered heavy woolen curtains on either side of the tree, effectively bisecting the room and cutting off any view of the other half of the platform. I realized that it must be where Julea and Dana lodged. Two cots were arranged such that each had one end against the trunk, and each had one of the bedrolls from our supplies sitting on it, along with what looked like rustic pillows. Candles in small glass enclosures lit the room, and a metal stove on a stone platform across from the trapdoor seemed to be providing the warmth I felt upon entering. Opposite it was a small table with a basin containing fresh water. On the whole, considering that it was two stories in the air in the middle of a hostile wilderness, it was quite comfortable.

Kelly considered the curtains and, obviously aware that we were not alone, held a finger to his mouth. I nodded. In a brief time and in absolute silence, we settled in for the night.

CHAPTER FOUR

—JULEA—

Of all the fantastic, bizarre, and – to use Aeryk's word – surreal things that the day had held for us, perhaps the most amazing was this; that night, I slept soundly.

I should explain, and to do that, I will need to go back to where it all started for me.

On a late summer's day that had been mostly full of necessary duties but had thankfully afforded me time for a pleasant ride through the Imperial gardens, I received an envelope from my mother requesting my presence in the throne room. As this was unusual, at least, and an absolutely terrible portent at worst, I tensed immediately. I gave a cursory consideration to my clothing in the nearest mirror – Oh well, nothing to be done about that now, I thought on seeing the smudges of dirt on my riding pants – and I hurried off. On my arrival at the palace, I sought out and informed the chamberlain of my arrival in the main antechamber. Several moments passed, then the massive golden doors swung open, admitting me into the throne room of the Empire of Yorch.

Stepping through the doors into the throne room was like crossing the threshold of another world. The chamber was a cavernous hall some three hundred feet from the entryway to the throne platform opposite. Twelve massive, black marble columns, shot through with veins of gold, supported the arched ceiling some sixty feet above, where a large dome of glass, inset in the ceiling just beyond halfway to the throne, allowed in the blue of the sky and the glow of the early autumn sun. The walkway to the throne also made of marble, black down the middle and white at the edges, and was itself seventy feet wide. It was slightly raised from the stone floor beneath and framed by well-manicured plants all along its edges. Two side rooms, one to each of the left and the right, met the walkway just past halfway in the chamber and served as space for more substantial state functions. It was in this place; truly an intimate venue; that my mother – Ardallah Niconnal bar Morrisia, the Empress of Yorch – wanted to have a chat with me.

I walked the length of the cavernous room with a quick step that I tried to keep from looking overly hurried. I glanced up at the bright blue sky through the dome as I passed beneath it, before reaching the presence of the throne itself. The Throne of Yorch sat precisely in the center of the higher of two platforms. The first, where a petitioner would stand to have an audience with the Empress, was fifteen marble steps up from the main floor. From there, another seven steps ascended to the level where the gold and ivory seat itself, with its ten foot high back and ornate golden sigils inlays, was placed surrounded by four twenty-foot tall glass windows that overlooked the city of Yorch and the Eastern Ocean.

I climbed the fifteen steps, stopped on the audience platform, and waited. The throne was empty, but I knew better than to break with propriety. I stood quietly with my hands folded together in front of me.

"You are going to the Western Kingdom, daughter," said a voice.

"Am I?" I said.

From behind the throne stepped a tall, straight figure with long, snow-white hair pulled back in a braid and a golden crown. Her dress was the purest white and covered with a mesh of gold that caught the sunlight through the windows and gave the suggestion of a swarm of fireflies. Her hands were held identically to my own, and I was aware that we shared a similar preoccupation with our posture. Empress Ardallah walked casually around to the front of the throne to stand before me. She regarded me for a moment.

"You have come to our presence dressed… like that?" she said.

I glanced down at the gray riding britches and the flecks of mud they had accumulated that I had not sufficiently dislodged earlier. My coat too was less than pristine; my afternoon ride had been little more than chasing wild foxes through the brush, and that does present a particular challenge to tidiness.

"I did not wish to prolong your wait, Your Highness," I said, bowing my head to hide my grin.

The Empress turned to pace in front of the throne, but I was sure I saw a slight eye-roll. "You are going to the Western Kingdom as my ambassador," she continued, choosing to drop the discussion of my dress altogether. "A request for aid has come to our ears from their king, and we would have you negotiate the terms of our involvement."

"I know very little of that area of the world, ma'am," I said. "I would expect that we have practiced negotiators who are much more learned in such things that would be better —,"

"There are. Without question," she said, cutting off my argument, "But we wish to send you. We have reason to believe that the Western Kingdom will figure prominently in the future, and the presence of our own daughter will be significant in the ties we wish to form."

I bowed my head but gave it another try. "Of course, Your Highness. But I have so little understanding of their ways. Surely—,"

"There is little you need to worry of," she said, cutting me off again. "They are a rural people with little cohesive history and no validated record of their ancestry. And more," she paused for effect, "they have no standing army."

"Ridiculous," I said aloud before I could prevent it.

"It is true," she said, forgiving at least this once my lack of propriety. "But their land is rich, if rather sheltered. And more, they have certain resources they don't even know they possess. We desire to secure a partnership before they become aware of them. And we wish to prevent others from becoming aware."

I scrambled in my mind, but I had nothing left. "I understand, Your Highness. When do I depart?"

"We are preparing a small vessel to take you and your handmaiden to one of their port cities even now. If our interests are made obvious, there will be significant competition, and that too must be avoided. Also, we understand that there is a local challenger that is looking to involve himself in their affairs for reasons of his own. Therefore you must understand that your discretion and stealth are preeminent in this. You will be leaving within the week. We will have all other necessary information secured for you for your assignment on board the vessel that will bear you there."

I bowed low, then said, “You mentioned my handmaiden? Did you mean my personal guard?”

She waved her hand, dismissively, “Whatever you wish to call her. Yes. We desire her to accompany you.”

I bowed my head again. When I looked up, I saw her descending the last few steps to the audience platform, stopping right beside me. Sidelong, she looked at me, then gently laid her hand on my cheek.

“Do be careful, Julea. I don’t do this lightly, and I will miss you while you are gone.”

I felt myself smile at the warmth of my mother’s hand before she withdrew it from my face. She turned and glided back up the seven steps before stopping at the top and looking back over her shoulder.

“Besides, you are our heir. Your loss would be an inconvenient challenge,” she said. Then without another word, she disappeared again behind the throne.

And so, from that day to the day we found ourselves in the camp of a bandit clan, I had found decent sleep to be elusive. I’m sure that’s understandable. Especially including the other…, complication, I found myself mostly surviving on latent tension and conscious intention; forgoing almost all genuine rest. Imagine my surprise, then, when for the first time, well, ever, Dana nudged me awake the next morning.

“Jules? Are you okay?”

"Hmm? Dana? What's the matter?" I managed to slur as consciousness slowly began to return.

"Nothing," she said both confused and amused. As I opened my eyes, I could see that she was standing by the cot on which I was laying with her hand still on my shoulder, "Unless you count just how very far out you were just now," she continued, "In any case, we need to get going. Everyone is gathering in the common area down below, preparing to get back on the road soon."

An old friend used to say to me that one should always remember to enjoy the first few minutes after waking, before "the hawks of morning" – the worries and concerns of the waking world – found their way back to your mind. I never understood how to enjoy the window where you aren't thinking about something because the minute you realize you aren't thinking about it, you are. While Dana was speaking, my personal 'hawks' swarmed into my mind, and abruptly, I was fully awake.

"How much time?" I said, already swinging my legs around to sit up.

Dana stepped back as I got my feet to the floor and stood beside her. "We have a little time yet," she said with a gentle smile, "I brought up some food for you," she pointed to a small tray of bread and cheese sitting on the table. I looked around and saw that the wool curtains that had been hanging in the middle of the room were gone. I looked back at her.

“They were awake and gone when I got up,” she said, guessing correctly at my unspoken question, “but Lord Aeryk and Kelly were already down below, so I took them down.” I was pulling on my leather armor and starting the process of fastening the buckles on one side. Dana came over and buckled the other as we talked. We had slept in clothes, of course, and there was no time to do much primping. “Kelly was talking to Gadai when I went down,” Dana continued, “I think he was trying to get a guide or two for the rest of the way.”

“Whose idea was that?” I asked, just a hair sharply, I suppose.

“Gadai’s, if I heard correctly. He seems to think that we could be at Castle Sterling by nightfall if we ride hard with a good guide. That would shave almost two days off our expected time,” she said. It was more information than I had asked for, which was usually a sign of Dana trying to appease me preemptively.

“That would be worth the effort,” I agreed, “Anything that makes this shorter.” I unintentionally emphasized the word ‘shorter’ as I tugged at the last buckle.

Dana smiled cautiously. “Absolutely.”

She finished the other side, and I went over to my boots and began pulling them on. Dana stood, watching me.

"Did you get the rest of our belongings?" I asked.

"You danced with him," Dana said, ignoring my banal question.

I sat up and stared at her. She looked back without flinching. We were firmly in 'friend' territory in this, not 'official', so she was doing the thing that I most valued about our friendship; she was challenging me.

"He asked," I said, realizing that it was a weak reason even as I said it.

She didn't react.

I stood and grabbed my cloak, draping it over my shoulder. "It's beneath my station to reject a proper request," I added.

She remained unfazed. I looked back.

"It was fine," I said with a little sigh. "He told me a little about Gadai and how they knew one another. Nothing important. He's still..., him."

Dana took a breath and relented. "Okay, Jules. That's fair. I didn't mean to pry."

"Don't worry," I said, smiling at her, "I am fully aware of the situation and the possible dangers. But," I put my hand on her arm, "don't stop keeping an eye on me, okay?"

She squeezed my hand in return. "Of course, your

Imperial Highness," she said. I kicked her in the shin.

"Fine. Let's go," I grumbled.

Our newly formed party left shortly after I got to the ground. Our horses had been brought out to us and appeared to be fully rested and tended. Covertly, I looked once again at the beautiful stallion Kelly called Locksley. I love horses; I always have. There is little that I'd prefer to do than to ride full speed over hill and meadow on a willing horse. In my position, I had access to the best bred of the best lines in the Empire. Despite that, never had I seen such a fantastic animal as Locksley. Every single muscle and proportion was perfect, and his temperament and intelligence appeared unparalleled. Of course, Dana had told me Kelly's story of the horse, which was itself incredible, but truthfully, all I wanted to do was to ride him with all the speed he could bring to bear.

"My lady?" Aeryk said suddenly, shaking me out of my thoughts. In his hand, he held the reins of the horse I had been riding. He offered them to me.

"Thank you, your lordship," I said, taking them and turning away. I mounted and rode over to where Dana was waiting.

A few moments later, Kelly gave one last embrace to Gadai, mounted Locksley, and we left under the guidance of a half dozen of the forest people.

That day proceeded in a way that was, for a ride through a supposedly untamed and dangerous forest of treachery and awfulness, quite dull. There were occasional noises from the dark tangle of branch and vine just beyond our view, but always our guides seemed to be both unimpressed and completely confident. If I were to be asked to retrace their path, of course, I would be at a complete loss. I had spent a fair share of my time as a child wandering about the forests near Yorch – under the watchful eye of the Imperial Guard, obviously – and I was comfortable in the near wilds. Honestly, I still enjoyed wandering the woodlands at home. But this was like nothing I'd ever experienced before. Having no point of reference as to our path made the entirety of the ride disorienting. As the day wore on, though, I became almost complacent in the saddle.

So of course, that was when the Aosta Forest decided to remind us all what it indeed was.

We rode along between the two trios of Gadai's clan, with one of them guiding us all from the front and two immediately behind him to either side. The six of us had been milling about in the middle, sometimes two abreast, sometimes three, and at this point, I was between Aeryk and Dana while Kelly was just ahead and the two guardsmen from the port city behind. In the very rear, the other three of the forest people mirrored the three in front. The drowsy, trance-like atmosphere I mentioned above was in full effect, until it wasn't. Perhaps the sleep I'd had the night before helped me more than I realized because I was the first to notice the change. The rhythmic hoof steps of our horses had gradually become no longer rhythmic; in fact, the sounds had ceased altogether. I looked down and saw the pathway beneath us appeared uneven. And seemed to be moving; even wriggling.

"Dana!" I spat. She turned with a start and looked down to follow my gaze, suddenly alert.

"Kelly, the ground!" she called, and as she did, I saw the lead guide snatched off his horse by what looked like black vines or tentacles. They had extended from beneath the leaves on the forest floor and with frightening speed pulled him to the ground. Dana already had her blade out and was directing her horse in a sideways motion to close the distance between us. I felt my horse pitch as if it tried to take a step and slipped on unsolid ground, and I looked to see the black things wrapping around the animal's foreleg. All around us, both from below and from above, dozens of the black tendrils reached out toward us.

"Shadow snakes!" one of the other guides called, his sword now hacking at the sinewy black things. I drew my own and swung a forceful chop at the tentacles on my horse's leg. The sword bit as if into hard, boiled leather and it did little damage. The thing twitched but held the animal fast. By now, every one of us was in motion. Aeryk was only a few feet to the left of me, his horse already immobilized by the crawling black horrors. He was furiously whipping his staff, deflecting as best he could an array of the tendrils reaching out for him from the branches above. Dana had succeeded in getting to me and was now pressed tightly against my right side. She was hacking at the things reaching out from both above and below us. The lead guide that had been first pulled down to the ground was now barely visible beneath a mass of blackness. Behind me, the red-haired guard that had accompanied us – Markh, I believe he was called – had been pulled down along with his horse, and they were visible beneath the black mass. It was then that I felt something grab my left ankle and calf. It felt like a hangman's knot had seized me and begun to both pull and squeeze. I hacked at it with my blade to no avail.

"No!" I shouted in reflex. I looked around for some, any, ideas when I saw Kelly. He had tucked his legs up onto the saddle and was balancing on Locksley's back while the stallion pranced, never keeping more than two feet on the ground at a time. It looked like a wild dance and were the situation not so dire; I would have laughed. But it wasn't a dance, and each step Locksley took seemed aimed to be at one of the reaching tentacles; as an attack, it was only marginally successful, but it was keeping him from being entangled. Kelly, black blade in hand, was hacking at a cluster of tree-borne tendrils that were reaching for him from above. His sword seemed to have no interest in or difficulty with the leathery toughness of the things, and with each swing he made, it cleaved completely through the creeping horror. At the sound of my voice, Kelly looked over and saw the shadow snake working its way around my leg. Instantly, he leaped off of Locksley's back and onto the treacherous ground. The vicious black blade continued its work as he hacked his way to my side and freed me with a stroke.

"The heart," came the croaked voice of one of the guides behind us, who was now suspended up in the air by several of the tendrils. Turning, we saw that he was feebly pointing to where we could see a small red flower to the left of the path. A thrashing cluster of the nightmare tentacles surrounded it, making the crimson petals bright against their blackness. Kelly turned but saw now that his legs were tightly entwined by the wriggling things, slowly pulling him down. He struggled and made to strike again at them when one of them trapped his forearm. He looked up to Aeryk, then called out to him.

"Get the heart!" Kelly shouted, heaving the sword

toward him with his off hand. Deftly, the marquess dropped his staff and in a fluid motion, caught the flying blade by the end of the handle. He threw himself off his horse then, landing and tumbling into a roll that put him next to the red flower. With a guttural groan, he sank the blade into the center of the bloom.

There was a horrific noise; like sheets of glass grinding against one another. The black tendrils twitched and writhed. I heard a groan and a snap like that of wet timber breaking. Then, suddenly, the black things fell limp and dropped away.

Everything went quiet save for the sound of the horses prancing on their newly freed feet and whinnying their disapproval. I looked to see Kelly face down and half buried under the dead, black things. My heart skipped, and the rest of the world seemed to disappear.

"Kelly!" I shouted. Without a thought, I jumped off my horse, dropped to my knees, and grabbed at the mass of black tendrils covering him. They were heavy; warm and slightly damp like giant black pasta. As I grabbed the largest of them from across his shoulders and heaved it off of him, he rolled over and coughed, then let his head drop back.

"Well, that was awful," he said so weakly I almost missed it.

"Are you okay?" I said, my voice soft.

He lifted his head and looked at me, his gray-blue eyes looking unblinking into mine for a long moment. *Oh god.* In a flash, the memories came back, one in particular clear and bright.

I knocked gently on the door, and it swung open slightly. Through the opening, I could see Kelly standing in silhouette, his back to the window. He was looking at an array of cloth piles laid out on the bed. At the sound, he looked up at me.

"Hi," he said before I could back away, "come in."

I entered, unconsciously nudging the door shut behind me as I did. His room was not excessively big, though it was still well-apportioned and comfortable; as all the rooms in the palace were; with a large bed at one end and a stone hearth at the other. There was a warm fire there, warming the room comfortably despite the winter's chill outside. Kelly was arranging clothing and other sundries on the bed, no doubt in preparation for packing them. The late afternoon sun reflected through the window behind him, bathing the room in a warm honey-gold glow. He looked at me and smiled, still holding a folded bundle of cloth that appeared to be one of his shirts. It is also possible that thought crossed my mind because he was, in fact, shirtless; clad only in a pair of black pants. Unbidden, my eyes surveyed his lithe body. He turned briefly to set the cloth on the bed with the rest, and as he did, I could see the fresh tattoo of a swooping raven on his right shoulder.

"I'm sorry, your highness," he said, "Let me throw on a shirt."

His comment jarred me, and I flushed a little, realizing that I had been staring just long enough to draw his attention. "Oh, don't worry about it," I said, trying to sound casual, "please don't."

He looked at me, one eyebrow slightly raised.

"I mean, of course," I said, suddenly desperate to correct the implication, "you can do what you wish. You aren't bothering me." *Wasn't he?* I thought.

He smiled warmly, stepping back from the bed. *Oh. So, we're really not going to get a shirt*, I thought. "What can I help you with?" he said, folding his arms across his chest.

"I just came to see when you were leaving so that we had time to see one another before. The court, that is. For a proper goodbye," I said, though I wasn't sure what those words meant.

"Ah. Well, I intend to leave sometime tomorrow, and I think I heard that – weather pending – the captain plans to leave with the tide in the morning." He gave a little shrug. The winter winds on the ocean were not a sailor's friend, but they were reasonably predictable this time of year, so the departure time was likely.

“That is what he said,” I nodded, “so then, we do have the remainder of the evening. To say our goodbyes, that is.” I added awkwardly.

He took a step toward me, coming around the bed until only a couple feet separated us. He smelled like cinnamon and wood. “We do,” he said, “I’m glad it’s on much better terms than our last conversation.”

I remembered the argument we had when he told me he had accepted the appointment from my mother, and we discussed what that would mean. He would publicly be quitting service to the throne and seen as a deserter. Despite the incredible honor, it would all be clandestine. We..., disagreed on it at first.

I smiled self-consciously. “Me too. I was a bit...” I floundered for a word.

“Harsh?” he offered.

“Bitchy,” I said. I looked up at him sheepishly. I didn’t want this. I liked things as they were; his presence as my bodyguard was reassuring. I told myself that, at least. But it was an assignment from the throne and a high honor. He couldn’t have refused, and I did understand that in the end.

It was his turn to suppress a laugh. Then just as quickly as it came, the smile faded, and he gazed at me very intensely, his gray-blue eyes seeming to look at me and through me at the same time. He took another step forward, and before I knew it, he had taken my hand in his. For some reason, I made no effort to pull away.

"Hey now," he said, much more seriously than I was accustomed to, "don't talk that way about my princess."

I shrugged. "I think we've noted that – publicly, at least – I'm not going to seem very much like your princess," I said very gently. He glanced down to the floor for a heartbeat, then returned his gaze to me.

"Not an argument I wish to have again," he sighed, "But I suppose that's true. Then let it suffice not to say that about someone I care about very much." He squeezed my hand as he spoke, telling me more than a thousand words could have.

"Kelly...," I said, but for some reason, I was having trouble finding words. I had, in retrospect, no idea when I came to him what I wanted to say. I had solely trusted that it would come to me as it usually did. Instead, despite all my training, the right words refused to present themselves.

"You are exceptional at this," he said, "You're going to make a great empress."

I balled up my right fist – my left hand still in his – and playfully punched him in the chest as I laughed. He caught my hand as I did and held it there, drawing me closer.

I looked up into his eyes again. They seemed different as the laughter in them faded. There was a sadness I could now see in his face. A shadow of the life he was leaving; the one that had been. I opened the fist I had hit him with but left my hand gently on his chest.

"Jules," he said, his voice just above a whisper, "I told you – saying goodbye to you is the fight I can't..."

He trailed off.

"Then don't," I whispered, leaning closer, "not yet." I pressed against him, and our lips met. I felt an eruption of heat coming from him and inside myself all at once, a warmth that mingled and swirled in my mind and shut down all thought. There was just him; his lips, his smell, his body, and the heat.

It was later, and the sun had long since set; the only light remaining in the room was the dwindling fire as Kelly opened the door. He looked down the hallway in both directions before he waved me out. With quick steps, we made our way to a small sitting room some distance from the door before we stopped.

I looked up into the gray-blue eyes. Even here, even after, I could see there the same feelings – the same connection – that I felt.

"Julea," he said, then paused.

"I know," I said, "it changes nothing. Nothing in the

real world, anyway. You are now the Imperial Raven."

"And you are still the Heir to the throne."

I nodded. A long moment went by.

"But," I said.

"Exactly," he said, "But."

Then and there, where anyone could have seen, though no one did, Kelly took me in his arms and kissed me one more time.

"I'm good. Thanks," he said from the mound of tentacles, making his voice loud enough for everyone to hear. Then he pushed himself to his feet and offered me his hand. I took it, dazed as I was for multiple reasons, and stood up. "Everyone! How are we?" he called out.

"I'm a little pissed-off," came Aeryk's voice from the far side of the path. It had a strange gurgle to it, and as we turned, he stood up from where he had stabbed the 'heart.' An iridescent green ooze that had gushed from the flower covered him, and he was spitting some of it out of his mouth. "But I'm not hurt; if that's what you mean," he finished.

"Primarily," Kelly said, extending his hand as if waiting for something.

Aeryk lifted the sword. "What the hell is this thing?" he said. "It sank into that..., whatever that was..., up to the hilt and I barely pushed on it. And look! It's the only thing on me that doesn't look like a butterfly threw up on it."

"It's my sword," Kelly said somewhat more severely than I might have expected. He waved his hand at the marquess, who stalked over and reluctantly handed it to him, still spitting. "And it's special," he said, calmly sliding the blade back into its sheath.

Aeryk looked down at the goo all over his clothing. It indeed did look like a butterfly had thrown up on him. "Special?" he grumped, "Oh, of course, it is. Special sword, special horse. Do you have a special bath somewhere, Lord What's-your-real-name?"

Kelly looked at him for a moment. "Not my fault you can't stab a monster with your mouth shut," he said. And there it is, I thought.

Aeryk glared at him for a long moment, then shook his head with a grin. "Fine. It's..., fine," he said as the tension and frustration drained from him. He vainly continued to brush at the prismatic slime all on his clothes.

I turned to Dana, who was still on her horse. She had the reins to mine in her hand as well, and she was looking at me meaningfully before she looked over to Kelly. "I'm okay," she said.

Two of the guides in front of us and all three that were at the rear had come through unscathed, and the Clemon's soldier that I had taken to thinking of as the "other" one –

Phranc, I believe? – suffered only some bruising. Markh, however – the one with the odd red curly hair – had been crushed by the creatures, the guide that had been leading us. Kelly walked over to Gadai's men where they stood around their fallen companion while Aeryk took the militiaman aside.

"'E was fightin' hard," Phranc said to the lord through tears that he fought vainly against, "but when it started dyin', it twisted 'im and...," he paused, gathering himself. "'Is neck broke, mi'lord," he finished. I had the sickening realization that his neck was the snapping sound I'd heard. The color drained from my face.

Aeryk put his hand on the man's shoulder. "We'll be sure his bravery is recorded, okay?" he said, "You'll be the one to report this day. Do him proud."

The man nodded, wiping tears away.

Dana and I watched while the group of men began to dig shallow graves to the side of the trail away from the dead shadow snakes. I looked at her determinedly, and instead of the reaction I expected, she nodded and dismounted. Together we joined the rest in digging the shallow graves and burying the bodies with collected stones. It was grueling, but also necessary and proper.

And in what felt like a disrespectfully short time, Kelly addressed us all from Locksley's back again.

"We only have a few more hours in the forest. We've learned an important lesson just now; we can't ever let our guard down again." He looked at the makeshift graves. "Quiet and alert. The price has already been high enough," he said.

It was true, though. By that time, the sun was committed to setting, and we were bathed in twilight. We were once again in woods that seemed much more like those we had begun our journey in and like the woodlands of home – an area of high trees and open forest floor. It was at that point that Gadai's remaining people bid us farewell. There was a kind of sadness on their faces, but it seemed like an old sadness; one they had known before, and one they expected to see again. I stopped the last one before he passed by on his way home.

"Tell Gadai," I paused, then continued, "that I am grateful," I said. It took him a moment, but he nodded soberly before waving goodbye to us all to disappear into the forest.

The remainder of our group continued through the trees under Kelly's guidance again but without the fear of the unknown terrors of the Aosta dogging our steps. We emerged from the edge of the forest onto vast open grasslands as the sun set and left us awash in the light of the waxing moon. We went back to our protective formation, with Kelly at the front and Aeryk and the remaining guard from Clemons behind; Dana stayed at my side. Judging by the movement of the stars, we rode like this for about an hour before we came upon a road and turned to follow it. I realized, looking back to where we had come from, that we had been riding uphill since we left the forest, and were now about even with the tops of the tall trees we had ridden through. It was hard to estimate in the dark, of course, but the shadow of the woods in the distance was still a barely visible contrast against the night sky. After the tragedy at the vines, our party was left very somber, and that coupled with the renewed weariness of the long journey left us riding in a silence broken only by needed direction from Kelly and the steady rhythm of the horses' feet.

After a time, he pulled us to a halt and waved for Aeryk to come forward. He explained, loudly enough for us all to hear in the nighttime quiet, that he estimated we would be approaching Sterling not long thereafter, although traveling at night made it difficult to predict. They agreed that it would be wisest if Aeryk were in the lead position as we approached, as our arriving after darkness had fallen, and nearly two days early, would be somewhat unexpected, and we would be looked at warily until we were identified adequately as traveling with the marquess. Aeryk fell into the lead position, and we began to ride again. Dana glanced at me and without so much as a word dropped back to the rear-guard position with the militiaman, leaving Kelly to ride at my left. We maintained the silence as we rode for a while until Kelly spoke.

"Is your ankle all right?" he asked, his tone hushed as he looked down at my leg where the shadow snake had ensnared it.

"It is," I assured him, "There will be some bruising, make no mistake," I continued, reaching down and rubbing the side of my boot, "but nothing worse than I've had before."

I saw him nod. "That time you got thrown," he said.

I nodded. "The doctors believed I might not walk correctly ever again, remember? They told my mother to expect it. Compared to that, this is nothing."

"You did walk a little oddly for a bit," he said. In the glow of the moonlight, I saw him look over to me with a little grin.

I involuntarily smiled back at the memory, "It only affected my dancing. It was unfortunate that there was a reception so soon afterward. The Empress was not pleased." I chuckled, then caught myself and quieted again. Memories, I reminded myself, are a tricky business.

Sensing the shift, he looked back forward. "Well, we'll have you back in more appropriate surroundings shortly here. The worst is over."

Of all the qualities that can be ascribed to the man called Kelly – and I can think of many – "prophet" will never be one of them.

The moon was high above us as we came upon the city of Sterling. While it was in no way comparable to the majestic spires and massive walls that made up Yorch, for what it was, the city was impressive. It lay in a semicircle around a small hill with a central plateau; that being the summit of the large hill that we had been gently ascending since we left the forest. The city was divided into three parts that could be discerned even in the semi-darkness. First was the outer city, a sprawling, undefined collection of homes and smaller buildings – some currently lit with firelight, most not – that dotted the land and through which we would pass first. Then at the base of the central hill was a large wall divided into sections by watchtowers and illuminated by torches. Beyond that was the second part of Sterling and the first area that would fit my definition of a proper city. It was built on the sloped ground surrounding the central hill and was much more densely inhabited. It would be here, I knew, that more of the wealthy and noble would live and work, protected by the wall. Markets and the temple would also be there, and likely most of the trappings of what could be called true civilization. Finally was the peak surrounded by its own sectioned wall inside of which the tall stone towers of the castle itself were illuminated and visible from the entire area.

"Castle Sterling," Aeryk called back, pointing, "Home of our king. We've made it." He nudged his horse to a faster pace, and we followed suit. Shortly, we had passed through the outer city and arrived at the wall. It was a well-built if utilitarian affair, twenty-five feet high and solid stone cut to fit tightly together. We followed it as it wound around to the north until we came to a gate; one of several entrances that gave access to the city proper. As we approached, we could see that there were already a dozen guards standing in the arch, which was half the height of the wall and just as wide. The portcullis was open, but a cluster of men stood before us, blocking our path and looking at us gravely. In the torchlight, I could see that they wore the blue of the militia that we had seen in Clemons, but even on my first impression, it was clear that they were both better armed and trained. They stood in two ranks, the ones in front holding bucklers and blades, while the second rank held long pole-arms. To a man, they wore heavy leather on their chests, arms, and legs. Aeryk stopped us several feet back, then stepped forward alone.

"I am Lord Aeryk Escrios of Claire. My father, Duke

Rojer, has sent me to deliver a message to His Majesty, King Ronald. I seek an audience," he said with his tone as formal as the words he chose. I noted his commitment to propriety again, incongruous though it was in his current state. The iridescent ooze from the shadow snake thing had dried on his clothing, having resisted his persistent efforts to clean it save where he was able to wipe it from the metal scales of his armor. Still, he sat tall and noble in the saddle as he addressed the garrison. No one moved at first, and then a voice came from the shadows beyond the gate.

"Strange time for a courtesy call," said the deep bass voice. A shadow moved, and it looked to me that a section of the stone wall broke away and was shuffling out toward us. I blinked; the small child inside me suddenly convinced that I was seeing a stone troll from bedtime stories advancing on us. Involuntarily I nudged my horse slightly back and behind Kelly and Dana. I only excuse that by saying that I was quite drained.

The figure that came into the torchlight was almost as impressive as the imaginary troll I had conjured, though. The man towered over the other guards by a full head at least and was one and a half men wide at the shoulder. He was dressed in the colors of the guard but wore a tunic decorated with golden chains over a full chain-mail shirt that covered his arms as well. In his right hand, he held a massive double-bladed axe casually.

He spoke then in the deep voice we'd heard a moment before. "There are many reasons to seek access to the king, but few of them appropriate in the middle of the night. What is your business?"

"Private," said Aeryk, facing the giant directly, "it is for the king's ears alone. He is expecting us."

The tall figure looked Aeryk up and down, then motioned with his left hand. One of the spear-bearing guardsmen stepped forward. Without looking away from our group, the two men held a brief conversation, after which the smaller man ran off.

"Stranger, you should be praying right now," came the deep bass voice, "that you are expected. It will bother me not even a little to gut you all if I wake the king, and you are lying to me." As if to underscore the threat, he swung his axe up into a two-handed grip.

I heard a low hiss come from Kelly as he tried to get Aeryk's attention. He nudged his horse and came back a couple of steps, still facing the gate.

"What is going on?" Kelly whispered, "Doesn't anyone in the guard know you?"

"Secret mission," Aeryk said. "The guards wouldn't be expecting us, so they're cautious. Like we expected."

"Which was the reason you took the lead," Kelly said

with a little exasperation, “so why doesn’t someone recognize you? You’re the son of a duke; at least the captain over there should know who you are.”

There was a pause, and I watched Aeryk. He seemed to consider something before he spoke.

“Well, I haven’t been here in a while.”

“A while?”

“Twenty years,” Aeryk said.

Kelly blinked. He looked over to me and blinked again emphatically, then turned back. “I’m sorry? I don’t think I heard you right,” he said.

Aeryk now turned his horse more toward us and spoke in a low voice, “I have been occupied at home, learning to manage my province. Our relationship with the other provinces was secondary, and…,” he shrugged a little, “that was my father’s concern,” he said. His demeanor was defensive, and if I had been made to guess at the time, I would have said that he was embarrassed at being challenged openly.

But Kelly was undeterred. “You’re your father’s heir, and you haven’t been to your liege lord’s home in your entire adult life?” he grumbled, “That’s an interesting approach, your lordship.”

Aeryk’s eyes narrowed. “So how did you handle it when you were being groomed to rule your father’s lands?

Oh wait," he snapped, "that's right. Never mind."

They glared at one another. Aeryk lifted his eyebrows in a challenge, and I saw Kelly's eye twitch, though he held his tongue.

"Gentlemen," Dana said, breaking the spell, "our hosts?" She nodded toward the gate where the dismissed guard was returning. We turned in time to see him come up to the captain and whisper in his ear, then step back into rank.

"It looks like," grumbled the ax-wielding giant, "the king will see you. Dismount and follow me. Stray at all, and I'll have you killed where you stand."

We were moved quickly through the streets on foot, and much of it was a blur. The palace guard took our horses, gear, and weapons from us at the gate, and it occurred to me to wonder how Locksley was taking to being herded together with the other animals. Ultimately, we ascended a long stone staircase that led to the upper wall and the castle itself. Dana had taken up her position next to me, and I could see from the look on her face and the tension in her stride that she was fully engaged in the 'protector' side of her role. Kelly too stayed near; just two paces ahead of us. He also was keeping, I noticed, well behind Lord Aeryk, and I wondered which one of us he was protecting by staying where he was.

We entered the castle proper at the top of the stairs.

Rather than the main gate which I could see off to our left, we entered through a heavily secured side door that led to a small, unadorned chamber. Our escort stopped us here, and the leader of the guard disappeared through a door on the other side of the room. My leg ached. I wondered when I'd have a moment to pull off my boot and inspect just how much damage there had indeed been. Then, I wondered if I'd be able to pull off my boot without screaming. I looked up just in time to see the captain return.

"This way," he said and stepped back out of the door. Aeryk went through, followed by Kelly, me, Dana, and our remaining companion. We entered a reasonably sized stone chamber that was apportioned as an office of some sort, dominated as it was by a central wooden table that was covered with papers and other miscellanies. Above it hung a metal fixture with multiple candles that lit the room so brightly after the darkness of outside that I felt my eyes flinch closed before they slowly adjusted. At the far end of the place from where we entered, a tall man stood wearing a heavy fur cloak. He looked to be middle-aged but somehow seemed far older – even a glance in his eyes gave an impression of insight honed by many years. His hair had once been dark, but a life of care and service had left his head wreathed with the gray of wisdom which stretched down into a well-cropped beard. He had the look of one that had once been a capable warrior but was now in a phase of his life where he was better suited to the guidance of men than the dominance of them.

"This is King Ronald the First Kastellian of Sterling, Ruler of the twelve provinces of Lochhaven," the captain said to the room. He turned to the king and bowed low and said, "Your Majesty, I give you Lord Aeryk Escrios, Marquess of Claire." Straightening, he turned and gestured toward Aeryk.

Aeryk bowed low. "Sire," he said.

King Ronald nodded to him. "Hello Aeryk," he said plainly. His manner was not far different from that of Lord Myk in Clemons; more polished, perhaps, but still plain-spoken. He continued, "It's nice to see you again. I only remember you as a small boy."

"Yes, sire," Aeryk said, his cheeks flushing.

"You are here much sooner than I anticipated," the king continued. "How did you manage the trip so quickly?"

"I had some…," Aeryk hesitated, "remarkable help. I'd like to introduce them to you. By your leave."

The king nodded and smiled, then turned to look at the rest of us. Kelly bowed, as did Dana. I waited.

Aeryk beckoned first to Kelly, who stepped forward. "This man has been integral in getting us here, and, truthfully, saved my life when my trip first started," he said, and with that, the awkwardness between the two men seemed to evaporate. "He's called Kelly," Aeryk finished.

Kelly bowed his head again. "My privilege, Your Majesty," he said.

The king looked at him for a long moment. At first, I didn't realize what was wrong, but then the king spoke.

"My privilege as well, sir knight," said Ronald with a nod of his own, "Your reputation precedes you. How did you come to be in my lands?"

A flash of understanding came to me then. Isolated as the Western Kingdom was, King Ronald was still a man of authority and reach. He would be no stranger to the doings of the wider world. Unquestionably, he had heard tales of significance from the east, and possibly those had come from some involved directly. Kelly would be no stranger to him, but his presence there and under those circumstances, I'm sure the king saw was a cipher.

Without hesitation, Kelly responded, "Simple coincidence. And I hope any reputation you're referring to isn't too...," he took a breath, "concerning."

Ronald shook his head. "Not at all. You are welcome within my borders." He turned to Aeryk.

The marquess stood agog but recovered quickly. "And this is Lady Dana of Yorch," he said, indicating Dana.

She stepped forward and bowed. "Lady Dana Lunavale bar Donnara, Silver Spar of Her People, and

Guardian of the Court of Yorch."

"Lady Dana," the king said, "you are most welcome. Your order is well-known and universally respected. And if you are one of the Guardians of the Court, then that would mean that our ambassador here…," he looked at me. I stepped in front of the others to stand before him.

"I am Princess Julea Niconnal bar Ardallah, Light of Our People, Heir to the Golden Throne, and Emissary of Yorch," I said. I've always found my title to be pretentious, but formality was necessary when it was appropriate, and so there it was.

"I'll be a son of a –," I heard Aeryk mutter behind me, but I kept my eyes on the king.

"Imperial Highness," Ronald said, letting the implications of my presence sink in. "Please let your mother know that she honors me by sending so auspicious a representative."

I nodded. "I will; and thank you, that is very gracious. As it is, I bring my mother's greeting and good will to you and your lands."

Ronald nodded in thanks, then said, "I apologize for the rather in-auspicious nature of this meeting. I promise you we will be much more appropriate tomorrow. For now, please allow me to have you and your companions taken to accommodations where you can refresh yourselves after your journey."

"My thanks again," I said. "We are exhausted from the road and its challenges."

Aeryk stepped up then. "Sire, one of the guardsmen from Clemons, a young man named Markh Rindros, died while we were journeying here through the Aosta Forest. Would it be that his brother here could be sent back to Lord Myk so that his family can be comforted?"

The king looked around the room briefly as if he was waiting for someone to correct what he had heard. When that didn't happen, he looked back at Aeryk. "The Aosta Forest?" he said, "So that's how you made the trip so quickly." He sighed in a way that evinced a man with the weight of the world on his shoulders. "That's sad," he said. "Your request is, of course, granted. He may return to Clemons as soon as he wishes. In the meantime, let's get you all some rest. Captain?" The captain of the guard stepped forward.

"I'd like to formally introduce you to Rohb O'Laird, captain of the castle guard," the king said with a gesture toward the captain. He nodded sternly toward us. "Rohb," Ronald continued to him, his tone becoming more informal, "can you see to their horses and make sure their personal items are brought here for them?"

Captain O'Laird nodded and with a couple of giant

steps swept back through the stone doorway that we had entered and disappeared. The king turned to another man that had been quietly and up to then all but invisibly standing in the far corner of the room. They exchanged some brief words before the king turned back to us.

"Vasily will make sure you are guided to your accommodations," he said, gesturing to the small man, "Princess Julea, we will plan to meet tomorrow afternoon after you have had plenty of time to refresh yourself. In the interim, please accept my hospitality. And the rest of you as well. Now I bid you goodnight." With that, he turned and left the room. Vasily held the door and waited quietly for us.

Kelly turned to Dana. "So I don't forget to do it later, let me say it now. Congratulations; I didn't know."

She looked at him, obviously unsure of what he was referencing.

"Silver Spar," he said with a smile and a bow of his head.

"Thank you," Dana almost whispered. She flushed, and I knew it was both because of his show of respect and at the simple fact of being the center of attention. I smiled slightly at her modesty, but more at his acknowledgment of her status. The ancient Order of the Silver Spar had been established generations ago as a way to acknowledge and promote those that had served the Empire with exemplary honor and skill but were not of a royal bloodline. It was only granted by the Empress – or Emperor, in times past – and only to the truly unparalleled. As such, there had been only a small number in recorded history that had ever achieved the rank, and never had there been more than two concurrently. Dana was, in fact, one of only three that had been accorded the title in over two hundred years and was the sole active member of the order.

"It's a tremendous honor. Few have deserved it as she does," I said, though I immediately thought better of it. So much of what I was thinking and feeling inside was coming out with two meanings; I realized that – to Kelly in particular – this was another example. While I may have meant such jabs on occasion – and let's be clear, I assuredly did – I didn't intend to be prickly just then. Nonetheless, I saw what I thought was a shadow pass over Kelly's face before he turned away.

Vasily cleared his throat, and in a sing-song voice said, "If you would be so kind as to follow me, I will show you to your rooms." He beckoned again at the door. Kelly shot a look at Dana and I and then turned and walked out. Aeryk waited by Vasily for us, undoubtedly feeling that it was inappropriate to leave before we did. Dana looked at me.

"I know," I said quietly, "I know." One by one, we exited the room.

The next day, dressed in full finery, I stood before the throne of the Western Kingdom. Or Lochhaven, I surmise, depending on to whom you were speaking.

King Ronald and I had agreed to meet after midday, which gave me the entire morning to review the documents and notes that had accompanied me from my mother, as well as to make myself presentable. The room I had received was spacious and quite well-apportioned, but for me, the most important thing was the heated stone basin filled with lavender scented water. The flames stoked in the hearth, I took advantage and allowed myself the luxury of a long bath. The dirt and dust of the road lifted away, as well as the residual aches that days shipboard and on horseback can bring. I evaluated my left leg and saw that it had adopted a deep shade of bluish purple from my calf to my ankle, but that there appeared to be no functional problems. On request, the palace serving women provided a soft cloth strip for me and an ointment that smelled like tea. I can't be positive of its actual effect, but it did seem to make the tenderness there less by the time I dressed for my meeting with the king. Dana arrived at my chamber as a small lunch came, and together we ate before the final preparations. I had packed a silver-trimmed black dress for my audience with King Ronald, and she helped me put it on. It was long;

its silver stitched bottom hem brushed the tops of my open black shoes. It had a high collar, with a strap that came around my neck in the fashion of a choker and bore a green gemstone clasp in the front. The neckline swooped in from the shoulders to the middle of my chest, while the back was open. The long sleeves too started on each shoulder and came down my arms and ended in wide bell openings at the wrist. Dana finally sat the silver circlet of my office on my head, and thus adorned, I left to meet with King Ronald.

The throne room of Lochhaven in Castle Sterling was in the exact center of the hill on which the castle stood. The guard led me from the building we lodged in through an open courtyard to its oak framed entrance opposite the main gate. Towering wooden doors swung open as I approached, and I found myself walking into what seemed more like a conservatory than a throne room. The entrance opened onto a broad bridge arching over a pond that curled around the entire circumference of the sixty-foot diameter room. Stone statues and tapestries decorated the outer walls, set in small, arched insets for the first fifteen feet. Above that, more statues alternated with tall multicolored windows for the remaining thirty feet of the room's height. The center; an island in the middle of the pond; was the actual summit of the hill, and it was here that the throne itself was built. It consisted of a broad platform of stone with another piece of raw stone jutting up at a right angle behind it and shaped like a wide, immense arrowhead. It looked as though the arrangement had been natural, though there was an intricate starburst pattern carved into the stone above the throne seat. The platform as a whole was wreathed in greenery that hugged the edge of the pond and rustled with a slow current in the water, the source of which I could not identify.

In the center of this, below the starburst, was a couch-like seat upholstered in red cloth; the throne of Lochhaven. I say it reminded me of a couch rather than a throne as it was wide enough for two and the back was low. It didn't seem like any throne I had ever encountered, but King Ronald sat perfectly at home on it as I came over the bridge to the central platform, leaning forward with his elbows on his knees, and watching me approach.

"Your Majesty," I said as I entered. I bowed my head.

"Princess Julea," he said, sitting up straighter and placing his hands on his knees. We were on the same plateau, I noted. It was unlike the two levels in my mother's throne room. It created an entirely different feeling for the discussion.

I began my prepared statement. "I bring the greetings of the Empire of Yor—,"

"Please," said the king, holding up a hand. "May I say something first?"

I stopped. It broke protocol, but I nodded, “Of course, your highness. It is your home.”

Ronald smiled at me in a way I can only describe as gentle. He half turned and looked at the stone backdrop behind himself. “Amazing, isn’t it?” he said. It was rhetorical; he didn't wait for an answer. “I’m told that my ancestors found this hill with this rock formation on top and decided to build a city here,” he continued, “I don’t know if that’s true or not, but it would explain why the city is here instead of somewhere more obvious, like on the sea, or a river. But here it is, and it’s been a good place for...,” and here he gestured to the stone images, “for a long time. Good enough to build this castle, this city, and this kingdom around.” He turned back to me. “You see, that’s the symbol. The solid rock of this hill, this place; it means something to our people. All of us,” he said, and I knew he was talking of the entirety of the land. He continued again, “I know the proprieties of a discussion like this. I daresay that I helped define them. And I am willing to follow each and every one of them if that is your preference.”

I looked at him carefully. “But?” I said.

He smiled, again gently. “But,” he sighed, “for the sake of my land, I would love to just talk like people. I will,” he reached up and removed the bejeweled golden band from his head, “set my crown down. You set your script aside. We can talk. I would like that.”

The Empress would not be pleased, I thought. All that work on the negotiation strategy and paperwork for nothing. I smiled broadly and removed the silver circlet from around my head. "I would like that very much, too."

"I need help," Ronald said then, leaning back comfortably. He casually tossed his crown on the other end of the couch-throne. "I've been complacent. We worked so hard to achieve peace here among ourselves that we weren't paying attention beyond our borders."

"What you've achieved here is a miracle," I said sincerely.

"Thank you," he replied, "and as true as that may be, it is only a local miracle. The king to our north is a serious threat."

"Mathu," I said.

He cocked his head at me, then shrugged. "I should have expected you to have done your research. Yorch is well known for its – oh, let's call it – caution," he said.

I let the implication pass. "You need support, and that's something we can supply," I said. There had been a whole speech that my mother had prepared — volumes of negotiation instructions that the political geniuses of the court had sent with me. I chose again with great satisfaction and conviction to ignore all of it. "But Yorch has a price," I concluded.

Ronald nodded. “I can afford a tithe to the Empire, and minimal taxes on imports from your merchants.”

“And that you will do,” I said calmly, “and one thing more.”

Ronald sat up straight. For the first time, I could see, he did not have a handle on what was coming next. “And that is?”

I paced a little to one side, mostly for show. I meant it to look like I was deciding whether to reveal a secret, though this was my intention – indeed, the entire reason – for my coming at all.

“There is a mine in your lands. I believe it is near your northeastern border and overseen by a man called Duglas,” I started.

"Duke Duglas Dasous of Auron," Ronald confirmed, his brow furrowed.

“The mine has recently begun producing gems,” I said.

“Emeralds,” the king said, “The miners uncovered a new vein just this last year.”

I stopped pacing and looked directly at him. “The Empire would like exclusive access to the mine’s product. In perpetuity.”

The king looked at me for a long time. “The Empire wants an emerald mine,” he said as if to confirm what he heard.

I nodded. “And one sample of its product to return with me to Yorch.”

“A trade agreement, one mine, and a box of emeralds and I will have the Empire’s support?” he said, pulling the whole discussion together.

“Indeed,” I said. I withdrew a tight scroll from the fold of my sleeve and held it up. “Sign this agreement and your concerns about outside threats will vanish into the mists.”

King Ronald stood and paced in front of the throne for several moments. I waited, holding the scrolled document in my folded hands and keeping a blank look on my face.

“We are not a vassal of the Empress,” Ronald said, “Ever.”

“Of course not,” I said with a shake of my head for emphasis, “You would be allies. This treaty, as written, includes a covenant of peace. The Empire will not act against a signed ally. Ever. Of this, I can speak with authority.” Which, I grudgingly had to admit, was why my mother had sent me. A guarantee from the current generation and the next was a powerful bargaining strategy.

He was still pacing. Rationally, he had to agree. But it was my experience that people – well, okay, mostly men – didn’t like to negotiate as the distinctly weaker party. He needed to believe this was good for Yorch too; that somehow he was bringing something valuable to the table. How much do I reveal? I wondered.

"The threat to your north is very credible," I said, "and while the Empire is not at all interested in such squabbles unless they involve an ally, we believe that working alongside you has a much better chance of being beneficial than if this Mathu swallows your kingdom."

There, I thought. That should feed the pride monster without revealing anything about the Empire's goals.

He paced some more. Finally, stopping right before me.

"I am going to trust you, Princess. Partially, because you seem to be speaking in good faith, and partially because we spoke plainly with one another here today. And also; because I don't think I have any other choice," he said.

"You can trust me, Your Highness, because I am speaking in good faith," I said. Then after a pause, I continued, "But yes. You have no other choice." Maybe I had a pride monster of my own, I thought.

He sighed again, another sigh that carried the overwhelming weight of authority. Turning back to the throne, he picked up his crown. Setting it back on his brow, he sat and looked back at me.

"My ministers will reread the agreement, but if it is as we've discussed, I will sign it before the end of the day," he said.

I set my silver circlet back on my head. "It is as discussed. It will be an honor to have such an agreement between our two peoples," I said.

He approached, and I nodded to him, handing him the treaty. He took it, and then took my hand, which he kissed the back of gently. He stepped back, and I nodded my head again. We had slipped back into the formalities for which we were both bred.

"I will send for you when the documents are complete," he said. Then he turned and went back to the throne.

For the second time in what felt like too a short period, I turned and left a grand throne room with much on my mind.

CHAPTER FIVE

– KELLY –

God's teeth, but that woman could get under my skin.

I looked around the room that Ronald's administrator had led me to the night before, and was still annoyed. It wasn't the accommodations; they were spacious and very comfortable. The room's contents centered around two focal points, one at each end, with the entrance in the middle. To the left of the door was a massive stone fireplace surrounded by heavy upholstered furniture on, and surrounded by, rugs made of overlapping furs. To one side of the hearth was a stand on which was a basin for water and a kettle that could be used to heat it in the fire, and finally, an alcove where a large stone bath sat. It had been filled with fresh hot water the night before when the porter showed me to the room; to be fair, using it did improve my mood a bit. On the other side of the hearth were sideboards with a variety of decorative pots, bowls, and other such items carefully arranged on them. The walls bore paintings of various levels of quality, but all tastefully hung and serving well the purpose of warming up the bare stone. The other side of the room was home to an enormous four poster bed that looked very much like it had been carved out of the trunks of four trees. It sat atop a wooden platform that was two steps up from the stone floor and was framed by thick wooden beams. A carefully arranged pattern of crosspieces that mimicked the look of branches covered the entire assembly. The bed itself was thick and clean and as soft as a cloud looked. Aside of the bed's platform was a large armoire containing several soft robes and clothes of various sizes in it, and a smaller cabinet which contained my equipment taken from me at the gate when we arrived. Every aspect of the room bespoke the comfort and safety of royalty.

So, of course, I was enjoying none of it simply because Her Nibs took a cheap shot at me about a life I claimed to no longer want. Instead of wallowing in the depravity of the giant bed until they found my desiccated corpse some months from now, all dried out because I refused to get up from its cloud-like glory, I had woken at dawn and brooded half the morning away.

Very noble, I scolded myself; *you should be proud.*

It wasn't that I hadn't done anything. I had enjoyed the use of the bath the night before and had slept for some hours. The exhaustion of nearly being killed does help in that area. But once those distractions were over, it seemed like my brain wanted to spend some quality time reevaluating all the decisions I had made over the previous few years; since, as I'm sure is clear, that is always helpful.

By mid-morning, I found myself perched in the window on the side of the room overlooking a large field some forty feet below where the Palace Guard of Castle Sterling seemed to be in training. There were a fair number of the guardsmen of Sterling that had come out onto the field that morning and started sparring with one another. This seemed to me to be an excellent distraction, so I decided that I'd get a closer look. Or at least I'd try. I had no idea how much freedom we had as visitors to the castle; it wasn't impossible that the training grounds would be off limits. I finished dressing in some of the clothing provided by my host – my own still being covered with the filth of the road and heaped in a corner the night before – and made my way downstairs and in what I hoped was the appropriate direction. Whatever the policies of the castle were, no one challenged me, and in a short time, I stepped out to the fringes of the field.

At first, and for some time after I arrived, the scene was one of random sparrings. One on one, the guards would test one another's attacks and defenses, sometimes pausing to make suggestions, sometimes knocking each other to the ground as they pushed their opponent's skills. At one end of the area, a contingent of archers performed target practice from a variety of distances and stances. It was peculiar, but I found in myself a feeling of familiarity, if not nostalgia, that was very comforting.

All this went on for some time, before the distinctly identifiable figure of the captain, Rohb, came out from the shadowed overhang across from where I was watching. As they noticed his entrance, the other guardsmen one by one stopped their exertions and turned to him expectantly.

"Time for the Trial!" he called loudly, and with that, a cheer went up. "Adh has the list and will be posting it on the board. You have half an hour to prepare."

One of the men near Rohb – Adh, presumably – held up a large sheet of paper with what looked like a spiderweb drawn on it. Again a cheer went up, and the crowd of men followed as Adh went to a large wooden signboard and fastened the paper to it. I walked out to where the captain still stood.

"The Trial?" I said. He turned at the sound of my voice.

"This field is for guardsmen only," Rohb said, "There are stiff penalties for civilians who are caught here."

I shrugged. "Okay, but humor me for a minute," I said smiling, "What's 'the Trial?'"

He glanced back over to the men. None of them had acknowledged my presence as they focused on looking at the posting.

"An internal contest of sorts," Rohb said, his voice lowered, "Good for morale, and keeps them sharp. We match them up by what we think of their skills and have them fight."

"That's got to be hard on your archers," I said.

Rohb ignored me. "The combats are quick, and either obvious defeats or scored by Adh and me – Adh is their training master – and then the winners move on through until we have a final fight and a final winner."

"What's the prize?" I said.

"Coin. A weekend off duty. And pride. Mostly pride."

I looked over at the cluster of men, some of whom had now turned back to see us talking. Rohb looked and noticed, as well. "Well, that's it then," he said, "rumors or no, you have to go."

Rumors? I thought. I looked at him again. "You said there were 'stiff penalties' for being here. Since I've got to pay penalties anyway, what's say I stay and watch?" I asked. The only thing waiting for me back inside, I knew, was more boredom and time with the disquiet in my own mind, and watching a little competition seemed eminently more productive than that.

Rohb looked at me carefully, then glanced over to the men. Some of them were coming back in our direction now, apparently curious about the newcomer on the field. A gleam flashed in the captain's eye, and he grinned at me in a way that I found unsettling.

"I've got a better idea," he said to me, then in a loud

voice reminiscent of a caller at a town faire, he continued, "Boys! We have an unwelcome visitor on the field! Now we all know that's not allowed!" The men began to grumble loudly in their support for the captain. Rohb stalked to one side, strolling around me like I was a horse he was considering buying. "Some of you have heard," Rohb continued in the same voice, "that this particular visitor has a bit of a rumor going around about him. One that has to do with the high and mighty Empire! Now I myself think that it's nonsense. I mean, look at him! Hardly seems like what we've heard could be true, does it?" The men began to mutter and voice support for the captain's words. Some laughter rippled through them. He stopped his pacing right in front of me.

"Does it?" he said, glaring at me.

I narrowed my eyes. "Depends on what you've heard," I said, keeping my voice quiet. "But I'd be glad to help you figure it out." A tiny crack opened to the burning flame buried inside me.

"Then this is what we'll do," he said, loudly again and with a broad smile that made me realize that I had said exactly what he was hoping I would. "The Trial begins in twenty minutes! When it's over, the winner will have half an hour to rest, and then he will face our visitor in a final contest. If he wins, we double the prize!" The men cheered. Rohb turned and looked at me before saying, "And we'll have our answer, won't we?" The men cheered again.

I looked at him and waited for the cheering to die down before I answered. "As you like," I said, giving him a slow nod.

And so the Trial began. I found a seat on a bench not far from where I had initially entered and which afforded a view of the entire field and set to watching.

Shortly after noon – and after several rounds of skirmishes – I saw Aeryk come through the entryway onto the field, looking around. Seeing me, he purposefully stalked over and stood next to me.

"What exactly are you doing?" He asked.

"You aren't supposed to be out here," I said, watching the field, "They made that pretty clear when I came out."

Aeryk sat on the bench by me. "Kelly, everyone in the castle is whispering about the visitor who's going to fight the guard! This is stupid."

I ignored that last part. Aeryk, I had realized over the days of travel, got very tense, very quickly, and with no filter. "His house, his rules," I said, nodding toward Rohb who was out in the autumn sun.

Aeryk looked from me to him and back. "Whatever's going on, I'm sure the king will give you dispensation for breaking a rule you didn't know about. You don't have to fight in a stupid contest."

"Oh, I know that," I said, turning to look at him for the

first time, "but, see, I want to."

Aeryk furrowed his brow, "What? Why?" he said.

I turned back to the field and watched as another round ended. "Because. Because that guy?" I said, pointing at Rohb, "that guy pisses me off. Doesn't make sense. Isn't smart. I know all that. But still," I said with a slight shrug.

At this point, I'm sure it's clear that I was simply looking for an outlet for my frustration. The thing is that I knew that even then. I just didn't care.

"Winner!" Rohb cried out, holding the man's hand in the air. A cheer went up from the other men now gathered around the combat area, forming a ring in the center of the field. Rohb and his winner turned in a full circle, allowing him to enjoy his moment of triumph. Gradually, the cheering subsided, and finally, Rohb put his hands down. At this, the entire group quieted quickly. The captain turned and looked over to where I was still sitting, and I took that as my cue, so I stood and walked out, stopping across from them in the ring of men.

"We have now the makings of our grand finale!" Rohb announced, "Our trespassing visitor, the man called Kelly, versus Samhn Fayette ban Rothson, first lieutenant of the Palace Honor Guard!" Another cheer. Honestly, I was starting to think they cheered just because they liked it.

"Samhn Fayette ban Rothson", and it was not lost on

me that Rohb had used the Imperial form of his name, was about my height with a nest of curly brown hair and a mustache that ran from his upper lip to the edge of his chin. He wasn't small – larger than me, at least – but he wasn't a giant like Rohb. I extended my hand to him, and he looked at it as if I had been mucking out the stables. I cocked my head a little and retracted my hand.

"Sawn?" I said, intentionally mispronouncing his name, "Interesting."

"Samhn," he sneered, correcting me by over pronouncing it and making it sound like he was saying "Sa-ou-n."

"Oh yeah," I said, "that's much better."

Rohb stepped between us and addressed the crowd again. "The final battle will be joined in one half an hour. Return here then for the theater!"

"Just one thing," I said, matching his volume if not his carnival barker's tone. Rohb turned to me with a start, and the men froze. "There's one order of business we haven't considered," I said, "The spoils of victory."

Rohb shook his head. "That was addressed. He will receive double the normal reward of coin and time."

"No, no, no," I said as condescendingly as I could at the volume I was maintaining, "I meant for me."

A low murmur went up in the crowd. Rohb looked at me, sternly.

"I mean," I continued, "what do I get out of this little game? You can't give me time off, and I don't want your coin. And actually," I looked directly at Rohb, "Considering how impolite you've been, I think I'm owed something."

Rohb scowled and said, "What do you want?"

"If I win," I said, now aiming for the carnival barker tone, "I want an opportunity to prove myself more emphatically," I squared off with the captain, "One on one, you and me. One last fight."

The low murmur became a rumble of loud conversations among the men. Rohb looked around slowly, then held up his hand to quiet them. He turned to me.

"If there is anything left of you," he said, "it will be my pleasure."

The cheer that arose this time was deafening, and I backed away from the center of the circle and went back toward the bench. Aeryk was staring at me. As I approached him, he shook his head.

"You're an idiot," he said. I shrugged and waved over one of the attendants. Aeryk waited as I requested appropriate practice armor and weapons from him, and he hurried away.

"I have some stuff to work out," I said, turning to the marquess. "Besides, it's not a mortal battle; no one is going to die here. It's just an exercise."

"You're fighting two men who seem to be very good at

what they do, and what they do is fight," he said, "and you're doing it for no reason. That is the definition of senseless."

I shrugged again. "I have reasons. Stuff to work out, like I just said," I replied, thinking of my brooding mood earlier. "This is a convenient release. Besides, I'm really only fighting one guy."

Aeryk looked at me as if I'd spoken another language. "Two guys," he said as if to a child. Helpfully he held up two fingers as if to clarify.

"One guy. The captain. The first guy – this 'Sououn' – doesn't count," I said, deliberately mangling the name.

"Doesn't count?" Aeryk said.

I shook my head. The attendant approached with a cart and left it by the bench. I picked up the various pieces of beige gambeson armor, and one by one began strapping them on. "Nope," I said, "What do you think I was doing here all morning? I was watching the fights for a reason," I looked up to where Samhn was seated across the field with some of the other guards. "I picked him out about an hour ago as the winner," I said, keeping my voice low, "He's got good moves; it was pretty easy to see he was going to be the finalist, but the man has no variety; almost everything he does is exactly the same every fight. Same sidestep, same cross stroke, over and over. Also? He got tagged on his left knee earlier, and he's been favoring it since." I slid the vest on over my shirt and started pulling at the buckles. Aeryk got up and helped me finish.

"Still," Aeryk said, "I don't know why you're doing this at all." He paused, a long pause like he was considering what he was about to say very carefully. It was especially unusual for him, so it got my full attention. He seemed to decide something, then looked out at the field as he spoke. "She won't hear about this," he said, "She went into the throne room a little bit ago. She won't be out for hours."

I cocked my head to one side. "This isn't for her," I said, "Maybe it's *about* her; that's not entirely clear in here –," I pointed to my head, "but it isn't *for* her."

Aeryk looked back at me and nodded. "Fine," he said.

"And also," I said, looking at Rohb across the field, "I just really don't like that guy."

Samhn stepped out into the middle of the practice field with all the confidence of someone that was either absolutely certain of their abilities or absolutely clueless about them. I had confidence as to which case was more likely for two reasons. First, I had watched him fight, and while he was far from incapable, he was unremarkable. Second, and more importantly, I knew that the guardsmen of these lands had never faced actual combat, and that made all the difference in the world.

Rohb had been busy over the previous half hour. Using black soot, he had his men mark out a circle on the ground some twenty-five feet across in the middle of the field. Around this, he had others drag benches on which now were sitting many men I could identify as participants from the morning combats among others I didn't recognize. To one side of the circle, several of the benches had men seated on them with drums in their laps. A large crowd of other people, many of whom I hadn't seen earlier; presumably they had only come when they heard about the special event; were clustered impatiently around the whole affair. When the time came, the captain stepped out into the circle and pointed to the drummers. They began to beat a march-like rhythm that rapidly drew the attention of all of the spectators. The focus now on him, Rohb pointed toward the far side of the field, and Samhn strutted out from the other entrance. He was met with a cheer, and I saw that one bench, in particular, seemed to be especially loud; probably these were the rest of the Palace Honor Guard. As Samhn took his place, Rohb pointed to where I had been all morning.

"... from the east, the challenger known as Kelly!" Rohb finished. I stepped out from the overhang and walked as calmly as I could through the crowd and into the circle, stopping in my place on the other side of the captain. I could feel the slight buzz in the back of my neck as the expectation of combat woke old reflexes, and the burning flame inside grew hotter. Already things around me were becoming sharper and slower, and I could feel the texture of the air with each breath I took. Not yet, I reminded myself, just a few more minutes.

Rohb was reciting the rules of the contest in the same carnival voice as he used earlier, but I heard very little of it. What I did hear was that the fight would continue until someone yielded, or it was clear that one or the other fighter couldn't go on. Entirely exiting the ring intentionally was considered to be a yield, but falling on the line itself required the attacker to relent and allow the fallen opponent to stand back up and come back inside the ring. Rohb looked from me to Samhn and back, and I realized that he had asked if we had any questions. Samhn shook his head, and I followed suit.

"On my command then," Rohb said, backing away until he was outside the ring. I faced Samhn and lifted my wooden sword and buckler into a guard position. He shifted his weight onto his back foot and raised his guard.

"Soon," I said.

"Sa-ou-n," he growled.

I grinned. "I didn't mean your name, back-birth," I said, "That was how long it will be before you kiss the dirt." With that, I released the restraints in my head and let the burning fire loose.

Samhn stepped once forward, keeping his weight on his back leg. He moved cleanly but with a slight awkwardness that belied the fact that he had reversed his stance because of his knee injury. I moved half a step to my right but feinted a second step. Seeing the feint, he hurried to his attack before I would be out of range. He shifted his hips and swung his sword in a half circle below my guard and toward my hip joint, where the armor pieces met. I had watched him do precisely that on better than half of his fights that morning, and in most cases, the blow struck the outer hip where the armor didn't cover well. The resulting shock of pain typically distracted his opponent enough that he quickly moved inside their defenses and from there would dominate them and take them to the ground easily.

Of course, since I had seen it so often, I was well prepared for it. I backed out of my feint step and dropped my shoulder with my sword angled down in a blocking position. His strike hit early and had built up no power. There was a mediocre 'crack' sound as the two wooden blades met and the end of his sword slid along mine until it was stopped at the top by the cross-guard. Samhn turned frantically to pull the weapon free, realizing that if he didn't, I would easily lock it against my blades hilt and my buckler and pull it away from him. The turn, though, shifted his weight to both feet and brought them very close to me. I dropped from my crouch to one knee, pivoted slightly and grabbed his right ankle with my off hand and lifted. His weight shifted onto the weaker left leg which was already at a bad angle, and he tumbled backward, landing squarely on his back. Reversing my grip on my now freed sword, I drove the end into the ground as I threw myself up and forward, landing with my knee squarely in Samhn's chest and driving all the air out of him on impact. I thrust the edge of the buckler into his exposed throat and raised my sword high for a head-strike.

"Hold!" Rohb's voice cut through the battle haze, and I looked down at Samhn. He was gurgling to breathe as he had no air in his lungs, and I was both kneeling on his chest and pressing on his windpipe with my buckler. Slowly I stood up, and he rolled over on his side, coughing and gasping for breath. I looked at the guard captain. He had rushed in from the edge of the circle and was standing only a couple of feet away and staring at me with a mixture of anger and disbelief.

I narrowed my eyes. "Round one," I said, then turned and walked back to my bench through an opening the observers now made in the circle.

I'd like to say something here about how I wasn't proud of trouncing the lieutenant of the Palace Honor Guard. Maybe something about how I regretted the violence and was ashamed that I had done it only to blow off steam. The thing is that none of that would be really true. I was irritated and irritable. Having Julea around brought up all sorts of unsettled issues that I much preferred not to have on my mind. The guard captain and his men had been nothing to me but arrogant and unfriendly, and the snide comments about the Empire were particularly bothersome. So the truth is that it felt good to knock one of them on their arrogant western ass, and it would feel good to do it again.

Aeryk was looking at me as I sat down and continued to do so for much longer than I felt comfortable. I drank a little water and watched the guard milling about on the field, but soon I was done with it.

"Something on your mind?" I said.

He seemed to consider that for a bit, then finally said, "So when you said 'one guy' a little bit ago...,"

"Yeah," I nodded.

He raised his eyebrows and blew out a breath. "Well," he said, "I guess I did not see that coming." We sat in silence and waited. Rohb was across the field, getting his gambeson armor and practice weapons prepared. In place of a sword and buckler, he had a wooden representation of the double-bladed axe we had seen him carrying the night before.

"This isn't going to go as simple as the first fight did," I said, "I haven't had a chance to watch him in action, and variety of styles make all the difference. Do you know anything more about him?"

Aeryk flinched at that, and I remembered our disagreement the night before. "Not really," he said, "They say he's only been serving here for a couple of years at most. I believe he came from somewhere in the south."

"Whoa," I said, "In the south? Wait, did anyone say anything about his being one of the Talhas?"

"Actually, yeah, I think I heard someone say that word. Why, what's that?" Aeryk said.

I reached up and rubbed the bridge of my nose and then ran my fingers through my hair. "Well, that would explain the accent," I muttered to myself. I turned to Aeryk. "The Talhas are a tribal coalition from south of the Talte Bruite. Many of them have served in the Imperial army as foreign legionnaires. They're incredibly effective warriors and soldiers," I said, "That's probably why he is the captain. Well, that didn't make this any easier, but at least I might know what I'm dealing with."

Aeryk considered me. I'm sure he was wondering whether it was a good idea to try to talk me out of it again. Whatever it was, he decided against it, and we sat and waited in silence. Finally, some few minutes later, Rohb walked into the field and toward the ring. I stood, picked up the sword and buckler, and went out again myself without another word. As we approached the circle, the drums began again, this time beating an actual battlefield march. We reached the middle of the field at almost the same time and took up positions opposite one another. I lifted the sword in front of my face in salute, and he did the same with the axe before smoothly spinning it into a two-handed guard position. The tribute was the giveaway; he was a Talhas and had Imperial training. It was also the signal to start and thus given, the drums stopped, and the crowd cheered, and we began.

I was right; he did not rush in and engage as Samhn had done but instead stayed back and out of range, slowly sidestepping to circle me. I matched the maneuver, grateful for a chance to observe his movements. The buzz in my neck had returned, and again, the world slowed down. I stepped forward, reducing the distance between us, but keeping still out of his range. I knew that if he stepped in and attacked, between his long arms and the length of the axe, he would readily reach me before I could him. My only assets were going to be speed and what I hoped would be the unexpected. I edged slightly closer, now right at the edge of his reach. So close, in fact, that I couldn't be sure I wasn't actually within his range. But that was the risk I needed to take.

Rohb could see that I might have overstepped and come too close but didn't yet attempt a strike, instead choosing to reverse the direction of his circling steps. I followed suit, but too late realized that he had changed the angle of each step slightly after the reversal and had thus closed the distance a little more. And it was just as I realized it that the enormous axe swung at me. I had no time to think, and instinctively I threw myself backward in a roll that got me clear, but so narrowly that I felt the air as the axe passed behind me. I completed the somersault with my feet again under me and stood only to see the back of the giant man's hand swinging at my head. He had allowed the weight of the axe to pull him into a spin that he used both to propel himself forward and to aim a backhand strike where he expected my head would be; where I had conveniently actually put it. With no time to dodge, I instead took the blow on the side of my head and did my best to absorb it by rolling in the direction it sent me. Despite my efforts, his fist hit me squarely just behind the temple and sent me sprawling, my head crashing into the ground on the other side as I tumbled into the dirt. My vision clouded, and my ears rang, but I forced myself to keep rolling further. Just behind me, I heard the loud crunch of the axe coming down where I had been laying moments before. With my less clouded eye, I saw that I was now far enough to the big man's left that I would have a moment to get back to my feet before he could face me.

I pulled one leg under me and pushed to stand, but inspiration struck. I kicked off backward, instead of up, and wound up lying on the ground right behind Rohb's legs. I swung my blade at the back of one of his knees; I knew it wouldn't hurt him, but it caused his leg to buckle, and he stumbled forward to keep his balance. As he did, I got to my feet, grabbed my sword by the wooden blade end with both hands, and brought it up with everything I could muster into the open underside of his left arm. The corner of the cross-guard struck in the soft, unarmored part of the shoulder joint, and he howled with the surprising pain that made his arm go suddenly numb. I kicked him in his backside, and he stumbled forward, his one leg still wobbly from where I had struck at the knee. He turned back toward me and swung the axe, though his left arm had no strength and it came at me slowly enough that I was able to sidestep it easily. We faced one another again. My head was still ringing from the punch and the impact of the ground, and he held his axe only in his right hand, snarling. Abruptly, he stopped, stood straight, and dropped the axe. I almost rushed forward to strike when the sound that caused him to stop soaked through to me.

"By order of the king himself, this ends now!" The voice was high pitched and obviously unaccustomed to being at a high volume, but it was also unaccustomed to being ignored. I recognized it as the voice of Vasily, King Ronald's chamberlain. I looked around to find that, on the far end of the field, all of the guardsmen were down on one knee around him, while the others were in the process of doing so. I dropped the sword and buckler.

Vasily walked through the crowd into the middle of the circle with the stride of an angry school-teacher. He looked at Rohb and me in turn. "Captain, the king requires your presence. Now," he said. Rohb nodded, turned, and slowly walked off the field, cradling his left arm.

"You men will return to your posts, and the rest of you will disperse this instant," the chamberlain continued after Rohb was gone, "There will be no reward for this contest of yours, and indeed you are all fortunate that the king does not have more discipline enacted. Now go!" The men moved immediately, some few staying only to move benches back to their original location and generally restore the field to its normal state. Vasily turned to me and eyed me severely.

"Sir knight," he said, "you are a guest in our lands and our home by the grace of His Majesty. Your involvement in this dangerous and unsanctioned contest is not only inappropriate; it is all but offensive."

Blinking away some of the pain in my head, I said, "Begging your pardon, but 'unsanctioned?' I wasn't aware."

Vasily looked at me studiously, then in a much less judgmental tone said, "Am I to understand that you were unaware that His Majesty banned this 'contest?'"

Aeryk came up to stand behind me, which was good because I was finding this discussion getting in the way of my headache. "We were only told that visitors were not allowed on the field during the contest," he said. It was gilding the truth a little; they said visitors weren't allowed at all, but it was strictly true. Vasily rolled his eyes.

"I am certain that was to the end of keeping it secret," he said with a nod, speaking as much to himself as to us. "Very well," he continued, "please see your way back to your chambers and refresh yourself there. I will send up a physician if you feel a need?"

"I'm fine," I lied, "No harm done. But thank you."

Vasily nodded and turned to go, but I stopped him as an idea formed in my head.

"One question," I said, "what will happen to the captain?"

Vasily turned and looked at me, confused. "If it matters," he said, "he will likely be spending some time in our prison before he will be reinstated to the general company."

"You're taking his rank," I said.

"Of course," Vasily said, "There is a need for consequences in such things."

I nodded, but the idea that formed wouldn't go away. "Fair enough. May I speak to him?"

Vasily looked at me, "I will need to consult with the king."

I nodded and said, "That's fine; I will probably need to talk to him too."

"What are you doing?" Aeryk said, not for the first time.

"I have an idea," I said to him.

"Okay, sure. An idea. Am I going to like it?"

I thought for a moment while I gently rubbed at my head where I had been hit. "Probably not."

It was several hours later, and I was discovering that the so-called dungeon of Castle Sterling was in actuality nothing of the sort. Instead of being taken to a dripping underground pit of suffering – in other words, a dungeon – my guides took me to somewhere entirely different. The chamberlain and two of the Palace Guard – two that had not been sitting in the cheering section during my fight with Samhn, I noted – led me out of the training yard and through a labyrinth of passages that ended at the northeast corner of the castle grounds. From there, we entered into a small antechamber where a single guardsman sat behind a table in the middle. On seeing Vasily, he nodded curtly and stood, moving to a thick oak door at the back of the room. Sorting through a ring of stout keys, he inserted one into the door's mechanism and turned, releasing a dual latching system that retracted two metal rods that had been seated into the door's top frame and the stone floor respectively. He pulled the door open without a word and remained to hold it open as we passed through. Vasily guided us through a short stairwell that led half a flight down and through a door on the left-hand wall at the bottom. On the other side of the door was a long, curved hallway with a row of prison cells on the left and a long narrow window with bars across it on the right. It was just above shoulder height and provided a fantastic view of the surrounding forest to the north and east of Castle Sterling.

Vasily and the guards stopped at the door and gave every appearance of not going any further. I looked at Vasily with an unspoken question.

"Eight cells down," he said with a vague gesture of the direction he meant. I looked down the hall, then back at the chamberlain. He stood placidly.

"Right," I said with a nod of conviction, "thank you." I started down the hall until I found the eighth cell. On the way, two of the small chambers were open and had no occupants, giving me the opportunity to look inside. The rooms were small, no more than eight feet square, with a small cot on one side and a stone table built into the far wall. The doors were similar to the heavy oak one we had passed through in the office and locked in the same manner, but each one had a foot and a half square barred window in the middle of it. In one corner of each cell was a circular hole in the floor with iron bars fixed across it. I took a cautious look down and saw that it opened into empty space several hundred feet above the stone crags below. I realized that the whole prison area was suspended off of the side of the castle's northeast face over sheer cliffs. The circular holes allowed for dumping waste into the ravine below, but the iron bars and the long drop to the rocks below prevented that from being an escape route.

As I approached the eighth cell, I stepped to the outer side of the hallway, nearer the window. Just a precaution, of course. I had no idea how this discussion was going to go. I came even with the window in the door and could see the cot in the back of the room with two legs stretched out on it.

"I've seen worse," I said to the door. There was a silence, and then I heard the wood of the cot creak in protest to movement. A moment later, the window filled with the face of the former captain of the guard.

"Are you serious?" he grumbled. His voice was still hostile, but it was also weary.

I shrugged. "It's a little hard to tell just now. You rang my bell pretty good," I said, rubbing the side of my head for emphasis.

I thought I caught a quick smirk, but just as quickly as it came, it vanished. "What do you want?" he snarled, the hostility just a hair more convincing.

I leaned back against the opposite wall and folded my arms. "I heard what happened," I said, "you probably should have told me the whole thing was forbidden."

"Probably," he conceded, "and you probably shouldn't have come out at all. And probably I should have hit you harder."

I bobbed my head as if I was deciding something and said, "I agree with at least one of the things on that list. Maybe two. But the third?" I smirked, "just be happy with what you got."

"You just here to be an ass?" he snarled, "'Cause you are interrupting my rehabilitation." He moved away from the door.

"Talhas, right?" I said, and he stopped in his tracks. His face reappeared in the window.

"Say again?" he said.

"You," I said, "You're one of the Talhas. From the accent, I'd say, maybe Oaigoth?"

Rohb's head came close to the door so that his features were more visible. He appeared to be leaning down on the crossbeam of the door. "I am Robh of the O'Lairds. My people are from the north west of the city. Ours was the last of the independent clans to unite under the banner of Oaigoth."

I nodded. "I've fought alongside many of the Talhas, members from many of the clans. As warriors, they were the best of the best. And among the most honorable of people that I've ever known," I said.

Rohb narrowed his brows and glared at me. "Right," he snarled, "What's with all the flattery?"

"Not flattery," I said, standing and pacing a couple of steps, "Verification. I wanted to know if the 'rumor' was true." I smiled at my little reference to earlier, though if he enjoyed it, there was no sign. "In truth, I have a proposition."

No response.

I continued, "As you knew from our arrival last night, or I guess this morning, the ambassador came here for a private meeting with your king. The reason it's private is that there is a pretty significant threat from—"

"Mathu," Rohb said, cutting me off, "He's been a point of discussion here for a while."

"Exactly," I said. I had forgotten that as the captain of the guard, he would have been privy to those conversations. "We made it here by doing the unexpected. We cut across the Aosta Forest and avoided any of the mercenaries we know are looking for her."

"The Aosta Forest," he repeated. There seemed to be some grudging respect behind the words, but it was hard to tell.

I leaned back on the wall. "Yeah," I said, "We had help, but even so it was a costly path. And more importantly, we have lost the element of surprise. There will be a much tighter noose to slip through for the return trip."

"Giving the sell-swords a lot of credit, aren't you?" he said.

"Not when Edword Ribald is one of them I'm not," I said.

There was a long silence; then, a grumble came from the cell door that took me a while to recognize as laughter. "You people surely stepped in it, didn't you?" he said as the laughter died off.

I shrugged in agreement. "So I have convinced the king and the marquess that we could use the good arm of a seasoned warrior. You know," I said with a little grin, "maybe one that is recently out of work?"

There was a long silence. I looked up and saw that the outline of his head was no longer visible in the window. I waited.

"What do I get out of it?" his voice came from further inside the cell.

I had prepared for this one. It had taken no little discussion with Aeryk to get him to support my plan with the king, but he had, and we had a deal ready. "The prison sentence will be lifted, and the king has agreed to reinstate you to the position of lieutenant," I said. I had aimed for his full rank, but King Ronald and Vasily had stood firm on the idea that there needed to be consequences for the tournament. It was clear to me that this illegal competition had been an ongoing problem between them, and I wasn't going to be able to make any headway against it, so when they offered even the reduced rank, it felt like a win.

I waited, but if I'm honest, I knew it was just a formality. Men like Rohb would rather face the storied horrors of the Talte Bruite than sit unoccupied in a prison cell.

"I want two things," he said.

"It's not actually a negotiation," I said, "it's an offer. Take it or leave it. This result is all the king and the chamberlain will allow."

"This don't concern them," Rohb said, "just you."

I straightened and stepped closer to the door. I could

see him standing a foot or two back from the window with his arms folded across his broad chest.

“What do you want?” I said.

“Two things,” he repeated, “one now, and depending on that the other after we’re done.” He stepped closer to the door, and we could see one another clearly through the barred window. “First,” he said, his tone hushed, “I want a straight answer. Are you really the Blackcrow?”

I froze, and the hair stood up on my arms as he watched me. So that was it; that was the ‘rumor’ that had been going around. The Blackcrow. The traitor. The Imperial pariah, condemned to walk the world in exile. I matched the gaze of the big Talhas through the bars as I felt the crawling in my flesh at what I had to say next.

“I am,” I said, my voice flat.

He maintained the gaze a moment longer, then eased back from the bars. “Two,” he continued, “When this is over, we finish what we started today. For real.”

Ten thousand thoughts rushed in simultaneously, and not one of them was useful. My mind had pulled up history, reason, rationality, and even rage to respond to the warrior’s challenge, but ultimately it was all flushed away by one thing; I would have done the same thing if I were in his place.

“If that’s what you want,” I said, “then I accept.”

“Then get me out of here Blackcrow,” he said with a

little extra growl added to the name. He continued, "Let's get the princess home."

The first rays of dawn were becoming visible in the eastern sky when our little band assembled; together again this time in the throne room of Castle Sterling. The remainder of the day before had consisted of carrying the agreement I had reached with Rohb back to Vasily and securing his release and then returning to my room to prepare to leave. The plan Aeryk and I had discussed with King Ronald – while we were negotiating the release of the man that seemingly wanted nothing more than to have a chance to kill me – was to leave in the early morning hours through a secret passage built into the throne room. Its original intent was to allow the monarch to escape should the castle ever come under siege, and as such, it hadn't been open in generations. Such was, I guess, the struggle of living in a land that had never known open war.

We stood together in the massive throne room and waited for King Ronald. *Why is it that all throne rooms have to be so large?* I wondered, *Is there a contest that I'm unaware of?* Vasily had brought us there individually over the course of an hour before first light, and through private back halls generally reserved for the king alone. As a result, even the guards at the doors did not know we were inside.

Julea was standing off to one side of the group with a

look of concern on her face. I knew the look well enough from prolonged exposure to it, so I walked over to her.

"Coin for your thoughts," I said.

She turned to me as if only then noticing I was there. "Hmm? Oh, right," she said absently.

I cocked my head. Seeing this, she began to come back from wherever her mind had gone. "I'm sorry," she said, "It's been a long few days."

I nodded. "Everything all right?" I asked.

"Yes," she said, all business suddenly, "With one exception that I believe will be taken care of this morning, everything is fine." Suddenly she locked her focus on me. I braced for what I knew was coming. "How's your head?" she asked.

"Sore," I said, absently reaching up to where I'm sure there was a fair-sized bruise hidden only by my hair, "but it's fine."

"Of course," she said calmly, "I cannot imagine what it would take to crack that head of yours. Years and years, and I've rarely ever seen anything penetrate it." The corner of her mouth curled in the tiniest grin.

And she's back, I thought. "So you did hear," I said, "Aeryk owes me a coin." She shook her head disapprovingly before walking away. *Good work. We're very much making progress, Kelly*, I thought ruefully.

One of the sculptures of what I presumed to be dead

kings suddenly shifted with the sound of stone grinding revealing a passage behind. From the shadows, King Ronald emerged and came around to the central plateau in the room. He bore a wooden box in his arms a little less than two feet long and maybe eight inches wide. It was shallow, a hands-breadth high if that, but latched shut with metal bands and a large lock. He approached the princess and handed it to her. She passed it to Dana, who had come up next to her, and turned back to the king. Ronald produced a small key and inserted it into the lock, opening the latch and then the box.

"What's that?" Aeryk said from over my shoulder.

"Don't know," I said, craning my neck, "It looks like a box of..., coins, maybe? Or gems?"

Aeryk craned his neck as well, but the king had closed the box, apparently receiving the approval of the princess. "Token for the treaty?" he guessed.

"Could be," I said, "I mean, that's not usually an Imperial thing to do, but I guess it could be."

Dana turned away and put the box with the rest of their supplies while Julea turned back to the king. The key, I noticed, seemed to disappear, and I smiled at her sleight of hand; she had been a good student.

"It's time," I called out, and the party gathered in front of the throne. Ronald stepped over to the throne seat and stood in front of it, facing us.

"I am sorry your stay couldn't have been longer," he

said, “but time is of the essence for my people. You will find that I have ordered your provisions restocked, and of course, you know your personal items were cared for by the staff. The exit you will take will lead you to a seldom used road due north of the city. Last evening, we had horses prepared for you at a small roadside inn not far up the road where the remainder of your belongings await as well.”

I saw Dana look over toward me with a look of concern and knew that she was thinking of Locksley. I gave her an ‘it’s-all-right’ motion with my hand and turned back to the king.

“Sir knight,” he said directly to me, startling me. “Your instructions as regards your horse were seen to as well,” he said. I bowed my head, even as I felt a little like a boy caught talking during the instructor’s lecture.

“Lieutenant O’Laird of the Palace Guard has consented to accompany you and will serve as your guide for the early parts of your journey, as he knows the land well. I will say good-bye now, as it would be best to do what we can to draw attention away from this place until after you depart.” He stepped forward to stand before Julea. “Imperial Highness,” he said in the gentle voice he’d used when we arrived, “Thank you. This agreement between us means the world to my people.”

Julea reached out and took his hand, making a small nod with her head. “It has been my pleasure to meet you,

Your Majesty," she said, "May this agreement be the start of a long and mutually beneficial relationship."

Ronald nodded in return, turned, and left back through the entrance through which he had come. The statue ground it's way back into place, and we were alone.

Rohb walked up to the throne seat, grabbed the backrest and heaved it forward. For a moment, nothing happened. Then the distant sound of counterweights rumbled from beneath the bridge. Slowly at first, the near end of the bridge lifted off of the center area where we were standing and rose up into the air. After a couple of minutes, the bridge stood up perpendicular to the ground. As it had risen, stone barriers rose and blocked the water on either side of where the bridge had been, exposing the wet rock floor of the pond. Near us, next to the edge of the plateau, a section of the now exposed floor dropped away and revealed a dark tunnel going down nearly vertically.

Dana looked from Rohb to Aeryk and finally at me. "You're mad," she said matter-of-factly.

"Begging your pardon, my lady," Rohb said, "But this is the best way out. There are only six people in the world that know that this exists, and three of them are in this room. If we're leaving quietly, this is the way." He turned and, with his pack of supplies on his shoulder, worked himself down into the tunnel opening. With a careful look around, he grabbed a small handhold and descended into the darkness.

Aeryk looked at the hole and said, “So, no torches.”

“No,” I said, “no torches. The king was worried that the light could give us away.”

He slowly worked himself into the tunnel, fussing with his cloak and clearly unhappy that he was likely to get his newly laundered clothes befouled so soon.

Julea grabbed her pack and without a word stepped forward and followed the marquess into the tunnel. Her supply pack was off balance with the addition of the box, and as she descended into the opening, she readjusted it repeatedly as she strove to keep her balance. I watched her, knowing full well that any offer of assistance I made would be met with irritation. I looked over and noticed Dana watching her as well. She looked at me.

“She’s so stubborn,” I muttered.

“*So* stubborn,” Dana replied. Then she too went into the tunnel.

I looked around the throne room once more. A strange feeling, manifested itself, almost like an itch in my mind that I couldn’t quite reach. But I was utterly alone. I thought of the Clemons guardsman that had ridden here with us, reminding myself that he had left for Clemons the day before and was no longer in our party. Stupid, I thought, That’s not a useful thing to think about right now. I climbed down into the darkness.

The tunnel that had seemed nearly vertical only

stayed that way for a few feet before the floor became more sloped and easier to navigate. It was a good thing too since once the tunnel bent to its new angle, the meager light that came down from the throne room quickly dropped away, and we were left in complete darkness. Just a few paces from there and the telltale grinding of stone on stone told us that the way back had sealed itself. Now unable to see, every other sense rushed in to try to compensate, and I can still easily remember the smell of wet earth and stone carried on the cool of the subterranean air. I realized abruptly that must be the reason behind the 'no lights' rule; somehow there were ventilation ducts that connected to this tunnel, and there was an off chance any torchlight would be visible through one. It was deathly quiet, which amplified the only sounds that were present; the scrape of our footfalls on the stone, the distant drip of water, the occasional whistle of air through the unseen shafts, and every so often the skitter of some small creature or other that had made the tunnel its home.

"Ah!" Aeryk said, in a whisper that sounded like thunder in the silence.

"What?" hissed Dana, then she too made a startled sound.

Moments later, something bumped into my left leg about halfway up my calf. It was soft but substantial, and just as quickly it was gone. I kicked backward, but only managed to graze something with the toe of my boot that elicited a quiet hiss.

I have to say, I am really, really glad it was dark.

We walked like this for a long time; the only change was that the tunnel was, bit by bit, leveling off. By the time we found the exit, it was entirely level, if not slightly sloping up. Gradually too, as the ground was getting more comfortable to walk on beneath our feet, there were hints of light filtering in from in front of us. Consciously or not, everyone quickened their pace, and while there were more frequent stumbles on the rock-strewn ground, we came quickly to the opening of the cave hidden behind a large boulder. We came out of the tunnel into the middle of a copse of trees.

The day had the kind of gray light that came from heavy overcast, and the air smelled like rain. The breeze, though gentle, was on the cooler side of pleasant. But no one cared. It could have been a torrential downpour or a blizzard, and we would have been happy just to be out of the tunnel. In the shelter of the trees, everyone sat for a brief rest before continuing. Dana and Julea sat on a fallen tree trunk across from Aeryk and me.

"So what's in the box?" Aeryk said, pointing at the wooden box in Julea's gear. I will say this about his lordship; if there was something he wanted to know, he was more than willing to ask, even if it was something that was probably none of his business.

Julea looked at the box and back to the prince. "A surety from your king to my mother. Part of the promise that we pledged in our agreement."

Aeryk nodded then said, "I'm glad the agreement is going forward. So, does the great Empire always ask for gemstones as part of a treaty?"

There was a tone of both pride and condescension in the nobleman's voice; he seemed to be simultaneously proud to reveal that he already knew the contents of the mystery box and yet also convinced that something as mundane as an exchange of valuables was beneath her station. Which, I have to say, seemed odd, as it was my experience that exchanges like this were really the fundamental role for people of high-born station.

Julea, though, was unaffected. "Just a box of emeralds," she said, "A request from the Empress that your king was happy to oblige."

Emeralds.

There was more said, but I didn't hear it. My stomach had fallen into my boots. If that box contained what I suddenly realized it must contain, then my only choice was that I was going to have to steal it.

INTERLUDE

The small group of travelers emerged from the bundle of trees hiding the secret tunnel they had used and found themselves traversing a field of rolling grassland. The air was thick with moisture, and each step they took through the wet grass released a shower of dew on their boots. The dampness amplified the coolness of the wind – now more than a light breeze – and invoked on them a chill that their cloaks were only able to blunt.

After walking thus in discomfort for much of the morning, they reached a small road that in short order led them out of the openness of the fields and back into the shelter of the tree line. The massive dark-skinned barbarian leading them told them then that they would shortly arrive at the inn where their horses and supplies were waiting for them. The knowledge that they would soon be riding again, coupled with the fact that the shelter of the trees provided some protection from the dampness and the wind, buoyed their spirits and made the walking a bit more comfortable. And so they pressed on.

The tall woman felt it first, from somewhere at the very extent of her senses. Something was not right. Her alertness raised, she slowed her steps slightly, without straying too far from her princess, and began to sweep her gaze around the woods to either side of the path. The black-garbed warrior with them must have felt it too, she saw, as he was now looking around actively – his cloak swept onto his back to free his hands, the right one of which now resting on the hilt of his sword. The alertness went on for several minutes, until, as they were reaching the crest of a small hill, the peace of the hike was abruptly shattered.

The dark-skinned giant was still at the forefront of the group and had stepped one stride past a large tree at the top of the hill when a long piece of timber some six inches in diameter swung down across the path from behind the trunk. It hit the big man squarely in the chest; knocking him several feet back and leaving him breathless and stunned on the ground. Suddenly, there was a rustle of noise from the forest all around them. A crowd of shadowy figures – appearing as if from the brush itself – advanced on them. On reflex, the woman warrior stepped in and took a position with her princess right behind her, facing this new threat from the forest with her blade drawn. The attackers rushed in, dressed in mottled black and brown and brandishing broad-bladed cutlasses. The sounds of steel on steel rang out as the battle began.

The fighting was ferocious, but brief, as the small group was overwhelmed by the number of their foes. Two men had gone to where the giant still lay on the path from the impact of the trap and bound him before he could recover enough to resist. The dark-haired nobleman had felled several of his attackers in the first few moments of the battle but was soon dragged to the ground where they held him fast. The tall woman had been driven toward the middle of the road as she fended off the slashes of two of the whirling cutlasses. The warrior in black had been pushed in the same direction, and they found themselves back to back, their swords flashing as they parried blade after blade.

"Go high!" she growled, and then dropped to one knee, spinning her blade in a full half-circle to her right at knee height, slicing across one of the men's legs and leaving him crumpled on the ground. Her companion, gripping his sword with both hands, spun in the same direction at shoulder height on the opposite side. The black blade struck the cutlass of one of the attackers about two inches above the cross guard, shattering the steel blade and leaving the man holding a handle with a jagged stump on it. She finished her pivot on her knee and stood, once again back to back with her partner but now in the opposite direction.

"Drop it!" said a deep voice. The two warriors turned. A couple of feet away, a tall, dark-skinned man stood pressing a curved gold and silver knife with a serrated edge into the princess's throat. A small trickle of blood was visible at the leading edge where it indented her skin. He had his other arm wrapped around hers and used the leverage to hold her up and off balance. The tall woman felt her companion shift his weight and realized with a cold shudder that he was moving to attack.

"Okay!" Her voice croaked out, strange to her own ears. She dropped her rapier from her hand. There was a tension-filled pause that lasted until, with a guttural snarl of frustration, her companion dropped his sword as well. Immediately, the attackers that had been surrounding them rushed in and grabbed their arms.

"Better," said the man holding the princess, his knife still poised. "You two," he continued, turning and jutting his chin toward two more of his men, "take an' hold this one." With one motion, he took the knife away from her throat and shoved her hard toward them, where they quickly grabbed her and held her fast.

He wiped the tip of his knife against his leather-covered thigh and slipped it back into a horizontal sheath on the back of his belt. Putting his fists on his hips, he surveyed the area briefly before he spoke. "All right, maggots!" he shouted. The remaining attackers gave him their attention while maintaining hold of their five prisoners. "Get this lot bundled! We got a bit of a ways t' go t' get back to the ship!" he said. "And grab these sorry so-and-sos that are lyin' about too," he pointed indiscriminately at the forms of those of the men that had fallen, "They'll be mannin' the bilge when we get back t' sea." There were shouts of "Aye, Cap'n," as the men began got to work. The captain looked around again, then stepped over one of the fallen men and picked up his sword. He walked over to the man in black and the tall woman warrior. He looked her up and down and made a smacking sound with his lips, then smiled a predatory grin at her. She sneered in return, eliciting only a deep chuckle from him. He walked past her to stand before the man.

"'Member what you said?" he asked. The warrior snarled and struggled a moment at the grip of the men who each held one of his arms. The captain took a step to one side and viciously jammed his knee into the warrior's stomach with enough force to double him over even through his armor. The man coughed out all of the breath in his lungs as he lurched forward from the blow, and as he did, the captain brought the metal hand-guard of the cutlass down on the back of his head. He slumped.

"Kelly!" shouted the princess, struggling against the two men holding her to no success; they held her tightly.

"Dry yourself," the dark-skinned man said to her over his shoulder, now kneeling beside the sagging form of the other, "he ain't dead." The captain leaned in a little further. "Naw," he said quietly, "ye ain't dead, are ye, Blackcrow? Not yet, anyhow." Casually, he backhanded the captive man's head as he stood up. "Stuff something in his mouth and tie all of 'em up tight," he said, "then take an' get them all on the cart right away. There's bounty waiting."

Bound and blindfolded, the five prisoners were taken some distance and thrust unceremoniously into a cart. There, under the watchful eyes of their captors, they were carried for an unknowable amount of time until they felt the carriage come to a halt and they were dragged off, across a soft, sandy ground into cold waters, and loaded onto one or the other of two small boats. After a short row, they could feel the boats being hauled up out of the water. Still blind, they felt as they were thrown onto the deck of a ship. Then dragged or pushed or pulled, they were taken down into the hold where the telltale sound of metal bars scraping and locks clicking told any of them that were able to hear that they were in the cells of the ship's brig.

The dark-haired nobleman had carefully not resisted any of the actions of his captors, and as he had hoped, they had been less careful with him as a result. Little by little for the entire trip, he had worked the blindfold – which they had not tied very tightly on him – looser, allowing him now to nudge it up over his brow and look around. He was in a small wooden box with strips of steel reinforcing the sides. On one side was a door with a small window that allowed in the feeble light of a hanging lantern. Opposite the door, the wall sloped out slightly which he recognized as the inside of a ship's hull. A small rectangle set high in the wall served as a vent that allowed some fresh salty air in, though it was obviously close enough to the waterline that occasionally a wave would splash up and a spray of water would moisten the already damp floor. He stared at the vent, noting the faintness of the light beyond. The sun could not have yet set, he knew; there simply had not been enough time since they had been taken for it to be nightfall yet. Awkwardly, he crawled up the sloped wall until he could see through the small vent hole. The masts of the ship cast long shadows on the passing sea and confirmed his suspicions. The vessel was headed north. It may be that pirates had taken them, but that wasn't who was their true captor. That could only be King Mathu, and they were being taken to him.

CHAPTER SIX

– JULEA –

I still can't get the dripping sound out of my mind. With everything else that I experienced there, it's incredible to me that I still wake up some nights thinking I hear the dripping.

In the dim light, I could make out the general layout of the dungeon, or at least the part in which I found myself. My cell was long – more than twenty feet from end to end – but only a few feet deep and built of massive, well-fitted stone blocks. It was oriented such that the hallway outside, which I had been ungraciously dragged down to be left here, ran the full length of the room along one side. The hallway floor was higher than that of the cell by some four feet, which served to reinforce the feeling of being left in a pit. A heavy iron grating ran at an inward sloping angle from the hallway floor to the stone ceiling above me for the full length of the room, and a bolted gate in the middle served as the only door. The back wall and corners of the room were shrouded in impenetrable darkness as the only light was what was feebly making its way in from the sconces in the hall outside through the iron bars. I could see no indication of an outside window anywhere, and the cold, stale air bit at my nose. Everything was damp, and from somewhere unseen in the darkness was the steady, wretched sound of the dripping.

I sat in the corner of the cell against the half wall below the iron bars to benefit from as much of the light as possible, my bare feet pulled up and my arms around my knees. I couldn't tell how long I had been there, but even more troubling was that I very much didn't know how long I would be.

We had been imprisoned in the ship for the entire journey, with only meager water rations and no food. Our captors came to us once we were at sea and removed our blindfolds, as well as confiscating our armor and what little equipment we carried. Being able to see again was a relief, but by then there was actually very little to see. The pirates – for it was apparent that was what they were – were only interested in making sure that we didn't get loose, so other than occasionally checking on us and providing the water, they left us alone in the cages for what I believe to be the two days of the trip. The small windows on the cell doors were staggered just enough to prevent us from seeing one another, though we did manage – while it required shouting over the sound of the waves – to confirm that we were all relatively unharmed. It appeared that Dana was in one of the cells that were further away from me, and as a result, I couldn't speak to her directly. I wondered absently if she were seasick, and if the emptiness of her stomach made it better or worse. *Of course, it's worse;* I chided myself; *we're trapped in tiny boxes and bouncing in the waves. If that doesn't fill up the misery quotient, the food situation isn't going to make much difference.*

The setting sun glowed orange on us as we disembarked under the pirates' watchful eyes at what was probably the end of the second day. We were removed from our cells and fitted with steel manacles that bound our wrists together by a short length of chain. Then we were either dragged or prodded at sword-point onto a high-sided cart attached to two horses. Once there and the entryway then locked into place, the cart began a slow, plodding rise up a sharply ascending road. The ascent was so steep at several points that we had to struggle to keep our places and not tumble to the back of the cart bed. As the last of the light of twilight began to fade, we rounded a bend, and an immense black castle came into view. It jutted out of the outside edge of an angled cliff face, and that location combined with the angular design of its walls and spires gave the impression that it had been carved out of the black stone of the cliff itself and was clawing at the sky. The road again turned slightly, and we flanked the massive structure, allowing a full view of its entirety. The black stone walls, turrets, and towers were illuminated at irregular intervals by large sconces of fire that burned reddish-orange against the obsidian stone. If ever a building could look angry – or evil – this one accomplished the feat.

"Chateau Flint," muttered Aeryk, "Exactly as described."

A moment passed before Kelly said what I was thinking. "Described by who?"

The prince jumped a little and looked over at him. Since we had left the ship, our captors had allowed us minimal opportunity to talk, and we had used it mostly to reassure each other that we were more or less unharmed. Kelly; after a muttered assurance that he too was 'fine'; had not spoken at all, and instead become silent and seemed very focused on watching everything around us at the same time. So when he posed the question to Aeryk, it was jarring.

Aeryk shrugged. "Just from what I've heard around the court," he said. I saw Kelly looking at him intently even after the prince turned away and I wondered what he was thinking. He noticed and looked back at me, then gave me a wink before I looked away. He was trying to be reassuring, I knew. Doing that with the tension between us – and considering the situation we were in – was noble, but awkward. I turned back to the imposing castle and decided that I didn't feel reassured at all.

The pirate entourage guided our cart through the high black gate of the castle and across a circular courtyard to a giant staircase that we would shortly learn led to the audience chamber and the throne. We were directed off of the cart and up the stairs, where the castle's guardsmen awaited. The group of men, fifteen in all, encircled us and brandished their short spears. After a moment, the pirates stepped back, and the soldiers arranged themselves into formation around us. Beyond our new captors, I could see Edword making his way around where we were standing and heading toward the large black and red doors opposite the stairs. He took a position in front of the doors and waited. I looked around at my companions again. Rohb and Aeryk were immediately in front of me, while Dana had found her way to my side. She quietly reached her hand over and briefly held mine, and I gave her's a gentle squeeze of reassurance before I let it go. Behind me, I saw Kelly, still actively looking around at both nothing and everything. We waited like that for some time. Finally, the two doors swung open; each pushed from inside by a matched set of guards who then held them as first Edword, and then we, entered Chateau Flint.

We were ushered into the entryway which was a hall, perhaps some forty feet long by ten or so feet wide, lit by smaller versions of the angry looking red and yellow sconces from outside and flanked by alcoves on both the left and right. I ventured a glance into one, noting that another guard was standing there, and the niche itself appeared to extend much farther than I expected. I wondered if they were in truth camouflaged doors to a larger troop muster. I didn't have time to think on it too long as we continued without pause the rest of the way into the castle proper, and before what appeared to be the throne of evil itself.

As we exited the hallway, the ceiling of the black chamber soared fifty feet up, and the walls fell away from us almost that far to either side. We stood on a black stone walkway that led to the throne at the far end of the room. To either side of the path was a deep channel that disappeared down into darkness and then out of which the rough black stone of the outer walls gradually rose. The edges of the walkway were gilded with gold and illuminated every few feet by small torches; the combination gave the illusion that the glossy black path was lined with fire on each side for its whole length. At the far end, the walkway expanded into a broad dais. Mounted high on the back wall was one of the large sconces like that which illuminated the outside of the castle on our approach, the light of which glistened off of random flecks of gold in the unfinished back wall. On a raised platform immediately below the sconce was a tall golden throne that seemed to glow in the reflected light. On the throne was a man.

Edword stopped several feet back from the bottom step of the throne's platform and bowed his head momentarily. I looked back and forth at my companions again. Dana and Kelly had found a way to place themselves on either side of me with Rohb and Aeryk on the other side of Dana to my right. Behind us, the phalanx of guards that had escorted us spaced themselves out evenly on the platform and had each dropped to one knee, though they kept their eyes carefully on us. I turned back to the figure on the throne. As if on cue, he stood and stepped forward. He was clad in polished steel armor from head to foot that reflected the light from above at least as much as the golden throne itself did. A thick black cape trimmed at its edge in golden rope was wrapped around his chest from his left shoulder to under his right arm. The golden handle of an Imperial style long-sword hung at his left hip. On his head was a golden crown atop long, unkempt, black hair that framed his face and continued down to a thick black beard. But it was his eyes that made my blood run cold. They were green, piercingly so, and open too wide, despite a slight furrow in his brow. He looked out at us as if seeing us for the first time, though the walk up the pathway had taken several moments. He smiled broadly, but the smile never touched those eyes.

"Captain Edword," he said, his voice butter smooth, "we are pleased to see you have been successful."

Edword stood very still, and even though he had not moved, it was apparent that he was on alert, as if something was not right to him. "Of course I was," he said nonetheless,

"I present to you the ambassador of Yorch and her protectors." With a flourish, he turned and waved his hand as if drawing attention to treasures on display. After a moment, he turned back and faced the king. "And that makes the contract fulfilled on my end."

"It does," the king continued in the same silky tone, "indeed. No doubt, you are looking for our side of the bargain to be fulfilled." Edword nodded, the hint of a grin tugging at the corner of his mouth. The king strode a little to one side, much as I recalled my mother doing when she was about to deliver an unpopular statement. "Your ship."

"If I hear right, it's ready for me. I will take an' load her up, and our business will be done," said Edword.

"It's a remarkable vessel," said the king. He strolled a bit before he continued, "Our shipwrights tell us the design is remarkable. You are to be complimented."

Edword took a breath to respond but then held it, as if guessing what was coming.

"So remarkable in fact, that we wish it to be the flagship of our royal navy," the king finished.

The pirate's muscles flexed at the words as he visibly restrained himself from whatever his reflexes nearly made him do. He looked from side to side at the king's soldiers. The men had stood and stepped in by a pace, closer now, not only to us but to him. He turned slowly back to the king.

"That ain't the agreement," he said in a barely

restrained growl.

The king turned back and walked forward until he was immediately in front of him. "The agreement was for *a* ship. A ship based on your design. You will receive such. But," he looked down at his gloved hand as if he saw a smudge on its glistening steel surface, "it will not be *this* ship. This one is ours."

"That wasn't the contract." The anger in Edword's voice was more pronounced now, and his volume rose as he spoke. "It took almost a year to build this one!"

"You can always leave," the king said, his tone still smooth but now cold, "it is your choice to refuse the payment we agreed on. Either way, this ship stays."

Again I saw the pirate's muscles tense, but this time they stayed knotted as he and the king stared at one another. The castle guards were now standing at guard, holding their weapons in a ready position.

Without looking away from the king, Edword snarled, "Of course, King Mathu." I couldn't help but notice a strange note in his voice as he said Mathu's name; as if there were some unspoken meaning to the words.

"Excellent," the king said, immediately resuming his saunter around the throne. "Perhaps you would be interested in serving in our royal navy while you wait? We are always looking for good men."

"That's a kind offer," Edword said, and I could hear

him choking on the words. “I will take an’ consider that, Your Majesty,” he finished.

“Very well,” the king cooed, “you may go.”

The pirate nodded his head stiffly and turned. He looked briefly from one to the other of us, but if he had something to say he thought better of it. He strode past us and out of the room.

“Now then,” the king said, turning to look at the five of us, “let’s get to the real business at hand, shall we?” He walked down from his platform and approached me. From behind, I heard the sound of the guards shifting, and though I couldn’t look, I expected that they were moving in closer to be better able to protect the king as he came near to us. He stopped in front of me and folded his arms.

“We are especially gratified to have you in our presence,” he purred quietly, “though it is regrettable that we will ultimately have to dispose of you. It won’t do to have the empress hunting for her ambassador in my lands.” I felt the weight of his eyes looking me up and down as he unfolded his arms. I gritted my teeth, suddenly keenly aware of the closeness of the armed men behind me as he stepped very near to me. “But perhaps,” he said almost hoarsely now, “we can spend some of the intervening time getting to know one another better.” He was close enough now that I could smell him, leather and steel mixed with the blood-like metallic scent of his breath. He reached up toward my breast. I balled my fist by my side, and as his hand came to rest on me, I took a step back and brought my fist up with all the loathing I felt with the intent to break his disgusting jaw.

Except that isn't what happened. As I tried to step away, I collided with one of the guards who had moved behind me, and he held me fast. The king caught my swinging fist with his other hand before it had any power behind it, and I saw his mouth open in a broad smile. He took a step back and backhanded me across the face with his free hand. There was an explosion of pain as the metal gauntlet collided with my head and spun me half around. He still held my right arm by the wrist, which is why I only whirled part of a full turn, but by then I was so off balance that I was left dangling from my trapped arm. The world swam, and I could not follow what happened in those next few moments. There was an explosion of motion and sound near me, and at some point, I was let go to drop awkwardly to my knees. More noises came through the haze as my vision slowly cleared, and I looked up. Dana, two of the guards standing over her, was down on one knee next to me, her hand on my shoulder in concern.

"... all right?" Her voice came to me through the haze. I nodded, but before I could say more, the two men pulled her away. Able to see again, I looked up and saw four of the guards standing around the bloodied form of Kelly, lying next to where the king had been standing. All four of them held their short spears in both hands in the manner of simple clubs, and I saw the blunt ends of the shafts spattered with blood. The king was back on the platform and supporting himself on the arm of the throne, his back to us. He stood that way for a short time before he stood straight again and turned around, his too-wide eyes glaring at Kelly.

"Take him to the furnace!" He growled in a voice like a caged animal. "Wake him before you light the fire!" The guards around Kelly bowed, then lifted him by his arms and began to drag him out.

"Wait!" the cry came from my own throat unbidden. "Don't!"

The king looked at me, icily, but the guards kept going.

"I call for mediation," I said, my voice an echo in my own ears.

"Hold!" the king barked, lifting his hand. He came again off the throne platform and toward me. "Mediation? What could you possibly be able to negotiate with?"

"I am a princess of the blood," I said, realizing only then what I was doing. "I speak from the authority of the Golden Throne of Yorch."

"Jules!" Dana said; her shock at the realization of what I was doing evident in her voice.

The king's eyes flashed. He looked to Dana and the rest, all held fast by the guardsmen I could now see, for verification before he turned back to me.

"You are of the blood? A child of the Empress?"

"I am," I said, squaring off my shoulders. I felt the bruising beginning on the side of my face, knew my clothes were bedraggled from the journey, and was weary to the bone, but I knew who I was and that how I would present myself meant everything at this moment. "And I negotiate for our lives with the authority of my mother," I finished, looking into his ghastly green eyes without flinching.

The king looked back and forth from one to the other of us. His face went through several expressions before settling back into the mask of control he'd had when we'd entered.

"Tell me," he said, his voice again a purr, "even if I believed you are what you say you are, what precisely would you bargain with that I do not already have?"

"An alliance with Yorch, of course," I said, making it sound so obvious that I was surprised I needed to say it. "We came here to discuss terms with the Western Kingdom. Her Imperial Majesty has no interest in precisely *who* the Western Kingdom is. Treat with me and allow me and my companions to return to Yorch and not only will you have prevented our agreement with the Western Kingdom as it is but you will have achieved an alliance that will prove very profitable for all of us." My mind was racing; I was inventing each point as I said it to convince him. I felt a cold sweat breaking out on my skin, and my chest felt tight, but I maintained my posture and my tone.

The king had remained still in front of me as I spoke, close enough that once again, I could smell the leather and steel. He stared into my eyes without blinking, as if he were reading my thoughts directly.

"Why would I believe that a daughter of the blood would come here?" he asked with a slow shake of his head. "Your story stretches credence far too much."

"Here," came a quiet voice. I turned. Dana stood, her arms still held firmly by two guards but with a proud gleam in her eye as she glared at the king. He looked over contemptuously but furrowed his brow in interest.

"Look here," she said, nodding her head down and looking toward her chest. The king walked over and tugged at the collar of her shirt to reveal a silver necklace. As he tugged it out with his finger, a small charm – a circle of silver around an upward pointing arrow, etched in intricate knot-work – slid out along the chain and flickered in the reflected light. The king looked at it in surprise, glared at Dana, then spun back to me.

"A Silver Spar!" he said, his voice rising with excitement. "If this," he flicked his hand toward Dana, releasing the charm, "is a Hero of the Empire, then what you say must be true. You *are* of the blood." He began to laugh, a maniacal sound that echoed through the chamber.

I looked over to Dana, who returned my gaze steadily. *I'm with you;* the gaze told me though she made no sound, and her jaw was visibly tight.

The king turned back to her, roughly seized the necklace and pulled it free from her throat. He stalked back to the throne, still laughing and looking at his prize. On reaching the seat, he carefully wound the chain around itself into a knot to restore the loop. Then he placed the necklace over the corner of the throne's back, leaving it to dangle in the light, and stood looking at it as one might a priceless painting, ignoring all of us for a long moment.

I swallowed. "Then you will negotiate," I said.

"Indeed," he said, "I have so many prizes to negotiate with! A princess of the blood. An Imperial Silver Spar. And a box of what I can only assume are Kelian emeralds." His eyes narrowed at me at this last pronouncement, and I felt my blood froze.

"Oh yes, dear lady," he said, reaching down behind the throne and retrieving the box Ronald had given me. The broken latch hung limply from the lid as he opened it for all to see. The raw green crystals glittered unnaturally in the torchlight. "I know why the Empire is here. I am insulted that you would think I didn't."

"You don't...," I began.

"Silence her!" he nearly screamed. Two of the guardsmen reached out and grabbed me in the same manner as the others. "I will unleash the power of these stones, and then I won't *need* your mighty Empire! I certainly won't need you. The world will bow before me and me alone!"

Everything went silent. My blood, which had gone so cold before, seemed to have drained from my body. I looked at the floor. The whole plan seemed to be falling apart, and I was rapidly starting to think that there was nothing left that I could do about it. Just then, though, I heard a quiet laugh. I looked over to see Kelly standing unsteadily between the two guards who had lifted him from the ground. His voice was weak, but he was unmistakably chuckling.

The king wheeled on him. "Are you laughing at us, fool?"

Kelly let his chuckle run out before he answered. "No, of course not," he said, then let another laugh out.

The king came off the platform in a flash, his cape snapping behind him as he rushed over and grabbed Kelly by the hair, pulling his head back. "How dare you!" he snarled.

Kelly looked at him directly despite being held. "Sorry. Again, very sorry," he said, some of his usual snark still there behind the weakness in his voice. "But are you sure those aren't just, you know, *emerald* emeralds? I mean, Kelian emeralds are the sort of things from children's stories. You know, myths. Like unicorns."

The king released his hair and stepped back.

Kelly stood with a little more weight on his legs now

and continued, "I only think it's a risky thing to be betting on, especially if you can negotiate with the Empire over something more concrete. Like, say, a princess of the blood."

The king looked over at me, considering.

Kelly kept going, his tone becoming very conspiratorial. "Maybe you keep her and her keepers alive until you're sure, right? Or you don't, find out you've got a box of run-of-the-mill emeralds, and the Empress ultimately feeds you casually to her dogs on a Sunday afternoon for killing one of her daughters."

The king's arm moved so fast I didn't even see it swing. It cuffed Kelly alongside his head and sent him collapsing into the two guards that held him.

"You forget your place, fool," the king said, looking at his limp form. He turned and walked back to the throne, where he sat down regally and made a gesture with his hands to his men. The guards dragged us all to the middle of the dais before him.

"Take these to the jailer's for punishment," he said to the guards, sweeping his hand to indicate all of us. Then he paused, thought briefly, and pointed at me. "Except that one," he said slowly, "we'll save her for later. But the one in black," and here he pointed at Kelly, "tell them that he goes first. While they are still fresh. Afterward, have them put in the lowest dungeon until we decide our next steps." He turned and looked at the open box of green gems sitting next to the throne in silence.

From there, we were dragged out, and I was separated from the rest of my companions. Half pushed, half dragged, I was taken down one stairwell after another until somewhere deep in the vaults of the jagged mountain that was the castle, we reached the dim, wet, and claustrophobic dungeons. They unlocked and opened the angled door and threw me into the cell. With a loud sound of metal scratching against metal, the heavy lock slid back into place before they turned and left the way we had come. I made a quick survey of my surroundings, revealing the cell as I described previously. There was, quite simply, no way out. I settled down in the pale glow of the torchlight by the hallway and waited. With, of course, the ever-present drip, drip, drip.

The distant sound of a door opening and closing shook me out of my thoughts, and I turned to look through the iron grate and down the hallway. Shortly, the figures of two of the castle guard appeared, dragging something wrapped in a heavy cloth bag behind them. On reaching the cell door, they dropped the bundle on the hallway floor and unlocked the gate. They peered into the cell until one of them, a short, stocky man with a braided beard sticking out from below the face-guard of his helmet, saw me and drew his sword.

“Get back, you,” he snarled, poking his sword toward

me through the bars. I eased myself toward the back of the cell and into the corner, which was the furthest away I could be from them. The other guard, once I had done so, opened the door and shoved the bag through it. The bundle made the short drop onto the cell floor, and from it came a grunt as it landed heavily. My breath caught; I knew what was in the bag, though part of me would have been happy to be wrong. The guards, after first testing the cell door to verify it was again locked, turned and went back the way they had come, leaving me alone with the bundle that I was both dreading and desperate to open. Cautiously, I approached it. It wasn't indeed a bag; more of a large burlap cloth knotted together strategically so that it would stay closed. There were stains on it, ranging from dark red to brown; it was impossible to say whether they were old or new, or whether they indicated things they had dragged the bundle through or something that was oozing from the inside. I tugged at the knots at one end, finding that they came undone rather easily. I pulled the cloth aside to reveal the battered form of Kelly.

My voice caught in my throat as I looked at him lying unmoving on the ground. The left side of his face, the only part visible in the half-light, was a deep purple from his hairline all the way down to his jaw, and there was a trail of dried blood tracing from his ear down to his neck. He lay still as death, and the darkness of the cell closed in around me so tightly that I couldn't breathe.

An eternity passed, and then I heard it. Almost too quiet to rise above the sound of the water in the distance, a low gurgling rasp of breath came from him, and his eye twitched. I reached out and gently touched his cheek, and he flinched, then slowly looked up at me.

"Princess," he croaked, his voice no more than the shaping of a sigh into sound.

"I'm here," I said. Kelly started to move, trying with great effort to push himself up on his elbow but only accomplishing a feeble roll onto his back. I moved closer and gently helped him until he was leaning against the half-wall under the iron grating. The right side of his face was less bruised, but another smear of dried blood ran from a large cut on his lip onto his chin. The burlap still half covered him, but it had moved aside enough to show the torn remains of his black tunic. He sagged with exhaustion for a moment once he was in position against the stone wall, but then straightened with great effort and looked up at me.

"What did they do to you?" I breathed, more as an exclamation than as a question.

The unbruised right side of his mouth curled into a weak grin. "Lots. But nothing permanent, I don't expect," he said, "though those guys very much seem to enjoy their jobs." The attempt at a cavalier attitude was for me, I knew; to reassure me. He turned his head as if to look at me more clearly. "What about you? Are you okay?" he asked.

I nodded. “I’m fine. They took me straight here,” I said.

Kelly sagged back a little as if relieved. “We bought time,” he said, “I wasn’t sure he would listen to what I said after our little tussle.”

“I missed some of that,” I said, touching the bruised side of my face, “what exactly happened?”

“He shouldn’t have hit you,” he said, looking down, “I wanted that to be clear. So I hit him back.”

I looked at him a moment, caught between emotions. “That was stupid,” I said suddenly and without thinking.

He coughed and winced. “Maybe true,” he said, “but then be sure you tell your girlfriend that when she gets here. The only reason it was me and not her is that I was just a little faster than my guards, and she wasn’t. Honestly, is it so bad that we wanted to protect you?”

I thought about it for a long moment. “I’m sorry,” I said then, “I didn’t mean ‘stupid’. I’m just saying things these days. You were trying to defend me; that was really quite noble, I suppose.” I went quiet for a moment, actually making an effort to consider my words. “You have been nothing but honorable and reliable since this journey began. I haven’t been..., very kind..., to you. My words are coming out before my thoughts, I think. I apologize for all of that,” I said.

A wistful look crossed his face. “You have had your

reasons, my lady," he said then, "I can't fault you for it." With effort, he leaned forward and pulled the remnants of his shirt aside to reveal his right shoulder blade. There I could see the black tattoo about four inches across. It was a raven, its claws down and its wings behind it as if it were taking off or alighting. Across the bird's image was a white scar shaped like a bolt of lightning – seared into his flesh as if by a branding iron, if somehow oddly smooth. After a moment, he pulled the shirt back into place and leaned back against the wall wearily. He looked back up at me. "I've surely given you cause," he finished. He let his head drop back and closed his eyes.

I watched him for several moments before I realized he was asleep. I moved over and sat next to him, gently pulling him against me so that he was more securely – and, I hoped, comfortably – supported. I pulled my feet back up and waited. And once again, my mind fell again back into memory.

"How dare you! How dare you seek to keep secrets from me! I require the secrets of those stones! I am commanding you to tell me what you know!" The words echoed off the marble walls in the enormous throne room of Yorch. My mother stood on the audience platform; her face radiant with unveiled fury.

"I see that, Your Majesty," said Kelly, kneeling on one

knee in the center of the platform and meeting her gaze steadily. He wore his formal attire – a brilliant white shirt under an embroidered, double-breasted black and silver waistcoat, high boots, and a simple black cape over his left shoulder. His sword hung from a black baldric on his left hip. His gloved hands were folded on his right knee as he knelt on his left. He was utterly still as they spoke.

"And you are defying us? Here before our throne? The one you claimed to serve? You would turn your back on our Empire?" Her voice was raised in both volume and pitch. She was not quite shouting, but for her, it was the equivalent of a blood-curdling scream. I was watching from off to one side of the platform where I stood, both literally as well as figuratively between them.

"I am not," Kelly said, his voice steady and quiet. The difference between her rage and his placidity was so shocking that I saw my mother flinch as if physically struck. She glared at him, and I could see her wrestling the anger inside her down as she forcefully shifted to another approach.

"I have heard the sages say," she said, strolling across the platform now, once again in control of her feelings, "that there is an old proverb that tells us, 'it is the curse of men that they forget.' Have you heard this?"

"I have," Kelly said, "I can't speak as to sages, but my father used to say that often."

"Indeed," Her Majesty said, "he must have been wise as well. If what they say is true; if it is a curse to forget; then it seems that the kindest course one can take is to help another to remember. After all, if we forget important things, how can we possibly make decisions properly? Or even continue living?" She stopped a few steps from where he knelt.

Kelly observed her cautiously, waiting for her to continue. When she didn't, he replied, "I see the wisdom in that, ma'am."

My mother nodded. I sighed inwardly; as I had seen her do the same thing before. It was her way to seize control of a discussion. Once she had the reins of the conversation, so to speak, she allowed no other reasoning besides the one that she was presenting. Most of the time, it meant that the actual discussion was already over.

"So, let us then recall some things that we can hold as truth." She began strolling again, coming toward me as she spoke this time. "You are a fortunate young man, are you not?" she asked.

"I have believed so, yes," Kelly said.

"Indeed," she continued, "I believe we can say that unreservedly. You were trained by several Imperial masters privately, availed yourself of a broad education, and served in the Imperial army before even meeting the mandated minimum age."

Kelly nodded, still watching her.

"Despite not being of noble birth, you rose in the ranks and were a decorated captain," she stopped a few feet from me and turned to him. He remained motionless as she continued. "You found a home in our court; again, you – a common-born man. You have eaten at my table. And we were on the cusp of awarding you the Silver Spar – the first to receive such in a generation. But instead, we went further. We made you the Imperial Raven. Because of our trust."

At that, Kelly bowed his head to her and said, "Yes, your highness." He took all of this silently, his eyes only darting at the mention of the Silver Spar.

"As our Raven," she continued, "you have served the interests of the Empire again and again in circumstances – unique circumstances – that we could not address through other channels. You became, in short, even more trusted."

Kelly looked back up at her and took a breath to reply, but she continued before he could.

My mother took a step toward him, preparing the *coup de grace*. She lowered her voice to one that was almost tender and said, "And you are very close to the most precious prize I have, which, were things to progress as I envisioned, could have truly apportioned you among the high born." Making sure he was looking at her eyes, she slowly turned and looked at me. Kelly followed her gaze, meeting my eyes. There was something in his look. Longing? Sorrow? An apology? I wasn't sure.

"And now you are telling me," the Empress continued, turning back to him, with a snarl in her voice that held all of her anger and disappointment, "that you are going to throw all of that away and betray the Empire?"

Kelly looked at me a second longer, then turned to her. "No, ma'am. I'm not betraying the Empire. I'm saving it. I'm sorry you don't see it that way."

She stood as still as a statue, her eyes boring into him. To his credit or his curse, he didn't flinch and met her gaze stoically.

She took a small pouch from the fold of her dress, opened it, and dumped the contents into her hand. The little pile of greenish dust would perhaps have fit comfortably in the palm of a small child. She glared at Kelly over it, then turned to one of the small torches that lined the throne's platform. With a flourish, she threw the powder into the fire. There was a crackle, the torchlight became green for a moment and rose a foot or so higher than before, then it quickly returned to normal.

"Nothing," she said in a barely restrained fury, "though I *know* of what they are capable. Things I have heard from eyewitnesses. What I have seen with my own eyes!" She brushed her hands together as she stepped back toward him. "I will know how to unleash the power of these gems," she said, "and where to get more. It is our birthright!

The power they yield could defend our borders forever!"

"Or it could destroy Yorch and everyone else," Kelly said, allowing his own voice to rise for the first time. "Your Highness, I don't doubt that you would use the power of the emeralds for the security of Yorch. But can you say that all of your ministers will? All of our generals? I can't. And all it takes is one. One leak and our world could tear itself apart. I am sworn to protect the people of the Empire, not just the one on the throne." He shook his head. "I won't have that on my conscience. Or yours," he said.

"I will have you executed for treason!" she hissed. Turning, she started up the stairs to the throne. I felt my stomach sink. I took a step to follow her when I heard Kelly's voice, once again peculiarly calm.

"No, ma'am. You won't," he said.

She wheeled to look at him. He remained on his knee, hands still folded, but he was looking at her with a glint in his eye.

"Won't I?" she said with a snarl.

"No," he said, "you won't. The law does not provide for the execution of an Imperial agent by the throne alone. You need a parliament of the nobles. And I know you don't want all of them to know about these gems." Kelly stood up, finally forgoing the formality he had been maintaining. He squared his shoulders and looked at the empress ruefully. "Besides, all you accomplish by doing that is proving how right I was to keep the secret," he said.

I have seen my mother's rage only rarely in my life. Her whole existence is the delicate dance of behaving as she must to accomplish her goals rather than letting rage – or any emotion, really – show. But there, in the silence of the throne room, I saw such a look of anger and hatred cross her face that I was truly frightened just to be near it. She turned away too slowly as if struggling to maintain even the control required to do that much. She ascended the seven steps to the throne platform, turned and sat on the gold and ivory Throne of Yorch.

"Very well," her voice came out cold and without feeling. A moment later, a phalanx of the Imperial Palace Guard appeared, appearing from hidden entrances on the sides of the audience platform. They marched forward and stood around Kelly, who hadn't moved. Last into the room, darting past me after the guardsmen had gone by, came the Imperial scribe, Larissa. She walked up onto the throne platform and stood next to where my mother sat. Once there, she braced a small wooden slate with paper on it on her arm and picked up a quill in her other hand. As the empress spoke, she began to write.

"Be it today known that we, Empress Ardalla Niconnal bar Morissia, Gloriana, Sola, Lunis, and Stelis, declare this day that the position of Imperial Raven is by me terminated. No longer will that title and role be filled in any manner by any man, woman, or creature," she said. So that was it; she couldn't kill him, but she could take his position away. I felt my heart skip as I looked at Kelly. He was watching the throne, and whatever he was feeling, he gave no indication. "Be it also known," she continued, "that for the good of the people of our beloved Empire, for the protection of our courts, our military, and our very lives, the former Raven is now declared Blackcrow. He is a traitor to all that we value. All of his lands and property are forfeit, and his name and ancestry are to be stricken from the record, never to be uttered. He is to vacate all Imperial lands and all of the lands of our allies before the rising of the full moon. Thus it is decreed."

My throat constricted, and I could barely breathe, yet everything became sharper and more precise; as if it were happening slower than it was. I saw Larissa busily committing the edict into a written pronouncement. One that she would give to the empress to sign before it was duplicated and distributed throughout the known lands. Everywhere it would be known. His life as he had known it would be over. Before the throne, the guards nearest Kelly on either side each took one of his arms. He made no move to resist but continued to stare at my mother.

She leaned forward and looked directly into his eyes. "You tilt with us, Blackcrow, so we will take everything you ever had," she said quietly, then turned to the captain of the guards. “The traitor’s brand,” she said, “then remove him from the citadel. If he is found on Imperial lands after the night of the full moon, the one who executes him will receive a generous bounty.” She stood and walked around to Larissa, pausing to look in my direction for the span of a single breath before moving on to disappear behind the throne. For me, the room washed away as tears filled my eyes.

I awoke with a gasp. The ‘hawks’ wasted no time, and my current situation immediately came back to me. I turned to check on Kelly only to find him leaning against the side wall of the cell several feet away. He had the burlap cloth wrapped over his shoulders and turned to look at me.

“Sit down. What is the matter with you?” I said as I got to my feet and went to him. I reached to grab his arm to help, but he waved it away.

“It’s okay,” he said. His voice was stronger, but the unsteadiness in his tone was noticeable; at least to me. “I’m okay,” he said.

“You are not okay,” I said, brushing his hand away and sliding under his arm to put my arm around him for support. With some effort, I eased him down until he was again sitting on the ground, this time against the side wall. “Would you do the sensible thing and rest for a minute?” I said, “you don’t know what’s going to happen next; we need to take whatever chance to rest we get.”

He sighed, but ultimately relented and, leaning back on the wall, stretched his legs out in front of him. His arm was still over my shoulders, I realized, and I looked up at him to find that he was looking back at me. A charged moment passed, then he lifted his arm, and I slid out from beneath it. I stayed where I was though and leaned back on the wall next to him. We sat in silence for a long time.

"Before..., you know, back then...," he said quietly and a little wistfully, "I have to know. Back then, did you at all understand?" He sat with his eyes closed and his head leaning back on the wall as he spoke. I knew instantly what he meant but asked anyway.

"When you left? The fight with my mother over the emeralds?" I asked.

He nodded.

I thought back to that day, so fresh in my mind from the dream. My mother had assigned him to look into a small rebel tribe, and he had returned, followed by a rumor among the people of the return of the powers of old. No one believed it, of course. The court questioned my mother, and she questioned him. He denied it categorically. And then, just months later, a band of pirate ships off the coast was chased away in the night by, so the stories that flooded the city said, an unholy green flame that would not quench. Her Highness called him in for an audience, and he admitted the truth. But the method was a secret, he said; a secret that must never be known. He said it could mean the end of the world as we knew it. The empress was, as it is said, not pleased. Her fury was catastrophic. But he had never asked me what I thought. Until now. Until we were locked in a dungeon and had time alone. A rush of feelings came back over me, but my answer was one I had known for a long time.

"I do," I said, "I didn't. Not really. But I have had time to think about it. And yet, I also understand what my mother was thinking."

"Of course," he sighed.

"Oh, stop it," I said. "Just because I understand doesn't mean I agree any longer."

He said nothing. I took it as a good sign.

"You have to realize, every minute of every day; every decision; every word she ever uttered; every bit of clothing she wore; every, every, everything Ardallah does, she does for the good of the Empire. She worries and plans and plots day and night about what to do to protect it. Even more than herself. More than her children. More than anything." I felt an unbidden lump in my throat, and my voice wasn't as steady as I'd intended, but I continued. "You showed up with what she saw as a way to give the Empire a power that could secure its borders – take her persistent fear of the very worst that can happen away, at least a little – and she was only ever going to see that. You must understand."

He closed his eyes again slowly, then after a pause,

nodded. We sat in silence for several moments.

"But," I said after I was sure the point had been driven home, "I don't think that she was right. I think her personal worries and sacrifices make it impossible for her to see the emeralds for what they are. And they are what you said; a threat to everything and everyone if they are misused. What you did was right, Kelly. I believe that."

He sighed then, and it reminded me of the sigh of a laborer setting aside a great weight that he carried for a long time. I could feel him sag ever so slightly more against the wall. We sat that way for another long moment before I spoke again. Because I realized I had more to say. Words that I needed to have heard.

"But I did hate you. And I felt betrayed just the same," I said, the words tumbling out of my mouth without thought. Again. His head turned as he looked toward me, a look of confusion settling on his face.

"Wait," he said, "you just said that you understood."

I nodded and said, "I did. I do. I understand why you kept the secret of the emeralds."

"Then...," he asked, "what?"

I looked intensely at my lap, my fingers tightly knitted together as I spoke, my voice barely audible even to myself, "You left," I said, "and you didn't ever say goodbye."

"I didn't...?," he said absently.

"Five years ago," I said, looking up at him now, tears

freely streaming down my face, "you were sent into exile by the full moon – a full five days later – and you never came to see me. Five days! We were...," my voice caught.

"We were," he said, grabbing my hands. "We were. But I didn't know what you felt, and worse, I didn't know if I could do it. If I could have seen you and been with you and still leave you and not want just to jump off a cliff somewhere. Jules, I can face a thousand to one odds in a fight. Find me a real-life dragon, and I'll face it with two sticks and a rock. But ask me to see you and say goodbye forever?" He paused but never stopped looking at me. "I just couldn't. I never could."

We sat that way for some time, his hand on my hands, neither of us knowing what to say next. Finally, I looked back up at him. "I would have come with you," I said.

A slow, warm smile crept onto his face. "And I wouldn't have stopped you," he said tenderly, "and the armies of the Empire would have hunted us for the rest of our days."

I sighed, the truth taking all of the tension that remained out of me. I leaned back and put my head on his shoulder. He knitted his fingers in mine, and I closed my eyes and time stopped, for a little while.

I don't know how much later it was when I woke again, but when I opened my eyes, I was greeted by the sight of Dana sitting not far from us against the half wall. Even in the dimness, I could see that she bore more bruises than before, and there was exhaustion painted on her face, but she seemed to have fared better than Kelly had. The monster on the throne had been truthful; his torturers had done their most thorough work on him. Seeing I was awake, she turned and looked at me, an unreadable look on her face.

I smiled at her and gently, so as not to wake him, slid away from beside Kelly. I eased his hand onto his lap before I quietly slipped over to Dana's side.

"So is there anything at all you would like to talk about?" Dana said, weakly but wryly. Considering our situation, it was not the time for such a conversation, but then again, what else did we have to do?

I shrugged. "We talked," I said, "it was... it was good."

She nodded, looking back over at him.

"So. You had a thing for the Blackcrow," she said.

I felt my cheeks warm slightly. "He wasn't the Blackcrow when we... when we were close." I looked at her solemnly. "I don't know if I can explain it," I said.

And then, as if to prove myself wrong, I told her the whole story. My mother's quest for the emeralds, his defiance of her, his exile; I told her everything I could. She sat quietly and listened, which was one of the things I most appreciated about her, stopping me only to clarify details or to see how what I was telling her now related to what she believed was happening back then.

"And I'm sorry, Dana," I said at the end. "Sorry that I kept you away from all of this back then. From that part of my life. But I had to."

She patted my arm gently. "Jules," she said, "you're the princess of the realm. You are always going to have things you can't talk about with me. I am okay with that; it's part of being your friend."

"That's the same choice that Her Imperial Majesty makes all the time," I said, "I'm not sure I can live that way."

Dana looked at me steadily and said, "Your balance may well be different from hers. That remains to be seen. But he was the Imperial Raven, and you couldn't have spoken about that no matter what was going on personally. I wasn't even part of the court five years ago; how would that have worked? You did the right thing."

I put my other hand on hers. "Thank you," I said. I looked back over at Kelly's sleeping form and then leaned my head back against the stone.

"So, you had a thing for the Blackcrow," Dana said, a twinkle in her eye as she looked at me sidelong.

I felt the laughter build inside me before it broke from my lips. It felt good.

It wasn't long afterward that both Rohb and Aeryk were delivered to the cell as unceremoniously as the rest of us. They both arrived walking, however, and though their bodies bore the marks of the torture they had received, it was significantly less than either of my protectors. The former captain of the guard of Castle Sterling, in fact, spun the minute he hit the cell floor and tried to shove the door back open, only to meet the crash of the iron gate and the stub ends of one of the guard's spears. The crack against his head was audible and slowed him enough to give them time to secure the lock. Laughing at their enraged prisoner, the two guards left the five of us alone.

Rohb paced along the length of the cell, occasionally grabbing the iron bars and testing them. Huge muscles tensed beneath his dark skin, but the iron and stone of the grating remained unaffected. He continued to pace.

"Would you please stop that?" Aeryk said finally, "you're not getting anywhere, and you're driving me crazy." He settled on the ground a few feet from us. He seemed, except for myself, to have received the least attention from the jailers. He looked from Dana to me and asked, "Is everyone okay? Dana? Princess Julea?"

Dana looked at him a long moment before answering. Something in her expression was unreadable, but she shook it off and replied. "To varying degrees," she said, "Kelly took the worst of it." She looked over to where he was lying. Aeryk followed her gaze, and a look of concern passed across his face. "But we're all whole, from what I can tell," she finished.

"Serves his stupid ass right for charging the king," Rohb muttered, still pacing, but more casually and less like a caged animal.

Dana swept up from the floor in one fluid motion and stepped into the big warrior's path. He stopped short and looked at her. She peered directly into his eyes.

"Your mouth appears to be speaking words," she said calmly, "That might be something you want to look to." There was a moment of tension, then Rohb turned away and walked to the far end of the cell. Dana returned to sit back down beside me.

Aeryk, whose eyes had grown three sizes during the confrontation, turned back to me and said, "He seems fixated on those gems we got from Ronald. I think we're safe until he decides whether they're these 'Kelian' things or not. Do you have any idea?"

"That doesn't matter much," came a quiet voice from the corner. We all turned to see Kelly, now awake and watching us. "What matters," he continued, "is that we get those gems away from him at all costs."

CHAPTER SEVEN
— DENIS —

Dungeons, in my opinion, have a much worse reputation than they deserve. I like to think that I've become somewhat of a connoisseur of the various dungeons of the western lands, and I have to say that for the most part, there is something to be said of their superiority over sleeping on the streets. Or worse, in the wilds. Most of them I've experienced have been more or less humane; they serve as protection from the weather, often provide a small meal, and are a mostly dry place to sleep. All of which is not too shabby, if you look past the whole "loss of freedom" thing, which I've never really taken very seriously anyway. All of that said, the dungeon of this particular castle – Chateau Flint, they appeared to be calling it now – was only barely meeting my standards, and I actively thought that it was about time to move on when my new neighbors moved in.

I was lying in the back corner of my cell when I first heard the commotion; two guards mumbling to one another in low enough tones that I couldn't quite make out anything they said other than what sounded like the word 'princess.'

Keeping to the shadows, I moved a little closer to the bars to see what was going on in time to see them open the cell opposite mine and toss a blonde woman inside. They locked the door afterward and left without any further fuss. I say her cell was 'opposite' mine, but it was actually opposite and catty-corner, so only the furthest extent of my cell was properly across from the furthest extent of hers, and I wanted to stay out of sight, so I remained at the other end. I could make out her face in the torchlight for a short time while she stood by the gate looking back and forth along the bars and then surveyed the rest of the room behind her. *Pretty*, I thought. *Bit of the look of the high-born about her, too.* Before too long, she disappeared into the darkness and out of sight.

And that was the extent of anything that made her of interest to me. I couldn't see her anymore, and therefore she wasn't my problem. I went back to my corner and dozed for a while.

It was some while later when I heard the noises of the guards again, this time punctuated by the telltale grunts of them carrying/dragging something substantial. I went back to the bars and watched for the second time as they opened the door and shoved a big burlap sack into her cell. I heard a grunt as the bag hit the ground and winced a little. I waited as the guards left to see if there would be more to see with two of them now. It was, after all, the only entertainment I'd had the whole time I'd been "enjoying" the castle's hospitality.

There was a brief exchange from the woman with whomever they had tossed in with her, and I could only make out some of it. It sounded like it was a man, and one in a bit of a bad way at that. If I heard right, the king had him beaten because he —

— Did he hit the king? I could swear that's what they said. I didn't know him – yet – but I was starting to think I might like him.

They went quiet then, and I realized that he must have passed out or something. I decided that it might be worth my time to stay closer and see what happened next, so I went to the end of my cell closest to theirs and sat down in the corner and out of sight. It was again some time later when I heard a rustling and took a look around the corner. The man I had heard talking was at the far end of their cell, leaning against the wall and looking like he was only standing through sheer force of will. There was a significant blue bruise coloring the left side of his face, and he seemed to be breathing very intentionally; like someone doing their best to make it so that something that hurt, didn't. But what caught my attention most was the intensity of his expression; as if he were memorizing every stone in the cell and hallway. All this went on for a bit before he abruptly turned and looked directly at me. I ducked back down and out of sight. And that, oddly enough, was the first time Kelly and I ever laid eyes on one another. Someday, I'll have to tell a bard so that it can be appropriately noted for historical purposes.

It was just a moment later when the woman – the princess, apparently – said something that distracted him. They spoke some more, and this time I listened carefully while they talked about the Empire – that, of course, explained their fanciful, sing-songy, accents – and the fact that he had left there for some reason having to do with a fight with the Empress. I was keeping track, that was the second member of royalty I heard about him alienating in just two short discussions. I was really starting to like him. They got quieter, and what I could still catch sounded more personal than before, so I stopped listening and waited some more. Waiting is, you should know, one of my best skills.

Over the next I-couldn't-say-how-long, three more people were separately ushered in by the guards and dumped in their cell, with me sneaking a look each time. The first one they brought was a tall, muscular, brunette woman. She then had a quiet chat with the blonde princess and revealed that the man was something called a 'Blackcrow'. It didn't mean much to me, but it sounded like an excellent nickname. Later the guards brought a tall, brown-haired man, and a dark-skinned giant of a guy who unmistakably had some problems with self-restraint. He got himself cracked in the head by the guards when he tried to climb back out of the cell door after being thrown in, making him truly the most fun of them all. The minute the guards left, he started prowling back and forth and yanking on all of the iron bars like a caged troll. Nothing happened, of course, but he sure gave it his best.

More importantly, the whole group of them started talking more, and I listened to as much as I could. I learned a few things pretty quickly. The man, I now knew, was Kelly. The blonde actually was a princess, and her name was Julea. And in moments, I learned two things about the Amazonian brunette. First, she was called Dana. Second, when she stood up and made the enormous troll guy back off, I learned I might be in love.

Not long after that, their cell went quiet for a long time. It wasn't a surprise, as I figured that they were all probably exhausted and starved. So, I let some time pass – my world-class 'waiting' skills again – then I decided I would try to get a good look into their cell. I stood, only to find that standing precisely opposite me in the other cell and looking in my direction was Kelly.

"Hey," I said, aiming to be the very image of casual.

"Hey," he replied just as casually, "I thought I'd meet the neighbors." He was keeping his voice low, and I figured that the rest of his roommates were asleep. I couldn't help but notice that he had lost the hint of the accent I had heard before. I wondered if it was something that the blonde woman brought out in him.

"Actually, I like to think of myself more as a lodger than a resident," I said with a shrug, "But, sure. I'm Denis."

He nodded, and I saw that though there was still some stiffness in his movements, he wasn't using the wall for support anymore. *Must be a quick healer,* I thought. He started to speak. "I'm called —"

"Kelly," I said, cutting him off, "I heard."

I saw a couple of expressions cross his face pretty quickly, but he settled on a lopsided grin and a nod. "So you're not a 'resident', huh? How long have you been 'lodging' here?" he asked.

"Oh, I've enjoyed the red-carpet treatment here for a while. The walking spore on the throne insisted that I stay," I spat. He raised his eyebrows.

"'Walking spore,'" he said, considering the phrase, "Okay sure, that checks. Anyhow, what did you do to receive such a reward?"

I cocked my head. "Maybe we don't need to talk about that right now," I said.

"Just trying to get to know the neighbors, remember?" he said.

"Yeah," I said, "but we don't want to rush things, do we? A relationship has to grow natural. We start talking about some things too fast, Blackcrow, and it can lead to all kinds of unpleasantness."

He stared hard at me, and I could see that he got my

point. “Check,” he said finally, “another time for that, then.”

I smiled. “Anyway, I’ve been thinking that it might be time to go, though. You know, greener pastures and all,” I said.

“And you’ve just decided this? You’ve decided that you’re ready to leave the dungeon?” he asked with just a hint of a mocking tone.

“It’s time,” I said, manufacturing a sigh, “to bid all this luxury good-bye. But I do have two problems. The first is physically getting out of the castle. I have a plan, and while I don’t technically need it, it seems like it might be easier if you and your humongous friend there would help out.”

“My…?” he started, then glanced behind him, “Oh, Rohb. You mean Rohb.”

“Uh-huh,” I said, “He’s perfect, but he seems to need a leash or something to keep him on task. So I figure I need at least two of you.”

“I’m going to want to hear the plan first, you know,” he said.

“Rein in your horses,” I said, “I said I had two problems; that was only the first. The second is that I’m going to need to get out of these lands. The tosser upstairs is not going to let me go happily.”

“You are really going to need to tell me what you did,” Kelly said.

“Due course, due course,” I said, “Stick to the

moment. Can you come up with a way to get us out of the north?"

I watched him as he thought about it for a minute, then a slow smile crossed his face. He looked back across at me like he was about to get away with something. "I believe we can arrange that," he said.

I had no idea what he was thinking, but he sure seemed to be happy with it, so I let it go. "Okay," I said, "then this is my plan..."

He held up a finger. "Well, I have a couple of stipulations too." He paused to make sure I was listening. "The first is this," he continued, "I need to know the location of a shipyard. It's supposed to be somewhere north of here. Someplace private, probably only access for the navy, so it's not likely to be in a big town or anything. Do you know it?"

"Shipyard?" I asked, thinking. "Do you know how far?"

He shook his head.

"Well, it probably doesn't matter. I can only think of one place anything like that. It's about half a day's ride away. Did your ship get taken there or something?"

He shook his head and said, "No, but there is a ship there; I am pretty sure. The king mentioned that he had a ship built there."

I shook my head to clear it. "Wait. The king had a ship built? That swollen pustule spent money on a ship?"

"You sure you're not in prison for *lese-majeste*?" he asked.

"The what?" I asked.

"Never mind. Yes, the king had a ship built to pay off a sell-sword, but he decided he wants to keep it," he said, "I thought maybe we could use it more."

"Oh, okay," I said, "that makes more sense. Anyway, yes, I think I can get us there."

"Getting on board may take some effort. There would probably only be a skeleton crew aboard in dock, but we may have to, er, convince them, and that will probably take all of us. Are you savvy with that?" he asked.

"Not my favorite thing, but not a deal breaker. Sure."

"And," he said, stretching the word as if to avoid the rest of the sentence, "before we go, we have to retrieve some belongings the king took from us. Okay, just one belonging; a box of green gemstones."

I stared at him. He didn't look away. "You're joking," I said.

He shook his head.

"Anything important he's taken is probably in his private tower, you know," I said.

He nodded. "Sure. And I'm guessing you know how to get there," he said. Which was right, but that didn't make it less stupid.

"So you're suggesting that if I want to escape with

your help, on top of helping steal a royal ship, we need to sneak into the king's private room and steal a box of stones," I said.

He nodded again. "It's crucial, really," he said, "I wouldn't mention it otherwise."

"Seems like a stupid idea," I said.

"I see that," he said, "almost as stupid as helping a stranger I met in a dungeon to escape without knowing why he's imprisoned."

I scratched my head and thought about it. "These stones," I said after a moment, "you're sure the king wants them?"

Kelly nodded slowly, a grin on his face. "And losing them will stick in his craw no end," he said.

I shrugged. "Okay, deal," I said, "No one lives forever anyhow, right? You and your friends help me get out of here and out of the kingdom. I help you get your box of rocks and steal a ship."

"Seems fair," Kelly said, "so what's the plan?"

The distant sound of the guards' slow footfalls echoed its way down the hallway outside. I laid very still in the dim pool of light in the very middle of my cell and waited. Again, as I said, I wait exceptionally well. It didn't take long before I could hear the sure sounds of the guards approaching outside our cells, their steps pausing intermittently. I kept one eye open the tiniest slit, and through it, I could see one pause to look into my new friends' cell across the hall while his smaller companion stood and watched me in my cell for several moments. Then, both apparently satisfied that we were all still inside and asleep, they continued down the hall. After a moment, they were out of sight. I remained exactly where I was, unmoving though I could feel the excitement building inside me. Short bursts of energy that always came before the game began. I breathed through it, keeping myself still. After I don't know how long, I heard the guards coming back. I opened my eye again just a crack to watch and saw them as they reached the far end of my cell, walking back the way they had come. The tension in me grew, but I still didn't move. They were walking casually now, paying little attention to the contents of the cells that they had, in their mind, already checked thoroughly. A couple more steps, and finally they came up even with my cell door. With all the speed I could muster, I popped up from the floor. Taking a step toward the door, I jumped and grabbed onto the iron fixtures where the cell bars were seated into the ceiling stone. I swung back and kicked the door with everything I had. The door – the lock of which I had picked long ago – swung wide open and hit the nearest guard on his side, causing him to stumble into his companion. On my second swing, I threw myself out of the now open doorway and planted my feet on the hallway floor before I threw myself at them. Between my sudden added weight and the fact that they were already off-balance, they collapsed onto the iron bars of the cell across the hall. I rolled off the heap of their bodies and back to the other side of the hallway, stopping in a crouch facing them. Two furious guards were looking back at me at first, but their expressions turned suddenly to confusion and surprise when, as they tried to stand up, two massive, dark-skinned arms reached out between the bars and pinned them down. As they struggled, other hands reached through the bars, pulling their swords from their belts and grabbing at their arms and legs. I stood, kicked one of their short spears away, and grabbed the other. I spun it around in a tight arc, hitting the nearest guard squarely at the joint of neck and shoulder. There was a crunching sound, and he went limp. Reversing my grip, I pointed the sharp end at the throat of the other guard, still held in Rohb's sturdy grip. Kelly reached through the bars and grabbed the keys from the belt of the unconscious guard, then unlocked the cell door. One by one, he and his friends came out. He stood next to me, resting the tip of one of the captured swords at the throat of the still conscious guard. At this, Rohb released him and came out. We stripped both of the guards and put one in each of the cells we had occupied, locking the doors behind us. Quickly, we moved some distance down the hallway, finally stopping and ducking into a small storage room off to the side. Rohb and Dana took a position on either side of the doorway and watched for anyone who might be approaching, which was silly, really, since I knew full well there wouldn't be anyone coming for hours.

Kelly looked at me as we sorted the belongings we had confiscated from the two guards. "So, how long was that door of yours unlocked?" he asked.

"Few days," I said, "They rarely check it. If they do, they assume they made the mistake, since I'm still in the cell. They think it's funny I didn't escape. I think they're really stupid. It's just a game I play."

He stared at me for a long moment, then with a little shake of his head, he went back to the items we had collected. He handed one of the short spears to Rohb and took the one I had been holding and gave it to the brown-haired man that had been with them, who he called Aeryk. Then he passed one of the short swords to Dana – who I now thought of as my secret girlfriend – and kept the other. I looked at the spears and swords in turn, then gave him a look. His expression said something like, *there is no way you get a weapon*. I shrugged. Both of the guards had worn leather jerkins which weren't particularly heavy, but they were definitely better than bare skin and tattered cloth. He considered these. Neither would fit Rohb or me, for entirely opposite reasons of size, but he slid into one that fit pretty well. He tossed the other to Aeryk and turned to the remainder of the items, retrieving both of the guard's belts before finally looking at their boots.

"Wow," he said, "those are some small feet."

"No wonder they fell over so easy," I added.

There was a snicker from the blonde woman at that, and I decided, princess or not, she might be okay. He tossed the boots aside.

"Kelly, this is pointless," Aeryk said. We turned to find him with the leather vest, the one from the smaller of the two guards, barely over his shoulders and gaping open across his torso. "I think this makes it worse," he mumbled.

"Give it to me," Dana said and slid into it easily. Again, it wasn't perfect, but with the assistance of one of the two belts, it fit her suitably.

"Okay," Kelly said, "Next steps."

"What's the fastest way out?" Rohb said.

"Yeah," I said, moving over by the big man, "what is that?"

Kelly looked at me. "We have an errand to run, remember?"

Everyone in the room turned and looked at him.

"Yeah," I said with a sigh, "but I was hoping you didn't."

"What is he talking about?" said Rohb.

"And, come to that," said Aeryk, "why is he still with us? Who even *is* he?"

"We don't have a lot of time, so I'll be quick," Kelly

said. His voice was strained, in the way of someone trying very hard not to sound strained. "Formal introductions; Princess Julea, Lady Dana, Lord Aeryk, Lieutenant Rohb," he pointed at each as he went around the room, "and I'm Kelly. Everyone, this is Denis, the one I told you about when I explained the plan to get out of the cell."

"But –," Julea started, then stopped as Kelly continued.

"We – that is, the two of us – agreed to help one another. He shows us the way out of the castle and to a place we can get a ship, and in turn, we take him with us."

Rohb furrowed his brow at me, which is terrifying in a genuine way, and then looked at Kelly. "What's this errand you're talking about?"

"The gems," Kelly said, "We aren't leaving without the box of gems."

"That's crazy," Aeryk said, looking back and forth from one to the other of us.

"Don't look at me," I said with a shrug. I pointed at Kelly. "This is all your man's idea."

Julea stepped forward and took Kelly's arm from behind. "Are you sure about this?" she said.

He glanced back at her and then back to the group. "That box is the surety that seals the treaty with Yorch. Without it, even if we get free, the treaty won't be valid," he said. The other four looked back and forth to one another with somber expressions.

Obviously, none of them could tell that he was lying through his teeth, but that really didn't have anything to do with me, I figured.

"Okay," Dana said, turning to look at Kelly and me, "How do we get the box?" She and Rohb were still at the door of the small room and keeping an eye on the hallway outside. I smiled at her. She didn't smile back. So coy.

"Simple," I said, "We just have to make a short detour to the king's private chambers in the north tower."

There was a longish pause. Then Kelly jumped in. "And it isn't 'we', it's me," he said, then half shrugged and continued, "Well, it's Denis and me. The rest of you need to get out of the castle and wait for us to join you. If we don't make it, you need to get back to the south and warn them."

"Sorry," Julea said, "You are in no shape for this. You're not going traipsing into the most secure area of this fortress with some dungeon rat —"

"Hey!" I said.

"—when you can barely stand," she finished, pausing not at all at my objection.

Kelly turned to her and put his hands on her shoulders. "I understand what you're saying," he said calmly, "but you do know that I'm the right one for this. And I need him to show me the way."

"Do you just randomly trust people?" she said, a hint

of frustration in her voice.

“Mostly just forest bandits and dungeon rats,” he said with a little grin.

“Hey!” I said again.

“Okay,” Dana said, drawing everyone’s attention back, “If you two are going off to do stupid boy things, what do we do?”

No one spoke for a few minutes, and it dawned on me that they were waiting for me. “Oh, it’s my turn,” I said, “I was starting to think that this was a family discussion. Fine. Once we’re out of the dungeons, I’ll show you the direction you want to go. We’ll need to get to the kitchens. There are two or three supply doors in the lower levels of the kitchen stores that lead to a secondary courtyard. From there, it’s just a matter of getting on one of the supply carts and bluffing your way past the rear guard.”

“Bluffing?” Rohb said. There was enough tension in his voice that I thought of an overfilled wine bladder that was close to bursting.

“Yeah, bluff,” I said, “The other choice is to fight them. You might be okay with that, and you might even win, but you’ll bring the wrath of the entire palace guard down on you. Since you’re going to be my ride, I think that might be bad for both of us.”

“Bluff it is,” Aeryk said.

“Good choice,” I said, favoring him with a grin. “Then,

you just need to get far enough down the road that you're out of sight of the castle gates."

"Wait for us there," Kelly said, jumping back in, "We'll be along."

"What if you aren't?" Rohb said.

"Watch the castle," Kelly said, "If you see an alarm go up, just go. If you see guards coming out in your direction, go. Even if you feel like you've been there too long, go. Head south by whatever way you find."

Both Julea and Dana seemed unsettled at this, but neither voiced the objection that it was apparent to me they felt. Kelly's demeanor shifted, and he looked from Dana to Rohb. "The most important thing is that the princess and the marquess return home safely. That's your priority," he said. It seemed weird that he was suddenly talking to them like they worked for him or something, but even more weirdly, they took it; both of them nodded back to him curtly.

"Okay then," I said, "everybody ready?"

Silence fell on us then, and Kelly waved at me to take the lead. I rolled my eyes and, being entirely sure that no one was there, I casually walked back into the hallway. For the first several paces, I didn't hear them following me, but I decided that they would eventually figure it out and so I kept going. After a few more steps, there came the sounds of my newfound companions finally following me. We went down the hallway that lead to the stairs' entrance; the same stairs that had brought each of us down to our cells originally. I was still slightly ahead of the rest, and I began the long climb up the stairwell. The hallway we climbed through was bowed somewhat outward, and its walls were of the same rough-hewn stone as the cells we had left below. We went up; each flight of stairs stopping at a landing where there was a small torch set in a metal bracket, providing more than enough light to see. Before long, we began to ascend the final set of stairs. I took the first couple of steps up – the entrance doorway at the top visible in the dim light – before I stopped and waited for the rest of the group to catch up. I held up my hand, hoping that they would see it and get the idea. They did, stopping to wait while I listened. It only took a second to verify what I was afraid of, and I turned to where Kelly was standing to my left.

"I hear two," I whispered, pointing ahead, "Probably relief for our two friends back there."

He nodded grimly. I saw him turn and make several motions with his hand. Then he leaned close and said, "We'll take this. Stay here. Wait for my signal. Make a noise and then get low."

I nodded, then watched as he and Rohb crept up the remaining stairs until they were just a step or two below the door. I glanced behind me and saw that Aeryk, Dana, and Julea had backed down the way we had come, just far enough that the curve of the wall hid them. This left me alone, crouching low at about the halfway point. I looked back up and saw Kelly on the left side of the stairs and Rohb on the right. After making sure I was watching, Kelly raised his right hand and faced the door. A moment later, he dropped his hand.

"Oh, look! I'm escaping!" I called, very proud of my creativity. I dropped down onto my stomach on the stairs.

The door swung open almost immediately, light streaming in around the shadowed outline of a stocky soldier, one of the two people I had heard a moment before. He had come down two full steps before he registered the figure of Kelly on his right. He raised his sword to strike at him when, from behind the open door on his left, the shaft of Rohb's short spear came across into his lower shin. Momentum and a lack of balance took over, and he toppled and came crashing down the stairs, landing inches from where I was. At the same moment, Kelly sprang up the remaining stairs and into the room to get to the other guard before he raised the alarm. They were out of sight, but I heard a clashing of metal on metal as Rohb rushed up to join him. The guard on the stairs by me moved, his armor seemed to have taken much of the impact, and it looked like he was only stunned. I came up from my crouch, only to drop my knee down with all my weight on his helmet, smashing his head into the edge of the stairs where he lay. He collapsed and went limp as I quickly ran up the stairs and into the chamber.

The room was only about twelve feet square, with walls of stone built around timber supports. A small hearth filled the far corner with a healthy fire in it. After having been in the damp dungeon for so long, the warm, dry air was almost shocking to breathe, smelling as it did like burned weeds and tobacco. The walls were unadorned, and there was no furniture in the room save for a tall cabinet in one corner and a single table in the middle of the room. A scattering of papers that had once been on the table covered the floor. Kelly sat with one hip hitched on the table, one arm wrapped around his midsection. Rohb stood a couple of feet away, cradling his left arm. On the floor was the sprawled figure of the remaining guard.

"Great plan, guys," I said, looking at the two of them.

A moment later, the others came up, stepping around me while they surveyed the scene.

"Get...," Kelly started, but his voice came out breathless. He started again, "Get these two into one of the nearby cells," he croaked. Dana and Aeryk went into the stairwell to see to the first guard while I started to remove the equipment from the one on the floor.

"Are you okay?" Julea said, stepping around us and going to Kelly's side.

"Got the wind knocked out of me," he said weakly, "I'll be all right. Check Rohb."

The big man stood stoically, still cradling his left arm. She came over, and he reluctantly showed it to her. There was a deep dent in his left forearm that I am very sure wasn't there before.

"It's broken," he said, "That back-birth on the floor there caught me sideways with his sword. He'd have taken my head next if it weren't for him." He nodded toward Kelly.

"You need to be alive to try to kill me later," Kelly said, his breath more normal now. The princess looked back and forth between them, easily as confused as I was. The two men nodded to one another.

"So you're *both* idiots," Julea mumbled as she came over to me and took the belt from the unconscious guard. Expertly, she wrapped it around the deformed part of Rohb's arm and fastened it over his shoulder into a make-shift sling. Once again, I thought she might just be okay, princess or not.

Aeryk and Dana reappeared, dumping the armor and equipment of the other guard on the floor before dragging out the one whose stuff I had taken. Kelly was looking around the room for anything else useful when they returned. Dana locked the door and put the keys on the table. One of the leather jerkins did fit the marquess this time, but the boots were still a loss; too big for the women, nowhere near the right size for the rest of us.

I went to the door that would lead out and turned to them. "Okay, here's where it will get tricky. I don't know what time of day it is. If it's midday, we could be in trouble – there will be a lot of people around. Hopefully, it's early or late. What we need to do is get to the kitchens."

"All of us?" Kelly asked.

"Yeah," I said, "The more I thought about it, the more sense it makes that that's where we'll part ways. They'll go to the supply chambers, and we'll take the servant's halls up to the tower."

He seemed to consider this, then said, "That sounds reasonable, then what?"

"Then they find their way out on a cart, and you and I hope a really good idea turns up," I said.

Aeryk looked at Dana and said, "Again, *who* is this guy?"

We managed to sneak out of the dungeon area without incident, and after a glance out of the first window we could find revealed a night dark sky heavy with rain-clouds, I felt a little more relaxed. For whatever reason, the Great World was smiling on me again; the castle would have only the bare minimum staff awake inside, and we would be able to move pretty freely. With only a little wandering, I managed to get my bearings and suss out where the pantry was. Unchallenged, we made our way into the central work area. It was quiet and very dark, which told me that it must be very late rather than very early. By even the second watch, the kitchen staff would have been starting their daily baking chores. The princess, the marquess, and their bodyguards, after a sort of elongated goodbye to Kelly and me, headed off through the storage rooms and supply stores to find the service entrance which would lead them out of the castle. That's what I presumed, anyway. They could just as likely have been caught and killed on the spot, but we had no way of knowing once they were gone. We, in turn, found the servant's hallway entrance that would lead us to the king's tower and headed that way.

"Servant's halls," as they are known in most castles, are kind of a hidden, shadow floor-plan. Basically, the hoity-toity don't like to look at the people that take care of their palaces, so they have them built with hidden doorways and secret passages so that the nasty, dirty, ordinary folk servants can clean the rooms and stoke the fires and take the dishes and what-not without actually showing their ugly faces. The good part of this, if there is one, is that the fancier or prissier the part of the castle, the less they want to see the dirty commoners, and the more servant's halls there are. And that worked out well for Kelly and me. We managed to make our way to the bottom floor of the king's tower with only a little effort and no contact with anyone. Finally, we arrived at a door that when opened, led to a sort of staging area at the base of the king's tower; a functional space where personal items were stored, clean and dirty linens were kept before use or laundering, and other necessary supplies were stocked. It was illuminated by a dim torch, probably in case of need during dark hours.

"Okay," I said, surveying the room as I spoke, "I'm going to guess your box of gems isn't in the laundry."

"Probably not," he said, looking at the various shelves and bins that populated the room, "If I had to guess, I'd say it's most likely in some locked chamber upstairs."

"You're funny," I said with a shake of my head. "If these rocks are so important, he's sleeping with them."

Kelly looked at me, askance. "That is an awful thought," he said.

"If you want," I said, "I can waste our time by only telling you what you want to hear." I saw what I was looking for and started across the room.

"Well, it might be nice sometimes," he muttered before following me.

On the opposite side of the room from the hidden passage through which we had come was the 'official' door of the room; the one that, should the king himself require any of the supplies inside, he would use to enter. Immediately to the left of that door, though, was smallish wooden cabinet inset in the wall. Even in the dim torchlight, the wear on the latch was noticeable, which meant it was definitely what I was trying to find. Shoving the catch over, I pulled the doors open to reveal a large cabinet with two twines of heavy rope going through the center.

“Ah-ha,” I said quietly and began to climb inside.

“The dumbwaiter,” Kelly said. I couldn’t tell from his tone if he was impressed or disappointed; probably because we were whispering even though there still wasn’t anyone nearby to hear us.

I settled in the back and looked at him. “Well, come on,” I said impatiently, “Your dumb rocks aren’t going to wait forever.”

Shaking his head, he climbed into the box. It was a lot smaller with two of us inside, but I’d been in worse places with worse people, so I wasn’t too annoyed. Kelly reached back out and pulled the door shut before settling into final position. Just before it closed, I am sure I caught the hint of a grin on his face.

“Now,” I said, “we pull. And quite a bit too; if I remember right, this tower is really high.”

I *did* remember right; it felt like we tugged on that rope for a day and a half easily. Kelly would grab the line at the top of the box and pull down, while I would pull up on the other rope from the floor. The pulley system, designed to counterbalance the little chamber against its own weight, would make a gentle squeak and we would rise some three or four feet with each cycle. It was pitch black, of course, since we were in a wooden box inside a stone shaft. Intermittently, we would feel the open side of the box to see if we had reached another access door. We ascended the shaft for some time in silence, and I could hear Kelly's breathing becoming more labored. Well, I supposed that if I had been worked over by the jailers, I might struggle a little too. Around the time I noticed that though, I felt a ledge on the shaft wall.

"Hey, look at that," I said, "We're somewhere. One more pull." The little dumbwaiter slid up even with the ledge as we pulled, the front opening now filled with what felt like a wood door. I shoved on it, but it didn't budge, obviously latched from the other side.

"Shyte," I muttered.

"Very classy," Kelly said.

"Oh stop it," I mumbled, a bit cross that I hadn't thought about the latch on the doors. "It isn't like you're above saying it if you've got a mouth full of it."

"Excuse me?" he said, sounding genuinely surprised.

"Come on," I said to the dark place where I knew his head was, "Your blood is not even a little bit blue. You're surrounded by a bunch of them, but you're as common as —"

"As you are?" he cut in.

"Yep. And proud of it," I said, holding back a little anger that I was kind of surprised to feel. "So don't shine me on, okay?" I said. I pulled out the thin metal strip I had hidden in the rope that held on my pants – the one that I had used to pick the lock of my cell repeatedly – and slid it carefully and quickly into the seam where the door met the jamb. With a flick, the latch came undone, and the door swung open.

We got out of the dumbwaiter and looked around. The room we were in looked like it was intended to be a sitting room of some kind. It was large and looked as though it filled the entire diameter of the tower minus whatever was necessary for stairs and such. Narrow windows were spaced pretty evenly around the perimeter – barely more than arrow-slits – letting in what dim light the cloudy darkness outside provided. I could see a spattering of water on the edge of the nearest window which told me that the clouds outside had started to leak rain; the smell of which mixed with an overwhelming staleness as I looked around. The room looked as though a wild gale had passed through sometime in the recent past. Furniture of every type was scattered everywhere, tables lying on their side, chairs askew, even a couch that was flipped completely upside-down. Tapestries that had once decorated the walls were either heaped on the floor in the corners or hanging in shreds.

"Seems a little casual to me," I whispered to Kelly.

He glanced over at me before he started into the room. The expression I had seen in the dungeon when I first saw him had returned to his face, and I could see that he was trying to take in every detail around us. I walked to the left where the hearth was, two chairs lying on their sides at odd angles in front of it.

"Cold," I said, "Doesn't look like there's been a fire here for a long time."

"A long time," Kelly agreed quietly. "There's a layer of dust on everything. No one's seen to this room for a while."

"That seems very strange," I said, kicking gently at one of the overturned chairs and spinning it around which gave me a look at the upholstered front of the seat-back. The top of the wooden frame had a wedge hacked in it, and a dark stain trailed down to the seat. "Okay," I said, pointing, "that is definitely a very bad sign."

Kelly came over and kneeled to look closer. "Yeah," he muttered, "Very bad." He looked back at the stain, lost in thought.

"Hey, so," I said, "I'm pretty sure your box of rocks isn't here, though."

He looked back up at me, whatever he had been thinking about now put aside. "No, apparently not. Back in the dumbwaiter?"

I shook my head. "No. From here the 'acceptable' staff, —" I made air quotes around the word 'acceptable,' "— would bring the food either to the guests here or to the private royal chamber upstairs." I walked over to the side of the room opposite us, just to the near side of the archway that led to the official staircase. "But," I continued, "there would still need to be a second entrance to the upstairs.

Something that would allow the rest of the staff in and out."

"For?" he asked, still looking at the stain on the chair.

"For the staff that *isn't* handling food to use. The ones that deal with the garderobe, linens, cleaning..., stuff like that."

He stood slowly, turning to me. "You know a lot about this, eh?"

I nudged a section of wood paneling that swung in without resistance. "Yep," I said.

He followed me into the hidden stairwell. It shadowed the main stairs, rising at the same angle under the steps of the other. It would lead to a secret exit in the bedchamber that would be just a few feet from the actual door to the room.

"How is that?" he said, dropping his voice to a whisper as we ascended.

"Questions, questions, questions," I whispered back, "and always at the dumbest time." I put my finger to my lips, which didn't make a lot of sense in the darkness actually, but somehow, he got the point, and we fell silent. A few steps later, we reached a small landing, maybe as deep as the stairwell was wide. The back wall of the landing was made of wooden planks fitted together tightly to form a solid panel, and after feeling around for a moment, my hand landed on a wooden lever on the right side. A quick sweep of my hand toward the opposite side revealed one of what were likely two hinges positioned just a little above my height. I shifted to the right of the landing as far as I could, while Kelly took a step the opposite way, giving me room to move. I felt along the length of the lever to the metal pivot that affixed it to the wood, then on to where it fitted into a long vertical slot in the wall.

"When we get inside," Kelly whispered, "we sweep the room as quickly as we can. When we find the box, we get out immediately. No looking around for anything that isn't necessary." I remember him saying this – as you'll see – because it was stupid.

"Fine," I replied, "but you know it's going to be right by him if it's that important."

"Just sweep the room," he repeated, "I'd rather not get any closer to waking him and raising the alarm than I have to."

"Okay," I said in a whisper so quiet it was nearly a sigh. I leaned into the door and then pressed the end of the lever down, rotating it and releasing its catch from the slot. I put my hand under the metal pivot and pressed up, shifting the weight of the door on its hinges before I carefully swung it toward me. It opened soundlessly, and when there was enough of a crack, I looked out and into the king's bedchamber.

Okay, it was a closet. Or, more like a storage room. Either way, the door opened into a small chamber that was probably six feet by ten, or the width of the hallway and twice as long. A doorway arch in the middle of the left wall admitted a dim, grayish-blue light from the main chamber beyond. On the wall to my right, two shelves ran nearly from end to end, one at knee height and one about even with my head. A cabinet filled the other end of the room from floor to ceiling, barely visible in the wan light. The air was warm and dry compared to that in the stairwell – which had been more like that in our cells – and smelled of a mixture of fire and sage. We stepped out quietly, and Kelly eased the door shut behind us. The warmth in the chamber – even the stone floor felt warmer under our feet – was a welcome change from the damp chill everywhere else.

Kelly started looking through the shelves, squinting in the dim light to see if our box of rocks was there, I supposed. I went to the doorway to see if I could see into the main room. The area of the place I could see was in much better repair than the sitting room downstairs had been. A little to the left of the closet doorway I stood in was the entrance to the royal stairwell as I had expected. The hallway beyond, lit by the distant light of a torch, bent back and away from us at the same angle as the hidden stairs we had climbed. Not far away, I knew, would be an exasperated but competent member of the castle guard whose life itself would depend on his preventing the exact sort of thing my new friend and I were trying to do — the bluish-gray glow of cloud-filtered moonlight filtered through a rain-spattered glass pane across from the storage room door. I started to cautiously lean out for a better look at the rest of the room when I heard a click from behind me. I turned to see Kelly opening the large cabinet.

"Shh," I hissed, no louder than an exhale. I crept over next to him. "Honestly," I whispered, "do you even understand what 'sneaking' means?"

He gave me a disdainful look and turned back to the cabinet, swinging the doors open. He did it silently, shifting the weight the way I had with the passageway door so that the hinges didn't squeak. The cabinet opened to reveal a tall mannequin wearing ornate plate armor. Each piece was a glossy jet black with glistening gold trim around the edge. Despite the dimness, I could make out complex scroll-work decorating the surfaces of each of the plates, while in the middle of the breastplate was etched the sigil of an eagle etched in gold. Completing the armor was a matching black helmet with a golden faceguard sitting atop the head of the mannequin. Hanging on one side wall of the cabinet, next to the armor, was a similarly decorated triangular shield. On the opposite wall was a bejeweled long-sword. There were other miscellaneous items too, hanging banners and a few things on the floor, but no box.

"Come on," I whispered, "He's not going to have your magic rocks in the closet." I turned back to the doorway, but

Kelly stayed put. He stared at the armor for a long moment, then reached in and retrieved the long-sword from its mounting.

“I thought,” I said, keeping my slightly frustrated voice at a whisper, “we were after your gems. ‘No looking around for other junk,’ or something like that, you said.”

“I prefer the long-sword,” Kelly whispered, “And since this is here…” He slid the blade into the loop on the belt he had taken from the prison's guard. He offered me the short sword he had been carrying since we left the dungeon. I raised my eyebrow, unsure if he could see it in the darkness.

“Trust is trust,” he whispered.

I nodded, then brushed past him and the offered sword. I heard him take a breath behind me to say something, but he stopped as I reached over and picked up a leather bandolier with two daggers sheathed in it from the bottom of the cabinet. I slipped it over my shoulders quietly and looked at him.

“More my speed,” I said.

I could make out the curve of a grin on his face as we both turned back to the doorway.

“Okay,” I said, “let’s get to the main event then. The king is sleeping. Right. Over. There.” I emphasized each word by pointing in the direction of the unseen portion of the room. At least, I hoped he was sleeping. To be honest, with every moment passing, I was more and more convinced I was going to turn around and see the king and his guards standing right in front of me. But we had to pause so Kelly could get his stupid sword, so whatever. I craned my neck around the door-frame and finally got a good look around.

The room beyond was lit in the soft yellow of candles and dying firelight, giving the whole place a kind of dreamy atmosphere. It was a strangely shaped area, the stairwell door and the storage room we were in was off to the side of one end of the oblong space, whereas the royal bed itself sat mostly centered at the broader end opposite us. Dark wood paneling covered the outer walls from the floor to a height of four feet. The rest of the wall revealed the dark, black stone that the castle was mostly constructed of, the only difference being that here it was smoothed and polished so that the flickers of flames on the candles and in the fire reflected randomly from its surface. Thick overlapping rugs covered the majority of the floor, and only near the wall could the bare wood beneath be seen. The wooden trussed ceiling rose in the middle some fifteen feet, and a huge chandelier hung in the center, suspended from a chain and retaining rope that was in turn fastened to a pin on the wall opposite us. The large hearth filled most of that wall, next to which was a small doorway that likely led to the dressing area, the garderobe, and possibly a bath. The fire in the hearth, burning low now, would provide heat not only to the main room but all of those back chambers as well. The royal bed itself was an enormous, ornate thing that sat on a wooden platform two steps up from the floor. It was constructed of four massive wood columns, one at each corner, and topped by a carved wooden frame. Thick red cloth – velvet, probably – hung on each side, gathered to the corners by gold ropes. On either side, two heavy wooden tables stood with several candles on each. Between the bed and us was a small sitting area consisting of two heavily padded couches and a full-length mirror on a wooden support. The smell of the fire hung heavy in the air, colored with the scents of sage and cedar. The whole place felt luxurious and obnoxious at the same time.

I made a follow me gesture and quietly made my way into the room. Kelly followed, slipping the short-sword through another loop on his belt opposite the long-sword. I'd have to ask him later what in the world he needed two swords for as the only people I'd ever known with two swords were people who very much overestimated how useful two swords were. And they were almost all dead, too, so that was an important fact. I heard him hiss very quietly and turned. He gestured that he was going left around the room. I nodded and continued on my way to the right. In silence, we made our way investigating each table, shelf, and cabinet noiselessly, looking for the gems.

I want to state right here that I was sure the gems were going to be where we found them a few moments later, just like I said back in the stairwell, and if we had just gone there and gotten them, the next few minutes of our lives might have been smoother.

It took us a while to examine the perimeter of the room, including the time it took Kelly to investigate the areas beyond the fireplace – which were exactly what I thought they were, incidentally. Finally, we reached the bed. I was looking on the lower shelf of the table on my side when I heard the faint sound of wood sliding on wood. I stood up to see Kelly standing with a wooden box about two feet long in his hands. He gave me a nod. I nodded back, then glanced down to make sure the king was still asleep. My heart stopped. I looked across the room, then at Kelly, who must have seen the look on my face, because he shot a look down to the bed at the sleeping figure. I was already in motion, off of the bed platform and headed back the way we had come. Kelly followed me immediately, keeping himself remarkably quiet while carrying the box.

A step away from the storage room we had entered through; he hissed, "Hey! What's wrong?"

"Just tell me," I said in a very intense whisper, "Is that the guy that imprisoned you?"

He looked at me with a mixture of irritation and confusion. "Yeah, of course."

"Well, guess what? I've met Mathu a couple of times, and that guy?" I pointed at the bed, "That guy *ain't* Mathu."

The faintest hint of a shuffling noise came from the storage room. We shot each other a look.

"Stoking the fire," we said almost in unison. The fire in the hearth was low; we had both noticed it. So, of course, the house stewards would be assigned to come in and stoke it on some schedule, and they were about to find two escaped prisoners in the king's bedroom. We looked around frantically. The main entrance beckoned, but there would be guards – personal guards, actually – close by, and we weren't in a position to fight our way out. I started to head for the chambers beyond the hearth across the room – they were a dead end, but we might be able to hide there, I thought – when I saw Kelly heading toward the window. He had pulled off the leather vest and the remainder of his shirt which he tied into a makeshift sling for the box, hanging the whole thing around him over one shoulder when he finished it.

"Are you broken in the head?" I said though I found myself following him.

"It's been alleged," he said, "but only at the dumbest time." He nudged aside the window sash and climbed out.

Behind me, I heard the secret door squeak open in the storage room.

A nostalgic thought came as I climbed out the window into the cold, wet night. *Things had seemed so pleasant back in my cell.*

The clouds that had seemed to leak rain earlier had by now fully committed, and we emerged into a steady shower and chill, fall air. After the comfortable warmth of the bedchamber, the sudden shock was enough to cause my muscles to start to cramp, which was something they needed not to do as I clung to the side of the stone tower far above the ground. I blinked the rain from my eyes and looked around to get my bearings. Kelly was to my right, clinging as tightly as I was to the cold stone; both of us using the bottom ledge of the window we had come out of as a narrow finger-hold. From a distance, the walls of Chateau Flint appeared almost smooth, but up close – very close, in our case – the curved parts of the wall like the tower we were on revealed small gaps and ledges, and it was in these that we were able to wedge our fingers and toes. I chanced a look down and saw that the window we had come out of was on the north-most side of the tower, overlooking the ravine that flanked the castle's rocky perch. The upshot of this was that not only were we dozens of feet above the castle proper; we were also hundreds of feet above the ground. The craggy, rocky ground.

"Seriously thinking that the dungeon was better," I said. The sound of the rain swept my voice away, so Kelly didn't respond at all. A moment later though, we both looked up as we heard the 'thunk' of the window sash latching shut again. *Sure,* I thought, *why not? They probably thought they left it unlatched and it blew open in the wind.* Of course, that did mean that we unquestionably were stuck out here in the rain.

"Lovely night for it," Kelly said.

"You take me to the best places," I replied.

He looked up and down, over in my direction, and then craned his neck to look further to the right of us. I could see the muscles in his arms and back straining to hold on as his weight shifted with each tiny movement.

"All right," he said, loudly enough to be heard over the weather, "Two choices; up or down."

"What does up get us?" I asked.

"Well, off the wall, mostly," he said, "But not much else. Down, however, is a long way, and the longer we're out here, the more likely we go that way and not on purpose. The other option is to go this way," he made a little gesture with his head to his right as he continued, "The main castle wall joins the tower on this side about halfway down. But there is a short section of the wall that is flat, and it doesn't have much in the way of handholds."

"Look," I said, "let's just do it. Hanging out here talking it up is not a solution."

He nodded and shifted his weight again. Carefully, he adjusted first one foot, then the opposite hand, then the other foot, and finally he took his left hand off the ledge and moved it to another finger hold. I did the same and so, inch by inch, we made our way over and down the outside of the tower wall. After several minutes, my fingers went blissfully numb in the wet chill, which slowed me down more, but we continued to make progress until we were just a few feet away from the north castle wall, its narrow walkway the most beautiful sight I could imagine. Kelly had been right though, the tiny gaps and ledges that had been so helpful as we climbed disappeared as the tower wall slowly flattened. Finally, Kelly stopped.

"Well, that's it," he said. I looked down. The walkway was about twenty feet below us, and maybe five feet still to the right.

"Jump," I said.

He looked at me. "Jump?" he repeated, sarcasm dripping from his tone like the rain off our noses. "Who's broken in the head now?"

"Do you have a better idea?" I said, "'Cause I'd absolutely like to hear it if you do. Otherwise, yeah. Jump."

He looked at the walkway again. "God's teeth," he muttered. Then, without another word, he flung himself off the wall. I froze. Honestly, I didn't think he'd do it; I was hoping he would have another idea up his sleeve. Of course, he had no sleeves at that moment, so I should have known better. Time slowed down, and he seemed to hang in the air. His body arced through the night air toward the wall and a thought colder than the rain ran through me. *Shyte*, I thought, *he's not going to make it.*

Suddenly, his body half twisted, and he flung his arms out just as he reached the crenelated edge of the wall. His hands caught the top of the higher part of the battlement, and his body slammed into the stone with a grunt of pain I could hear even over the rain and wind. His momentum swung him around against the wall in an arc until, just before he would have lost the tenuous grip he had, he got one leg into the lower part of the battlement. Gracelessly, he scrambled over the wall and collapsed on the walkway, breathing heavily.

"Hey!" I called down, "that was great! So, uh, how about a hand?"

He looked up at me slowly from where he was kneeling. "What —" he paused to cough, "— what happened to 'jump'?"

"That would be crazy," I said, "Seriously, give me a hand here!"

He didn't move for several moments, and an unnerving concern started to grow in my mind. *What if he's hurt?* I thought, *how do I get down then?* Finally, though, he stood up, and after looking around, he held his finger up to me and walked out of sight along the wall.

"Wait," I muttered, "Sure. I'll wait," as I talked my voice got unintentionally louder until I was almost yelling, "I mean, I am very comfortable here on the side of a feckin' castle tower in the rain!"

As if in response, Kelly reappeared with a long pole in hand. He maneuvered it until he had it wedged into position straight out from the battlement so that it extended below me. Kelly nodded that it was ready, and as gently as I could, I let myself drop, catching the pole under my arms and across my chest as I did. It flexed with the addition of my weight, and there was a tiny cracking sound, but the pole held, and I slid along it as quickly as possible until shortly I was pulling myself up and over the battlement.

Kelly was leaning against the wall under a small overhang. His breathing was labored, and he had his hands on his knees. I shoved the pole off the side of the wall, letting it fall into the ravine outside, and came over to him.

"Jump," he mumbled.

I shrugged. "That was pretty amazing, though," I said, "I really wasn't expecting you to do that."

"You're an ass," he said, though he choked back a laugh.

"That's not new information," I said.

"No," he said, straightening up, "but you know what is?"

"The fact that the king isn't the king?" I offered.

"Yeah, that," he said, "Come on, we have to get out of here and meet up with the rest of the group."

I looked around. "I have a plan," I said after a

moment.

"Does it involve jumping?"

"Not as such, no."

"Then I'm in. Which way?"

"That way," I smiled broadly, "Toward the chapel."

CHAPTER EIGHT

— DANA —

My dad said to me that he knew what I was when I was only eight-years-old. Our neighbors the next farm over had a daughter who got married, and her father, a hard-old farmhand who worked the land from dawn to dusk without a smile or a frown, had a celebration and invited most everyone from the area. Even the landowner came, giving the new couple the gift of a year's free rent on their own plot of land not far away. Then, I didn't realize what an incredible gift that was; only that the party became much louder and more full of excitement after his arrival. There were other children there, but I kept to myself even then. It was because I tended toward solitude that I was not with the rest of the party-goers when the fire broke out just after night fell. Somehow the huge – to my eight-year-old eyes – bonfire had found a way to the nearby barn, and by the time the other attendees knew what was happening, the old wooden building was wreathed in flame and billowed smoke from its windows. Several of the men went to fill buckets from the water reservoir behind the house, and they were gone when the realization came that, though the barn had been empty of livestock, other children had been playing in and around it all evening. One of the girls – Viktori, a wispy blonde girl just a year younger than me – was missing. The flaming structure began to creak and groan as the fire split and twisted the dried wood. Through the brightness of the blaze, I caught sight of Viktori peeking out of a wide gap that had cracked open in the side wall. I didn't stop to think or say anything to the adults, I just ran. The heat from the flames made the night air feel like a blacksmith's forge, and the hot breath of the fire hit me like the worst desert wind I could imagine. I found a small pathway through the blaze to Viktori's side. I was coughing now, the smoke threatening to choke the life out of me and, I now realize, it might have if I had been just a little taller. She was dazed from the heat and the terror overwhelming her, and she wobbled on her feet as I grabbed her arm, pitching over as I tried to pull her out. The old barn creaked again, and the wall next to us, already undulating in my vision through the hot air, seemed to twist and lean. I pulled harder on Viktori's arm, dragging her across the ground in a desperate attempt to get out, but she was little more than dead weight. The wall creaked once more before it came loose from the blackened frame and collapsed, falling inward toward us. I threw myself on top of Viktori as the flaming planks of the wall crashed down. There was so much pain, and thankfully, I passed out. When I came to, I was several feet away from the remains of the barn, lying in a pool of water that had been dumped on me by the men when they returned with filled buckets. Dad told me later that he had led several of them to where he had seen me run into the barn and with their help – and the water – they had pulled the two of us to safety. Viktori was coughing somewhere in the distance. The hot air had burned her lungs, and she would always have trouble breathing, but she mostly recovered. The burning debris had severely burned my back from just below my shoulders all the way down to the tops of my legs, and it was long months before it could be said that I had healed. I carry the marks on me even now. But that night, what my dad said to me has remained with me even more than the scars have.

“I thought we’d lost you, Dana-girl,” he said through the tear-stained soot on his face, “I should have known. You’re always the one that runs at the danger, aren’t you, love? That’s just who you are.”

So when we left Kelly and Denis to their hair-brained plan to recover the emeralds, I had very mixed feelings. First and most logically, I felt that the whole thing was idiotic and that the token box of gems wasn’t worth any of our lives. But second? Ah, second. I genuinely wished I could have gone with them. Toward the danger.

“Dana?” It was Jules, touching my arm and pulling me back to my duty. We were already almost through the dark storage area, winding our way around a labyrinth of shelving units, stacked crates, barrels, bushels, and every sort of sack and bag. Every few feet, different smells wafted past me, from wet grain to onions to hay to coffee. The room was lit only by the splashes of light from the high-set windows on one side, making the process of traversing it and remaining stealthy a challenge.

"Sorry," I said, refocusing, "I was just thinking about those two idiots back there. It isn't worth —"

"Kelly knows what he's doing," Jules said. It was a statement of fact, not a defense, exactly, but still a definite statement. I narrowed my eyes in the dark and stopped, facing her.

"What is this really about?" I said. Even in the half-light, I could see the stunned expression pass across her face. "Really, Jules," I continued, "What is it that I'm not understanding here?"

There was a pause, and then she said, "You know all I can tell you."

"Excuse me," came Aeryk's whispered voice. He had been up ahead with Rohb but had doubled back to find us. "Can we save the chat for later?"

Jules looked in my eyes a second longer, then turned to the marquess. "Sorry. We got distracted. Let's go," she said as she followed him. Dutifully, I fell in behind them.

We continued around one last bend and came upon a

spacious, open area where the high-set windows allowed a little more of the outside light in, affording us a better view of the room. It appeared that we had found the loading area, a large stone chamber with a high ceiling and two large carriage gates inset in the wall below the windows. We came up behind Rohb, joining him where he was kneeling behind one of the nearby crates. I noticed that he was cradling his broken arm, only letting it go when we were close.

"There's our way out," he said without turning, "I don't see anyone, and other than you braiding one another's hair back there, I don't hear anything."

"That's enough, Lieutenant," Julea hissed forcefully.

"What's beyond?" I said.

Aeryk shrugged and, very quietly, slipped past Rohb and made his way around the perimeter of the open area, keeping mostly in the shadows. He moved slowly, scanning the room carefully every time he had the opportunity to duck back into the darkness. Finally, convinced he was safe, he walked over to the door. Lying flat on the ground, he pressed his face against the bottom of the first gate where the two heavy wooden door panels met. A moment passed, then he stood up and almost casually brushed himself off before he turned and waved us over.

"It's the merchant's gate all right," he said, "I can see an open area outside. No torches."

"No guards?" I said.

"Not that I could see," he said.

"Could be," Rohb said, "This isn't an outside gate. Guards would be at the outer wall, checking everyone in from there."

We all stood still and listened, but except for the slight tap of the initial spattering of raindrops on the windows above, the silence was complete.

"Fine then," Julea said. She stepped around where Aeryk was standing and threw back the iron bolt that held the doors fast. With a tug, she swung the left-hand door a few inches inward, granting us an easy view of the courtyard outside. The sky was dark, with thick clouds hiding the stars and turning the moon's light a sickly gray. The light of one small lantern – mounted on the stone wall between the doors – mixed with the moonlight and gave everything nearby a murky orange color. The courtyard itself was relatively large, maybe a hundred feet in diameter, nearly round, and bounded by a low stone wall. The design was such that a laden cart could both enter and turn around to leave without slowing the movement of others in the same area. As we had heard from inside, the weak dribble of raindrops had not yet made the ground wet, though there was the promise of more in the air. Several feet to the left of us was an empty cart with angled wooden side panels and a small bench for the driver at the front.

"No horse," Julea muttered.

“Not a problem,” Rohb said, “Some folk wouldn’t have one anyhow. They’d pull the cart themselves by hand. Whatever they had unsold would still be in the back to take home. Grab a couple of those bags.” He pointed with his healthy arm toward the stores in the supply room behind us. Aeryk and I slipped back into the supply room and grabbed a couple of the nearest large sacks, dragging them outside. Rohb had pulled the cart near to the door by the time we got back.

“Some hay too,” he said, “Something to spread around the bottom. Make it messy.”

I went back in as Aeryk heaved the sacks into the back of the cart. I glanced around the area, finally finding a hay-bale in the corner under several balled-up horse blankets. With a little effort, I got it over to the door, cloth bundles and all. Aeryk and Rohb broke the bale open and spread the hay on the floor of the cart. I shook one of the blankets open and draped it over Julea’s shoulders and then did the same for myself. There was a chill in the air that the random droplets of rain were only amplifying. Aeryk took a piece of the twine from the disassembled hay-bale and returned to the open door. He disappeared inside for a moment, then returned with one end of the string in his hand. He tugged at the open door to close it, and as it came even with the threshold, he pulled on the twine which slid out through the gap between them a short distance before breaking off. He pushed gently on the now closed door, and it held fast. He turned around and saw me looking at him.

"Covering our exit," he said, "I pulled the latch closed with the twine."

"I see," I said, "That was a good thought. Quite sneaky, in fact."

"I think I'm picking up bad habits," he said, tossing the broken twine into the dirt. He reached over and grabbed another blanket, draping it over his head.

Rohb turned to us. "Okay, up you two go," he said, motioning for Jules and me to get into the cart. He then turned to Aeryk. "You're in the driver's seat," he said. Without another word, he went around to the front of the wagon and lifted the shafts. Before anything could be said, he had gripped both, the left one wedged between his broken arm and his body.

Aeryk, now halfway up to the driver's seat, said, "Hey you don't—"

Rohb looked back over his shoulder and cut him off. "Oh, you gonna do this?" he said.

The big Talhas gave a tug on the shafts, and the wagon moved forward. Aeryk wobbled, not entirely seated yet, but then dropped into the driver's seat and settled in. It took Rohb a moment to get the cart steadily in motion, but shortly we were moving away from the castle and around the back access road. It twisted and turned around several outbuildings until we rounded a bend and saw the castle's outer gate come into view. Rohb slowed but didn't stop; I assumed he didn't want to lose the momentum he had built up before it was necessary. It would also have drawn undue attention, and I was sure he was aware we were going to have enough of that at such a late hour.

"Okay, I think we are approaching showtime," Aeryk said quietly. I nodded and crouched back down into the cart. Julea was already moving the sacks we had loaded onto the cart closer to to the front while scattering the hay more haphazardly around. She and I then crouched ourselves down and nestled behind the sacks, draping our blankets over ourselves. The smell of the closest large bag, now pressed tightly against me and warmed by my body, was of roasted coffee beans, which was so comforting that I reflexively took a deep breath and sighed. Aeryk shushed me quietly from his position above us, and I quieted.

"Late night," said an unseen and tired voice from somewhere off to the left of the cart.

"Yah," Aeryk said, "Livin' in 'ope that more'd sell didn' get me nuttin.'" My eyebrows rose unbidden. His crude accent was almost perfect, seemingly matching precisely that of the staff I had heard back in Clemons when we arrived. Sneaky and guileful, I thought. He's definitely picking up some bad habits.

Of course, I didn't know then what was to come.

"Bad day, eh?" came the other voice.

"Nah, no' bad," Aeryk continued, pausing for a yawn, "I was jus' hopin' ta 'ave a perfect day, git me? Make the wife 'appy."

I could hear gentle scraping against the side of the cart. Someone, the partner of the speaker most likely, was probably looking over the wooden side of the cart to see the load. I held my breath.

"Smells like barley," said a second voice. It came from the same direction as the scraping sound now; the opposite side of the cart near where I knew Jules was lying.

"Aye," Aeryk said, stifling another yawn, "an' coffee. No' a bad day, if you take me, jus' late."

I heard more scraping, echoing more loudly to me now through the wooden panels of the cart.

"Your man all right?" the first voice said again.

"'E will be. Got 'is arm 'tween two barrels o' beer. Made a nasty crunch, but 'e says it's fine. That's right, eh, Doug?"

"Nothin' to it," Rohb said with a grunt.

The rustling sounds around the cart faded. "On your way. Good morrow," the first voice said.

"Thank y' sir. And good morrow t' you," Aeryk said. There was a slight tug, and the cart shifted but didn't move. My stomach tightened; if Rohb couldn't get us moving, we would be by the guards longer, which was one place we needed desperately not to be.

“Here,” said the voice from behind us. Suddenly, something hit the back of the cart, and it lurched forward. The bag I had leaning against me shifted, which in turn tugged at the blanket covering my head. For a brief moment, my face was exposed, and I found I was looking directly at the figure of a guard right behind the cart. He must have kicked it to get us moving, I realized, which left him standing in the perfect position to see me. I closed my eyes and froze, hoping against hope that the shadows would keep me as well hidden as the blanked had. Nothing happened — no shouts from the guard, no sudden stopping of the cart, nothing. A minute passed. Two. Three. I opened my eyes again and saw the closed gate of the castle receding behind us. I let out a breath that I didn’t realize I had been holding. Still, no one spoke until, several minutes and a reasonable distance later, we turned around a bend in the road and out of sight of the castle. The cart started to bump and rock as we came off the road and stopped alongside in the brush.

“Don’t believe that worked,” Rohb said as Julea and I came out of our crouches, shoving the sacks back and shaking out the blankets.

“You don’t?” Aeryk said.

“I never thought it would,” Rohb said. He came around from the front of the wagon to stand at the back. “I was just waiting to crack some heads.”

I tossed the remaining blanket to the big man, and he caught it with his good hand, shaking it loose and then awkwardly wrapping it over himself. It was the same size as the other three but seemed much smaller across his broad shoulders. He climbed into the back of the cart with us as Aeryk stepped over from the driver's perch and did the same. I stood for a moment, re-wrapping my blanket around myself, and looked around at where we were. Rohb had pulled the cart several feet off the road and under the branches of a large oak which, though it had already begun to shed its leaves, still had enough clinging to its branches that the smatterings of rain were not yet heavy enough to penetrate. Behind us, the road bent back toward the castle, now some distance away and visible only through a tangle of branches. It also continued into the forest to the right. I moved to the back corner of the cart and sat such that, with only a turn of my head, I could see the road in both directions. I mostly watched the way back to the castle, though, waiting for a sign; good or bad. We sat in silence for a long time; the rain slowly going from the random splattering to a steady shower. Though the canopy of leaves above still provided some protection, more and more of it was coming through, and our blankets were beginning to dampen. It was, in short, becoming miserable. Moments later, I found out just how miserable it could be.

"How did he know?" Julea said suddenly after some

time. I looked over at her, reluctantly taking my eyes off of the castle. She sat against the opposite side of the cart with her knees up, her arms folded around them, and her head bowed. She let her words hang in the quiet for a moment before she lifted her face to look at Aeryk. "The pirate," she continued, looking at him with a glare that eerily reminded me of her mother, "Edword. He knew exactly where to find us. We left Sterling through a hidden passage that no one knew about, but there he was. How did that happen?"

We all sat in silence, quick looks passing back and forth between us. Not Julea though, she was only looking at Aeryk.

"I don't—" he started, but she cut him off.

"'Exactly as described,'" she said slowly, "That's what you said when we were taken to the castle. Kelly noticed it; he even asked what you meant. And you said that it was from what you'd heard around the court, but you hadn't been to court in years. King Ronald said as much when we arrived." Rohb was eyeing the two in turn now, watching the exchange with keen interest.

The marquess shifted uncomfortably where he sat as if looking for some way he could get out of the cart and away from the conversation. "I…," he began, and when he continued, a note of resignation tinged his voice, "This wasn't what was supposed to happen." He slumped, dropping his head onto his knees. Rohb leaned forward toward him from his place at the front of the cart, his features now hidden in shadow. Jules had moved onto her knees and was watching Aeryk intensely.

“What wasn’t?” she said, her voice soft but intense.

“You have to understand. The way I grew up. We were just a fat cow, ready for slaughter,” Aeryk said, and I saw that he obviously was reciting something he had long had on his mind. “Our lands, our people, everything - all of it. And no one seemed to care. The king, my father,” he veritably spat the word, “none of them. No matter what I ever said. Anyone could walk in and destroy our lives, and they were just fine with it.”

Julea narrowed her eyes but kept her voice soft as she spoke. “What happened?”

Aeryk looked up at her, his expression haunted. “Nothing. For a long time. But then I started to hear rumors. Just little stories at first, but more and more of them; the same things over and over. They came from merchants and traders, mostly, that traveled up here to the north on occasion. Some chieftain in this land had started uniting the tribes under his banner.”

“Mathu,” Julea said.

“Yes,” he said, “You have to understand. What I heard was that he was bringing peace to tribes that had been at war with one another for centuries. I was being told that he had rebuilt one of the ancient strongholds here and was using it as his capital. A proper castle and city. And he was encouraging trade, farming, real commerce. The makings of an actual kingdom."

"You mean that guy?" Rohb muttered, jutting his finger toward the distant castle.

"Then what?" Julea asked, ignoring the interruption.

Aeryk sagged further, his voice becoming smaller, somehow. "I sent a message. I said I wanted to build an agreement between our two peoples, but I needed help." He paused a long moment as if struggling to get the words out. "I said that we could be better neighbors if we could defend one another, support one another, but I needed his help to get our barons and dukes to agree."

"To agree to what?" Julea asked.

"To paying for a standing army," he said.

"So you essentially confirmed for him – someone that you only knew from trader's stories – that we actually didn't have an army?" Rohb interjected.

Aeryk looked at him, and a little bit of heat rose in his voice as he replied. "I did, yes. But I emphasized that our local militias were undefeated in all our history and so we were still a match for his little tribal bands. I'm not an idiot. But I said that I believed we could be better neighbors if we were both able to defend ourselves. And one another."

Julea's eyes stayed on him for a long moment, seeming to look right through him. Aeryk's brief show of bravado withered under the glare, and he dropped his eyes again. Then, raising her eyebrow, she broke her silence. "He didn't know he was only talking to the son of one of the lesser lords, did he?"

Aeryk turned to her but avoided her eyes. It was all the answer she needed.

"You pretended to be the king," she said. He nodded slowly, and his head sank.

"So when Ronald contacted the Empire...," she started.

"It had seemed to be working. The rumors about the "new threat" had my father nervous, and he was sending and receiving messages from the other members of the court. I was sure there would be a conclave in no time, and the word would come down to begin to build the army. But then I heard the real plan. One that I would never have guessed. Not only were we not going to build an army for our own defense, but they were planning that a foreign power – the god-forsaken Empire, no less – was going to have troops living on our soil." He hadn't looked up, but his voice had gone hard, a wave of hidden anger revealing itself in stages. "Unless I could somehow stop the process," he finished.

"You absolute arse-hat!" Though it wasn't above an average speaking volume, Rohb's voice seemed to boom out in the quiet. There was an explosion of motion as the big Talhas warrior lunged forward and collided with Aeryk; his momentum carried the two of them over the open back of the cart and down to the ground. Instinctively, the marquess wrenched himself loose and kicked at Rohb, trying to scamper on his back toward the road to put some distance between them. Rohb was launched backward and landed on his rear, awkwardly scrambling back to his feet and a moment later again hurling himself at Aeryk. He landed across him, pinning the smaller man to the ground. Their arms and legs seemed to flail wildly as they struggled. Aeryk punched at Rohb's wounded arm, now lose of the makeshift sling Julea had put on it, bringing a howl of pain from the big man. Rohb jabbed a punch into Aeryk's face in return, catching him just to the side of his right eye and driving his head into the gravel. He closed his hand around the marquess's throat as Aeryk, obviously dazed, reached up and clawed at Rohb's chest, finally grabbing the leather belt that had been the sling. He pulled on it, and it tightened around Rohb's throat.

At this, Julea and I jumped from the cart and flanked the two men. "Enough!" I said loudly enough to be heard over their tussling. They froze, though neither one released their grip. Julea, holding the short spear Aeryk had been holding up to now, brandished it near enough to their faces that they could distinctly see the threat. I rested the blade of my short sword on Rohb's shoulder. He looked up at me, the rage still on his face. "That is enough," I repeated, quieter but no less forcefully. The two men looked from me to Julea's spear point and then to one another. Finally, they each released their grip and Rohb moved off, allowing the other to get up. The two men knelt there on the ground, Aeryk catching his breath while Rohb coughed and cradled his injured arm. Julea came around to face them both, her stance ramrod straight; entirely in command.

"Lieutenant, that will be quite enough of that," she said, "I will tell you if and when the time comes to kill him." She looked over at Aeryk. "You understand that I am keeping that option open," she said.

He nodded, still kneeling in the rain.

"Then let us complete the tale. Your plan was failing. I expect that was when you contacted Mathu again," Julea said. Her tone was different, now. The gentle sympathy had been replaced by something more pragmatic; colder and far more decisive. I briefly thought again how much she seemed like her mother.

"I did," Aeryk croaked, his voice still recovering from the assault. "I told him – as the king – that the barons had resisted the idea and had contacted the Empire. But that I had someone we could trust and a plan that could still succeed."

"Why would he still be interested? His result seems insignificant, it seems to me."

Rohb had regained his feet and now stood opposite

me on the other side of the marquess. He held his left arm up gingerly and remained silent, but it was only by sheer force of will, I could see.

"I said that it was the Empire's idea. They came to us and wanted to open a relationship. But I knew it was just Imperial expansionism and that he would be next."

"You made us your threat. The hobgoblin to scare up what you wanted," Julea said. It was again a matter of fact, but I knew her well enough to know that that idea was burning her inside.

"All we had to do was stop or delay the talks with the Imperial representative," Aeryk said. "Of course, I had no idea that the representative would be the Imperial heir."

"So the sell-swords suddenly became worth it," Julea said, pacing a little. She was a couple of feet back from him, and still mostly sheltered by the oak. The pacing did nothing to dispel the comparison to Ardallah in my mind.

Aeryk nodded. "But they failed every single time. Nothing worked for them," he looked down again.

"Because of Kelly," she said.

Aeryk shook his head as he spoke. "Yeah. He somehow managed to chase off their ships; then found a way through the forest, so we never went on the road. Nothing worked. But then we got to Castle Sterling, and one of Edword's men contacted me."

"And that's how they knew about our way out," Julea

said.

“Just the inn,” his voice was almost a whisper now. “I think they just worked backward from there. And then...,” his voice broke. He put his face into his hands, sobbing. He sat that way for a long time before he continued. “I’m so sorry. I didn’t know,” he said, struggling to get the words out, “I didn’t know this was what he would do. I just meant to protect my people.” His voice disappeared into the sobs again.

Julea stopped in front of him and stood very still, her hands clasped behind her back. We were all the most bedraggled creatures by this point. What remained of our traveling clothes were torn and dirty from days of wear and abuse. We hadn’t eaten, barely had anything to drink, and were barefoot in a cold rain. But somehow, as she stood there before him, she still carried herself like a queen. She waited until finally he collected himself and looked up at her.

“It seems that you were deceived. It makes you a fool. But..., probably an honest one.” She shook her head but then leaned close to his face. “If Kelly doesn’t make it back, though, the cost of your betrayal will rather abruptly be much higher than the value of your life. Think on that,” she said, then turned away and walked toward the cart.

The rain, which had already graduated to a shower, started to come down harder yet as we followed the princess back onto the wagon. Aeryk went all the way to the front corner and sat down, clutching at the blanket on his lap. He moved slowly as if he had aged in the last few minutes, and his eyes, when visible, were red and raw and haunted. Julea and I climbed back up for whatever shelter our blankets and the cart were against the rain. I sat back down in the same spot, again to watch the castle, but this time I had Julea sit beside me where she remained more easily within reach. And that much further from Aeryk.

Rohb stood behind the cart for a moment while we all settled in, then looked down at his arm. It was misshapen, with a large bulge on the inner side that seemed to indicate the broken bone had shifted. He rested his right hand on the swelling and tightened his grip. Furrows of concentration and pain formed across his forehead for several seconds, and then there was a loud pop. He threw his head back in a groan that sounded more animal than man and staggered a step so that he was leaning against the cart. Julea and I looked at one another and then back to where he stood. It took him a moment to control his breathing, but finally, he reached up and took the belt from around his neck. He looked at the princess.

"Your Majesty? If you wouldn't mind?" He held out the belt.

A gentle smile crossed Julea's face, and she moved around me to recreate the sling for him.

"Do try not to get choked with it this time," she said

quietly.

Rohb nodded to her, a grateful look on his face. Possibly the least aggressive look I had yet seen from him up to that point. He climbed up and moved past us to the front corner of the cart opposite Aeryk, where he settled in and fixed his eyes on him. And so we stayed for what felt like an eternity until I saw the two riders.

It was very late – perhaps saying it was early is more accurate – and the undulating showers had left us very damp but not quite soaked through. The passing of time had begun to make my eyelids heavy, even as my anxiety grew. I had just looked at my companions and back to the road when I noticed distant movement through the thin branches screening my view of Chateau Flint. I could see it was two men on horseback, though the remaining rain and the branches conspired to hide more details of them until they were quite close. There were indeed two, hooded and cloaked, and their horses were laden with heavy packs. They were following the road leading into the forest from the castle and would pass very near our little camp; if such is the right term for a supply cart nestled beneath a tree. I nudged Jules and motioned for her to get low while I readied my short sword. Rohb saw this and, now also aware of the riders, shifted his position in his seat to prepare best for whatever might come. I stepped off the back of the cart and stood facing the road as they came near. They stopped a few feet from us, so I stepped closer to them, making sure I stood between them and my companions.

"Good morn, sister," said the one closest to me, his hooded head bowing in a nod, "What sad chance puts you on this dark and wet road rather than by hearth and home?" They were close enough now that I could see the decorative stitching along the edges of the heavy cloth of their cloaks and hoods. They were the religious symbols of the Church of the One, and I realized they were monks. I lowered my blade, which I had unconsciously been holding in a guard position, switched it to my opposite hand, and bowed my own head. I made a circle with my right thumb and forefingers and then traced a large circle clockwise in the air in front of me from my forehead to my chest and back.

"Peace to you, brothers," I said.

The monks flashed a glance toward one another, then they both returned the gesture. "Peace to you, sister," they said in concert.

There was a pause, and I waited while the two looked at one another again. Finally, the second monk made a shrugging motion and said, "Okay, I'm not sure that I know what comes after that."

"Me neither," said the first, reaching up and scratching at the back of his head.

I stared, and the realization hit like lightning. "Kelly?"

I said.

“Serves us right for not being churchgoers,” Kelly said, pulling off his hood.

“Don’t all you fancy folks have to go?” Denis said, removing his hood, “I thought that was a rule.”

“We have discussed how I’m not fancy,” Kelly said as he dismounted and walked over to me. We stood looking at one another, and I thought for a moment about punching him; it seemed like it would be very satisfying after the whole ‘peace-be-with-you’ nonsense. But instead, as he held out his hand to me, I found myself brushing it aside and embracing him.

“You’re probably going to be damned for pretending to be a monk,” I said into his ear after a long moment.

“That,” he said as we eased out of the embrace, “is unlikely to be the reason I’m damned.”

I shook my head. “I still think the whole thing was stupid,” I said, though I couldn’t seem to stop myself from smiling.

“Kelly,” Julea’s voice came from my right. She had come down from the cart and was already just behind me. I stepped back as he turned to her, and she grabbed him in a tight hug. He grunted, an unmistakable look of pain crossing his face though he made no effort to stop her.

“Well, this is all just swell,” Denis suddenly said, having dismounted and stepped over to my left, “but I think we should probably get ourselves moving. There is going to be no end of hell to pay when the castle starts waking up." He glanced back over his shoulder just a little nervously, or so it seemed to me. "Besides, monks wake up really early I hear, and they're going to be well and truly pissed."

Kelly and Julea separated as he turned back to Denis and I. "He's right. Let's get moving. Strap the horses to the —" he looked around suddenly, "Wait, where's your horse?"

"Right here," Rohb said, standing up in the cart. He glanced over at Aeryk – sitting frozen in place across from him – and then back to Kelly.

"Whoa," Denis muttered.

"Right," Kelly said, suppressing a look of wonder, "Okay. Sure. Then let's get our horses lashed up and get away from here. Denis, grab the packs off the horses and throw them in the cart. We managed to grab some supplies."

"Food?" Rohb said, still standing where he was.

"Food, clothes, some boots," Kelly said.

"Slippers," Denis corrected. They looked at one another.

"Fine," Kelly said, "Slippers. Better than bare feet."

"Comfy," Denis said.

"Fine," I said, shaking my head, "Give me a hand." Denis followed me over, and we pulled the overstuffed packs from off the horses and hefted them into the cart. He and Julea went about arranging the load while Kelly and I took the horses around to the steerage and started lashing their harnesses to the shafts. Kelly looked up at Rohb.

"Did you want to give us a hand here?" he said.

"Can't," Rohb said, "Guard duty."

"Guard duty?"

"Aye. Keeping an eye on our resident quisling," Rohb said. Kelly looked at him curiously as he turned his head to Aeryk, then back. "Seems our little lordship here has been busy swapping messages with our host back in the castle there for a while. Talked about things like how an ambassador was coming to Clemons and then how there was a secret way out of Castle Sterling. Things like that."

Kelly shot a look over to me. I nodded. "It's true," I said, "Julea uncovered the whole thing earlier tonight. He's admitted it."

Even in the dim light, I watched as a terrible look passed over Kelly's face. It was as if all of the horrors of the last few days played through his mind in flashes, all from a new viewpoint. He turned, his hand reaching inside his robe to what I'm sure was his sword, but I caught his arm before he got to it.

"Don't," I said, and he turned to look at me. "The princess is withholding judgment," I continued, emphasizing the word 'princess.' His body shifted as he consciously forced himself to relax. I let go of his arm, and we went back to affixing the harnesses. I could see that he was still processing what he had heard, and so for the next few minutes, we worked in silence.

“That’s very funny,” blurted Denis, his voice shattering the stillness as he climbed up onto the driver’s bench from the opposite side of the cart. Rohb, Kelly and I all looked up at him with a mix of shock and irritation. “No, think about it, Kelly, it’s kind of hilarious,” he said. He sat down on the driver’s bench and looked at us from one to the other.

I watched as Kelly’s furrowed brow suddenly began to relax, and a sad smirk appeared on his mouth. He leaned heavily on the horse’s flank and bowed his head, shaking it in a slow, sorry, back and forth motion. A humorless chuckle rumbled from his throat. I looked up at Rohb, but he was no help as he appeared to be as dumbfounded as I was. Even Julea, now standing in the cart just behind him, looked back and forth between the men with a look of confusion on her face.

“Oh, you stupid, stupid, blue-blooded idiot,” Kelly muttered. Through a gap in the wooden panel separating the inside of the cart from the driver’s area, Aeryk’s eyes were now visible, looking toward him curiously. “Tell me,” Kelly said more loudly, his eyes in Lord Aeryk's direction, “These messages. Were they sealed? Signet rings and wax or something of that sort?”

Aeryk slowly rose, standing where he was at the front

of the cart, wilted and silent.

"He couldn't have," Rohb said, "'Cause he pretended to be the king."

Kelly continued, never taking his eyes off Aeryk, "So of course, you didn't get a seal on the replies, right?"

"No," the marquess replied, his voice barely more than a whisper. "I couldn't ask for one since I didn't use one. It was good faith."

Denis started to laugh, stopping after a moment when he saw that he was the only one.

"Good faith," Kelly spat, tugging the last strap into place on the horse and then turning to Aeryk. "Not good faith on your part," Kelly said, his stare cold and hard. "And it turns out not on his part either. That man, the one you were dealing with? The one that had us all imprisoned and beaten? He's not even Mathu," Kelly said.

We all turned and looked at him, aghast. Well, all of us but Denis. He started laughing again.

"Full on right," he cackled, "We saw the guy in the king's bed; the same man you all saw in the throne room. Absolutely not Mathu. I've seen the real Mathu. I know the real Mathu. Hell's bells, he shook my hand and paid me once.. He's also irretrievably pissed at me and would have me strung up on site. So yeah, I know him, and you know what? That?" he pointed toward the castle, "Not the same guy."

"That's impossible," Aeryk said, finding his voice for

the first time in a long while.

"Afraid he's right," Kelly said, "To get the gems back we had to go into the royal bedchamber at the top of the tower. We saw him sleeping. Also, during the search, we looked inside an armoire in a storage closet. It was a display cabinet and inside was a custom suit of royal armor—"

"It was very fancy," Denis agreed.

"— that was all the wrong proportions for the man that imprisoned us," Kelly continued as if uninterrupted, "I for a moment thought that we were in the wrong tower until we saw him in his bed. Whoever he is, he's taken the place of whoever it is that does live there. The real Mathu, I expect. Think about it. Even the pirate knew something was wrong, remember? When we were in the throne room? The strangeness of his conversation with the king? He must have known something wasn't right."

"Why not say anything?" Julea asked.

"Pirate," Kelly said, his tone matter of fact, "I'm sure he was more interested in his payment than who was paying. And when he was told he wasn't getting his ship, that was positively all he was thinking about. Besides, who was he going to tell? The people he just helped kidnap or the lying piece of garbage he did it for that was reneging on the deal?"

"Speaking of that," Denis said, glancing back toward the castle, "We really need to get moving, you take me? Monks? Early risers? All of that?"

Kelly looked over at me, and I gave him a nod to indicate that my piece of the task was complete. In less time than it takes to tell, we all settled in the wagon while Kelly and Denis drove, directing us off into the forest.

The road twisted back on itself after a few yards and then began a slow descent. In a brief time, the distant glow of Chateau Flint dropped behind the hill rising behind us and was out of sight. I had stayed at the back of the wagon to play rear guard, watching behind us, but once the darkness took the place of our capture from my view, I felt myself relax slightly. The rain had been slowing little bit by little bit since Kelly and Denis had arrived, and it was now impossible to tell if it was still falling or if we were still getting the drips from the drenched branches above us. Turning my back to the road behind, I surveyed our little group. Kelly and Denis, in their stolen cloaks and with their hoods once again enshrouding them, were only dim outlines in the darkness where they sat on the driver's bench, guiding the horses through the night. The animals were moving slowly, but more from their inability to see in the murk than from the weight of the cart. Aeryk was seated back in the front corner; he wore his blanket wrapped entirely around him and kept his head down. Rohb sat across from him, ever watchful. Julea was opposite me, her head back as she watched the shadows of the branches above move past. I saw the small wound on her throat from where the pirate's blade had bitten into her and winced inwardly. *That shouldn't have happened*, my mind chastised me.

"Okay," I said, changing the subject at least for myself. "You said there was food?"

The shadows driving the cart exchanged some brief words I couldn't hear, then Kelly called back, "We grabbed what we could. It's no feast, but right now I imagine that doesn't matter."

All four of the packs, for there had been two on each of the horses, seemed to be overstuffed; the ties holding them closed pulled tightly. I untied the one nearest to me, and wads of cloth spilled out. I pulled them loose and found they were four monks robes not very dissimilar from what Kelly and Denis were wearing. I looked at them for a long moment. This is disrespectful, if not outright blasphemy, I thought. Just then, a chill breeze swept through the cart, and an unbidden shiver passed through the four of us. I looked down again at the robes and shrugged. I'll worry about my soul later, I thought, if there is a later. I handed one to Julea, a larger one to Rohb, and tossed one up near Aeryk, who didn't react. I shrugged into the one I had kept for myself, draping it over the tatters of my clothes and misfit leather vest. It was blissfully dry, didn't smell like a horse, and took away the chill that had been ever-present since our escape. In other words, for a brief moment, it was the best piece of clothing in the world. I may have moaned; it felt so good. I opened the next pack and found the “slippers” the two had mentioned. They were the monk’s footwear – short boots of soft sheepskin with a second layer on the sole. A leather strap wrapped around the upper part from the ankle to the top, making them effectively fit almost any foot size. I distributed these as well and found that I had been wrong about the robes. After being barefooted for hours on cold stones, and on gravel, and in the rain; putting the ’slippers’ on convinced me that *these* were truly the best pieces of clothing in the world.

The third pack revealed the food; a random assortment of fruits and nuts and bread that was slightly stale, though that didn’t matter in the least. At the sight of it, Rohb and Julea moved forward, and we quickly divided it up as evenly as possible, barely containing the almost animal-like hunger that rose within us. Julea took an apple, a few nuts, and a chunk of the bread and brought it over to Aeryk. He looked up, startled, and stared at her.

“You should eat,” she said. There was no edge to her voice, no further accusation, and no condemnation. She put the food on the robe lying where I had tossed it. “An honest fool,” she repeated her earlier summation, “but I believe I understand.” She turned and came back toward me, stopping only to look over her shoulder and say, “And put that robe on. You look a mess. For heaven’s sake, man, you’re the son of a duke." She returned to her original spot and settled back down. The marquess didn't move for some minutes, but eventually, he donned the robes and shoes, settled back into the corner, and ate.

I tugged at the fourth pack and pulled it open. Inside, nestled in some scraps of cloth for padding and secured with twine, were four bottles of wine and the box of gems from Castle Sterling. I looked at Julea. She looked at it for a long moment before she looked up at me, and there was a look of satisfaction on her face.

"Of course," she said.

"Oh hey," Denis called from the front, "I have dibs on one of those bottles."

"We'll share," Kelly said, holding out his hand.

"I knew we should have taken more," Denis mumbled as I placed one of the bottles in Kelly's outstretched hand.

Taking a second bottle, I opened it and passed it to Julea.

We slept. Well, what I am most sure of is that I slept, but when I opened my eyes again, I saw that the others were still sleeping and likely had been for some time. The exhaustion of our adventures had, it seemed, finally caught up to us. I could see a hint of light in the sky now, through the heavy clouds, but it didn't appear to be dawn yet. I also saw what looked like an animated exchange between Kelly and Denis up on the driver's bench. It ended a moment later, after some barely-restrained talking and hand waving, when Kelly stood and climbed down into the back of the cart, leaving Denis alone with the reins. He carefully made his way past the sleeping forms of Rohb, Aeryk, and Julea and sat down wearily on the other side of the coffee-scented sack against which I was leaning. He groaned as he settled in, and I imagined that the mistreatment he had gone through was making itself known now that we had a moment to rest.

"You trust him?" I asked, nodding toward Denis.

Kelly glanced in that direction, then looked back over to me. "Self-interest is a good motivator," he said, "and right now it is in all of our best interests to get where we're going." He paused a minute, considering. "But yeah," he finished, leaning his head back against the wooden side panel and closing his eyes, "I do. There's more to him than meets the eye. He seems to want people to think that there's less, but I have a feeling that's just for show."

I raised an eyebrow. "You've been doing very well at picking who to trust," I said, dripping in a hint of sarcasm.

He didn't react at first; then I saw his mouth twitch with a suppressed grin. "I am running a solid half and half, aren't I?" he said with a sigh. I considered him. His mop of dark-brown hair had been finger-combed in the rain and had dried in a haphazard, swept back style, unruly strands dropping randomly on his forehead. The bruise on his face, so dark just a day ago – was it already a day? –, was now only a faint shadow across his cheek. I leaned back against the cart side and looked up at the sky.

“May I ask you something?” I said.

“You can always ask,” he said.

“Why did you go back for those emeralds? Seriously, I don’t believe for a second that the agreement was going to hinge on a small box of semi-precious gems, and I don’t think you do either. But you went back and risked your life for them. I don’t understand.”

Very subtly, with a minimum of movement, he looked around the cart. The others were still very much asleep, and thus satisfied, he closed his eyes again and leaned his head back.

“Have you ever heard the old stories of the founding of the Empire?” he asked, his voice quiet.

“Sure. I heard about them as a girl. Everyone does; parents have been telling those tales for generations. Probably since there has been an Empire.”

“Do you believe them?”

“Of course not. They’re legends more than history. Myths. The city being raised from the sea. Fire from the heavens defeating invaders. There may be some truth to some tiny part of it, but..., no. Not really believe. How could anyone?”

“You’ve happened on a salient point. ‘Some truth to

some of it,' you just said. And you're right, just not about what parts may or may not be valid. In the tales, the mages of old conjured the miracles you just described with the aid of magical stones and such. Well, Kelian emeralds are the magical stones."

"Are you trying to tell me that the magic in the stories is true? Or that people believe that it is?"

"First of all, anything we don't understand is going to seem like magic. The first person to discover fire probably called it magic. So no, I'm not saying the 'magic' is real. But I am saying that there is truth to the stories. Stones and other such that have abilities that we don't understand."

I involuntarily looked over at the bag that held the wooden box of gems. "So those emeralds...," I started.

"The empress believes that a mine that was dug recently in Ronald's lands is a source of Kelian emeralds. Those," he nodded his head toward the bag. "She believes that if the Empire can get them and figure out how to put them to use, the Empire will be able to recapture the power it had in the old stories."

My mind reeled. That the mystical gems in the stories, the ones the ancient wizards used to do everything from immolating whole armies to flying to changing the weather – really anything they wanted to do – were real? It seemed unbelievable. That the Empress, or Julea, or Kelly believed it was confounding. That there might be a box of them in the cart with us was almost too much.

"Magical Kelian gemstones," I muttered.

"It's still not magic. It's just a little outside of what we can explain. But what Kelian emeralds are above all is dangerous, even if just because of what people believe. They can't be left in the wrong hands," Kelly said.

"So you went to get the box back. I understand now. It didn't make sense that you would leave for something so trivial and put the princess in danger. It wasn't trivial."

"Not at all. It was potentially catastrophic."

I leaned back, still trying to make my mind accept what I had just learned.

"And you're wrong about one other thing," he said, "I didn't leave the princess in danger. I left her in the best hands of all. She had you."

I looked over to see him staring at me, the gray-blue eyes unblinking. "Thanks," I said.

He rolled his head back and closed his eyes. "So I guess my trust count is better than you thought," he said as a broad grin crossed his face.

I woke again later to Kelly's gentle hand, nudging my shoulder. "Trouble," he said as I looked up at him blearily. Suddenly I was awake, coming to my feet and following him as he jumped off the back of the cart to the ground. Julea and Aeryk were at opposite corners in the front of the cart, both awake and watchful. She held a short sword that Kelly had given her, apparently having found another blade that I hadn't seen yet during his time in the tower. Rohb was now up on the otherwise empty driver's bench, splitting his time between watching the road and watching the marquess and the princess — each for very different reasons. I followed as Kelly led me several yards away from the cart, further up the road. We crept up to where Denis crouched behind a large bush. Seeing us, he waved us over, turning back to peering through the branches.

"I think we found your pirate friends," he whispered as we crouched near him. He made a gesture with his head, and Kelly and I leaned around the bush to see what he was talking about. Off the side of the road was a fairly large camp nestled in a small clearing. A fire was burning low, generating neither smoke nor much heat, while a cluster of men gathered around it. Some were standing, some sitting on logs or the ground, but they were all dressed similarly to the men that had grabbed us in the forest and brought us here. I looked up at Kelly, who seemed to be intently looking at the group as if waiting to see something specific. A moment later, from a large tent to the rear of the clearing, a tall, dark-skinned man emerged. Edword. Kelly pulled me back out of sight.

"The man is like bad weather," I muttered, "He shows up just in time to spoil everything."

“Edword Ribald,” Denis muttered. “Hell’s bells. You people are nothing but trouble.”

I looked at him sternly. “You are free to go, you know,” I said.

He looked at me, and a devilish smirk settled on his face. “Don’t think you get me,” he said, “I absolutely love trouble.”

“Shh,” Kelly hissed. He waved us back a few feet and looked at Denis. “How far to the docks, do you reckon?” he asked.

“We’re just a few hundred yards from the beach. From there the docks are probably another couple hundred. Pretty close,” Denis said.

“Why do you suppose Edword and a cluster of his men would be here?” Kelly said, this time looking at me.

“I don’t—” I began, and then suddenly I knew. “He wants his ship!” I said, cutting my own sentence short.

Kelly nodded. “I think you’re completely right. And he’s about to try to take it if he can,” he said.

Denis looked from one to the other of us. “So what?” he said, “I thought the idea was that we take the boat. Screw that guy.”

“I agree,” I said, stunned to find us on the same side of the issue.

“Or,” Kelly said, extending the ‘o’ for two beats, “Edword might just be an option we didn’t consider.”

"Excuse me?" I said. I cast a look at Denis who had the same look on his face that I was sure I had.

Kelly ran his fingers through his hair again and took a breath. "Okay," he said, shooting a quick look to me, "we may have to reset my trust counter again, but here we go. You're welcome to join or not." He stood up and stepped out from behind the brush, walking toward the clearing.

"Hell's bells," Denis snarled. He looked at me, then back to the retreating form of Kelly. He dropped his head and shook it, then he stood up and with a quick sprint, caught up to the warrior.

I watched them go before I turned away. I had taken two steps toward the cart when a quiet voice echoed in my thoughts. I stopped.

"To the danger," my father's voice said.

I hesitated another moment, then turned and ran to catch up to Kelly and Denis.

CHAPTER NINE

– DENIS –

"Parley," Kelly said.

We were standing about fifteen feet away from the small campsite with our hands in the air. Kelly was just ahead of me, and Dana stood to my left. She had rushed up at the last-minute right as the cluster of pirates around the fire noticed our approach. For a long moment, no one had moved, which I credit to the fact that what we were doing was so unbelievably stupid that they couldn't exactly decide if it was actually happening. I empathized; I couldn't be sure it was happening either.

"Parley," Kelly said again. I'll give him this; he was committed to the insanity. I'm sure he was aware that – presuming we survived this in any meaningful way – I was going to have some very specific comments for him.

Several of the pirates had stood now, their hands on the hilts of their blades or whatever other implements of destruction they carried with them and they approached us cautiously. I wondered, academically, how far I could get before there was an arrow in my back. I mean, I didn't genuinely intend to run, but it never hurts to consider the options.

“A damn fool,” came a deep voice from behind the cluster of men. I glanced over at Dana to see that, while she was keenly watching Kelly, her eyes would dart to-and-fro across the pirate band. I looked back in time to see the tall figure of Edword step to the front of others. He was actually about my height, his dark hair bunched into braids which he had collected in a bunch on the back of his head. A vest of dark leather armor covered his chest, though his prominently muscled arms were bare. A curved cutlass, longer than average, hung in a sheath on his left hip while the hilt of a dagger peeked out from behind his right side. He stopped just in front of his men, his arms akimbo.

“Seriously?” I breathed, noting the stance. Dana and Kelly ignored me.

“You think you can get parley from me?” the tall pirate said.

“I think, everything considered, you owe me at least that,” Kelly said, “And, I also think that you don’t have much of a reason not to talk. It isn’t like your employer back there is suddenly going to change his mind on your fee if you try to take us back.”

Edword’s eyes narrowed. “But what is in it for me?”

“That’s why we’re going to parley,” Kelly said, dropping his hands. As if on cue, one of the pirates to

Edword's right side lunged forward, his sword coming free from its sheath as he did. My hands went inside my robe to the hilts of the daggers I wore there, but as I got my hands on them, I realized I needn't have bothered. Kelly's robe swirled, and the long-sword we had purloined from the king's chambers flashed out. He met the attacker mid-stride, taking the impact of the other's stroke at the joint of his blade and its cross-guard. The sword seemed to spin like the spoke of a wagon wheel around the point of contact, guiding the cutlass up and out of range as it did. Kelly was already moving to the side, passing beneath the locked blades until both he and his sword were to the other man's right. He spun on his lead foot, whipped the sword around and struck hard at the exposed back of the attacker's head, just below the skull. It was a strike that could have taken the head clean off, and would have but that he struck with the flat of the blade. The impact still sounded hellacious, though; the sword let out a metallic ring that mixed with a dull wet thud from the contact with the skull. The man dropped to the ground like a bag of butcher's meats. Kelly placed his feet and swept the blade into a low guard position.

"Damn," I said. Because really, all of that took place in less than two heartbeats.

I looked around, fully expecting a wave of cutlass-wielding pirates to be surging at us. Dana had stepped up even with my left side, her blade also ready. But no wave came. The pirate captain stood looking down at the fallen man with a confused look of disgust and anger, and the other men stood where they were.

“Why not kill him?” he said. The men clustered behind him were on edge, it was clear to see, but not another one of them had even started to draw steel. Each was watching their leader with what I’ll charitably describe as ‘eager intent.’

Kelly held his guard, resting a steady glare on the pirate. “I came to talk, Edword,” he said, “I will fight if that’s what we have to do, but I’d rather not. There are more important things on the table right now.”

Edword considered him for a long moment. “I see your point,” he said finally. “Fine then. Important things first.” With one motion that was almost too fast to follow, he grabbed the dagger from the back of his belt and threw it, sinking it deep into the exposed back of the fallen man. The body twitched twice, let out a groan, and went limp. Edword turned toward his crew.

“Discipline!” he called loudly so that the assembled group of men could hear. “No one, and I mean no one, acts without my say so! You dogs hear me?”

In a synchronous chant, the assembled pirates shouted, “Aye, sir!” I’ve heard church choirs with less harmony than that group of pirates, honestly.

Kelly watched the display without reaction. Then

slowly, he let his sword drop to his side and relaxed his stance as the pirate turned back to face him.

"Second," Edword said, "we parley." He turned and, pausing to pull his dagger from the dead body, walked back toward the tent from where he had appeared. Kelly reversed his grip on his sword as three of the pirates broke away from the crowd and approached each of us individually. He handed the blade to the closest one to him, who took it with what I think was a kind of reverence before turning to follow behind the pirate captain. The other two approached Dana and me expectantly. Kelly gave us a knowing nod as if that made giving away our weapons an okay thing to do. I hesitated but noticed that Dana had already surrendered her short-sword. With a grumble, I reached inside my robe and unbuckled the bandoleer that held my daggers.

"Careful with those," I said to the pirate, "I just got them, and I'm going to want them back." He didn't react at all but just took the strap in his hand and retreated with his friends.

Kelly stepped over the corpse and closer to Dana and me. "Okay, the rules for parley are pretty simple," he said, "Only the participants – Edword, as captain, and me, since I called for it – will talk. We will have an equal delegation with us, so he will be allowed two men since I have the two of you. Whatever happens, accord or no, we are guaranteed free passage in and out of the meeting as long as we follow the protocol. Whatever we do—"

"We don't mention the others," Dana said. Kelly nodded and gave her a wink.

"Do we know if he knows about your magic rocks?" I asked. They both froze, fixing a stare on me. I looked back and forth between them.

"Oh please," I said with a puffed sigh, "I didn't survive this long without knowing that the time to listen is when people clearly don't want to be heard. You two and your little chit-chat in the back of the cart last night were practically sending up a signal that said, 'important info here.'"

Kelly looked at me for a long moment. It was not the best timing, but it suddenly occurred to me that if he wanted to keep these things secret, he would likely have no problem doing to me what the pirate had just done to the dead man. But true to form, Kelly just gave a resigned look to Dana, shook his head slightly, and then continued. "We don't; to answer your question. I think we keep that quiet too."

There was movement behind him, and we looked over to see that the pirates had formed a path from us to the tent. They stood at attention and intervals on each side, leading straight to the entrance.

"Here we go," Kelly said.

"Have I mentioned," Dana said to him under her breath, "how you take me to the most interesting places?"

"You know, I said the same thing," I said.

"Quiet, or I'll go back and trade you both for the grumpy Talhas," Kelly said.

Moments later, we found ourselves standing inside the big tent into which Edword had disappeared. It was oblong, like a squashed circle, and made of several layers of heavy canvas with a layered flap drawn back as the entrance in the middle of one side. Rugs and tarps of various sizes were scattered on the floor, overlapping one another and completely covering the ground beneath. The result was a relatively soft floor. Whatever they usually kept inside had been moved out; only two tables, one against the canvas 'wall' opposite the entrance, one slightly larger in the middle, and two chairs remained. On the smaller table, our weapons rested alongside the sword and dagger that Edword had carried. A coiled whip and two cutlasses joined these toward the far end. Dana and I were standing at one end of the space while across from us two of the pirate's men, probably his lieutenants and owners of the extra weapons on the table, mirrored us. Kelly and Edword sat on the two chairs opposite one another at the table in the center. A small lantern sat between them and to one side of the table.

"Take an' tell me, then," Edword said, wasting no time once they had settled onto the chairs, "why I'm even listening to you right now. What can you, in your stolen holy robes and broga, have to bargain with me?"

Kelly started, his voice calm and even. "I know what you want. We were there when your deal with the king was, so to speak, altered."

"Broken," the pirate interrupted.

"Broken," Kelly corrected, "I agree. But somewhere not far from here, there is a ship that he had built according to your design that he's decided to keep for his own. We will get it back for you."

I turned to Dana, but her only reaction was a small twitch in one eye.

"Bollocks," Edword said. "If, and when, I want my ship – my ship –," he emphasized, "I will march my crew up the beach and take it. You got nothin' to offer me."

Kelly cocked his head slightly. "True, you could do that," he replied, "but probably after a big fight that will likely result in your crew getting hurt and maybe even your new ship getting damage. Then, you will have to fight your way out of the harbor and off to open sea in whatever condition that leaves you in. Furthermore, you have to watch your back here in the northern seas for who knows how long even if you do succeed."

"Don't scare me," Edword scoffed.

"Or," Kelly raised a finger. "You could let me get it for you. No danger to your crew, and I give you a personal guarantee that there will be no damage to the ship."

"You bluffin' me."

"Possible, but what do you have to lose? If we get killed, maybe we take a few of them with us, which makes it easier on you. If we succeed, you get what's yours free and clear. And either way, your reputation stays intact," Kelly folded his hands on the table and waited. Edword observed him before speaking again.

"What's the catch?"

"Safe passage back to the Lochhaven," Kelly said, folding his arms, "for my companions and me. Unmolested and uncontested."

Suddenly it dawned on me why he had been so specific about not mentioning the other three. He didn't know it now, but if Edword realized the heir to the Empire was one of us, the opportunity for profit might overwhelm his good sense. Until they sealed the agreement, both of our high-born friends would be at risk. Kelly wanted the promise first before that could happen.

"Are you for real?" Edword asked, "You putting your necks on the line – and Mathu's guard is not a joke – for a free ride south?"

"Just what I said," Kelly said. Then he leaned a little forward, looked directly in the pirate captain's eyes, and said, "Rules of parley are that we don't lie, so let's get this out of the way. That's not Mathu, and we both know it."

The pirate stood and paced back and forth several times between the table and his men, his arms crossed while his left-hand stroked his chin. Finally, he stopped and put both hands on the back of the chair. He glared at Kelly across the table.

“I don’t trust a traitor,” he said flatly.

“You haven’t heard the whole story,” Kelly replied calmly. He allowed a slight grin to crease his lips. “On the surface, I shouldn’t trust a pirate either. But we both know that there’s more to that story too, *ist est nicht*?”

For the tiniest sliver of a second, Edword’s eyes flared at the foreign phrase. Then a solemn look settled on his face.

“We have an accord, Blackcrow,” he said gravely.

“We do, pirate.”

Kelly stood while Edword retrieved his dagger from the side table. He slid the blade across the thicker part of his palm, by the thumb, and then reversed his grip on the knife and handed it, hilt first, to Kelly. He took it, repeated the process on his own hand, and then they shook hands with a steady grip.

I looked at Dana who, reluctantly, returned the gaze this time. I rolled my eyes, and for the first time, was rewarded with a smile. I was, it should be known, very pleased with myself.

Kelly walked over to us, wrapping a small piece of white cloth around the gash on his palm. He looked up at us with a smile. “So, that went well,” he said.

Dana glared at him. “I thought,” she said, “when you

showed yourself to the pirates, that it was to get their help, not commit us to the same suicidal thing we were already going to do without them. What are you thinking?"

"I'm thinking that I don't want a war on two fronts. The last thing we need is to be taking over the ship from the guard and have the pirates arrive to fight us too. That's more chaos than I think we want," he said.

"I love chaos," I said.

"In the right dosage, yes," he said, "But not too much."

"If there's a right dosage, then it isn't chaos," I retorted.

Dana ignored the whole exchange and instead continued, "so we're still going to take a ship from a troop of the royal guard without help,"

Kelly snapped his fingers, resulting in a tiny wince as his fingers clapped on the fresh wound in his hand. He turned back to the pirates.

"Captain? Would I be correct in thinking that you still have the equipment that you took from us when you took us from the road?" he said.

Edword appeared to resist a reflexive need to lie, then said, "We do. Spoils of victory."

"Sure, but we're going to need that stuff back. If it's not too much trouble," Kelly said nonchalantly, "And possibly some livery for my new friend here?" He jutted a thumb at me.

"Wasn't part of the deal," the pirate said. They stared at one another for a moment.

"I'll tell you what," Kelly said, "That long-sword on the table belongs to the king. Well, one king or another. It was taken directly from his bedchamber. I'm sure that just the gems in it are worth more than the modest value of our equipment. It's yours. Consider it a balance for this little additional request."

Edword reached over and picked up the long-sword. I hadn't clearly seen it in the light except for the brief flash when Kelly sapped the now dead man outside, but as the pirate raised it for inspection, I got a much better look. The blade was a mirrored silver finish, terminating at a gold cross-piece inlaid with silver etching and three gemstones, a deep blue one on each end and a larger diamond-cut red stone in the middle. Silver wire wrapped the handle, and the golden pommel had a single yellow stone around an inch across centered in it. If I had taken it, it could have been one of the single biggest scores of my unsavory career. As it was, the pirate waved it around casually, a pensive look on his face.

"I realize you're partial to cutlasses," Kelly said. He made it sound as if they were haggling over a horse, which struck me as funny, considering that we had not long ago watched the pirate casually kill one of his crewmen.

"Deal," he said finally, before turning to the men

opposite us. “Take an’ bring the two gray chests in here. And before you bury Ewan, bring his clothes too.” He shot a look over at me with a disturbing smile. “Yeah,” he continued, “That’s ‘bout the right size. Sorry for the hole and the stains.” The two men snapped a nod and left ahead of Edword who, slipping the royal blade into his belt, collected everything on the table – except my daggers which were still in their sheaths – and walked out, leaving us alone. And almost entirely weaponless, I should note.

I tried for a gracious smile before I turned to Dana and let my eyes go wide. Kelly watched Edword go and turned back to us.

“We need to go get the others,” he said.

“Definitely,” Dana agreed, “and it might be wise to tell them what we ‘aren’t’ saying, too.”

“You mean the part about the magic rocks, the part about her being a Yorchian princess, or some specific combination of those?” I asked quietly. They both glared at me.

“Let’s just say it would be better if we didn’t talk about anything,” Kelly said finally.

“Are you planning on knocking Aeryk out or gagging him?” I said, “Because it seems like that’s a tall order in his case.”

“I’ll go,” Dana said. Just then, four pirates came into the tent in sets of two, each carrying a large wooden chest between them. They set them on the floor opposite us and walked back out without a word.

“They seem unfriendly,” I said.

“We are fresh out of the friendly, cuddly pirates you appear to be looking for,” Dana said, her voice flat.

“Whoa,” I said, “was that humor? I think that was humor.”

She turned to me, and I swear I saw the hint of a smile, but then another pirate came in and tossed a pile of miscellaneous clothing on the table. He sneered at me, then turned and stalked out.

“He was especially cuddly,” I murmured.

I walked over to the table and picked through the clothing, which was standard pirate livery – a bleached loose fit cotton shirt, dark britches, a heavy leather vest, and cavalier boots. I tossed off the monk’s clothing and got dressed. The shirt had a large red stain where the dagger had been sticking out of the dead man, but once I got it on, the leather vest mostly covered it; the hole from the knife was efficient and therefore small. The boots even fit comfortably, though I have to say that the holy slippers were nicer. I strapped my bandoleer over the armor and turned back to Kelly, who was shaking his head, and Dana, who had her hand over her eyes.

“What?” I asked.

“Nothing at all,” Kelly said. He looked at Dana and

smirked. I noticed a flush on her cheeks.

“Denis, we need to know the layout of the docks. There any way you can go for a quick walk?” Kelly asked.

I shrugged. “I’ll go have a look, anything specific I should be looking for?”

“Anything you can tell me, but don’t get caught. And don’t dawdle. Sooner than we like, I expect our host back there will come around to the idea that we came this way,” he said. He swung open the first of the crates and started to rummage through the supplies as he spoke.

“I could go fetch the others since I’m heading out,” I said.

“Lady Dana suggested she do that,” he replied, looking over at her. She nodded. “They can get changed while we wait for you,” he finished.

“So,” I said, scratching my cheek absently, “do you think Edword is going to feel like you cheated when she shows up with three more people?”

Kelly glanced over at the entrance to the tent before he answered. “It’s possible; but as far as he knows it doesn’t change the terms of our deal, so he may not even mention it.”

Dana looked sidelong at him. “Unless, of course, he realizes exactly who they are.”

“Right,” Kelly said with a grin, “Which is specifically what we’ve agreed not to tell him. Not yet, at least.” He stopped, bent to reach deep into the crate, and retrieved a black satchel with a shoulder strap. He pulled open the fasteners and rummaged inside as if he were taking inventory. He smiled.

"What, did you pack a lunch?" I asked.

He looked at me and rolled his eyes. "Go," he said, "time is wasting. Shoo."

I winked at Dana and slipped out of the tent.

If I had to guess – and with the cloud cover preventing me from seeing the sun clearly, I did – I was back in around an hour. The same two pirate watchmen that saw me go greeted me at the edge of the camp with a nod as I returned and then pointed me to a smaller tent off to the right. I entered and found the whole group again together. Kelly wore black from head to toe, including his leather armor, pauldrons, and bracers. The pieces were mostly unadorned, but several subtle touches were reminiscent of feathers. These reminded me again that I thought 'blackcrow' was an excellent nickname, whatever these people all thought about it. Rohb and Aeryk wore combinations of blue and black, which I figured must be a standard uniform in Lochhaven. Dana and Julea had loose fit tunics and britches. Over these, they wore armored leather corsets, boots, and vambraces, all of which were of the highest quality. As I entered, they turned my way.

"You all clean up pretty well," I said.

"Good timing," Kelly said as he saw me. It was close in the small tent and having six of us in there didn't help. Dana and Julea sat to one side on a small bench while Rohb sat on the other side on a crate. Aeryk stood by Kelly opposite the entrance. "What did you see?" he asked.

I dropped onto the crate next to the big man, which I'm sure made him no end of happy with me. I explained, "Well, we're not exactly set up for success. I went through the forest northwesterly for a few hundred yards – all uphill, mind you – until I got to a spot where I could get a good view. From there I could see the coast pretty well. Further out, I could see that the beach cuts in, around, and back out along a narrow peninsula so that it makes a small cove or a bay. I shouldn't say beach; it's more just a narrow space between the forest and the water, maybe a couple dozen yards at the widest between the water and the brush. The bay itself is almost black; it's so blue, so I'm guessing that the water gets deep almost immediately; maybe we're on something like the top of an underwater cliff or something. Anyway, the real news is, there's a full-on settlement of the army in the cove – cabins, bunkhouse, the whole mess. It surrounds a couple of very long docks that stretch out into the bay. I couldn't figure how the docks worked at first, but it looks like the pylons support them at an angle instead of straight down. Kind of like a big shelf, you take me?"

Aeryk, who was listening with a solemn look on his

face, nodded. He seemed less timid than he had since we found out that he was stupid, and now he spoke up. "The old stories say that the Superiors don't stop at the water's edge, they're just hiding. Maybe that means that the mountains continue under water. Building the docks with supports like you describe off of such a thing would make sense," he said.

It's still surprising to me how much you can learn by watching someone closely. Aeryk was standing near Kelly and seemed to be mirroring his expressions and even his stance a bit. I decided that they must have had a discussion and that the Blackcrow had somehow gotten him out of his guilt some, which was good because we needed all hands, of course, even if I wasn't quite sure that he deserved it.

"Did you see the ship?" Kelly asked.

I blew out a breath. "Yeah, I saw it. At least I think I saw it," I said. "Just at the edge of that narrow peninsula, maybe half a mile from where I was and as far from the dock as you could be and still be in the cove, there's a ship moored. I'm going to go out on a limb and say she's the ship we're looking for because that thing is very strange looking. She's got an odd-shaped bow; it almost looks like it's not entirely in the water at the front. And she's completely black. I don't mean shadowy; I mean it's as black as pitch. Or like your clothes there."

"That does sound like it fits," Julea said, "but you saw no other ships? None of the rest of the navy? There should have been at least two; there were two left after the attempt to take us in the bay at Clemons."

I shook my head. "Nope," I said, "just the one. And like I was saying, it's out by the mouth of the bay; nowhere near the docks." I kicked at the cloth covering on the floor. Unlike the big tent we were in when I left, only a single piece of heavy canvas was spread on the ground, so pushing it aside revealed the dirt beneath us. I drew one of my daggers and gripped it upside down. Leaning over, I sketched the layout of the bay in the earth using its small pommel. "The problem," I continued, marking the docks and the location of the ship, "is that there is no way we can get over there without going through the guards. They're patrolling around their port constantly, and you have to go through there to get up the peninsula. The only other way to the ship would be by boat, but even if we had a launch to go across the bay itself, they'd see us and be on us before we got close."

"Probably why it's moored where it is. They're trying to protect it in case the pirates move in force," Dana said.

"We're screwed," Rohb grumbled, optimistic as ever.

Aeryk stared at the ground as if I had hidden the answer there. "If there were some way to distract the guards...," he began.

"All of them," Julea added severely.

"Sure, I know it's not an easy thing," he said, "but hear me out. If something could distract them and draw them over here," he pointed with the end of the staff he had been leaning on to a spot that would be a short way inland, "we could get across the bay and onto the ship."

"That would have to be a big distraction," Dana said, "we would need two or three launches to get all the pirates over there."

"But we don't," Julea said, "we just need to get enough of them over to take the ship. We can pick up the rest down the coast. Remember, Denis just said that they don't seem to have any ships of their own."

I listened to all of this, and it seemed like they were getting a little more excited than they should be. Trying to be a voice of reason, I said, "So, we distract all the guards; the whole platoon or platoons or whatever. Then we sneak ourselves, probably Edword, and a handful of pirates across the narrow part of the bay and onto the ship, deal with whatever guards may be there, then we speed off down the coast and pick up everyone else." I glanced from one face to the other. "You don't see any problems with that? I mean, this is your serious plan?"

"Got a better one?" Rohb rumbled at me, which was the most positive thing he'd said about any plan to that point, so I considered that high praise.

"I don't," I admitted, "but come on. Let me just hit the highlights here. We first need a launch or something; which we don't have."

"The pirates do," Julea said, seeming to surprise herself. "I heard them. They kept some of the boats in which they landed here originally. Apparently, they use them for storage for the camp."

"Okay, fine," I said, "that's a point. And for reference, Your Highness, it is easier to plan if we know all of our resources."

Dana glowered at me, but Julea nodded politely and said, "I take your point, dungeon rat."

Rohb snickered. It was a disturbing sound.

"But there's a giant hole here in the room, folks," I said, "what in the world is going to attract the entire regiment of guards away from the docks?"

Silence fell, and I looked around the room, stopping at Kelly. He had been standing completely still and staring at my drawing for the entire conversation, though I was pretty sure that he was really somewhere else. The silence lengthened until finally, he broke it.

"Leave that to me," he said.

"Here we go," muttered Rohb, dropping his head.

Aeryk looked at him sternly and put his hand on his arm. "I don't know what you're thinking, but I'm utterly sure I'm not letting you go alone. I owe—"

"No one's going to do anything of the kind," Julea said, standing. "Acting as bait for a regiment of armed men for a plan that's insane from the beginning; that's ridiculous.

I forbid it."

That woman is unquestionably going to be a queen someday, I thought. I developed a whole second set of reasons not to do this right then, just because of her tone.

"I appreciate your input, Your Imperial Majesty," Kelly said, squaring up to her, "but as has been made readily apparent, I am not your subject." The two of them stood like that, all but staring one another down. For some reason, I had a vision of two wolves, figuring out who was the leader of the pack. But just as suddenly as it began, it ended as Kelly broke into a smile.

"Besides," he said, "I have no intention of acting as bait." He turned back to my sketch. "I'll talk to Edword and tell him to pick the men to go with you. There should be room for five; if it's a decent sized boat that is," he said as he stepped closer and squatted down. He pointed to the near shore. "You can set off here. Even with a bad tide, you won't have too far to go. We'll arrange a location to regroup with the rest of the pirates and me back in this direction when you get the ship; that should throw them off a little and give us more time," he said, pointing to a spot indicating a location further up the coast.

"Look, I am becoming a real fan of you and your wackiness," I said, "I've already had hours of fun musing on you jumping off a castle wall like an idiot. But if you're going to try to bait a regiment of men alone..."

Kelly looked around the room, then back at me. “You all keep saying ‘bait.’ I have no plans on baiting anyone. I’m going to terrify them.”

It was mid-afternoon by the time we had everything in place. I went back and watched the port for a while; if only to make sure there weren’t any surprises. Kelly and Julea had – after stepping apart from the rest for what I'm pretty sure was a charming discussion – both had to work to convince Edword of the plan, but only when Kelly assured him that there was no chance he or his men would be at any serious risk getting to the ship did he agree. By the time I got back, the launch was in the water and the other nine passengers – four pirates, Edword, and my companions – were waiting at the shore. Kelly stood off to one side, a black cloak draped over his armored form. I passed him as I headed toward the launch.

“You realize a bit of blue on there would bring out your eyes,” I said.

“What?”

“Nothing. I am hoping against hope you have a real plan here.”

He half grinned. “I’ll see you on the other side, kid,” he said, turning and disappearing into the treeline.

“‘Kid’,” I muttered, “whatever.”

A half an hour later, the ten of us sat bobbing in the

surf as the cold, misty wind came off the sea. Edword had afforded me a cloak; more of a blanket with a tie-off, actually; and the rest had their own which helped. The pirate, however, was having none of it and stood tall and bare-armed in the middle of the small boat peering into the distance.

“And he didn’t say what the signal would be?” he asked for what I'm sure was at least the tenth time.

“I think he said it’d be the hundredth time you ask,” Rohb growled. The pirate spun to look at him, and I saw Rohb start to stand.

“Wait,” Aeryk said suddenly. He was crouched in the bow with me, watching the bay off to our right intensely. He hadn’t spoken since we had been on the water or, more accurately, since Kelly had left. Instead, he had spent his time watching the shore and then, when we were in position, staring at the bay where the dock was. Now he leaned forward, his head edging out over the prow. A moment passed.

“There,” he said, pointing at the far side of the bay, “a tree just fell, right at the edge of the shore.”

I looked, but nothing seemed to be happening. I had just enough time to think of what I wanted to call the prince for getting jumpy about falling trees when there was a flash of what looked like green lightning from the spot where he was pointing. I blinked, the afterimage clear in my eyes, and by the time I looked again, a torrent of green and yellow flame blasted across the surface of the water in the cove. It was shaped like a cone and swirled in a funnel like a horizontal tornado as it stretched across the width of the bay. By the time it reached the opposite shore, the end of the cone was undoubtedly fifteen feet across if it was an inch.

"Holy shyte!" Edword said, stumbling back and sitting down.

The fire-blast hit the treeline on the opposite shore, and as if in response, a corresponding blast of flame exploded from there, this time launching upward at an angle into the sky. It was, if anything, more significant than the first, and since it wasn't skimming the surface of the water, it spread more widely with distance. The entire area was awash in green and yellow light. The docks, now on the opposite side of the violent blasts of flame, were utterly invisible to us.

"Hell's bells," I muttered.

I turned back to the rest of the passengers. "Row!" I yelled, amplified because I was actually as scared as balls. The pirates grabbed the oars and began to push us forward across the open mouth of the bay toward the other side. The whole time, we watched as the weirdest fires I had ever seen seemed to swirl and dance across the water and the sky. Clouds of steam rose from the bay the entire length of the flame blast, swathing the whole cove in a thick fog that glowed an unnatural green. The light of the flames themselves, now blurred in the clouds of steam, slowly began to fade, and by the time we approached the black ship close enough to throw a mooring rope on it, the light was gone while the fog had gradually wafted away.

"What happened to the beach?" Dana asked, pointing back. We all looked, and from where the first fire-blast had hit the shore, the ground was strange. In the center, there was a reddish glow, visible even from the distance we were. Around the edge, the land was black and smooth.

"Did it melt the ground?" Aeryk asked, stunned.

I stood, looking at the weird ground with a genuine uncomfortableness. It wasn't right, and looking at it wasn't making it more right, either. The pirate's voice jarred me back to reality.

"Hey! We got a ship to take an' steal here?" He pointed to the rope that he and his men had tossed up to the deck.

"Right," I said.

"Edword," Dana said, "You follow me up. Bring your men. If there's trouble, we meet it first. Rohb, you and Aeryk stay with Julea."

"Yeah," I said, "you all do that." I started to sit back on the bench.

"Oh no, dearie," she said, "You're coming with me at the front. Today you're my second."

Now, secret girlfriend or no, this was not a part of my

plan, and I said so.

"Come again?" I asked, "Are you sure it's not better for me to stay here? You know, keeping an eye on the shore and such?"

She didn't answer, but really, she did. I stood and walked over to the rope. Edword looked for the briefest of moments like he wanted to argue with Dana's direction but then thought better of it. He held the line as Dana started to climb, Edword followed, and then I went up. I looked down to see the pirates following me one by one, with never more than three of us on the rope at a time. On reflection, I could see that Dana had planned it out; there was no chance that the pirates would act against us on the launch with Edword there, and no way they would do it without a clear advantage with him gone. She had, cleverly, kept there from being any chance of any of us, particularly Julea, remaining with the pirates and at a disadvantage; just in case they didn't keep their word. It made me think about the whole arrangement for a minute. The exchange between Edword and Kelly had been much more than it seemed, I knew. I was sure Edword had been referring to the whole Blackcrow thing, which I honestly did want to hear about sometime, but Kelly said some things back that seemed to hint that there was more to the pirate than just being a pirate. For some reason, Kelly – who should have been the last person with cause to believe he could negotiate with him – did precisely that.

I got to the top of the rope and moved onto the deck next to Dana as I drew my daggers. A word about them, actually: They were very nice. The king had decent taste, assuming they had been his. They were a matched set, each ten-inch double bladed affairs with curled cross-guards and black leather-wrapped handles that fit just perfectly in my hands. I spun them through my fingers in a flourish just for fun, resulting in Dana's looking at me sternly. For the umpteenth time, I smiled at her.

We swarmed over the ship in silence, save for a slight jingling sound coming from two of the pirates who had chains draped across their leather vests. Decoration, I guess. Edword had silently directed the four of them in different directions around the deck of the ship, while he made for the captain's cabin in the middle of the main deck. Dana and I moved toward the rooms in the sterncastle, while one of the pirates went to the forecastle to do the same. The other three had gone quietly down through the cargo doors, both fore and aft. The ship was, as I had seen even from a distance, as black as night. Up close, the story was much more distinct and much weirder. The wood was neither painted nor covered in any kind of pitch, which had been my guess, but was really and truly black. Even where the wood had been milled or drilled, it was clear that the wood itself was black all the way through. The accessories aboard – the various ropes, pins, and so forth – were more typical, though anything that would take paint seemed to be painted either black or red. I suppose it was in keeping with the color of the weird wood and the general colors that were the signature of Chateau Flint. The fit and finish of the ship was something else; a far cry from any of the craft I'd been on in the past. None of them had the kind of skill and attention behind their build that this one had. While the hull of the ship was just as peculiar as it had seemed from my earlier viewing of her; her layout was fairly standard. She was a four-masted clipper, the mizzenmast slightly raked. She had two raised platforms above the main deck – the forecastle and the sterncastle. The sterncastle was where the helm was, while there were lookout positions and navigational aids on the forecastle. Below these were several rooms accessible to the main deck through doors, including guest quarters, storage, a galley, and so forth. The captain's cabin sat amidships separate from the rest of the upper facilities. Below were two open levels for cargo. The pantry, crew quarters, and other such would be down there as well. Of course, as I found out later, this particular ship had some wonders below that went far beyond the color of the wood.

But the biggest surprise right then was, as Dana and I made our way through all the rooms under the sterncastle, there were no people aboard. No guards, no sailors, no engineers, and no laborers. Nobody.

Edword came out of the captain's quarters and looked

at us across the deck. I held my hands up and shrugged. He looked around and got a silent agreement as each of the men reported in to him. We were alone.

"Take an' get movin' you dogs!" Edword suddenly called. We had been so quiet since we boarded that his shout seemed to me to be loud enough to be heard back at the castle. I turned to say something to Dana about it only to find that she had already rushed back to where we boarded, and the rest waited on our little boat. She called down, and a few moments later, Julea and Aeryk hauled themselves over the railing. I came and looked over the edge, to see Rohb awkwardly wrapping the rope around himself in preparation to climb up with one arm.

"Hey," I called down, "wait a minute. Let me check on something." I turned and jogged over to Edword, who was busily directing his men around the deck.

"Where's the davit?" I said, interrupting him, "I think we should haul the launch aboard."

Edword looked at me steadily. "You a sailor," he said.

I shrugged one shoulder, neither to agree or disagree.

He nodded for a second, then pointed to the forecastle. "Off the starb'rd bow. There's a winch," he said, turning back to his men.

"Aye, Cap'n," I said before I could stop myself. I hustled away before there were any questions, cursing that some reflexes, once learned, couldn't be shaken.

It took a few minutes, as Rohb had to row the little launch alone and with a broken arm, but he got to the bow, attached the ropes we dropped down to him and waited while Aeryk and I worked the winch to bring the little boat aboard. Once it was up, the three of us pulled it into the designated recess where it fit nicely.

"Weigh anchor!"

Edword's call came almost the instant we finished, and I heard the telltale sound of chains cranking below us, lifting the heavy anchors from the sea. We had the very definition of a skeleton crew, but they knew their work well enough that the ship moved in a wide arc the minute the mainsail dropped, turning us back and toward our rendezvous point with Kelly and the rest of the crew.

While Rohb joined Edword on the sterncastle by the helm, Aeryk joined the four sailors. It was clear he'd never worked a day on a ship in his life, but I have to give him credit for trying, and on the whole, he did more good than harm. Honestly, that's probably the first time that was true for him in the whole adventure, but that wasn't so much my business. I found Dana and Julea on the forecastle where they were watching the shore slip by and talking in low tones.

"Did you tell her about the magic rocks?" I said as I approached. They turned to look at me. I'm going to call the look they gave me; 'severe.'

"I did," Dana said. She looked toward the princess. Julea wore a very dour expression as she turned to me.

"That was not for your ears," she said with the same imperial tone from earlier that day. I sighed.

"Do you know," I said, reaching up and nonchalantly scratching behind my ear, "how very little I care?"

Both women froze. Dana immediately looked at the princess as if for a signal as to how to respond. Julea looked at me as if I had struck her.

"Don't get me wrong," I said, "You seem like a nice lady. It seems like you'll be a great ruler. But you have the same problem that all you fancy people have; you think you get to decide everything for everyone and that you're always right. See, the problem is all the 'every-s' and 'always-s.' You sleep, eat, breathe, belch, and everything else just like these pirates and me and all the people you will be making decisions for, and you think you know better— always. And here's my little tip, lady princess; you don't, and you can't."

From the corner of my eye, I could see a war in progress revealed on Dana's face. She was frozen, maybe in shock and maybe because she was waiting for Julea's response. She was also obviously furious and was maybe seconds away from trying to take my head off. I decided to focus on Julea, who was looking at me stoically.

"Kelly respects you," I said, continuing, "Seems he has other feelings about you too, but I don't care about that. He respects you, and that's enough. I will help get you home, and I'll do it gladly. But don't ever tell me what I am and am not allowed to know or I am and am not allowed to do."

We stood there for what felt like a long time. The princess never took her eyes off mine, and I really couldn't have told you what was going through her head. That was more than a little disquieting, to tell the truth. Finally, she nodded.

"You are a singular man, dungeon rat," she said, just a little smirk on her mouth.

"Yeah, I get that a lot."

"Battle ho!" Edword's voice rang out over our discussion.

Dana looked up, then went over to the port bow. "Battle ho?" she echoed without understanding.

"Uh-oh," I said. Julea and I followed over to the port rail, flanking Dana on either side. After a moment, I saw what had raised the alarm. Not far ahead, the tree-lined shore opened up into an open field that abutted the beach. In the middle of the area, a cluster of men stood with their backs to the water while a crowd of soldiers and horsemen faced them from the opposite side.

"Is that...," Julea asked.

"The crew," Dana said, "and Kelly."

"Shyte," I added.

Rohb and Aeryk were suddenly right behind us,

watching the scene.

“Damn fool,” Rohb muttered.

“I would love to disagree,” Dana said quietly, “but this time I don’t think I can.”

“We have to go,” Aeryk said, “We have to get to the launch and go.”

“We’ll never make it in time. There’s too many.” Rohb said. It seemed strange to me that he was upset about this.

“Y’ just needs to take an’ slow them down,” Edword said, rushing up the stairs to where we were, “Give me a little time.”

“For what?” I said.

“Just take an’ trust me,” Edword said, glaring at me.

“It won’t matter,” Aeryk said, “Look. They're almost overrun already.”

We looked back over to the shore, and it truly did look bad. The horsemen were running in a circle around the men now, pinning them in a small cluster and keeping them from being able to move, which would have been their best defense. It wouldn’t take long for the slaughter to be over.

And then, for the second time that day, there was a green flash. It wasn’t as large as either of the ones in the bay, but it was no less startling for its effect. The telltale green lightning resolved once again into a blast of green and yellow flame, this time from the middle of the circle of horsemen and out toward the water. The funnel of fire, more focused in its smaller size, stretched out over the sea and across our path, not a hundred yards ahead. I felt a blast of heat as it stretched out over the open water, and all of us flinched involuntarily. A second later, the screams of men and horses filled our ears as the sounds of the horsemen who had met the flame head on drifted across the water. I looked back, and the cavalry was retreating to the far end of the field.

"Kelly," Julea muttered.

"Time," Aeryk said.

"Not enough," Edword said.

"But we can give you more now," Dana said, "Let's go."

And just like that, we were in motion. The five of us shoved the launch from its resting place, boarded, and were within moments, pushing ourselves with the oars toward the shore. I had no idea what we were going to do when we got there, but by god's teeth, we were determined to do it. We hit the beach with all the momentum that Aeryk and I could muster as we rowed, and at the first impact on the sand, we were all out of the boat, weapons in hand. The rest of the pirate crew saw us hit the shore, and a shout went up. Within seconds, Kelly came out of the crowd. His cloak was missing, but he seemed otherwise whole. I jogged across the beach toward him but stopped almost immediately. A thin black coating of something covered the sand where the flames had touched it, leaving a shiny pathway from the inner part of the shore in a continuous line to the water. As I stepped on it, it cracked and gave way, my boots sinking into the sand beneath. Kelly reached me as the others came up.

"They don't seem terrified," I said when he got close enough. "I pissed myself a little, but they seem okay."

Kelly shook his head as everyone closed in. "It's a different regiment. The ones from the dock ran off north along the coast. They may double back later, but this isn't them. These came from the castle," he said. He was breathing hard, but not so much that he was unclear.

"How do you know?" Julea asked.

As if in answer, a booming voice came across the battlefield. "BLACKCROW! You have stolen my prize! You have stolen my treasures! I will have your head!"

"That's how," Kelly said. We all looked to see, across the battlefield, the king who wasn't a king sitting on a warhorse in full armor.

"Edword said he needed time," Aeryk said, surveying the armored men regrouping around the king.

"He was unspecific as to how much," I added.

Kelly looked back and forth, his eyes landing on Julea.

"Don't," she said, that commanding edge in her voice again, "There was no way I was staying on the ship."

Kelly nodded. "Fine," he said, "then let's go buy some time." He turned his back and faced the pirate crew gathered around us.

"Your captain," he said, his voice loud, "says there's a coin for each sword you bring him from these lads. What do you say?" He raised his sword overhead. A roar went up from the pirates. Suddenly there was a whirl of motion as the pirate crew charged across the open space.

The six of us spread out in twos. I shadowed Kelly as he went up through the middle while Dana and Julea went toward the thinner grouping of soldiers to the left. Aeryk and Rohb – who was, I now realized, wielding an axe the size of my entire body with his good arm alone – veered toward the cluster of soldiers to the right. I had some misgivings, but I couldn't deny that at first, the strategy was working well. The pirates were spreading the attention of the soldiers, which kept there from being overwhelming numbers in any single encounter for any of us, and the sandy footing was enough of a challenge to the mounted guardsmen that they lost much of the speed and agility benefits of being on horses. Even so, the soldiers of the north far outnumbered us, and I started to wonder how long we could keep this up.

Kelly's sword sang with every strike, and more than once, I watched it bite entirely through the armor or the blade of the one attacking him. I had seen a glimpse of his skills earlier – I was wearing the evidence, in fact – but in full-scale battle, it was something else entirely. He moved almost like he was following the steps of an elaborate dance; the blades and weaponry of the attackers clumsily coming at him while he spun, bobbed and weaved around them. He didn't waste a single movement as he cut a swath of destruction down the middle of the field.

Over the sounds of the fight, I heard a dull thudding to my side and turned in time to see one of the cavalrymen coming up at full gallop, heading right for my companion. Kelly, busily parrying the attacks of two soldiers, was facing the opposite direction and unaware.

"Hell's bells," I muttered. I crouched and waited. The rider saw me and drew back his sword, intending either to kill me or to ward me off. He did neither. He swung sidelong at me, adding his strength to the speed of his horse. I reversed my grip on my daggers and, just as he came within range, I moved – toward the horse's flank. For a fraction of a second, I could see the rider's eyes go wide as I came inside of the arc of his swing. My shoulder bounced off the horse's side, and I could feel the heat and sweat of the horseflesh as I rebounded. I rolled with it, letting the contact spin me on one foot until I was facing the opposite direction. My daggers flashed; one upwards at a reverse angle where it bit hard into the rider's sword arm above my head; the other laterally, down and low, where it sliced cleanly through the saddle's strap and lodged into the heavy leather of the seat itself, pulling it out of my hand. The horse abruptly slowed as it felt the belt go loose and the rider tumbled forward and down to the ground, his feet still in the stirrups.

Kelly turned and saw him as he fought to get free from the saddle and right himself on the ground. There was a loud 'clang' as the black blade came down on the rider's helmet, leaving him unconscious. Kelly looked at me.

"You're welcome," I said, pulling my escapee dagger from the fallen saddle, "You need to watch your back more."

"No, I don't," he said, "You were there."

And that's when the arrows started flying. More to the point, it's when I noticed the arrows flying because one sliced open my left arm as it flew past me.

"Ow!" I said, appropriately.

"Down!" Kelly yelled as we both dove for cover. There was a rain of arrows that lasted for several more seconds as shafts dropped into the ground all around us. Many of them sticking indiscriminately in the fallen, pirate and soldier alike.

"Dana!" The scream sliced through the chaos of the battle as well as if it had been in a quiet room. I looked around, but crouched down as I was I couldn't see where the voice had come from. I looked over to Kelly, who had shouldered himself up on the unmoving form of the soldier I had so recently dismounted. He was looking back and to our left, a look of what I can only call horror on his face. In a single motion, he was on his feet and in full out run, heedless of the last of the wave of arrows that still skittered around us. I rolled up onto my own feet and, clutching my left arm, which was now slick with blood, I followed.

The field wasn't overly big – maybe fifty or sixty yards of open area – which contributed to the feeling of chaos with so many of us fighting. As a result, it didn't take us long to reach the source of the cry. Julea, spattered with water and dirt and blood, was kneeling on the ground with Dana propped up on her lap. Two soldiers were coming toward them from our right-hand side, close enough that they'd reach them before we got there.

"Down!" I shouted, flipping the dagger in my good hand so that I had it by the tip. Kelly dropped into a roll that carried him forward as, with just enough of a leap to get a better angle, sent the blade flying an into the gap between the nearest attacker's helmet and collar. He dropped silently amid the sounds of the battle behind us.

Kelly completed his roll and came up to his feet, managing to keep nearly all of his forward momentum. The second of the two soldiers, his step slowed with the slightest hesitation as his partner fell, found himself a scant few feet short of his prey when he was disarmed and brained in a flurry of strokes from the Blackcrow. We reached Julea and Dana's side and saw the reason for the cry. Dana lay back on the princess's lap, her eyes looking up at the clouds without really seeing them and her breath coming in short gasps. The thick brown shaft of an arrow was sticking out of the left side of her chest just below the shoulder at an upward angle. I looked at Kelly gravely and could see from the expression on his face that he knew as I knew what the angle meant. It meant the end.

There was, I'm sure, still a battle going on around us, but I honestly don't remember any of it. I felt like the world ended just a couple feet away from the four of us, and if there was anything beyond that, I couldn't have told you.

Julea looked up at Kelly, tears spilling down her face and leaving streaks in the dirt on her cheeks. He dropped to his knees and took Dana's hand. Her eyes twitched to look at him in so far as she could see anything.

"You...," she said so quietly that I almost couldn't hear her.

"Shh," he said, "Don't talk. Just hold on. We'll—"

Her head shook slightly, but it came out as more of a spasm than anything. "Should have... been... you," she said haltingly. Kelly looked at her, confused.

"The Silver Spar," Julea said, her voice barely more than a hiss, "She's saying it should have been you."

A look of anguish passed across Kelly's face. He made a motion like he wanted to speak, but no words came out of his mouth. He looked up at Julea, and for a moment, a look of shared torment passed between them. Then, almost as if they reached an agreement without even speaking, the expression on Kelly's face twisted into something else.

It was rage.

And just like that, the spell was broken. Kelly leaped to his feet and took off at a run. I turned to start to follow when I saw where he was going. Just a few yards from us, the king was approaching on his horse, two of his cavalry by his side. Kelly was running directly toward him, black blade in hand.

I risked a glance back at Julea and Dana. A few of the pirates were nearby, but no soldiers threatened, so I ran after Kelly.

The king saw him first, coming straight across the field toward them like a vengeful wind. I saw him motion to the two others, obviously his personal guard, who nudged their horses forward. I was too far away to help as the two horses reared and thrust themselves forward with the intent to kill my friend. I willed my legs to go faster, but just then a colossal shape slammed into the horse on the right. There was a crunching sound that was all but drowned out by a battle cry that made my blood curdle. The horse tumbled sideways from the impact, and as it fell, I realized that the shape was Rohb, following through the collision onto the horse and bringing the giant axe down on the rider. In the same second, I saw another figure alongside plant the end of a staff on the fallen horse and vault over the melee to land on the other rider. Aeryk wrapped himself on the soldier, and his momentum carried both of them from the horse's back and down to the ground.

Kelly ran past them without breaking stride and bore down on his target. The king, realizing that he was going to have to defend himself, lifted his sword and nudged his mount forward to meet Kelly. It seemed apparent to me that he had not been paying attention to the Blackcrow in the earlier parts of the battle or he would have run screaming. He swung his blade down with a furious cry as Kelly closed in. He kept the swing narrow, though, and turned his horse just enough that Kelly couldn't catch the blade on his own. It slipped under his guard and slid across the black armor just below my friend's chest. Kelly rolled off of the strike, spinning completely and bringing his blade down hard. There was a screech of metal on metal, and a howl of anguish as the king's sword dropped to the ground.

Along with his hand. And a pretty good part of his arm.

The horse cantered as the king released the reigns to instinctively clutch the crippled stump that had been his right arm. He turned his head to see where Kelly was, only to find him already alongside, the black blade in motion and powered by all the rage and power the Blackcrow could put into it. The impact when the sword hit him was enough to unhorse him, and he fell to the ground hard.

I had been running to catch up the whole time, so I got to Kelly's side as he dropped onto the fallen king and ripped the helmet from his head.

"Where is it?" Kelly raged at the fallen man, then, with a single punch that drove the other's head into the ground, he reached into the collar of the armor, coming out with a small silver chain in hand.

"You filth!" Kelly said, his rage coming out in every sound. "You don't deserve this! This isn't yours! It was hers!" Each word brought a fresh fury, and he punctuated each sentence with a brutal punch to the fallen man's face.

We might still be on that beach, in fact, or be killed by the remaining soldiers, except that there was suddenly a noise from the water that I have a tough time describing. It was like a reverse thunderclap, or maybe the sound of pulling a cork from the hugest bottle ever made. In any case, it was deafening and stopped Kelly mid-punch. Opposite the water, near the treeline, a rain of spears dropped from the sky. It was like the arrows from earlier, but each projectile was the size of Aeryk's quarterstaff, and it was going the opposite direction. I looked around and saw the pirates throwing up a cheer.

"Edword," I muttered.

The soldiers panicked, both at the noise and the rain of spears. They broke whatever formation that they had left and took off running for the shelter of the woods, leaving the pirates to retreat toward the beach.

"That's our cue," I said to Kelly. He didn't move, except that his hands were now tightly squeezing throat of the king, who was looking increasingly purple.

"No, really," I said, "We have to go."

"I'm. Not. Finished," Kelly said.

"Kelly," I said, then I took a breath. "Kel," I started again, "this won't help her. But we still can save Julea and do what she wanted done. We might even get to say goodbye. But we have to go now."

There was a very long moment where I didn't think he was going to move, but finally, he dropped the choking and only partly conscious king back into the dirt and picked up his sword. He stood and looked at me, blank-faced and dead-eyed. He was caked with mud and the king's blood, and a wide gash was open in the front of his armor.

"Let's go," he said, turning away from the fallen king and heading toward the shore.

By the time we got to the beach, the first group had taken the launch back to the ship, including Julea and Dana. Kelly and I moved over to be out of the cluster of the pirate crew and to wait for our turn on the boat.

It was there that, moments later Rohb and Aeryk found us. Both were dirty and banged up, but seemed mostly intact. Aeryk started to go over to Kelly when I grabbed his arm and shook my head.

"What's going on?" he said, turning his head slowly from Kelly to give me his attention, "We were across the field when we saw that little bit of insanity there. What were you thinking?" He again said this last to Kelly, who hadn't turned and was still looking away at the forest and the retreating soldiers.

"Hey," I said, drawing the prince's eyes back to me, "Don't. It's Dana. She... she fell."

"Fell?"

"Arrow," I said, as clearly as I could.

I have never seen someone crumble inside before my eyes before. As what I meant became clear to him, I could see his mind mentally drawing the direct line from his actions to this moment, and then watched as the whole world shattered in his mind. He stumbled backward and nearly fell over.

Rohb, standing close, dropped his head and muttered, "May the One be merciful."

"Merciful?" I almost shouted as I wheeled on him. I suddenly felt a fury that I didn't know I even had as the stress of the battle and unbidden feeling of loss swirled and fed it. "Seriously? Are you pulling that right now? Where's this One of yours, eh? Where's the much-storied mercy, huh? Don't placate me with your ritual-ish words right now." The heat in my voice hung in the air, and I saw even Kelly turned at the sound. Rohb looked squarely at me for a moment, then quietly turned away.

And we stood on the shore of the cold sea and waited.

CHAPTER TEN

— JULEA —

The room was, like the rest of the ship, black, though that was not what made it dark for me just then.

The captain's cabin was a raised rectangle in the middle of the main deck of the ship. We had entered through the door, which faced aft, into an area with several chairs and a relatively large table in it. The tabletop was recessed perhaps an inch or two and contained several rolled-up charts, weights, and pins that would be used to hold them open while the captain would consult them, and various navigational paraphernalia. From there, we went through a small doorway in a wall that divided the cabin into two parts. Here we entered the captain's private room, where we found walls lined with storage cabinets, a small built-in couch, and a bed. Edword had greeted our launch when it got to the ship, and on seeing Dana's limp form insisted on being the one to carry her. He then had bidden me follow him in here. Now, he lowered her gently onto the bed.

"Won't be the last blood on that bed, I don't expect," he mumbled to me as I watched. I would have responded, but everything seemed so far away. Since we left the beach, I had been moving as though I were in a dream – like I was a character in a story; merely going through motions absently with no will of my own. I turned and looked back at Dana and saw that the ragged breathing she had been doing since she was wounded had slowed. I didn't know whether to feel relief or concern. I honestly couldn't feel anything. My mind insisted instead on returning to the battle that had taken my friend from me.

We had made our way up the left flank of the battlefield with a good amount of success. Most of my childhood had included martial lessons with the Imperial masters as part of my education. It was much the same as the training that both Dana and Kelly had received, and while perhaps I don't have the aptitude or experience they do, I know how to acquit myself well. It wasn't lost on me that Dana had chosen the direction with a somewhat thinner apportionment of soldiers. I made a note in my mind to make a point of it later. Dana, however, was in her element. The return of her rapier with the remainder of our equipment was like giving her back a missing piece of herself, and she was conducting a master class on swordsmanship with it. Had I to estimate, she was taking on two opponents to every one of mine.

Thinking I could rectify the inequality, I took a course a bit further to her right, which separated us somewhat. As I understood it, our goal was to thin the enemy and prevent them from concentrating on any of us, so it seemed a sensible move. Just as I did, one of the pirates, who had been immediately ahead of me – a short, stocky fellow with an impressive beard – was knocked sidelong by the massive warhammer of an oncoming soldier, leaving me to face him alone. I held my long-sword in first position to keep as much distance from him as I could while maintaining a soft grip so that the hammer wouldn't snap it on impact should he strike at it. The soldier gave me a wild, animalistic snarl of a grin and advanced. I waited. He held the hammer in front of him with one hand on the enormous angular metal head and one on the base of the shaft. I remained still. Just beyond the range of my sword, he dropped the head and switched his grip so that both hands were on the bottom of the handle while the weight of the hammerhead swung down. The momentum built as he added his strength to it, swinging it around behind him, up and over his head, and aimed right for the spot I was standing in – where I had been waiting the entire time. I lifted my sword as if to catch the hammer on it and watched as the grin on his face became almost entirely feral. He brought his weapon down with all of his might.

I pulled my sword out of the feint and stepped one step quickly backward.

The warhammer slammed into the soft ground with a thud that I could feel through the ground beneath my feet. I watched as the wet sand where I had been standing was pushed forcefully aside, admitting the full hammerhead into the sandy earth.

The enraged soldier pulled on the handle, suddenly confronted with the fact that he had over-committed, but the ground held its new prize fast. I stepped forward again, putting my lead foot on the spot where the hammer was now embedded into the ground. More for sport than anything, if I'm to be honest. My opponent held fast on the handle of his weapon; the message that it was lost to him hadn't quite penetrated his dim wits. I brought the long-sword across, catching him on the side of the head just below the edge of his helm. He flipped sideways from the blow, his right hand stubbornly gripping the entrenched warhammer until it could hold no more such that he landed splayed out face up on the ground to my left. In two steps and a strike with the pommel of my blade on his head, I dispatched him.

I looked around to see where Dana was when I saw the shadow in the sky. It took another second for me to realize that the shadow was, in reality, a flight of arrow-shot.

"Dana!" I called, my voice sounding small through the cacophony of combat and the thudding of my own heart. She was some thirty feet away now, just finishing an exchange with one of the soldiers when she turned to my voice. She must have seen the look on my face and where I was looking because she turned in that direction. But it was too late. One of the shafts flew true and felled her before my eyes.

I crouched down by the fallen soldier as the remaining arrows pelted the ground around us, using him for as much cover as he could provide, though my heart was in my throat and I could barely breathe. The last of the arrows were still coming when I felt I could wait no longer. I scrambled up and, stumbling through the scattered array of arrow shafts and bodies, made my way to her side. I could see her struggling to get up, seemingly confused as to why her left arm wouldn't support her. As I reached her, she started to cough and collapsed back to the ground. Gently, I rolled her over and leaned her against me, the blood from her coughing trickling down her cheek...

I shook off the memory and came back to the present moment, where I was watching my best friend in the world dying before my eyes on a pirate's ship. Edword had left; presumably, he interpreted the fact that I was not responding when he spoke as giving him the leave to do so. I knelt down next to the bed.

"Note...," Dana said weakly. Her right hand moved uncertainly to a small fold of leather on her belt.

"It's okay, honey," I said, "Don't worry about anything."

"No...," she said. I couldn't tell whether she meant to say 'no', or was trying to say 'note' again, but I realized that she wasn't going to stop until I looked.

"Okay, okay," I said, as sweetly as I could muster. *No one taught me this, mother*, I chided in my mind, *I know what to say to anyone from a peasant to a king, but I do not know what to do now.*

Carefully, I reached into the small leather opening, pulling out an envelope folded in half. It was old and worn, stained where it had rubbed against the leather for who knew how long. I unfolded it and saw the remains of a broken seal of dark green wax.

"What is this?" I said. Her head twitched, and her eyelids fluttered while she strove to speak, but a racking cough seized her suddenly, and all words were caught away. I shoved the paper into my leather corset and reached over to try to calm her. A fresh bubble of blood spilled from her mouth, but the coughing slowed. She settled back, her breathing again shallow.

I knelt watching her for I don't know how long; time had lost meaning. So had anything else, it seemed, for it wasn't until they were right behind me that I realized that Kelly, Denis, and Edword had entered the room and that Kelly had been speaking.

"Jules," he was saying. He said it insistently, and in a way that made me think he had been saying it for some time.

"Kelly," I said as if from a distance, "You're here."

"I am," he said. His voice was ragged and tired. I turned to look at him and almost cried out. His black armor was covered in dried blood; and where there wasn't blood, there was dirt. His face and hands were cleaner, though, as if he had rinsed them off somehow. From far away, some part of my mind imagined him washing his hands in the seawater while he took the small boat from the shore. There was a wide gash across the armor on his chest, and when he moved, it yawned open slightly. I felt my eyes go wide and he must have noticed it, because his voice sounded different when next he spoke, and I could see him making an effort to appear less haggard.

"I'm okay," he said first, giving me a nod, "How is she?" He looked over at Dana and came up beside me next to the bed.

"It... won't be long," I felt the words catch in my throat. His hand settled on my shoulder as he stood beside me.

After a moment, Kelly glanced back over his shoulder at Denis, who turned to the pirate. "Cap'n," the other said, and I was stunned at how easily the word came off of his lips, "How soon before we go?"

"Jus' a couple more loads," Edword said, his voice low and almost reverent.

"Then," Denis said, dropping his voice, "if it's okay with you, maybe we should give them some privacy? I'll watch the door while you get us out to sea. If that's okay?"

I didn't see the pirate's face, but his tone was low and

solemn. "Aye, that's a good plan," he said, "I'll take an' get us out o' this gods-forsaken land."

The two of them moved away, and a moment later, I heard the outer door open and then close again. There was the sound of footsteps, and Denis returned.

"Okay, Blackcrow, you got your privacy," he said with a small nod.

Kelly took his hand from my shoulder and stepped back.

"Jules, what would you be willing to do to save her life?" Kelly said. His voice was very matter of fact, not emotional, and not excited. Most of all, he was deadly serious.

I looked up at him. "What? Anything! What are you talking about?"

"I'm going to try something – I mean, I want to try, by your leave – but if it works, there's a price," Kelly said, "I'm not saying that I want anything; I'm saying that saving her life will cost you. Both. If it even works." He shook his head, more at whatever he was thinking than at me.

"What do you mean?" A whirl of confusing feelings flooded my mind. I had seen miracles around Kelly – just that day, in fact – but I could not fathom what he meant to do.

"I'm saying that to save her, you may lose her," he said, his voice steady and quiet, "and it will change both of your lives forever. The only solace I can offer is that, if it works, she'll be alive, and you will finally have the answers to some of the questions that you've always wondered about."

I don't know if I expected help – or what I expected in reality – but I looked over at Denis.

"Ma'am," he said, much more seriously than I was expecting from him, "I really don't know what is happening right now. Haven't for a while. But I've seen shyte that turned me pale today, and I'd be willing to take a chance. And from the looks of her, if you're going to, we'd better take it soon."

There indeed was only one answer, and it took only a heartbeat for me to know it. "Do it," I said, "Whatever the cost."

Instantly, Kelly stepped back to the bed. Without standing, I moved over so that I was closer to Dana's waist while he knelt near her wounded shoulder. He unslung a black satchel from around himself, opened it, and began extracting the contents – laying them carefully out on the floor beside him where I couldn't see.

"What is that?" I asked, tilting my head a little but still unable to see what he was doing. Kelly didn't respond but continued to focus on his task. I looked back to Denis, who shrugged.

"We were standing on the beach. Feeling awful," he said in response to my look, "when this kid came up to us.

Pirate kid; maybe fifteen? He had that black bag in his hand. I saw Kelly with it back at the camp; it was with all the stuff of yours that Edword and his men had taken. Anyway, the kid comes up to us and says, 'Dis yern?' I think that's pirate-kid talk for, 'is this yours, good sir?' in fancy people talk. Kelly took it, stared at it for a second, then took off running to get on the next launch without saying a word. I told the kid that's how fancy people say thank you – seriously, I'm always translating for you all – and ran after him. We left Rohb and Aeryk on the beach; we moved so fast. I expect they'll have a lot to say when they get here."

"Lock the door," Kelly said suddenly. He reached up and undid the fasteners on Dana's armored vest and gently slid it aside so that it was out of the way of the arrow's shaft. With a small knife; I presumed one taken from the mystery satchel; he cut away the cloth of her tunic from around the shaft as well. The unobstructed image of the arrow sticking out of her flesh is one I will never be able to forget. I took an unsteady breath.

"I already did," Denis replied to Kelly's direction, "I wedged a chair against it and everything."

"Thanks, kid," Kelly said, then he turned to me and continued, "I want you to know, I've never actually done this myself before, so I only hope this will work."

"But what is this?" I said, excitement mixing with exasperation in my voice.

"After," Kelly said, "I'll explain everything after. For now, I need your help. Both of you."

Denis came closer and stood behind me. He was rubbing his fingers against his thumbs on each hand, and I realized he was nervous. I also realized that I could hear my heartbeat in my ears, and my chest suddenly felt very tight.

Kelly produced a small brass tube about half an inch in diameter with another, similar, brass tube partly fitted inside of it. They were each about four inches long; the inner one, which could easily slide fully inside the larger, was capped at one end, while the larger had what appeared to be an array of tiny protrusions on the opposite end. Each protrusion had a small hole in it. He handed it to Denis.

"You take this. When I say, you are going to put this end," Kelly pointed at the perforated end, "right on the wound. Push it tight against the gash. Then press the other end until the two tubes collapse together. Understand?" Denis considered the assembly for a moment and then nodded.

Kelly turned to me and said, "Okay, princess, I need you to keep the pressure on the wound when I pull the arrow out,"

"I thought it was better to push an arrow through than to pull it out – because of the barbs on the head," I said, thinking back to the healing lessons from my youth. Taught to me, ironically, by the same Imperial trainers that had trained me to kill.

"Normally," he said nodding, "but to push this through, at this angle, it would have to go through her whole chest, and that's not an option. I'm going to pull it out as gingerly and quickly as I can, and the minute I get it clear, put this cloth on there and keep pressing on it until I say, okay?"

I nodded. It made my head swim.

"Also, when Denis does his part, she is going to spasm. She will scream. Short of making sure she doesn't fall off the bed, there's nothing we can do to help that. If you try to hold her, one of you is like to get hurt. Try to stay clear and let me handle it. But be prepared for it and let it run its course."

Kelly reached down to whatever he had spread on the floor next to him and picked up a small, shiny wand about seven inches long. The last few of which were encrusted with a mixture of dark blue and yellow crystals. They looked like colored sugar, or pieces of painted quartz. A dusting of a white powder stuck to them haphazardly.

"Uh," Denis said, "what's that?"

"My part of the job," Kelly said. He looked from me to Denis, "Ready?"

I can report that I nodded because I felt my head swim again. I presume Denis did as well because Kelly leaned over, put his left hand on Dana's forehead, and whispered something in her ear. Her eyes fluttered, and she seemed to look at him for a moment before they closed again. He settled back and then took the clean end of the metal wand in his mouth, holding it there.

"Here we go," he said through clenched teeth. He placed one hand gently on Dana's chest, encircling the wound with his thumb and forefinger. With his other hand, he grabbed the shaft of the arrow. Gently, he rolled it back and forth in his hand, pulling up as he did. Dana's face twitched as the painful sensation filtered through to her. A moment later, he stopped and with a single steady pull, drew the arrow out of the wound. Dana gave a long moan that ended in a wet gurgle, but the arrowhead seemed mostly clean as it came away. Immediately, I shoved the cloth Kelly had given me onto the wound and pressed hard with the palms of my hands.

"Easy," Kelly said, his words slightly muffled, "Just a steady pressure. No need to push her through the bed." He tossed the arrow aside and took the metal wand in his hand. "Okay, get ready," he said.

A moment later and he tapped the back of my hands. I backed away and took the cloth from the wound. A fount of blood welled up from the hole, spilling over and down her chest. Carefully, adjusting so that it had the same angle as the arrow had, Kelly pressed the crystal-covered rod into the wound. He continued pushing until the crystals had slid entirely under the skin. Then he began to rotate it between his fingertips, first one way, then the other; back and forth a little at a time until finally, he turned it completely around.

"Den," he said, "Your turn." Denis leaned close, the strange brass tube in hand. With one smooth motion, Kelly pulled the metal wand out. It was clean; there was no blood, and, more significantly, there were no crystals.

Instantly, Denis pressed the end of the brass tube into place and pushed the inner one down until it was entirely inside the first. There was a quiet metallic hiss as the brass tubes slid together. He held it there, uncertain.

"That's enough," Kelly said, waving his hand as if brushing him away. Denis backed up, and we watched Dana, though I surmise that only Kelly had any idea what we were looking for. At first, nothing happened, though the bleeding had ceased. Slowly there rose a hiss like that of a kettle on a hot stove, coming from the wound site. I looked at Kelly, but his full concentration was on the wound on Dana's chest. Before my eyes, the red flesh turned pink, then white. Pale lines stretched out from the site across her chest in a tangled pattern, as if white vines were rapidly growing beneath the skin and pressing up against it. I glanced over and saw a weary grin slowly work its way across Kelly's mouth as he exhaled a long breath.

Dana began to cough. She coughed hard, blood coming up in bits of spittle and larger chunks where it had already dried inside of her chest. Then she screamed. It was a horrible, piercing sound. It was the scream of someone who has seen the very gates of hell yawning open for them. She convulsed, twitching and twisting on the bed. Another scream. She rolled, and it brought her to the edge of the bed where, before I could move, Kelly caught her in his arms and eased her back toward the middle. He sat there while she twisted and screamed for several more minutes, occasionally moving to keep her on the bed, sometimes blocking her flailing arms from slamming into either his face or the bed's wooden frame.

I slowly became aware of a pounding and shouting from the outer cabin door. I stood and went out to the other room, only to find Denis already there. He had his hand on the chair that was securing the door in preparation for moving it. I caught his arm, and he looked at me, confused.

"It may be best if you let me," I said. He gave me a long look, then with a lopsided grin, he stepped back.

I slit the chair aside and put my hand on the lock. I took a breath and straightened, willing the anxiety that had taken hold of me down and away. I waited until there was a break in both the screaming behind me and the pounding in front of me, then finally said, "One moment. I am coming. Please back away." Denis moved behind me as I paused – which was punctuated only by a deep groan from Dana in the other room – and then worked the lock to open the door.

The form of Captain Edword filled the door-frame, flanked by two of his crew. A short distance behind them, I glimpsed Aeryk and Rohb who were now standing and watching amid the movement of the pirates as they worked the ship.

"What in the nine hells is going on in there?" Edword bellowed.

I looked up at him placidly, folding my hands in front of me. "There has been a change," I said, using my most steady tone. I wasn't sure how effective it was, as my heart was still racing from the whole experience.

Edword looked at me, confusion and shock spread across his face. "What?" he said; the only word he managed to get out.

"A change," I repeated.

"A change," Denis echoed behind me.

"How in—?" Edword started.

"I assure you," I interrupted, and I gave a look over to Rohb and Aeryk as I did so, making sure they caught my eye, "All is well. It is. Give us but a little time to care for her, and you'll see."

Denis stepped up at this point, giving the pirate a nod. "It's true, Cap'n," he said, "I saw it myself. It's all fine." Edword looked at the two of us for a long moment in silence as he wrestled with his frustration. He furrowed his brow and made to step inside.

"I would take it as a kindness, captain," came a hushed voice from behind Denis and me. I spun to find Kelly and Dana standing in the door to the other room. She had her arm draped around Kelly's back and was wrapped in one of the sheets from the bed. Kelly had his arm firmly around her in return, and it was clear that he was providing most of the support that allowed her to stand. But she was standing and looking clear-eyed at the pirate.

Edword was aghast and looked around. His men were watching him in return for some clue as to what to do. After a good long look at Dana, he turned back to me, his face awash with confusion.

"She gonna be okay?" he asked. It was said quietly. He was not giving a command or making a display of his authority but instead asking an honest question.

"I think so," I said, "I do know that she's got a better chance now because of your forbearance."

He nodded, turned, and bellowed to his crew. "All right ye sea dogs! Get us to open water! Now!" Then he and the rest rushed off. In moments, Aeryk and Rohb were left standing alone outside the cabin. I gave them a gentle smile and held up one finger. Rohb nodded to me and put his hand on Aeryk's shoulder. After a moment, they moved to either side of the doorway and took position as guards. Aeryk gave me a last glance before I closed the door and I smiled an unspoken thank you to him.

I felt the ship shift beneath me as it began to speed up. It dawned on me then that I had no idea when the last of the crew had come aboard or if we had left the shore yet. So busy had I been with...

Dana. I turned, but she was no longer in the doorway. I rushed back through to the other half of the cabin. She was again laying in the bed, already asleep or nearly so, quiet and breathing normally. Kelly's equipment was all gone; I presumed it was back in the mysterious bag, which he had again draped across his shoulder. He was standing next to one of the cabinets and rummaging around inside when I entered. I walked over to the bed and sat down on its edge. Dana's face was calm and peaceful; her breath came deep and slow. I traced her cheek with the back of my hand.

"She needs to sleep now," Kelly said, "but I think – eventually – she'll be okay." He sat down wearily on the couch, wiping his hands and face with a small scrap of material that he had taken from the cabinet. "There are some more linens in there," he said, pointing to where he had gotten the cloth, "I think it might be wise to get the bed cleaned up and that armor off of her so she can rest better. I also wasn't sure that I was the best one to do that. In this instance." He smiled at me.

"I'll do it," Denis said from the door.

"That is very kind of you, dungeon rat," I said, though my voice was warm, "but unnecessary. I will take care of her if you don't mind."

He shrugged one shoulder and smiled.

"Why don't we let you do that?" Kelly said.

The two men had gone to the outer room while I cared for my friend. In the cabinet, I found another wrap for the bed as well as a nightshirt. I had a moment of hesitation – it was, after all, a pirate's linens – but I reminded myself that the ship was new, and the supplies onboard were likely fresh ones loaded by the palace guard under the order of the false king. The false king, I thought. We don't even know his actual name. Somehow that seems wrong. As gently and carefully as I could manage, I replaced the linens on the bed and changed Dana into the borrowed nightshirt. It took longer than I might have liked, what with her being deeply asleep and my own hands still shaking from the terror and triumph of the last couple of hours, but soon she was lying in bed again in reasonable comfort. I breathed a sigh of relief, exhaustion, and relief tinted by fatigue. I walked out into the other room where Kelly and Denis stood at the navigation table, examining some of the charts that they had spread out. I straightened up and folded my arms across my chest.

"I believe," I said, "that you owe me answers."

Kelly looked up from the table, his exhaustion again plain on his face. "I do owe you that," he sighed.

A piercing whistle came from the deck outside.

"Uh-oh," Denis said.

"What?" I said.

"Trouble," he said over his shoulder as he was already in motion toward the door, "The lookout saw something."

Kelly swept his hand through his hair and blew out a breath. "Of course," he muttered, more to himself than anything. He went after Denis out of the door, with me closely behind.

We came out onto the deck, where Rohb gave us each a nod as we passed him. Aeryk, however, was several feet away and coming back in our direction from the aft. He looked both pleased and concerned to see us.

"Tell us a story," Denis said.

"Three ships," Aeryk replied, looking at Denis and then back and forth to the rest of us, "dead ahead. They're spread wide across our path; no way around."

Denis cursed. "And we're hauling wind; they've got us."

"Look who knows everything." Edword snarled, approaching us from the fore of the ship so abruptly he might have wholly appeared from nowhere. "You just take an' sit back. We got some tricks of our own," he said offhandedly, never stopping as he continued past us toward the sterncastle, where he climbed up the stairs and moved quickly to the helm.

"What does that mean?" Aeryk said, turning back to

us after he passed.

"I think it means 'Watch,'" I said.

Behind me, Denis said, "Good translation."

"Let's do that, then," Kelly said, beckoning us as he followed Edword toward the steps that lead onto the rear deck. Rohb turned back to the doorway of the captain's cabin and retook his guard position. I cocked my head in an unvoiced question, but he only nodded. I smiled with an unexpected feeling of comfort and turned to follow the others.

On the rear deck, Aeryk, Denis, and Kelly had gathered at the railing on the port side. I joined them, standing just in front of Kelly, and could then see the threat as it had been described. Off to our port side, a ship was approaching, already just a few hundred yards away. It exactly matched the profile of the three that had chased Dana and I and our Imperial escort into Clemons just days before, and it was bearing down on us from about our ten o'clock position. Kelly touched my shoulder and pointed, drawing my eyes more to the fore of the ship. There, just a little aside of straight ahead, a second ship that matched the first was coming toward us, plowing through the water under full sail.

"The third is about our two o'clock," Aeryk said over the noise of the sea. He waved his hand in the appropriate direction. A crack of thunder punctuated by flashes of lightning rolled suddenly through the darkening sky to the south, as if there were not enough drama and the weather had decided to add some more.

"Well, this is a show," Denis said, "At least we'll go out with some fanfare."

"HO!" Edword's voice boomed and drew all of our attention. He was standing at the helm, a hand on the wheel while his crew moved busily around him, but he was pointing at Denis.

"Boatswain was taken in the battle," the pirate said, his voice clear in spite of the sound of the waves and the wind, "I need a pair o' hands. You handle it?"

Denis, unexpectedly, snapped a casual salute and shouted, "Aye."

"Smartly then!" Edword called back, suddenly leaning into the wheel and adjusting our course. Denis ran off across the deck, taking a station just in front of the pillar of the helm to one side, where a small brass pipe with a flared end protruded from the deck at about a man's height. I looked at Kelly, my eyebrows raised. He returned my look with a gentle shrug before he returned to the railing.

The rain came then; it spattered everything in little drops that made the wind cold on our skin and drew a gauzy haze across the horizon. I knew that the closest ship – whichever that proved to be – would try to grapple us, pulling our vessel to theirs with long grappling ropes while archers on both sides would trade fire from the deck. Do we have archers? I wondered idly. I felt the deck tip as the black ship listed to starboard under the pirate's hand, broadening the angle for the vessel approaching directly ahead. I knew he couldn't veer enough to that side to keep us out of range, as the third ship – the one I'd not yet seen but knew to be there – would then be too close.

"Furl the sheets!" It was Denis' voice, calling out from where he stood. The crew paused, and though some of them looked back to see where the command came from, they all began moving to the rigging. They hauled on the appropriate ropes, and our sails pulled up and into tight bundles on the masts. Almost immediately, the ship slowed.

"What's he doing?" I said, unable to keep the tension from my voice. I looked back to Kelly, but he didn't respond. He was watching the approaching ship, the center one of the three, and seemed to be counting. I followed his gaze and saw that it was nearly upon us. Already I could see the soldiers on the deck, still small figures but getting larger as each second brought them closer, preparing the grappling lines.

"If he has a plan, now would be an exceptional time," Aeryk mumbled.

As if on cue, from the helm, Denis barked the order, "Release!" into the brass pipe. There was a strange silence suddenly, the noise of the rain and the sea fading into nothing. My ears popped with pain as if I had suddenly plunged deep underwater. Then there was a sound; a rolling 'boom' that would not have been much different were we inside one of the thunderclouds above. The port side of our ship seemed to burst open like an overinflated wine-skin, black wooden hatches flipping back freely to release a blast of air that turned the tops of the waves into a mist. The same burst carried a barrage of the enormous spear-like projectiles that had driven off the soldiers on the beach as they rained down from the sky at the close of the earlier battle. At close range, though, they sped through the air supernaturally fast; flying in straight lines over the water toward the other ship. The majority of the shafts scored a direct hit, punching through the hull in a nearly straight array and pulverizing it into a shower of kindling and slivers. They continued straight through, and another hail of wooden debris sprayed out from the opposite side of our attacker. Their main deck, now unsupported, collapsed in the middle, sending the men tumbling toward one another and down to the lower level. The main mast, the sails still open, toppled forward, wreaking havoc on the foredeck.

And just as eerily as they had vanished, the sounds of the world returned. The rain pattered and the waves roared, but now there was the sound of screaming men and crunching wood echoing to us over the water.

"Take an' hang on to something!" Edword's voice

called out, and I looked to see him throwing a rope around his shoulders. Denis too was slipping a rope around himself that was tied to the nearby rails. I crouched down without asking and slid my arm through the railing while Kelly and Aeryk did similarly. At that point, I believe that I wouldn't have been surprised if we suddenly flew off into the sky on the back of a flying fish.

"Gangway!" Edword shouted. He leaned back and pressed his foot into a small niche in the bottom of the helm column below the wheel. The air suddenly felt..., wrong, I suppose is the word. The hair on my arms stood on end, and the smell of the sea disappeared, replaced by a metallic tang. I looked up and caught my breath. The rain was no longer reaching the deck. It was instead sliding away around us as if we were in a soap bubble. Then, the ship lurched forward as if pulled by the very hand of The One Himself. The water split off the bow with such force that it sprayed up in giant curtains around us that were surely half the height of the mast, while I was thrown back more powerfully than if I had been on a stallion bred for speed. I held fiercely to the rail, grateful that I had wedged myself in so tightly. Whatever the wizardry was that deflected the rain did nothing against the wind. It now tore at us with the force of a gale, clawing and biting at anything not fastened down. I dropped my head to shield my eyes from the wind's power, worried for a brief moment that it might be powerful enough to sheer the skin from my body.

This continued for I don't know how long; many minutes at least. Then, quite abruptly, it was over. It was as if the real world, having given us a brief license to break all the known rules of nature, suddenly decided to revoke that freedom. The ship lurched as we dropped from our supernatural speed, now bobbing in the sea severely for several moments as we continued to coast forward on sheer momentum. The rain returned, gentler though, sprinkling on a deck that was all but dry from the force of the winds. I stood, finding Kelly already up and leaning over the railing to look behind us. The other ships were nowhere to be seen.

"WOOO!" Edword called, and his crew joined in a deafening cheer.

"I don't...," Aeryk said after a long moment. He looked at me. He was pawing at his hair, trying to return some order to the chaos the wind had left it in.

I shook my head. "I have seen a lot today, your lordship," I said, looking out over the horizon, "I understand very little of it. But today – maybe only for today – we should just thank The One that so much of it happened in our favor."

He looked at me for a long moment, then in a quiet tone, asked, "Is she going to be okay?"

I looked over to the captain's cabin. Rohb stood again in front of the door and gave me a brief salute when he saw me. I nodded at him.

"Somehow," I said, turning back to the prince, "I think so. Somehow."

Kelly walked up just then, obviously hearing the last bit of our exchange. I looked at him quizzically.

"This wasn't me," he said, raising his hands in a gesture of surrender. He looked around at the ship and said, "I don't know for sure what this was."

I looked at him, and I could see that he was in earnest. I shook my head. I suddenly remembered being a girl and being spun around on a garden gate and then trying to walk. "There are too many things I don't understand," I said.

"And I owe you some of that if I recall," Kelly said, "Maybe it's finally time to talk."

It wasn't yet, of course. There were things to be seen to first. Kelly and the others gathered to confer with Edword; I returned to the cabin to check on Dana. Rohb opened the door for me when I reached him, nodding soberly.

"I put the belts on when he called for us to hold on," he said with what I took as a touch of sheepishness. I patted his shoulder and smiled at him.

The chairs in the outer room had not been fastened down, so they were tossed about by the ship's maneuvers, but the captain's chamber was unchanged. Dana remained quietly sleeping in the bed as I had left her – albeit with three canvas straps loosely fastened around her body. I reached over and undid them, sitting on the edge of the bed and looking at her. Gently, I moved the nightshirt to check on the wound to find that the white vines I had seen before had subsided, leaving only a bright star-like pattern where the actual injury had been. I smiled. She was already somewhat sensitive about the scars on her back; she didn't need anything more.

She stirred, her eyes flickering open and seeing me – actually seeing me this time. I smiled at her.

"Jules," she said, her voice still weak but very much her own. She tried to sit up.

"Shh," I said gently touching her shoulder to stop her, "You've had a long day. Apparently, you need rest."

The corners of her mouth twitched, and she laid back. "We're on a boat," she said.

"We are," I said, "Please don't throw up."

"Okay," she said with a sigh. "I think I like this boat anyway."

I watched as she drifted back to sleep, then went over and sat on the couch. I blew out a breath and looked down. The wind and rain had done an admirable job of cleaning the dirt of the beach off my clothing, and despite everything, I seemed almost human. Almost. I was sure my mother would have comments.

A wedge of paper peeked out of my armor, and I

remembered the envelope Dana had given me. I pulled it out and looked it over again. There were blood stains now added to the stains on the paper, as her blood had been on my hands when I took it from her. I shuddered and pushed the memory out of my mind. I unfolded the envelope again and looked at the mark from the green seal. I could barely see the imprint of the insignia, but when I finally made it out, my heart jumped. It was a wolf's head — the seal of the Empire.

I quickly opened the envelope and read the contents of the letter. A thousand thoughts rushed through my mind as I realized what I was reading and as the meaning of what I read hit home.

I had no time to think more, though. With a click, I heard the cabin door open. Quickly, I refolded the paper and replaced it inside my vest. Kelly poked his head into the room.

"Edword wants to move us into actual quarters for the rest of the journey. Something about his belief that we need to get rest. He's got a room for Dana already set up, so we can move her anytime. I think..., I think he wants to be the one to move her," he said with a wry smile.

I smiled back. "Well, he did insist on carrying her in here. Is our pirate captain sweet on my friend, do you think?"

He chuckled, then said, "Who can tell with him, eh? Anyhow, I wanted to come and make sure it was a good moment for us to make the move. And see if you were okay."

He cocked his head at this last, waiting for an answer.

"For now," I said after a minute, "I suppose 'okay' will suffice to describe it."

He nodded. For a moment, he looked like he wanted to say something, but then reconsidered. "I'll go get Edword," he said instead.

Shortly, Dana was resting in what would be our room for the remainder of our time on the ship. Once Edword left us, I busied myself with settling her in and putting our equipment in the cabinets. I found one of the full white shirts and a pair of britches and changed out of my clothes if only as a way to shake the events of the day off. Finally, I settled down on the small couch and, in time, drifted off into a kind of half-sleep with the letter in my hand.

The knock on the door was gentle, but I was no longer wholly asleep in any case. I rose, noting that it was quite dark now; only a pale glow came through the windows on the back wall, indicating that it was at the least late twilight if not later. I slipped the envelope and its contents, lying on my lap, into the cabinet where I had put my things and went to the door.

"Yes?" I said.

Kelly's voice came back. It was tired, and I thought that it was probably unlikely he had slept much if at all. "How's she doing?" he asked.

I looked back over to Dana's quietly sleeping form. "She's still asleep. Peaceful. She seems to be mending." I reached over to the lantern hanging over the small table beside the door and struck the sparker. A little flame came to life and painted warm shadows around the cabin. I adjusted its intensity to give the room sufficient light and hung it back up.

There was no sound from the door during all this, so I waited. "Let me know when she's awake," he said finally, "I need to talk to you both."

"You two are very loud," Dana said. Her voice was quiet and still quite weak, but I took the sass as a positive sign. "I'm awake now," she added. I looked to see that she was carefully sitting up and shifting so that she could lean against the wall into which the bed was built. She gave me a wan smile and a nod.

I slid the latch, opened the door, and Kelly stepped in. He had cleaned up since we had parted and now wore a light linen shirt and britches, no doubt on loan from the pirate's stores as ours were. The lantern's light revealed the weariness I had guessed at on his face, despite the smile he gave Dana when he saw her.

"Look who's still in the land of the living," he said.

"As I understand it, you're the one to blame," she replied.

"Guilty as charged," he said, his smile wavering a

little.

He walked over to where she sat and pointed to the site of her wound. She nodded, and he moved so as not to block the light while she slid the open collar of her nightshirt aside to reveal what remained of the injury. He leaned over and scrutinized it, then stood and stepped back to the table with a look of satisfaction.

"Is it okay?" I said, feeling the need to ask despite his apparent contentment.

"It is," Kelly said, sitting heavily in the small chair at the table, "It looks exactly as it's supposed to. It will be stiff for a while, but you'll be back to normal eventually."

Dana smiled and shifted in the bed; sitting up a bit straighter.

"Don't rush it," Kelly said, raising his eyebrows at her. "You bled a lot; you're going to be plenty weak for a bit." She leaned back again, suitably chastised.

I sat on the bed near her and looked at Kelly expectantly. He leaned forward with his elbows on his knees and looked at the floor. The lantern light played across him as it oscillated with the gentle sway of the ship. Dana looked from one to the other of us with a look of concern. I waited; whatever was coming, it had to come from him. In time, he looked up and began to speak.

"I want you to understand how strange this feels to me," he started, "I have lived, to this point, a life that has been dominated by secrets. Some that are mine, many that aren't. So to talk about this – this in particular – feels all manner of wrong."

"What are you talking about?" Dana said, confused. I reached over and laid my hand on her leg.

"Revelations, Lady Dana," Kelly said, "I am talking about revelations; ones that may explain many things. Years ago, when we first knew one another, you will recall that I left the army and my position in the palace guard, correct?"

We nodded. This part of the story, at least, was not new to me, though some of it – some great pieces of it – would be to Dana.

"I did not quit," he said, "though it was meant to look that way. I was, in truth, recruited. Selected by the empress herself as her Raven."

Dana's eyes grew wide. "That's a myth. There's no such thing," she said.

"There isn't now," I said quietly, drawing her gaze to me, "but there was. He was the last." I looked at him steadily.

"I tell you this for two reasons," he said, "One, it will help you to understand how the rest of what I tell you happened. And two, I want you to be able to know that what comes next is also a fact. I was Empress Ardallah's Raven – her agent, her eyes and ears where others couldn't go. I was a sneak and a thief and a liar, and all of it for the crown. Until I wasn't."

He stood up and paced in the small area before the door, his hands folded behind his back. “My duties led me to the Talte Bruite – the Crushed Lands. Rumors of the dangers there had the Empress concerned, and she wanted to know all I could find out. She nearly found out nothing. Shortly after I made my way past the borders, I got attacked by a pack of animals of a kind I’ve never seen before; ones I can’t even rightly describe to you, nor would you want me to. I was, in fact, killed.” He looked over to us.

“Um,” Dana said, “No, you weren’t.” She glanced at me.

“Well,” he said with a dismissive shake of his head, “not permanently.” He shrugged and resumed pacing. “I was found by a group of..., hermits, I guess? Though I don’t know if you can be a ‘group’ of hermits. Well, a group that has cut themselves off from the world. Monks, maybe? I don’t know. That’s more accurate, at least. They did for me basically what I just did for you; they brought me back.”

“How?” I asked. “How did you – or they – or anyone, for that matter?”

Kelly gave me a stoic look. “It’s the gems, Jules. They’re not just stones. With the proper preparation, they can make, well, miracles.”

I thought about the wand he had used on Dana. The blue and yellow crystals on its end suddenly clearly in my mind. “But they weren’t emeralds,” I said.

“There are all kinds of them,” he explained, “Kelian emeralds happen to be the most powerful, for sure. They're also almost exclusively destructive.”

I looked over at the cabinet where I had put the box of gems from King Ronald. I felt anxiety – a fear – take hold.

Kelly must have seen me looking, because he said, “Don’t get me wrong. All of them are completely inert unless they’re treated and combined with various other ingredients. But when they are, what they can do is incredible.”

I looked back to Dana, who was looking down at the now healed wound on her chest. I couldn’t tell what was going through her mind, but she looked pensive as she touched the white star-shaped mark.

Kelly sighed and sat back down. “I stayed with the monks for a long while – my wounds were pretty extensive – and while I was there, they taught me how it all worked. And they swore me to secrecy. You see, they believe that the Talte Bruite is the wasteland that it is because of a terrible accident involving the power of the stones long ago. They have a legend that tells of an ancient nation that misused them and nearly destroyed the world.”

My mind reeled. Everything he had done – being branded the Blackcrow, leaving, becoming a wanderer – all of it was to keep this terrible power secret. “Do you truly believe that?” I said, unable to hide how stunned I felt.

“I don’t know,” he said with a shrug, pushing his hand

through his hair, "but I do know what the gems can do in even small doses. Do you know how much I used back in the cove so that you all could get to the ship?" He looked at us for a moment, then held up his cupped hand. "Less than would fill my palm," he said gravely.

I looked at him, then over to Dana. Her eyes were on his hand, but unfocused, as if she were doing mathematics in her thoughts. It only took a moment for her to put the pieces into place.

"Someone wanted the secret," she said, looking at him severely. He looked down, his eyes flashing to me for only a moment.

"My mother," I admitted, "She found out."

He nodded, his face sad. "When I came home," he said, "I kept the secret. For a while, it was fine. But I was stupid, and the secret got out. Word spread of the reappearance of the 'ancient powers of legend,' and Her Majesty wanted to know the truth. More, she wanted the secret of the gems. Eventually, someone traced it back to me. She commanded me and I...," he sighed heavily, "I couldn't."

I reached up to brush an unfallen tear before either of them noticed. His life – our lives – had been so twisted by this secret. I felt a fit of impotent anger roil inside of me, and I stood, unable to contain it. "Why did you have to learn the secrets in the first place?" I blurted, "Why not just leave the monks to their secretive ways and leave it alone?" I was outraged now, the words chasing one another out of my mouth. I glared at him.

"I had no choice," Kelly said. He sat down and looked at me with such a sober pain on his face that it stopped my anger cold. "I had to learn," he said, "because unless I did, I wouldn't be able to use the stones myself. And if I couldn't do that...," he paused, the weight of his words pulling at him, "If I couldn't do that, then I would die all over again."

The room fell silent, even the gentle splash of the waves outside seemed to pause. I looked into his eyes as what he said settled in on me.

"I was dead," he said unblinking, "Now I'm not. The monks used the stones to bring me back. But without continued treatments, the effect will fade. I'm dead all over again."

Time froze for a long moment. No one spoke or moved as the weight of truth brought us all crashing to earth.

"Then, so am I," Dana said quietly, her situation now more evident to her. Kelly slowly nodded.

I spun on my heel away from them, weeping silently. It was horrible. It was wonderful. My friends were alive, but they weren't. Again, my mind whirled as I faced the thick glass windows and watched the sea through my tears. I saw all of it as little vignettes flashed through my mind; the gems, their power, the Empire. The part of me that was heir to the throne was now planning and plotting – drawing conclusions and making decisions – while the woman inside me curled up into a little ball and wished for it all to go away.

This new silence stretched on for a long time, none of the three of us moving or speaking. Finally, I reached up and wiped away the remaining tears from my cheeks and straightened, folding my hands in front of me and turning around.

"She cannot return to Yorch," the heir to the throne said with my voice. "I will not have her put in the position where she may be humiliated or killed for this cursed knowledge."

Dana looked up at me, aghast. "What?"

"I am sorry, Lady Dana," I said, allowing the cold of my office full control, "You are not in exile – though that would likely be my mother's judgment, I am certain. I do not wish that to happen. I wish your name and your rank to remain yours so that perhaps one day you will be free to return. However, for now, you cannot serve in Yorch any longer. It is the only way that you will not become what the Blackcrow is. Or worse." Inside me, very deep inside, the woman was screaming; screaming into the darkness how wrong, how horrible, how unjust it all was. Outside, I looked at my lifelong friend steadily. There were tears on her cheeks now, flowing freely from her unblinking eyes as she held my glare.

"I was told there would be a price for your life," I said,

briefly glancing over at Kelly, “And while I am horrified by what it turned out to be, I would pay it again that you live. It may perhaps be best that I didn’t know then; mayhap, I would have let my judgment be clouded. As it is, this is the right of it.”

Kelly stood and looked at Dana with sadness in his eyes. “When you’re feeling up to it, we can talk more. There are things you will need to know,” he said. He seemed wrung out; thin and tired.

Dana nodded, wiping away tears. “Would you leave now?” she said, her voice quiet but harsh, “I’d like to be alone for a while. I need to rest.” She turned her face away from either of us and toward the window.

“Of course,” Kelly said. He looked at me for a moment, and I could see the pain I – we – were feeling reflected in his face. Then he turned and left.

I walked over to the bed and put my hand on Dana’s arm. She didn’t move.

“You are my best friend,” I said, barely more than a whisper, “I love you.”

Dana swallowed hard and nodded, seemingly unable to do more.

I turned and left the room – and her – and closed the door behind me.

I sat alone on the foredeck, watching the clouds wheel

past the fragment of the moon that occasionally peeked out in the night sky. The crewmen that worked the ship at night were few, and all of them cut me a wide berth as if my desire to remain alone hung like a warning sign over me. I leaned back against one of the forward trusses on the starboard side, staring up at the sky and wondering how everything had come to be as it was.

"You look cold," said a quiet voice. I turned to see Denis approaching from the stairs. He had a blanket in his hand and held it out to me. He wasn't wrong, though the persistent chill in the air was more of an afterthought as I was mostly numb. I considered the bundle of cloth as he held it out for a minute, then finally took it without a word and wrapped it around myself. It did ward off the cold I hadn't realized I felt. He waited while I did so, and when I finished, walked a few steps past me to lean on the railing and watch the sea. Neither of us spoke for some time.

"Pretty night," he said, eventually.

"Yes," I said.

"It's funny, isn't it?" he said, still watching the horizon.

I watched the sky for a long time before I responded, but he waited in silence.

"What?" I said.

He waved his hand as if to take in the whole of the sky and the sea. "All of this. It can kill you dead as sure as night and day. It's relentless. Merciless. And it doesn't care about you or me or anyone at all." He paused. "But," he said with a sigh, "here you and I are. Two different worlds, two different lives, and it draws us both out here. It's amazing."

I looked again into the sky. I couldn't say why, but I felt a tear drop fall down my face.

Denis turned to me, leaning sideways on the railing. "I don't know all about what happened today; I know Kelly said that there was a 'cost' for what we did. I also know he seems well and truly miserable right now. And I know you're out here watching the sky at midnight with tears in your eyes. I'm not looking to interfere. As someone who has tried to avoid it most of his life, all I can say is this; sometimes doing the right thing hurts."

He looked at me for a long moment as if making sure that I had heard what he said. I cast him a thin smile.

"I'm not suggesting you miraculously just 'feel better'," he said shrugging, "Just that the pain doesn't make it wrong. You two saved her life. One way or another, that happened."

I nodded slowly, and he turned back to the railing and the sea. Several long minutes passed. Eventually, he straightened and looked at me, squarely.

"Don't stay out here all night; the cold and wet aren't good for you," he nodded to me and walked away.

A few minutes later, his words still ringing in my ears,

I went below, curled up in my bed, and drifted into a dreamless sleep.

CHAPTER ELEVEN
– AERYK –

The days aboard Edword's ship following our escape from Chateau Flint were, for me, as a long slow march to my final doom. Each hour brought me closer to my homeland, where I had no doubt, I would be facing the repercussions for my actions. I had no idea what my ultimate fate would be, let alone the specific personal reprisal from King Ronald or my father. Censure certainly. Imprisonment was very much a strong possibility. Was the loss of my birthright or exile possible? Was execution? Every option seemed, at least at one time or another over the days at sea, to be the one I was sure to face. And given the consequences already inflicted on my new friends during our adventure, it would be hard to make the case that I didn't deserve all of it.

To keep the dark thoughts at bay, I decided that it would be best to occupy my hands as much as possible. I had come through the last few days physically whole; a fact that did nothing to soothe my ongoing feelings of guilt; so I offered myself to the pirate captain for whatever tasks he might deem me as capable of handling. As a result, I spent those days doing menial chores such as swabbing the deck and minding the lines. It kept me busy and staved off for a time, the prophecies of my demise that haunted my thoughts. I did, in fact, begin learning the sailor's trade, and while it was only a brief stint, I was as surprised as anyone to find that I had a natural knack for the sea and that I was actually enjoying what I was doing. I worked from dawn to dusk, eschewing the standard 'shifts' that the crew used, and when such tasks were not occupying me, I tried to learn what I could. Each day ended when I, exhausted, collapsed in my cabin into blissful unconsciousness until the next morning when I began again. Thus, my contact with my companions was sparse. I did speak with Denis daily, for he too was spending his time in service to the pirate. He obviously had some history on the sea as well, which Edword found useful and so he continued to fill the role of boatswain as needed. Such were his duties that we were brought into contact regularly, if only briefly. Rohb came out on the deck for a bit of fresh air quite often and would give me a nod or some other acknowledgment when he did, though little more. He had needed to realign the bones in his arm again, having renewed the original injury when he collided with the horse during the battle. Here on the ship, the makeshift sling Julea had fashioned from his belt was replaced with a splint and wrapped appropriately by the ship's surgeon. Kelly, when he came up, spent a good deal of time near the helm, talking with Edword and Denis about I knew not what. Most other times, he remained below, as did Julea and Dana.

Edword had taken us far out on the Teardrop Sea and in a circuitous route south. His destination, he had explained on the first evening, was to be Clemons, and he believed that staying far from the nearer shore would lessen the chance of being intercepted by foe or friend. The result of this course was an extended journey of just over five days, but one that would be less eventful. There was no quarrel on this last point; we were all happy to avoid any more excitement than necessary.

I was standing on the fore-deck on the fourth day at about what the crew routinely called the 'second dog watch,' or what I would have previously called the late afternoon. I was coiling up the lines that directed the foresail – I was still working out the proper names for all of the rigging – when I heard booted feet coming up the stairs. With a glance, I saw Kelly approach. He was – we all were – wearing the ubiquitous white shirt and tan pants of the ship's stores. Kelly had added a wide leather belt from which his black blade hung. We had asked about the supplies aboard the ship when we first found them. Edword explained that the things aboard, apart from the personal items his men carried with them, had to be naval supplies that were stowed by the guard when the ship was still intended to be kept by the 'king.' He seemed somewhat maliciously pleased that we – and his crew – were making use of them.

"'Evening, your lordship," Kelly said. He had been somewhat quiet since the escape; as if something were troubling him. I had briefly pondered what it could be; after all, we had escaped alive and whole – including Dana – and we would soon be back to safety. I knew there must be something I was missing, but the cloud of my personal future was far too dark for me to see much beyond.

"Evenin'", I said.

"You're really taking to this sailor thing, aren't you?" he said, and I could hear the grin on his face in his voice. I shrugged, finishing the coiling of the lines before me.

"It seems I am," I admitted. "I have to admit; there's something to the idea of a life at sea."

Kelly sat on the railing, wedging his foot around a strut for stability. "I expect it seems particularly attractive to you right now," he said, considering me carefully.

I shrugged. "Cleaning out the bilge sounds significantly better than returning to the wreckage my life is about to become," I said as I looked up and gave him a grave look.

He drew a long breath and sighed, then turned and looked into the distance. The sun, bright in the late autumn sky, had landed on the western horizon, bathing everything in a pinkish-orange light. A gentle cross breeze heralded the coming of a chilly night. Autumn, it seemed, had come in full now and the nights held the promise of the winter that was just a few weeks away.

"What do you think will happen?" he asked, turning back to me.

I finished coiling a second loop of rope while I thought. I had, as mentioned earlier, considered a host of possible futures in my private thoughts, but being asked out loud collapsed all of the possibilities down to the real question; what will happen to me? I stepped over to the railing and leaned heavily against it.

"I would bet on imprisonment if I were pressed to," I said, and hearing the words aloud made it seem self-evident. "What I did – no matter my motive, you know – but what I did will be seen as treason," I paused, letting the thought sink in on us both. "King Ronald will seek to be lenient, because when it comes to it, he is a good man, and possibly a little too noble-hearted for his own good. But the law is the law, and he does need to keep the dukes and the other nobles on his side."

"And your father?" Kelly said, his arms folded as he listened.

I barked out a bitter laugh. "Lord Rojer is one of the ones the king will most need to appease, and he will be far from lenient in his appraisal. If anything, my father will be one of the voices pushing for exile or death."

Kelly looked at me a long moment as I stood staring at

the deck. I knew that I was acting as harshly in my judgment of my father as I was accusing him of being to me, and I felt struck by the terrible realization that, despite our best efforts, our parents do live on in us for good and for ill. I shook the thought off with a shrug.

"Besides," I continued with a sigh, "the truth of it is that I am guilty of treason. I impersonated the king, lied to what I at least believed was a foreign power, and conspired to aid in the unlawful abduction of a foreign ambassador. It's quite difficult to put a noble face on that, Kelly, no matter how hard you try."

A rueful chuckle came from him as he turned again toward the sea. We stood there for a long time before he spoke.

"Have you ever considered not going back?" he asked.

I felt the strangest sensation pass through me at his words. "What?" I said.

"Don't go back. If you know you're facing that kind of judgment, why do it?"

I stared at him. At first, I was waiting for there to be some indication of humor; something to tell me he was joking. But none came. He was in earnest, and I had never even considered the idea.

"I have to go back," I stammered, the words driven out of my mouth by a lifetime of lectures on duty, "I have no choice."

"Sure you do," he said. He hopped off his perch on the rail and turned around to lean on it next to me. "Look out there," he said with a flip of his chin toward the sea, "I can tell you from experience, it's a big world out there. And some of it is not even trying to kill you. You should see it."

I stood still, unconsciously shaking my head as if my body itself were resisting the idea.

"Aeryk," Kelly said, his voice somehow quiet and firm at the same time, "I understand the need you feel for penance. You made a mistake, and people got hurt. I'm not going to pretend otherwise, and you shouldn't either. But like I said to you back at the camp, you can't change the past. What you can do is make every decision going forward with the intent to do better. You've been tilting with your mistakes ever since you realized what they were, and you're a better man for it. I honestly don't know that any actual justice will be served with you sitting in a dungeon in Castle Sterling."

His words rolled through my mind like a herd of cattle; bumping and shuffling against the anxieties I had been holding there for days. He was mad, of course; crazy. There was no way I could simply walk away. Besides, a firm voice in the back of my head that sounded suspiciously like my father said, *who is he to give that kind of advice?*

"That's a fair point," I unintentionally said aloud to the voice. Kelly looked at me, confused. I turned to him and said, "It does seem that it's a bit inconsistent of you – of all people – to suggest I do something like that, doesn't it?"

Kelly chuckled, but it had a strange, sad quality to it. "Ah, maybe you're right. I'm probably not on a real high plateau of wisdom in matters like that, am I?"

I decided not to answer. Instead, it seemed like a good time to change the subject. "How is Dana? I've been meaning to check in but...," I let the sentence drop for fear it would result in us circling back around to the previous discussion.

"Sure," Kelly said, taking the cue, "Physically, she's doing really well." I got the intuitive sense that he was holding something back. By then, I had become very used to that with him.

"You said 'physically,'" I said.

He nodded, taking a long slow breath before he spoke again. "There are complications. Changes she is working through. She's not going back with the princess."

I looked at him hard. "What?"

"Complications," he repeated, "The wound she took will not allow her to continue as Julea's personal guard. She – well, they – decided that it would be better not to return to Yorch."

He was watching the sea, never once turning to me. I slumped, looking out at the water, now wine-dark in the light of the sunset. "That couldn't have been easy for her," I said.

"No. It wasn't," he replied.

"And Princess Julea?" I asked.

"She was the first to realize the situation," he said, "and she has accepted it. She is..., I think the phrase is 'a singular woman.'" He shook his head gently with a shrug.

I nodded. "She is that," I agreed.

We stood that way for a long time, until the light had nearly left the sky. Finally, he stood and faced me.

"We should be back in your lands by day after tomorrow," he said.

"So I understand," I said, facing him. He nodded, a pensive look on his face.

"I appreciate it, Kelly," I said, knowing that he was thinking about my fate.

"Just–," he said, then paused. He nodded to me before he began again. "I just hate to see a good man wasted."

"How fortunate for you that it's not entirely apparent whether I'm a good man," I said, with a smirk.

"Not your call to make, your lordship," he said, "I know better."

He looked at me for a moment and then, after clapping his hand on my shoulder briefly, turned and walked down the stairs and across the deck, on his way to his quarters. I leaned back down on the railing, lost in thought until long after it was dark.

We came in sight of Clemons harbor early in the

forenoon watch a day later. The previous day had been one of heavy rains and wind, and while I spent my time working below decks, the remainder of our little party stayed in their rooms. As a result, our last day at sea was for me a solitary one where I spent much of the time deep in thought about the future. Now, the sun had returned, and the heavy rain clouds of yesterday were naught but a memory as the sun glowed bright and clear in an azure sky. Seeing the harbor, its tall tower looking out on the sea, brought with it thoughts of youth and home, and made the conclusions I had reached during my meditations the previous day even more evident.

Edword had his crew hang a white flag off the mast during our approach as a precaution. While it was unlikely that anyone would identify the black ship as a pirate vessel; it was after all on its maiden voyage; he felt that prudence should rule the day. He brought us up short of the docks and dropped anchor a goodly distance out in the harbor. Then, using a small piece of shined metal, flashed a light to the watchpoint on the shore. In short order, a small ship left the dock and came toward us. It, too, was flying a flag of peace.

"Guards of the coast," Edword said. Our little band had gathered on the fore-deck near where the pirate captain was standing for the encounter. It was the first time I had seen the women since we had made our escape, and the first time I'd seen Dana since her brief appearance in the captain's cabin. She seemed, against all reason, to be entirely well. She stood by Princess Julea, her rapier belted around her borrowed pirate livery, tall and straight, clear-eyed and alert. There was, though, a difference about her; a sadness that just seemed to touch her eyes. On further consideration, I noted the same quality in the princess, appearing when she thought no one was looking.

The other ship now drew up close. From her foredeck, an armored member of the Clemons guard stood. He raised his hand in salute as the vessels drew to a close enough distance for conversation.

"I am captain of the dock watch, serving the Lord of Clemons. What's your business in our harbor?" called the other.

"Hail, Captain," Edword said, "I have no trade and no business in your harbor. I have come on behalf of these several souls who bade me return them to your port, and so I have done."

I raised my eyebrows while glances passed between my companions and me at Edword's unexpected etiquette.

"Which souls?" said the watch captain as he squinted in the sun at us.

"My companions and me," I said, stepping forward, "I am Lord Aeryk, Marquess of Claire. We left your city some days ago and have now returned. Guide us to Lord Myk, and everything will be made clear."

The captain stepped back as if he'd been struck. He

turned to the men behind him, and animatedly gave them instructions. Then he turned back to us. “Weigh your anchor, Captain. We will guide you in to dock.”

They cast a line over to us as they came about, and Edword had it fastened to our bow. Then the other ship drew wind and led us into the harbor and to the nearest dock. Shortly, the crew made us fast and laid the gangplank in place.

And thus, we arrived in Clemons.

Home.

— DANA —

The sunlight was, to put it bluntly, painful after all the days in our cabin, and I honestly felt more than a little unsteady when we finally disembarked. I would never have expected that I would be less settled on the dry ground than on a ship, but there I was.

I wouldn’t have expected a lot of things.

By the time we reached the end of the dock and were on the shore proper, Lord Myk of Clemons had already rushed down from the tower to meet us. I say ‘rushed’ as he was only partially put together; his armor hung loose and unfastened, his hair was unkempt, and he didn’t seem to have any weaponry with him at all. On seeing Aeryk, he rushed forward and grabbed him in a bear hug that I thought might break the younger man in half.

"How in the name of The One did you get here? We thought you were dead!" He blurted, looking from one to the other of us. Rohb, Edword, and Denis stood at the back, and if the Lord of Clemons had any thought about the newcomers, he gave no hint.

Aeryk eased himself out of the hug but kept his hands on Myk's shoulders. "That is a long tale, my friend," he said with a warm smile, "and one that would be best told after we've rested up a bit. Is that acceptable to you?"

"Of course!" Myk roared happily. "I have rooms in the tower, but..., what about the sailors that brought you here? Do they require lodging?"

Aeryk looked back to Edword, who shook his head. "The crew's fine, sir," he said, "and I will be looking to fill some vacancies, so it will be best if I can take an' find an inn nearer the docks? By your leave?"

Myk nodded, still in a fit of delight at our arrival. "Of course, of course, Captain," he said, "but I insist on your presence for dinner tonight. We will be celebrating!"

A devilish glint shone in the pirate's eye as he gave a sideways glance to Denis. "That's very hospitable of you, your lordship. I'd be pleased."

For a moment, I thought that it would be good to let Myk know that he was offering to entertain one of the most infamous pirates on the sea, but then I stopped myself. In a world where down had become up and duty had become a death sentence, who was I, I now wondered, to say that the pirate shouldn't eat with the lord of the city.

"Come then," Myk said with a tone that encompassed the rest of us, "come and get some refreshment in my home."

He turned then, his arm around Aeryk's back and began to walk up the hill to the Tower. Rohb and Denis followed behind, with Denis looking around and taking in the entire city. I wondered if he had ever been to Clemons before. It was apparent that he had been a seafarer for some of his days, after all. I mused for a moment if I should consider a life at sea for myself, before a clear memory of my constant seasickness made me reconsider. *Though you haven't been sick on this trip*, I realized rather suddenly. Was it because of the healing? In truth, I knew very little of my new condition, and I hadn't been the most open to hearing more during our journey.

Jules looked up at me and smiled gently, then followed Myk and his entourage. I fell in step with her; an old habit that wouldn't be of use for very much longer. Behind me, I heard Kelly's footsteps as he brought up the rear. I knew we needed to talk. He said he would explain my situation further. I, though, had stayed in my room and slept most of the trip, both because I was recovering and because I had no desire to face the truth. Yet, Jules had been there, and together we talked as we always had, though I feigned exhaustion whenever she tried to bring up the new future ahead of me. I had no desire to face that until I had to.

And now, here and in relative safety, I saw that I did.

The Tower of Clemons spared us nothing for our return. After a brief wait in the entry chamber, we were each ushered up to separate private rooms in the tower. Interestingly, I was given the quarters that Julea and I had shared on our first visit, as Myk insisted that we would all have "the best he could offer." The Person-I-Was, as I had named the old stage of my life, would have said such was unnecessary, but the new me was delighted at the chance to be by myself. A young serving girl – no more than an ascended child, really – brought a small plate of meat, bread, and cheese moments after I arrived in the room. She put it, along with a bottle of wine, on the small table at the end of the bed and with a nod, turned and left me alone. I ate the food with relish; the salted rations on the ship were, while not the worst thing I'd ever eaten, something that barely counted as food, and at a time when I felt as hungry as I could ever remember being. As it was, I could not imagine that the feast promised for the evening could be any more satisfying than what was on that platter.

With my stomach now pacified and my second cup of wine in my hand, I looked over to the bath in the far corner of the room. It was obscured behind a wooden screen, but visible from my seat on the edge of the bed. Neither Julea nor I had paid it any mind on our first stay, we were too busy looking for danger everywhere, but now it seemed quite fully as inviting to me as the meal had. It appeared that it had been prepared in advance, and was filled full with warm water – translucent wisps of inviting steam still wafting off the surface. In moments, I settled in and drifted into a fugue.

It was sometime later, and I was out of the bath, standing before the metal mirror in the corner. I stared closely at the white star on my chest, where the arrow had killed me but hadn't. The skin was smooth. When I closed my eyes and ran my fingers over it, it was indistinguishable from the flesh around it. It felt neither too sensitive or numb; rather, I felt my fingers on it as I ever had. It was so different from the scars on my back which...

Something, I realized, was different there too. I turned, and in the imperfect reflection, I saw that the scars on my back – the scars that had been there since I was a child – had changed somehow. The irregular texture, the blotches of color, the thicker and less flexible patches, were gone. Instead, a white swirl, the color of the star on my chest, replaced them all. I bent my arm around and realized that sensation had returned to the area as well. In my reflection, I saw my eyes like saucers and a tiny grin pulling at my mouth. And there in the image of my face, the objective truth confronted me again. My body – and by extension, I – had changed.

A gentle knock on the door snapped me back to awareness. “One moment,” I called, suddenly realizing that I had been standing naked for a very long time. I grabbed the long cream-colored robe from the hook by the mirror and bundled it around myself.

“Come in,” I said, still slightly flustered. There was a rattle of the latch, but the door remained fast.

“Oh,” I said, remembering the lock, “just a moment.” I opened the door to find Kelly standing outside. He saw my robe and glanced away politely.

“I’m sorry,” he said, “I was hoping we might have a chance to talk. It can wait.”

“No, no,” I said, “it’s fine. I think our talk has waited long enough already. Come in, please.”

I stepped back and aside as he entered. He looked around the room carefully as he did, habitually noting the details. It seemed as if he had taken the time to clean up as well. He was dressed now in the blue of the Clemons guardsmen; fresh clothing no doubt provided by the lord of the tower. I walked over to the two chairs placed on the near side of the room across from the bath and sat down, adjusting my robe carefully. He followed suit and joined me. We sat quietly for a long moment.

“So,” I said.

“So,” he replied.

I reached up and brushed my hair back with my

hands. I had washed it and brushed it out after the bath, but it was still hanging in wet strands, which I pushed away until they hung down my back over the robe. I looked hard at him and squinted as if to show my concentration. “You said that I need some sort of ongoing treatment. What does that mean, exactly?” I asked; there seeming to be little reason for preamble.

He raised his eyebrows, accepting the admittedly direct nature of my question, then leaned back in the chair. “First of all, I need to tell you that even the monks weren’t entirely sure how the gems work; they had several theories, but nothing conclusive. What I’m telling you is from my own experience. The stones don’t— they didn’t really heal us; not in the sense that we’re back to normal. We were as good as dead; you don’t heal from that. What they did do is to replace or fill in for the parts of us that stopped working. They’re part of you now, the same way they’re part of me. They replaced the damaged bits.”

“How can that be?”

He shook his head. “I don’t have any better answers. It’s a mystery. Like so many things about them.”

I nodded, not entirely satisfied.

“The most important thing to remember is that they don’t do anything alone. They only work in combination with other ingredients. It’s like a fire in the hearth that needs wood to burn or it stops giving off heat.”

"So this ongoing treatment is like that; we have to feed the fire?" I asked.

"That's how I look at it."

I nodded. That part I could at least understand, and I needed to have something I could understand to process any of it. "How often?"

He stood up and, as was his habit, paced back and forth across the room from me. "It seems to depend," he began. "The harder they work, the more they do, the sooner you need to add to the fire. At least at first, you'll probably need it more often. Actually, how are you feeling now?"

I shrugged. "Tired, but that's been true since the battle. Why, what should I look for?"

"Pains around the wound area. I let it go too long a few times when I was first getting used to it, and it felt like being stabbed all over again. Now it's more of an ache when I let it go, though that's maybe because I try not to test my limits anymore. And I've been doing this for a while now."

I looked at him, and my curiosity must have shown on my face. He pulled at the lacing at the collar of his tunic, loosening it as he walked over and stopped in front of me. He leaned over and pulled the collar down and away so that I could see. A broad white line about three inches long traced a path down and to the left from the middle of his chest.

"It was a bone spike that looked like a butcher's knife, and it went straight through me, bones and all," he said.

Absently, I reached up and touched it with my fingers, but much like the white lines on my own body, they were indistinguishable from the rest of his skin.

He coughed and stepped back, pulling the laces tighter again.

“I expect that you’ll feel it in a day or two. That’s when you’ll know,” he said, sitting back in the chair again.

“Some other things are different,” I said, thinking about the scars on my back. I absently reached up to my right shoulder.

“Sure,” he said, “you’ll probably notice a few strange differences. Mostly you’ll find that you heal pretty quickly from minor things – bruises, exhaustion, what-not. Best not to draw attention to that, by the way. People get curious. Then they get superstitious.”

I nodded, then said, “So I need to learn how to do this treatment then. And where do I get gems? And how do I do that when I don’t even know where I’m going?” I was starting to talk too fast, but saying it out loud was acknowledging the truth of it all, and I had been doing very well not doing that.

He leaned forward and rested his hand on my knee. “One step at a time, Dana,” he said, “one step at a time. First, let’s talk about how to do the treatment. Meet me tomorrow, and we’ll find a place where I can teach you. Tonight let’s just enjoy that we’re alive, okay?”

I smiled at him then. I owed him a lot, I realized. Not

only was he trying terribly hard to be positive about everything, but he had actually saved my life. Granted, he probably did that for Julea, I thought, but that wasn't such a bad thing, was it?

He stood then and turned toward the door. "Okay, I will see you tonight at the feast," he said. He reached the door and took the handle before he stopped as if suddenly remembering something.

"Oh, right. I nearly forgot," Kelly said, reaching into a small pouch on his belt. He pulled out a light silver chain and looked at it before handing it to me. "I believe this is yours," he said.

The small circle of metal flickered in the light – my Silver Spar medallion. I took it gingerly.

"Our friend back there had it around his neck at the battle. I went back for it; I thought you should have it," he said. He seemed almost embarrassed.

I looked at it, my mind full of all that it represented before, and what it meant that he had retrieved it. I looked up at him, unsure of what to say.

"I washed it," he said suddenly, breaking the tension, "but you may want to do it again, because really – yuck." He smiled at me.

I stood and pulled him into an embrace. "Thank you," I whispered.

He held me in return for a few moments, then gently

stepped away. "My pleasure," he said before he turned and left, closing the door behind him.

I pulled at the clasp and moved to put the necklace around my neck and then stopped.

"Yeah," I said quietly, "Definitely wash one more time."

— DENIS —

Say what you will about fancy people – and I'm sure whatever that is I've said worse – but they can really put on a shindig when they want to.

We gathered in the late afternoon in the banquet area of the Tower of Clemons for the celebratory feast that Lord Myk had declared at the dock. I was, personally, less than thrilled at the prospect of a long night of sitting around with the landed gentry no matter how good the food might be. I had been more than happy with the plate of finger food and the bottle of wine I had gotten when I got to my room. And the bath. Don't ever let anyone minimize the absolute joy of a nice warm bath. Food, wine, and a bath, people, that's the dream. And in fact, I dreamt about all three because after I took a nice long nap, waking just in time to reluctantly dress and go to the feasting hall. A very fancy dress shirt and black pants were left in the room for me, along with a maroon velvet waistcoat, and, thus fancied up, I went down to dinner.

Imagine my surprise when I came into the brightly lit and festively apportioned banquet room and found an actual party. Several dozen people that I hadn't met milled around talking and drinking. At the far end of the room, a long bar was in place, and several of the servants were busily pouring wine and ale into goblets and tankards. Across from me, at the near end of the room where the main door was, five musicians dressed as flamboyantly as I'd ever seen men dress, provided a background of cheerful music. The far wall opposite me was full of windows that overlooked a narrow balcony over the northwest side of the bay, the opposite side from where the docks were, and the sea reflected the sunlight from the setting sun. In the middle of the room was an elaborate arrangement of tables that gave the impression of a single table that wove snakelike through the length of the room. It was there, seated at the center-most section, that first I saw some of my friends. Myk, the lord of the city, sat to one end of the middle section with Aeryk to his side. They seemed deeply invested in a conversation that even from a distance, looked too serious for a party. This, I decided, I wanted nothing to do with. At the other end of the same section, Kelly, Julea, and Dana were seated and engaged in a quiet discussion. I had finally pinned Kelly down while we were at sea and he had let me in on the details of Dana's recovery. Short but sweet, she wasn't going back to the Empire, and everyone was sad. That, it appeared, was what was on Julea's mind when she and I met on the deck that night. I had said all I could to her then and had nothing of any value to say to Dana, so I decided on a higher purpose and headed to the bar where Edword and Rohb stood, each with a tankard in their hand and certainly more than one already down their throat.

"Hey! It's the dungeon rat," Rohb said, gruffly but amiably.

I bowed with feigned cordiality. "Are either of you looking to get into any deep or meaningful discussions?" I asked. They looked at one another for a moment in confusion before letting go with laughter.

"Excellent," I said, "then I'm staying here with you." I leaned over the bar until I had the attention of one of the servants, and moments later I had a mug of my own, filled with a dark brown ale as good as any I'd ever had.

The night went on as such nights do. The music and merrymaking – and the alcohol – eventually broke up the deeper discussions going on in the room and a real revelry was made of it. The Imperials even seemed to relax, with both of them actually joining in at one point during an honestly pretty sketchy song the musicians played. The discomfort on Princess Julea's face when she realized what the lyric "hoist the mainsail" actually referred to made me laugh hard enough that beer came out of my nose. Some time later, I looked around to find Kelly, only to see that he was standing alone outside the large windows, facing the water. I looked around until I saw, near the end of the bar, the small exit door that led out on the balcony. I went out to find him standing with a chalice in his hand, watching the starlight of the night sky twinkling on the black water.

"It's cold out here," I said first.

"It is," he replied.

I sat on the small stone ledge that formed the railing of the balcony. This side of the tower was built almost flush with a medium sized cliff, and from here a fall would drop you directly into the waters of the bay. Or on a rock.

"You're verbose tonight," I said, taking a pull of the latest in a long line of ales.

He looked at me and said, "I am all out of words, and you have a remarkable vocabulary for a dungeon rat."

"You know, I don't know if I'm overly thrilled with how that nickname seems to be sticking," I said.

"That does always seem to be the way," he replied. Unconsciously, he shrugged his right shoulder; the one where the scarred tattoo was.

"So what do you do from here?" I asked, taking another sip.

He sighed. "I'm not sure," he said. "I was heading back toward the Talte Bruite when I came through here originally. I had an idea to go see the monks again, but, I don't know if it matters," he said with a shrug.

I nodded.

"Honestly? I am tempted to head back north of the Superiors; maybe find out what happened to the real Mathu. I hate the idea that we left that walking sewage on the seat of power there."

I chuffed. "I'm going to guess that his remaining hand is full after what we did. There's no chance that the majority of Mathu's army knew it wasn't actually him on the throne. I'd bet five gold coins that there's a little civil war going on up there right now."

"Maybe," he said, his gaze unfocused as the idea rolled around his head. "That's a nice thought. Not a guarantee, though. I hate leaving things unfinished."

"I guess I can see that. That guy is a piece of work."

Kelly turned to me now with a stern look on his face. "You should come with me," he said.

I returned the look, confused. "Come again?"

"We make a pretty good team," he said, cocking his head as if the idea had just occurred to him. "Together I think we have pretty good odds, whatever we face."

"Your odds," I said. "My odds are spectacular if I don't go with you."

"Den, we haven't known one another very long, and there are a lot – a lot – of questions I have about you. But I know two things for sure; one, you're incredibly capable. I've rarely fallen in step so naturally with an ally before, in or out of a fight."

"Flattery is nice, but you're going to have to buy me way more drinks before I sleep with you," I said.

"And two," he said, unfazed, "you are much more honorable and noble than you pretend. Probably than you even want to be."

I didn't have a reply to that. In fact, I sort of felt uncomfortable; exposed, even.

"So what do you say?" he asked. He extended his hand and continued, "I can't promise we'll wind up at more parties; probably there are more dungeons in our future, honestly. But it won't be boring, and it will always be for the right reason."

I stared at his hand. It was a dumb idea. I was, I reminded myself, happy with my knockabout ways. Really. I was.

I continued to look at the hand. This was so dangerous. The gems, the crazy fire, and the even crazier 'bring someone back from the dead'; it was so much more than anything I wanted to deal with. Nice and simple was always the best.

I watched my hand reach up and take his. To this day, I can't say what I was thinking. Then again, I make the best decisions of my life when I'm not thinking. This one was just a perfect example.

"North again?" I said. "Really? Can't we go somewhere

warm for the winter? Euticha maybe?"

"We'll talk about it," he said, a broad grin on his face.

"Fair enough, Blackcrow, but I'm telling you now; you get me killed, you're bringing me back from the dead, or I'll haunt your eastern arse for the rest of your days."

"Sure thing, dungeon rat. That's a deal."

– KELLY –

The party ended late, though I started to make my exit not too long after talking to Denis. Dana and Julea seemed to have left some time before we returned and were probably already hunkered down upstairs. Edword had gone long before, headed back down to the dock quarter where he was lodged. Aeryk was nowhere to be found, and Denis had stalked off to refill his tankard. I put my chalice on the bar and turned to go when Rohb appeared from nowhere. He had been drinking all night, but other than a mushier quality to his usual snarl, there seemed to be no effect.

"We've business, Blackcrow," he said, squaring up to me.

I sighed. "Right, right. Fight to the death. I remember. Can we do it later?"

He stood still and unblinking, a wall of a human that I couldn't even see around, much less avoid. He was glaring at me intensely.

"No," he said finally.

"Now?" I said, raising my eyebrows. "You want to fight now? Tell me you're kidding."

He shook his head. "I mean, 'no' I'm not going to fight you," he said.

I stood dumbstruck, sure that I had heard him wrong. "You're not?" I asked.

"My intention was to fulfill the law of the Empire. The same law my father and grandfathers fulfilled. You've been branded as Blackcrow, and that meant that I was honor-bound." He reached his good hand toward me, then past my shoulder where he retrieved his drink from the bar and took a long pull of it.

"But now?"

"But now," he said with a swallow, "I've fought by your side; seen you risk everything not only for the princess but for the Empire's needs. My eyes don't see a traitor, Kelly. I see a loyal man."

I was speechless, both from the unobscured sincerity of his statement and from the fact that he had – for the first time I could recall – called me 'Kelly' directly.

"So go on your way, Blackcrow," he said, smiling a little as he did, "and I will go on mine. And if you ever have the need, my axe is yours."

I nodded to him gravely, relaxing now and leaning back on the bar. "Where will you go? Back to Sterling?"

He grunted, a tiny grin wavering at the edge of his

mouth. "No. I been summoned back to the Empire."

I raised my eyebrows again. "The Empire? Is that right?"

"The princess. She reactivated my commission. She has, I guess, the authority to do that. She's appointed me as her personal guard," he said, the last coming somewhat awkwardly. It took me only a second to see why. Dana was no longer available to serve the Empire or Julea, and that left her without her guardian. So she had chosen the Talhas for the role.

"Lady Dana recommended me," he said after a pause. He added it reflexively, as if to ward off any objection. But I gave him none and nodded calmly instead.

"That's an honor," I said, my voice grave, "and I can't think of anyone better suited."

He seemed to accept that, and the tiny grin returned to his face. "Supposedly the Empire will have a ship here within the next few days. A flotilla of ships from the Imperial Navy has been patrolling off in the northeastern part of the Teardrop Sea. They're waiting for word that the ambassador – the princess – is ready to return home."

"I wondered about that," I said. "Were they informed about any of the... er... mishaps?"

"Not that I know of," Rohb said, "I reckon they'd have been here in force if they had."

"Fair guess," I said. I took a breath and looked at him.

"Well, Lieutenant—"

"Captain," he said, the grin breaking wide on his face.

"Captain," I corrected. "I will be there when you leave for a proper goodbye, but for what it's worth; it's been my privilege."

"Mine too. Sir," he said, giving me a curt bow.

I patted him on the shoulder of his uninjured arm and stepped around, making my way out of the room and toward the stairs while my mind pondered the strangeness of fortune.

The next few days passed in a blur of activity, each of us occupied with what we thought of as necessary business. Edword spent all of his time at the docks, interviewing new sailors to make up for those that were either lost in the battle or had decided to leave his employ, which was common enough for such crews. We heard almost nothing of him, but the sight of the fantastic black ship in the bay was strangely comforting. Denis, with the assistance of Myk's house steward, was collecting together the supplies he felt he would need for our travels, and so spent much of his time in the markets. Myk told me that he had sent word to Castle Sterling when we first returned of our arrival and that he was caring for us and that the messenger – who had made the round trip with incredible speed – reported that the king was sending along our abandoned belongings from the inn we had never reached. Over the same time, the princess found herself to be the darling of the court in the Tower, followed around consistently by the ladies of Clemons as if they could somehow capture a bit of her cachet. She acted above it all, though I knew her well enough to know that secretly she enjoyed it. Honestly, it was a relief to me, as I knew that her impending trip home, without Dana, would be weighing on her heart and so any distraction was a blessing.

As for me, I spent most of the next two days with Dana. I taught her what herbs to combine with the gems, how to grind them into a paste, and how they should be applied. Together, we collected all the necessary tools and supplies, and she assembled them into her own version of the leather bag I carried. She was a good student, but the sadness in her eyes returned each time we took a break. I decided it was best not to press; this was her pain, and she would have to cope as she wished.

It was the close of the second day after our return, and I was sitting on the end of one of the docks, leaning against a support pole and watching the sea when Edword quietly walked down the pier and stopped a couple of steps to my right. He had his hands on his hips and took a long, distinct breath as he looked off into the distance. I watched him, though he hadn't looked in my direction or acknowledged me at all. He stood silently, his head panning back and forth before finally settling on looking at his ship off to our right.

He sighed another satisfied breath.

“She’s a beauty,” I said.

“Aye,” he said, “an’ she’s all mine.”

“She’s... a bit of a mystery,” I said, testing the water. The ship still fascinated me, and I wondered if there was a chance that he would tell me more.

“Like all beautiful women,” he said with a note of finality. I took the hint and went quiet. “I got a question for ye, Blackcrow,” he said.

“Is this a quid pro quo question?” I said.

“Naw,” he said, “just a question.”

“Let fly,” I said, letting my head drop back against the wooden support behind me.

“This lordling friend of yours, Aeryk,” he said, folding his arms across his chest, “seems like a solid man. If ye discount the ‘traitor’ bits, that is. And that seems like that’s something we do these days. Anyway, you think that way?”

“That he’s a good man? Mostly. Depends on why you’re asking,” I said.

Edword made a dismissive gesture. “He wants to take an’ sail with me,” he said.

“Does he now?”

“And I want to know what you think of that,” the pirate finished, “one professional to another.”

I thought for a moment, listening to the rhythm of the waves. If there was one thing that I knew, it was that the right answer and the sensible answer weren't always the same answer.

"He is a solid man," I said, "with the potential to be even better. He's green. You take him and train him, and you'll get more than you give."

"You believe that?"

"I do," I said.

A silence fell that lasted a while as we both watched the darkening sky as the sea splashed, and as the air got colder.

"I'm leavin' with the dawn," Edword said. "I got no desire to see Imperials, and I reckon they'll be here before midday."

I nodded, more to myself than to him, as he still hadn't looked in my direction. "That's probably a good move, all considered," I said. Then I stood, brushing myself off and facing him as he finally turned toward me.

"You need anything...," Edword said, letting the sentence trail off.

"Likewise," I said. The pirate reached out, passing my offered hand and grasping my forearm. It was a custom from ancient days; the grasp of warriors who met on the field of battle. I returned the gesture. After a moment, he released my arm, turned, and walked up along the walkway as quietly as he had come.

The next morning, I came down from my room to a

scene of chaos. A contingent of men from Sterling had arrived and was gathered outside the tower. At their center fussed an older man, my height but stockier, his head and face full of a carefully coifed mixture of gray and black hair. He wore the blue and black uniform of the nobles and guards of Ronald's lands, but his version was stitched ornately with gold thread and accompanied by golden jewelry. He was pacing back and forth in the courtyard, barking out questions to whoever he happened to be closest to, whether noble or servant, while Lord Myk stood at the far end of the space with a blank look.

I listened carefully to the blustering for several minutes before Denis sidled up to me and asked quietly, "Hey, what's going on?"

I tilted my head to him, still watching the scene. "I could be mistaken, but I think Lord Grumpy over there is Duke Rojer of Claire. He's looking for his son."

"Aeryk?"

"Yep. Except Aeryk sailed with Edword and his men about two hours ago at first light."

"He did what?" Denis said, almost too loudly.

"Yep," I said, keeping my tone quiet as a reminder. "It looks like our boy has opted for the life of a pirate."

"I'll be dipped," he said incredulously.

Across the courtyard, the duke paced and muttered and grumbled.

Duke Rojer had, though I doubted it was from the goodness of his soul of which little was on display, brought with him our remaining belongings as well as the compliments of the king. As a result, I spent the rest of my morning repacking my things and restocking my supplies. The sun was high by the time I finished and, leaving my packs on my bed, I made my way up to the tower roof for some air. I emerged to find Julea and Dana, standing together at the tower's edge and watching the sea. I thought for a moment, then turned to go back down when Dana called out.

"Are you leaving so soon?"

I turned back to see both women looking at me expectantly.

"Oh, I, ah, well...," I sputtered. Really, I was stammering; my mouth seemingly came unconnected from my mind. "I didn't want to intrude," I finally managed to get out.

"No sense starting that now," Julea said, and the two of them laughed at my discomfort. Giggled, even. I smiled involuntarily; it was good to see them happy. I walked over to where they were, so close to where Julea and I had met that first night, and we all turned to face the sea. In the distance, still very small, two ships under full sail were approaching.

"I believe those are for me," Julea said as we all took note of the tiny shadows on the water. She was still smiling but I swore I could see a bit of wistfulness in her eyes that hadn't been there a moment before. I looked away quietly, leaving her to her private thoughts.

Dana sighed, and Julea threaded her arm around her friend. They didn't say anything – so many words had been already used, I was sure – but instead, they just stood in their embrace and watched the two small ships that brought their future.

"How about you, Dana? Have you decided what your plans are?" I said, looking over at her. In all the hours we had spent together over the previous days, I had studiously avoided asking her about her future. The question felt impolite, uncomfortable in a way that comes from trespassing into private things.

To my surprise, she shrugged almost casually. "I don't know," she said, and the words came out lightly as if she were talking about choosing a dress. "I was just telling Julea, I woke up today with the oddest feeling. For the first time in my life, I don't have a responsibility or a duty to anyone. It's like I've been wearing a hat that was very tight for a long time. It wasn't uncomfortable, but it was always there and now..., now it's off. I still feel it, if that makes any sense, but it's not there. I don't know how to feel, but I feel – good?" She looked over at me with a half smile.

"Good for you," I said.

"Of course, I'm sad to leave my friend," and at this, she looked back to Julea, "and I'm absolutely in the dark about where I'll go next, but I think that's probably okay for right now."

I turned back to the water, losing myself in thought. So lost was I that, when I finally turned back, Dana was gone and Julea and I were alone on the tower. She looked at me and smiled.

"Where...?" I said, looking around.

"I asked if she could give us a minute," Julea said. "Didn't you see her go? Are you slipping, Blackcrow?"

I chuckled. "Maybe. Might be time for me to settle down on a farm and raise chickens."

She chuckled. "You could," she said, folding her hands characteristically in front of her as she pulled her shoulders back, "but then how are you going to invite Dana to come with you and Denis?"

I looked over at her.

"Oh please," she said, "I've known you far too long and too well not to know that is exactly what you were just thinking about."

I felt my jaw moving as if it were trying to say something, but no words came out. "You're a little scary," I said finally.

"So I've heard," she said, smiling. "You should know

that she is waiting for you to ask, as well. Nothing she told me, but I know her even better than I know you."

"Better?" I said, lifting an eyebrow.

"You know what I mean," she said, a hint of color hitting her cheeks.

We fell silent for a moment. Then I heard a rustling and turned to find her holding an old piece of paper.

"Lady Dana," she read, "As you will no doubt have heard by now, I have resigned my commission in the Imperial guard..."

I froze, memory sweeping in as she read words I had written years before.

"... Know that I can offer you no explanation, as I know that no reason that I am free to give you would be sufficient. I write instead to ask for you to do what I know you would do freely without my request. Julea will be the Empress one day, and she will be the greatest to sit on the throne since the days of legend. This, I know as well as I know the sun will rise. She lacks only one thing, and that is a friend she can trust, who will challenge her, who will disagree with her, who will love her, and who will support her. In short, she will need you." Julea paused for a moment, scanning the brief closing words of the note that followed, then folded the paper and looked up at me.

"I wrote that when I became the Raven," I said quietly, staring at the paper in her hand. "I knew I wouldn't be at court anymore, and…"

"And you wouldn't be there for me," she finished.

I shrugged. "I didn't know that I'd ultimately be even further away," I said.

"Prescient, all things considered," she said, her voice quiet.

I let my eyes drift up to her face. Her expression was placid, and a gentle smile rested on her lips.

"I didn't understand," she said. "I thought, maybe, you wanted to be away. That I had misread things…" She looked back down at the paper.

"No," I said, looking at her steadily now. "I accepted the posting because it was my duty. I truly thought – happily – that I'd eventually be serving you on the throne. But that's…, that's not what happened."

She stepped closer to me, reaching out and taking my hands in hers.

"We have been dealt… unfortunate cards," she said, looking up at me.

"I would have had things be different," I said. She came yet closer, looking into my eyes. We hung like that, on the edge, for a brief eternity. I wished at that moment that it actually could go on forever. But ultimately, she looked down and away, resting her forehead on my chest.

"But they aren't, are they?" she said, her voice muffled against me.

I planted a gentle kiss on the top of her head, then with a sigh said, “No, they aren’t. No matter what we want.”

We stood like that for a long moment. Finally, she stepped back and straightened again, her hands dropping from mine – finding their home folded in front of her.

“That time is past,” she said, the cool steel of her office; the strength she tapped into when she needed to think more than feel; had crept into her voice. Calmly, she brushed the tears from her cheeks as she turned back to the water.

I turned and headed toward the trapdoor, but stopped after a couple of steps.

“But..., Your Highness?” I said. She turned.

“The past is the past; that’s true. But it did happen. And it did mean something. And for me, it always will,” I said.

She hesitated, and even from a distance, I could see her eyes sparkle with new tears.

“Please take care of my friend,” she said quietly.

“By my life or my death, I will,” I said – an old warrior’s oath; one she would recognize.

She smiled, a little sadly. “That is unacceptable. You are to take care of both of my friends – that includes you.”

I smiled back at her. “Safe journeys, my lady. I will see you off at the docks later,” I said and bowed. She turned back to the water as I left the rooftop.

The following day, I was walking with my packs slung over my shoulders, following the road out of Clemons that had once led Lord Aeryk and me in. The air was crisp and carried the smell of fallen leaves across the broad fields to the south.

"But it's stupid," Denis was saying. He rode to my left, struggling to keep his cantering horse slowed to my walking pace. "He was going to give you a horse," he finished.

"I know," I said.

"How long are you going to walk along carrying all that stuff? We're not even going to make it to an inn before you collapse." He pulled back on the reins as his horse lunged forward. It was a pretty animal, dark gray flecks against a white coat with a black head, tail, and legs. It was young too, which explained its excitability.

"Leave him be," Dana said, riding along on the other side of Denis. "I'm sure he has a plan."

"Sure," Denis said, "a plan. Maybe he'll make a tube of fire, and we'll all fly away. By the way, why are you here again? Not that I'm unhappy with it, but how did that happen?"

"Someone has to watch over you two," she said. There was a note of playfulness in her voice that seemed new, or at least more pronounced. I smiled to myself.

I looked around and, satisfied that we were far enough from the city, I stopped. Loudly, I whistled. I knew it was asking a lot, and if it didn't work, I knew I'd never hear the end of it, but I had to try. I waited. Denis watched me the same way you look at a lunatic, hoping they don't hurt themselves. Dana turned her eyes to the distant forest, watching. For a long time, nothing happened, but then, when even I was beginning to wonder, there was a motion at the edge of the trees, and a beautiful brown and tan stallion emerged, galloping across the open field toward us. I smiled.

"Oh, for the love of The One," Denis said.

Locksley slowed and walked over to me, greeting me with a nuzzle of his great head. I petted him for a bit, returning the affection he offered before I loaded my supplies and equipment on his back and climbed up. Denis watched all of this with quiet amazement. He looked at Dana, who gave a disinterested shrug as if she were unimpressed.

"I do have a question," he said as we started to move again.

"Is it about the horse?" I said.

"Nope. I'm choosing to act like that's a completely normal thing for someone to do. That's what she's doing," he said.

"What?" Dana said; the picture of innocence.

"No, I have a question about the emeralds. You know, the big box of gems that we risked our lives for so that they didn't fall into the wrong hands?"

“I seem to recall those,” I said.

“The same ones that we just sent back to the Empire with Princess Julea? The same Empire that neither of you can go to because the gems are dangerous?”

I nodded casually.

He looked from Dana to me. She was watching me, concerned. I wondered if she had even thought about the box since she had been wounded.

“That isn’t a problem?” he said.

“No. Because that box is full of emeralds,” I said.

They looked at me. I waited.

“Yeah…,” Denis said, the pieces not entirely falling into place.

“Wait,” Dana said in a flash of understanding, “are you saying those were just emeralds?”

“Yep,” I said, “I checked while everyone was asleep on the cart and Den here was driving. Natural, normal emeralds, nothing more.”

We rode in silence for a few minutes as it sank in.

“But you didn’t say anything,” Denis said, eyeing me.

“Better that Empress Ardallah spends her time on those than on trying to find actual Kelian emeralds,” I said, somewhat smugly.

Dana looked at me for a long moment. “And Jules?”

“Better she doesn’t know,” I said, sighing. “Let Empress Ardallah focus her ire on me, eh?”

Denis started to laugh. It was quiet at first, then he slowly lost himself in it, doubling over and nearly laying on the back of his horse. It was infectious, and soon, all three of us were laughing. And so we went, following the road to wherever it might lead us, our laughter echoing off the hills.

EPILOGUE
– WILLM –

The days and weeks after my humiliation were marked in pain and blood. A portion of the army was now made aware that it was no longer Mathu on their throne, and initiated a coup to remove me from power. It was only by my foresight in replacing the soldiers closest to me with men loyal to me personally and placing those whose loyalty I could buy into positions of authority that I was able to hold my throne. As it was, though the days of battle were costly in lives and coin, I endured. Moreover, the land is mine now in my true name rather than my being forced to masquerade any longer as the boy king. I rule now as King Willm Steinhargh the First. I have... endured.

But the pains remain with me. My arm is the most constant. The ache there, I am told, will never fully heal; something about the weapon that severed it left the severed end unable to heal itself properly. Weeks have passed, yet it weeps blood still. The mechanical horror I wear on it now is as much a marvel as it is an abomination. The finest minds I could buy or coerce helped me create my new 'hand,' and though it is in part a testimony to their skills and my brilliance, it remains a monstrous thing. Even now I look at it, the tiny gears and springs in the hidden machinery whirring and grinding with each tug of command from the controls in my left gauntlet. I loathe it. In whispers that they believe I don't hear, the servants have begun calling me "King Steelclaw." I choose to allow this, though I will select some of the laziest to torture. If I am to have the name, then I will earn the fear that must go with it.

But that pain is in truth less than the pain of my memories of that day. That morning, I had everything I could have dreamed in the palm of my... hand... and it was taken from me by meddling fools. The Heir of Yorch was in my power! And a cache of the fabled weapons of ancient Yorch – Kelian emeralds – as well. Taken from me— from my bedchamber no less!— by the disgraced Blackcrow and some vile gutter-living chattel that had been festering in my stronghold's dungeon. Spirited away by the accursed pirate on my flagship! To have lost all of that and nearly my – *my* – kingdom as well? To these vermin? It is intolerable.

There will be a reckoning. My pockets are deep, and the world is small. The Empire will afford no protection to the exile and his cohorts.

I will have my vengeance.

Glossary

Adh

Ah

Training master of Castle Sterling

Lord Aeryk Escrios,
Marquess of Claire

AY-rick es-KRI-os,
MAR-kess of Klair

Heir to the house of Escrios, masters of the Lochhaven province of Claire

Aosta Forest

ae-OST-a

A heavily overgrown, old growth forest in the northeast of Lochhaven. Legendarily home of terrifying monsters and a few hardy bandit clans.

Empress Ardallah Niconnal bar Morrisia of Yorch
Gloriana, Sola, Lunis, and Stelis

ar-DAHL-uh ni-CON-al bar more-IS-e-a of York,
glor-e-AN-a, SOL-a, LU-nis, STEL-is

Ruler of the Empire of Yorch.

Claire

Klair

One of the twelve provinces of the kingdom of Lochhaven. A wealthy land in the south, governed by the Escrios family.

Clemons

KELM-ons

A quiet seaport town in the south of Lochhaven.

Lady Dana Lunavale bar Donnara,
Silver Spar of Her People

DAY-na LOON-a-val bar don-NAR-a

Personal guard of Imperial Princess Julea.

Lord Duglas Dasous,
Duke of Auron

DEW-glass da-SOOS,
Duke of aw-RAWN

Master of the province of Auron in the northeast of Lochhaven; known for its rich mines.

Edword Ribald

ED-ward RI-bald

Infamous pirate.

Esterwynn

ES-ter-wine

An immense river forming the western border of Lochhaven.

Euticha

YOU-ti-ka

An independent trade city on the coast of the Great Eastern Ocean, far south of the Empire of Yorch. It serves as the trade and passage gateway to the kingdoms of the south.

Gadai Marran

Ga-DAY MAR-ahn

Disowned son of the Archbishop of the Church of the One, now living as a bandit.

Princess Julea Niconnal bar Ardallah,
Light of Our People, Heir to the Golden Throne

Jew-LAY-uh ni-CON-al bar ar-DAHL-uh

Daughter of Ardallah and heir to the Imperial throne.

Kelian emeralds

Ke-LEE-an

Green gemstones that, according to ancient Yorchian legends, can be used to access mighty power.

Lochhaven

LOCK-hav-n

A provincial kingdom to the west of the Empire of Yorch, ruled by Ronald I.

Larissa Coffey

lar-IS-a KOF-e

Imperial scribe to the Throne of Yorch.

Markh / Phranc Rindros

Mark / Fraunk RIN-drus

Guardsmen and brothers in service of Lord Myk Peralta of Clemons.

King Mathu

MAT-hew

Recently emerged ruler of the tribes north of Lochhaven.

Lord Myk Peralta,
Baron of Clemons
Myk per-AL-ta,
Baron of KLEM-ons
Master of the port city of Clemons, a city-state in the south of Lochhaven.

Lord Rojer Escrios,
Duke of Claire
ROW-jer es-KRI-os.
Duke of Klair
Master of the wealthy province of Claire in the south of Lochhaven.

King Ronald I Kastellian of Sterling,
Ruler of Lochhaven
RON-ald kas-TEL-e-an,
Ruler of LOCK-hav-n
Primus inter pares (first of equals) of the Parliament of Nobles of Lochhaven.

Captain Rohb O'Laird
Rob Oh-LAY-rd
Captain of the guard of Castle Sterling, and former Talhas soldier in the army of the Empire of Yorch.

Lady Sherilyn Voelkel of Traverse Bay
SHAR-i-lin VOEL-kal of TRA-verse Bay
Daughter of the Baron of Traverse Bay; the northernmost province of Lochhaven abutting the Superior Mountains.

Samhn Fayette ban Rothson

SA-win fay-ET ban ROTH-son

First Lieutenant of the Palace Guard of Castle Sterling.

Talhas

TAL-hass

A tribal culture from the highlands of the Southern Lands; Well-known as skilled warriors in service to Yorch.

Talte Bruite

TAL-te BRUT-ay

The "crushed lands." A massive area of untamed wilderness to the southwest of Lochhaven covering most of the continent. Legendarily, it is a land of horrors and mysteries.

Teardrop Sea

Teardrop Sea

A large freshwater sea separating Lochhaven from the western land mass where the Empire of Yorch resides. It empties into the Great Eastern Ocean in the north.

Baron Vasily Roussos of Sterling

Va-SEEL-e ROUS-us

Chamberlain (household manager) of Castle Sterling.

Victori

Vic-TOR-ee

Childhood friend of Lady Dana

Willm Steinhargh

WIL-m st-EYE-n-hark

King in the north

Yorch

York

The largest and mightiest nation in the known world.

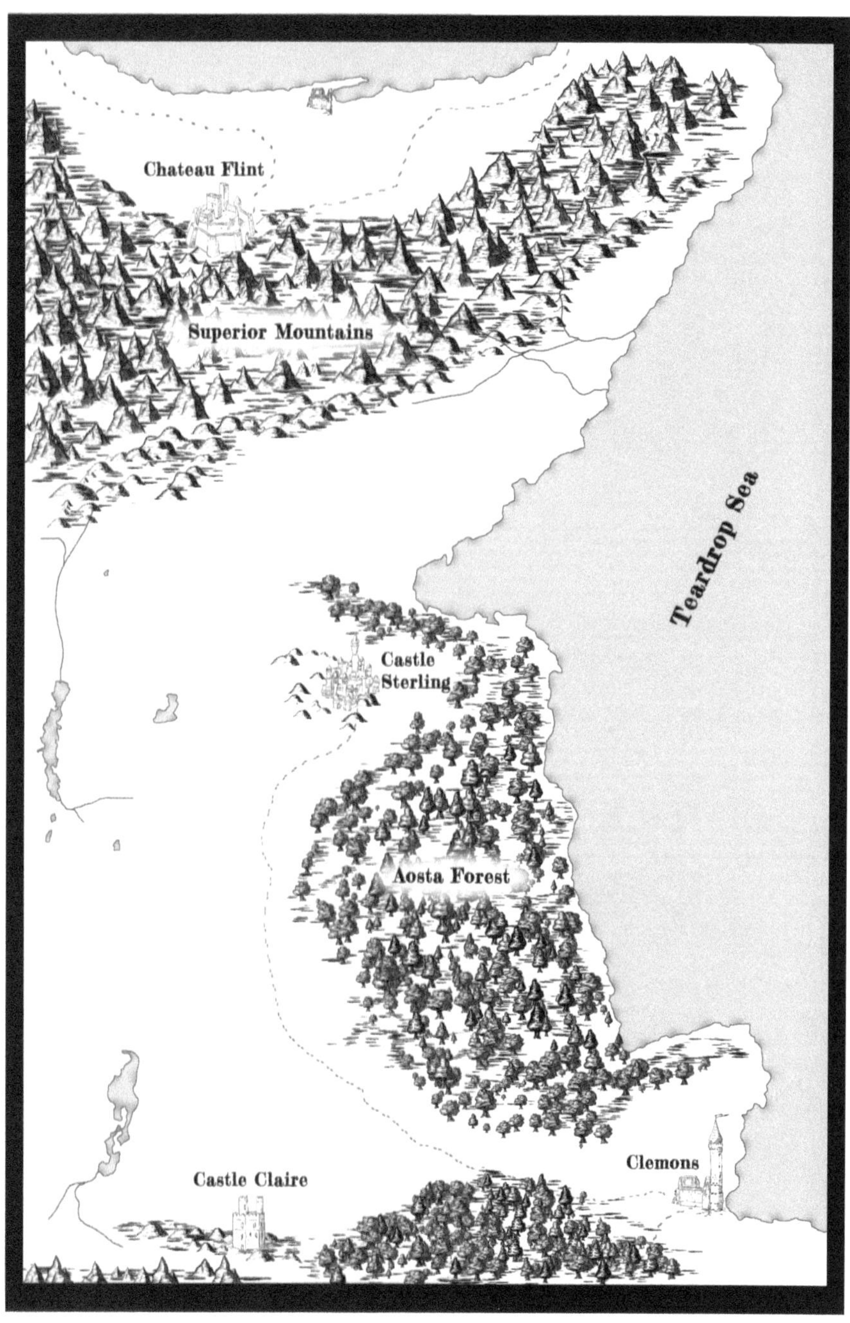
Chateau Flint
Superior Mountains
Teardrop Sea
Castle Sterling
Aosta Forest
Clemons
Castle Claire

www.ingramcontent.com/pod-product-compliance
Lightning Source LLC
Chambersburg PA
CBHW030542310726
48979CB00010B/1994/J

9781733408301